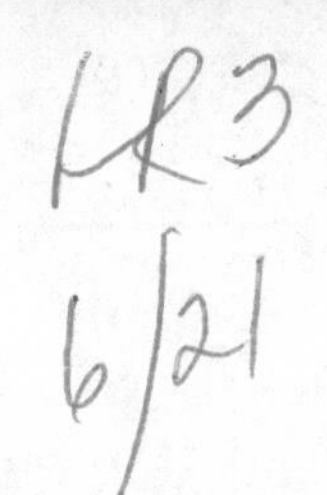

THREE HOURS IN PARIS

Books by the author

Murder in the Marais
Murder in Belleville
Murder in the Sentier
Murder in the Bastille
Murder in Clichy
Murder in Montmartre
Murder on the Ile Saint-Louis
Murder in the Rue de Paradis
Murder in the Latin Quarter
Murder in the Palais Royal
Murder in Passy
Murder at the Lanterne Rouge
Murder Below Montparnasse
Murder in Pigalle
Murder on the Champ de Mars
Murder on the Quai
Murder in Saint-Germain
Murder on the Left Bank
Murder in Bel-Air

THREE HOURS IN PARIS

CARA BLACK

SOHO CRIME

Published in the United States by

Soho Press, Inc.
227 W 17th Street
New York, NY 10011

Black, Cara, author.
Three hours in Paris / Cara Black.

ISBN 978-1-64129-258-0
eISBN 978-1-64129-042-5

1. World War, 1939-1945—Secret
service—France—Paris—Fiction. 2. Spy stories. 3. Spy stories
4. Historical fiction
LCC PS3552.L297 T47 2020 | DDC 813/.54—dc23

Interior map © Mike Hall
Interior design by Janine Agro, Soho Press, Inc.

Printed in the United States of America

10 9 8 7 6 5 4 3 2 1

For those who lived this and the ghosts

"War is a political instrument, a continuation of politics by other means."
—Carl von Clausewitz, *On War*, 1832

"Everything you do is going to be disliked by a lot of people in Whitehall—the more you succeed, the more they will dislike you and what you are trying to do."
—Admiral Hugh Sinclair, Chief of the Secret Intelligence Service (MI6), April 1938

"It was very frustrating to have to observe the course of battle with just a single grenade in one's hand."
—Lyudmila Pavlichenko, Russian sniper in the Second World War, 309 confirmed German kills

"Never was so much owed by so many to so few."
—Prime Minister Winston Churchill, August 20, 1940

Sunday, June 23, 1940

Nine Days into the German Occupation of Paris

Montmartre, Paris | 6:15 A.M. Paris time

Sacré-Cœur's dome faded to a pale pearl in the light of dawn outside the fourth-story window. Kate's ears attuned to the night birds, the creaking settling of the old building, distant water gushing in the gutters. It was her second day waiting in the deserted apartment, the Lee-Enfield rifle beside her.

Will this really happen?

She moved into a crouch on the wood parquet floor in front of the balcony and winced. Her knee throbbed—she had bruised it on that stupid fence as the parachute landed in the barnyard. She smelled the faint garden aroma of Pears soap on her silk blouse, which was dampened by perspiration. The June day was already so warm.

She dipped her scarf in the water bottle, wiped her face and neck. Took another one of the pink pills and a swig of water. She needed to stay awake.

As apricot dawn blushed over the rooftop chimneys, she checked the bullets, calibrated and adjusted the telescopic mount, as she had every few hours. The spreading sunrise to her left outlined the few clouds like a bronze pencil, and lit her target area. No breeze; the air lay still, weighted with heat. Perfect conditions.

"Concentrate on your target, keep escape in the back of your mind," her handler, Stepney, had reminded her en route to the airfield outside London Friday night. "You're prepared. Follow the fallback protocol." His last-minute instruction, as she'd zipped up the flight suit in the drafty hangar: "Always remember who you're doing this for, Kate."

"As if I would forget?" she'd told him. She pushed away the memory that engulfed her mind, the towering flames, the terrible cries, and looked him straight in the eye. "Plus, I can't fail or you'll have egg all over your face, Stepney."

As dawn brightened into full morning, Kate laid her arm steady on the gilt chair on which she had propped the rifle. From the fourth floor her shot would angle down to the top step. Reading the telescopic mount, she aligned the middle of the church's top step and the water-stained stone on the limestone pillar by the door; she'd noted yesterday that the stain was approximately five feet ten inches from the ground. She would have been able to make the shot even without it—three hundred yards was an easy shot from one of the best views of the city. Next, she scoped a backup target, referencing the pillars' sculptured detail. She'd take a head shot as he emerged from the church's portico, fire once, move a centimeter to the left and then fire again. Worst-case scenario, she'd hit his neck.

With a wooden cheek rising-piece and a telescopic sight mount on its beechwood stock, the Lee-Enfield weighed about ten pounds. She'd practiced partially disassembling the rifle every other hour, eyes closed, timing herself. She wouldn't have time to fully strip it. Speed would buy her precious seconds for her escape before her target's entourage registered the rifle crack and reacted. Less than a minute, Stepney had cautioned, if her target was surrounded by his usual Führer Escort Detachment.

Her pulse thudded as she glanced at her French watch, a Maquet. 7:59 A.M. Any moment now the plane might land.

Kate sipped water, her eye trained on the parishioners mounting Sacré-Cœur's stairs and disappearing into the church's open doors: old ladies, working men, families with children in tow. A toddler, a little girl in a yellow dress, broke away from the crowd, wandering along the portico until a woman in a blue hat caught her hand. Kate hadn't accounted for the people attending Mass. Stupid. Why hadn't Stepney's detailed plan addressed that?

She pushed her worry aside. Her gaze focused through the telescopic sight on the top step, dead center. Her target's entourage would surround him and keep him isolated from French civilians.

That's if he even comes.

The pealing church bells made her jump, the slow reverberation calling one and all to eight o'clock Mass. Maybe she'd taken too much Dexedrine.

But she kept her grip steady, her finger coiled around the metal trigger, and her eye focused.

A few latecomers hurried up the church steps. Kate recognized the concierge of the building she was hiding in. She'd sneaked past the woman yesterday, using her lock-picking training to let herself into one of the vacated apartments. An unaccustomed thrill had filled her as the locked door clicked open—she'd done it, and after only brief training in that drafty old manor, God knew where in the middle of the English countryside.

After the flurry of the call to Mass, a sleepy Sunday descended over Montmartre. The streets below her were empty except for a man pushing a barrow of melons. He rounded the corner. The morning was so quiet she heard only the twittering of sparrows in the trees, the gurgling water in the building pipes.

The wood floor was warm under her legs. On the periphery of the rifle's sight a butterfly's blue-violet wings fluttered among orange marigolds.

8:29 A.M. Her heart pounded, her doubts growing. Say her target's plans had changed—what if his flight landed tonight, tomorrow or next week? She wondered how long she could stay in this apartment before the owners returned, or a neighbor heard her moving around and knocked on the door.

8:31 A.M. As she was thinking what in God's name she'd do if she was discovered here, she heard the low thrum of car engines. Down rue Lamarck she saw the black hood of a Mercedes.

Several more followed behind it, in the same formation she'd seen in the newsreels Stepney had shown her. She breathed in deep and exhaled, trying to dispel her tension.

She edged the tip of the Lee-Enfield a centimeter more through the shutter slat. Kept the rifle gripped against her shoulder and watched as the approaching convertibles proceeded at twenty miles an hour. In the passenger seat of the second Mercedes sat a man in a white coat like a housepainter's; in the rear jump seats, three gray uniforms—the elite Führerbegleitkommando bodyguards. She suppressed the temptation to shoot now—she would have only a one in five chance of hitting him in the car. Besides, that might be a decoy; her target could be riding in any of the cars behind the first Mercedes.

The second Mercedes passed under the hanging branches of linden trees. A gray-uniformed man with a movie camera on a tripod stood on the back seat of the last Mercedes, capturing the trip on film. She held her breath, waiting. No troop trucks. The cars pulled up on the Place du Parvis du Sacré-Cœur and parked before the wide stairs leading to the church entrance.

This was it. Payback time.

The air carried German voices, the tramp of boots. And then, like a sweep of gray vultures, the figures moved up the steps, a tight configuration surrounding the man in the white coat. He wore a charcoal-brimmed military cap, like the others. For a brief moment, he turned and she saw that black smudge of mustache. The Führer was in her sights now, for that flash of a second before his bodyguards ushered him through the church door. As Stepney had described, five feet ten inches and wearing a white coat. In her head she considered his quick movements, rehearsed the shot's angle to the top step where he'd stand, the timing of the shot she'd take, noting the absence of wind.

The church door opened. So soon? Kate curled her finger, keeping focus on the church pillar in her trigger hairs. But it was the woman with the blue hat, leading the toddler in the yellow dress by the hand. The little girl was crying.

Why in the world did the child have to cry right now?

It all happened in a few seconds. A gray-uniformed bodyguard herded the woman and child to the side and the Führer stepped back out into the sunlight. Hitler, without his cap, stood on the top step by himself. He swiped the hair across his forehead. That signature gesture, so full of himself.

The wolf was in her sights. Like her father had taught her, she found his eyes above his mustache.

Never hold your breath. Her father's words played in her head. *Shoot on the exhale.* She aimed and squeezed the trigger.

But Hitler had bent down to the crying toddler. Over the tolling of the church bell, the crack of the rifle reverberated off limestone. A spit of dust puffed from the church pillar. The child's mother looked up, surprised, finding dust on her shoulder. Any moment the guards would notice.

Concentrate.

As calmly as she could and willing her mind still, Kate reloaded within three seconds, aimed at his black hair above his ear as he leaned over, extending his hand to the little girl's head, ruffling her hair. The guards were laughing now, focused on the Führer, whose fondness for children was well-known.

Kate pulled the trigger again just as Hitler straightened. Damn. The uniformed man behind him jerked.

As the shot zipped by him one of the guards looked around. She couldn't believe her luck that no one else had noticed. She had to hurry.

Reloading and adjusting once more, she aimed at the point between his eyes. Cocked the trigger. But Hitler had lifted the little girl in his arms, smiling, still unaware that the man behind him had been hit. The toddler's blonde curls spilled in front of Hitler's face.

Her heart convulsed, pain filling her chest. Those blonde curls were so like Lisbeth's. Why did he have to pick this toddler up just then?

Killing a child is not part of your mission. This time, the voice in her head was her own, not Stepney's. Agonized, she felt her focus slipping away.

Now. She had to fire now. Harden herself and shoot. Ignore the fact the bullet would pass through the little girl's cheek. That the woman in the blue hat would lose her daughter.

The hesitation cost her a second.

The uniform slumped down the church pillar. A dark red spot became a line of blood dripping down his collar.

Hitler was still holding the child as she heard the shouts. She hadn't yet taken her shot when all hell broke loose.

A guard snatched the little girl from his arms. Guards forced Hitler into a crouch and hurried him to the car. In the uniformed crowd now surrounding Hitler a man pointed in Kate's direction. Through the telescopic sight she saw his steel-gray eyes scanning the building. She could swear those eyes looked right at her.

Sunday, June 23, 1940

Le Bourget Airfield outside Paris | 9:00 A.M.

"Thirty-six hours," barked the Führer, pausing at the plane cabin door. Despite the heat, he was wearing a leather trench coat. It was bulletproof, and after what had just happened at Sacré-Cœur he refused to take it off. "*Verstehen Sie?*"

"*Jawohl, mein Führer.*" Gunter Hoffman blinked grit from his gray eyes.

Thirty-six hours to find the sniper.

The cabin door slammed shut and the Focke-Wulf taxied down the airstrip. Gunter was thirty-two years old, a Munich homicide detective in the Kriminalpolizei before he'd been folded into the Reichssicherheitsdienst, RSD, the Reich's SS security service. He sucked in his breath. He knew his job; he'd headed the southern Bayern section. But he'd never investigated solo in an occupied zone.

Beside him, Lange, the trim Gestapo agent, stood at attention until the plane's belly lifted off the runway. "Better you than me," Lange said, shielding his face from the hot engine's updraft. "I've got Berlin and Lindau's successor to deal with." He nodded to the stretcher carrying poor Admiral Lindau's corpse. The admiral had taken the bullet intended for the Führer. Lange would be accompanying the body to the troop transport plane at the refueling depot.

After the shooting, Hitler had instructed the guards to round up all the Sacré-Cœur churchgoers, as if any of them would know anything about the gunman—but of course the Führer's orders were to be followed. Gunter would have chosen to head the detail to comb the surrounding buildings for the sniper, but he had ordered him and his superior to accompany him to the airfield.

For the duration of the car ride, the Führer had issued wild demands: "Bring me that little girl, my good luck charm." "Take the priest and his parishioners to the church crypt and get the truth out of them, you know how." He raged at suspected traitors. "My suspicions were all correct. I knew it as soon as I saw those reports. This plot started in London. I'll pay them back."

After months on the job, Gunter had grown to distrust the man who led the Third Reich. At home in Munich, he focused on his work, kept his head down and avoided the Reich's inner politics. But today he had attracted the Führer's attention, for better or for worse.

"Better dig up a few suspects for the chopping block, eh?" Lange said.

The Führer's penchant for mock trials before the *Fallbeil,* a stationary guillotine, was well-known, but Gunter would conduct his investigation his own way—to the extent he was allowed to. "I'm still a Kriminalpolizei, Lange. We follow the law."

When he'd heard the shots fired at Sacré-Cœur, Gunter had caught sight of the glint of the rifle in a fourth-floor window. The sniper wouldn't get far. Chances were the squad had already apprehended the shooter and the Sicherheitsdienst, SD, the SS intelligence, had the shooter waiting for Gunter's interrogation.

Lange shook his head. "Our Führer's as slippery as an eel in the Elbe. How many times has he escaped death? But you already know all about that."

There had been eight attempts on Hitler's life on record since the National Socialists' rise to power, and Gunter knew that almost double that number hadn't been reported.

But he didn't voice agreement; he didn't trust Lange. After

seven years under National Socialism, Gunter knew better than to comment on the Führer, lest Lange twist his words and backstab him Gestapo-style. How often had Gunter witnessed someone slip up and make an untoward remark, leaving behind nothing but an empty desk.

"My job is to bring the perpetrator to justice," Gunter said instead. The standard line.

As Gunter turned away from the still-smirking Lange, his boss, Gruppenführer Jäger, a broad-shouldered dark-haired man in full SS regalia, strode toward them from an airplane hangar.

"I'll be following the Führer," Jäger told Gunter. "He insists." His words were politic but his expression conveyed his chagrin. No man was a hero to his valet and no Führer to his security chief. "I'm leaving the investigation under your control, Gunter."

"Of course, Gruppenführer."

"The Führer himself requested I put you in charge, Gunter. Such an honor."

An honor, yes, but being on the Führer's radar was a double-edged sword. Life changed in a moment—just yesterday evening he'd been in Munich, checking decoded messages that reported a possible British parachute drop in France, when his assistant, Keller, took a call for him.

"Your wife told me to tell you she's frosting the *Kuchen*."

Gunter could still make it home in time. How often did his daughter turn two years old?

He'd slipped that evening's reports and his daughter's present, a Steiff teddy bear, into his case. Before he could make it any farther, though, Keller had brought him Jäger's telegram, which summoned him to the airfield immediately for a flight to Belgian HQ at Brûly-de-Pesche, to continue on to Paris early this morning.

Gunter could almost smell the Schokoladenkuchen. *Ach*, why on his daughter's birthday?

He blinked again, still trying to dislodge the stubborn grit from his eye, bringing himself back to the dusty runway. "A privilege, Gruppenführer."

"Make us proud, Gunter," said Jäger. "You excel at the hunt. No one assembles the pieces better than you, putting order to the chaos."

"Danke." He hoped his boss would leave it at that and let him get to work.

Jäger nodded. "Your uncle trained you well."

Gunter's mother had abandoned him as a child on his policeman uncle's doorstep. He'd never known his father. Gunter counted himself lucky to be raised by his uncle, who had made sure there was always a coat on his back and bread in his school lunch pail, even during the hungriest days of the Weimar Republic. His uncle, a stickler for order and detail, had provided young Gunter a sense of safety he'd never known with his mother. No wonder he'd followed in his uncle's footsteps. He'd found a great sense of purpose in police work, a world where his efforts produced tangible results.

"An honor to be of service," Gunter said, a repetition of what they'd learned to always reply at the police academy. "I'll assemble a team and report back to you as soon as I have news, and liaise with the SD at the Paris Kommandantur."

Jäger took Gunter's arm. "You will issue reports only to me. Am I clear? No information to SD, or anyone else. No assembling a team."

"Jawohl, Gruppenführer, but without contacts on the ground . . ."

"I'll see you're in communication with the right people." Jäger tapped his thick fingers together. "Your cousin Eva's biology professorship is up for tenure at Universität Bayern, isn't it?"

What business was it of his? Gunter's heart beat hard in his chest.

"My old friend Professor Häckl heads the science department," said Jäger. "He could smooth the way to tenure for her. But if that business with the Jew came up, well, it might be a bumpy road."

His silly little cousin Eva's affair, long since over, was a vulnerability that never went away. It had almost cost his uncle his police position a few years ago. Gunter, who had his own family now, had to be careful.

But Jäger had never put personal pressure like this on him before. His boss's job must be on the line. That meant Gunter's was, too.

Jäger stuck a cigarette between his thick lips. Lit it and inhaled. Gunter always thought those lips were mismatched to his otherwise long features. "You will keep me exclusively informed of findings."

Already Gunter didn't like this. He wondered if he was being set up to be the fall man. But what choice did he have?

He nodded. "*Jawohl,* Gruppenführer."

Part I

Eight Months Earlier

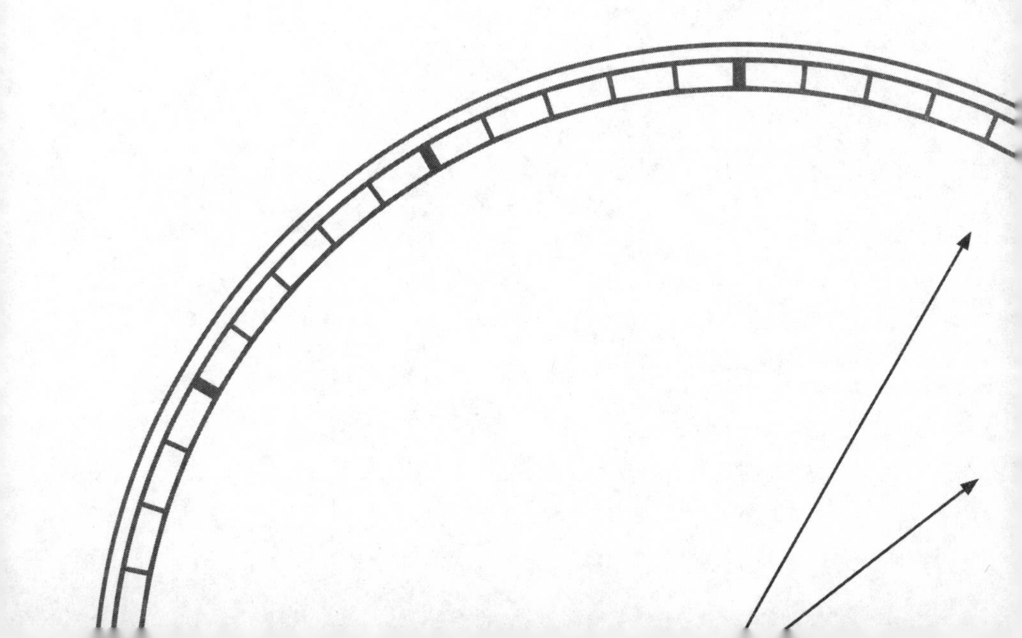

October 14, 1939

Scapa Flow, Royal Naval Base,
Hoy, Orkney Islands, Scotland

In the naval munitions factory, Kate Rees pushed her hair under her bandana and shouldered the Lee-Enfield rifle. The indoor firing range sweltered. The late-afternoon sun bathed Lyness's converted brick works in an orange glow. It was her last round testing the rifle, then off her aching feet. She couldn't wait to go home to her husband, Dafydd, a naval officer on weekend leave from his engineer's unit.

The piercing whistle blew the all-ready.

Kate put her eye to the sight and lined up the bead at the tip. Calculated the air current rustling the factory rafters. Focused on the black target rings three hundred yards ahead.

"Fire," boomed a voice.

She squeezed the trigger ten times. Reloading and firing at ten consecutive targets. A bull's-eye each time.

Sherard, the line supervisor's work coat stretched tight around his middle, ticked a checklist as Kate shelved the Lee-Enfield into the satisfactory bin. He pointed to a man with sparse brown hair combed across his crown. "Gentleman wants a word, Yank."

Still called her Yank even though she'd been working here almost a year.

"Impressive," the man said, his English accent like cut glass. He leaned on a cane. "Where did you learn to shoot like that?"

"I grew up on ranches in Oregon," she said, couldn't help the flicker of pride in her voice. "My father taught me to hunt when I was a little girl."

"What are you doing *here*?" he asked, his tone making it clear he wondered why anyone would come to this godforsaken Orkney island unless they were under military orders. She got that all the time. Hoy's naval base at Lyness and Rinnigill required security clearance and was considered a hardship posting, although both bases now employed a civilian workforce of locals and non-locals: secretaries for the various departments, staff to work in the laundries and canteens. Twelve thousand shore-based personnel were billeted here at camps and installations all over the island.

"I married a naval engineer."

"We've got a job for you."

"Already got a job." The military often scouted around the rifle factory and test range. Women were recruited for all types of work these days. She didn't think much of it.

"It's government work, and a bump in pay. In Birmingham."

A bump in pay sounded attractive. But not Birmingham. She'd gotten accustomed to this wild, desolate place.

"My daughter's a baby, too young to move to Birmingham. And my husband's stationed here," she said, thinking. "Why not a rifle instructor position here in Lyness?"

"Women as rifle instructors?" Sherard snorted.

Why not? She'd qualify.

"We only recruit rifle instructors from the army. No civilians," the man said. He handed her a card. "Let me know if you're interested in Birmingham."

When Kate got home to their cottage, Dafydd was rocking Lisbeth to sleep on the chintz settee. His curly dark hair glinted in the flicker of the coal lamp as he read the card she'd tossed on the table. "A government job offer in Birmingham?"

"I like this job here." And this windswept Orkney island—its sheep, rainstorms, Neolithic sites and Viking stones, the diamond-like stars in the black sky and murmur of the sea at night. Reminded her of home in a way. She liked the buzzing activity on the naval base, which had kicked into even higher gear since the September visit of Winston Churchill, First Lord of the Admiralty. Dafydd had told Kate about Plan Q, the strategic army defense plan for the Royal Navy Fleet Base. There were to be upgrades to the roads, underground fuel stores built and a massive wharf in the emerging naval dockyard to be constructed. Orkney was the best of both worlds to Kate—an untouched wilderness and a hive of human industry all at once.

She kicked off her shoes. Shut the window and pulled the blackout curtains, a new regulation, blocking the panorama of Scapa Flow harbor, dotted by charcoal shadows of a warship.

"Glad someone appreciates my long-legged Yank's talents." He brushed her cheek with his palm. Lisbeth, their sleepy-eyed eighteen-month-old, squirmed and caught Kate's hand in her chubby fist. Dafydd winked. "We certainly do."

Happy he was home for a long weekend leave, she snuggled up next to them. Kissed Lisbeth's tiny pink toes until the baby laughed.

"Should I go down to the pub and bring us back some bitter?" Dafydd said in a low voice. "We can pretend it's wine and spend an evening *très intime.* It might be the last for a while."

She sat up. "What do you mean?"

Dafydd pulled her back, kissed her. "There are reports that the Luftwaffe's flying surveillance."

"How does that affect you? Not your job, is it?"

"More than ever. I've been assigned back full time to the officers' barracks."

Kate felt a pang thinking about Dafydd toughing it out in the barracks. "Those horrible Nissen huts? They're like tin cans."

Meanwhile she and Lisbeth would enjoy the comfort of the granite crofter's cottage they'd made home. It reminded her of something out of Grimm's fairy tales, full of nooks and crannies and odd angles, yet snug. She looked around at the paraphernalia of their family life here: Dafydd's sketch pad, Lisbeth's toys scattered across the quilt, the neat pile of folded diapers, the teapot covered by Mrs. McLeod's crocheted tea cozy and sitting in the middle of the rustic farm table.

"You and Lisbeth shouldn't be on your own here."

Not this again. "We'll manage, Dafydd. It's not like you'll be far away. We'll see you every day." She and Lisbeth had had lovely days going down to meet him at Rackwick Bay, collecting seaweed on the beach, Lisbeth tottering through the sand, fascinated with the round pebbles. Kate and Dafydd had laughed at the startled sheep they'd discovered when they had clambered over the island's moors to a prehistoric stone cairn, Lisbeth carried in their arms. A limitless sky, the sea everywhere.

"Look, Kate, Scapa Flow's strategic defenses need an overhaul. The antiaircraft system is from the last war, the anti-submarine nets still need repairs, a lot of things aren't as safe as I'd like them to be. Better for you and Lisbeth at my ma's in Cardiff."

She couldn't stand the thought of the cramped townhouse in Wales, living again with her prissy mother-in-law, who folded bandages for the Red Cross, and Dafydd's half-blind retired RAF colonel father, an air warden with spare-the-rod, spoil-the-child opinions on child-rearing.

"But I've got a job, Dafydd," she said. "And Lisbeth's so happy with Mrs. McLeod when I'm on shift."

A jewel, Mrs. McLeod. She lived next door and coddled Lisbeth as if she were her own grandchild. She babysat on Friday nights so Kate and Dafydd could go out dancing—they'd both learned to dance local reels at Longhope. Mrs. McLeod rented them this cottage for a "pittance," according to Dafydd. Took in their laundry. Baked for the men in Dafydd's unit. The Orkney locals offered warmth and welcome—in contrast to the Brits on the base, who had never made Kate feel particularly comfortable.

"It's safer down there, and better for you and Lisbeth."

She didn't want to argue during the precious time they had together.

"Okay. But it's harder for you to visit on leave," she said, nibbling his neck. "And how would we play cowboys and Indians?"

"You're changing the subject." He rubbed the baby's back.

"What about all your repressed British schoolboy urges? Don't you want me to get out my cowgirl boots?"

Dafydd grinned.

"That's why you married me," she said. She wanted to snatch Lisbeth off his lap, tuck her in the crib and straddle him. "Admit it."

And for a moment his smiling eyes went serious. He took her hand, kissed it. "You're unlike anyone I've ever known, Kate," he said. "Who'd have thought I'd find a cowgirl in Paris. One I'll never let go of."

He'd gone to Paris to paint and had come back to Britain with her instead of a portfolio.

She draped her arm around his shoulder and pulled him close. Inhaled him—his musky smell she loved. "Like I'd let you?"

"You're the sexiest thing in boots this side of the pond," Dafydd said. "If there are more like you in Oregon . . ."

She nuzzled his cheek. "I'm the last one."

Lisbeth's pale pink eyelids fluttered like butterfly wings. Kate leaned down to kiss her and felt Lisbeth's little breaths hot on her cheek. Sometimes she couldn't believe that she and Dafydd had made such a beautiful thing together.

Lisbeth finally fell asleep with her favorite rattle and Kate and Dafydd ended up under the quilt, laughing and trying to be as quiet as they could. Later, warm in Dafydd's arms, his legs wrapped around hers, she put away her worries until tomorrow.

In the middle of the night, Lisbeth's cries woke Kate. She cradled the baby and felt how warm her daughter was.

She sponged her with cold cloths to cool her down. Crushed a quarter of Pulverette no. 67, the brown pill Mrs. McLeod swore by for its analgesic and fever reducing properties. Kate filled Lisbeth's bottle with warm milk, added the crushed pill and shook it. Lisbeth drank little, listless and burning with fever. Fifteen minutes passed, but nothing had changed. Worried, Kate switched on the lamp and roused Dafydd.

"Her fever's high, Dafydd. We have to do something."

Lisbeth's little legs and arms jerked in Kate's arms. Then her eyes rolled up her head. Her body went limp. Panic filled Kate. Everything she'd been doing must have been wrong.

They had no telephone but Mrs. McLeod did. "Go next door, call the doctor."

"She's not there. She went to her daughter's on the other side of the island this afternoon," said Dafydd, pulling on his pants. "That's a febrile convulsion."

"What?"

"I had one as a child, my mother told me. Kate, the convulsion itself isn't serious, but the danger is that it could mean meningitis."

People died from meningitis.

Here she'd been trying to bring down the fever on her own, wasting precious time, when the situation was too serious for that.

Kate grabbed his keys. "We're taking her to Doctor Tavish."

They drove in Dafydd's staff vehicle, a Tilly, an Austin converted into a military utility rust bucket, over the bumpy pitch-black country road, flying past blacked-out farmhouses and cottages. These were the accommodations Orkney could furnish naval families on wartime deployment on the island.

It was a moonless night, the air thick with a web of fog. Dafydd cursed into the darkness as he drove. "Can't see a bloody thing."

Kate grabbed a flashlight from the glove compartment. Its weak beam was little help. Lisbeth felt so warm, so still in her arms.

On Rinnigill's outskirts, she pointed to a dark stone cottage. "That's Doctor Tavish's."

Dafydd hit the brakes. Kate gathered Lisbeth to her chest, climbed down from the Tilly. Even in her fever Lisbeth was clutching her favorite rattle, which jingled softly as Kate ran up to knock on the cottage door. "Doctor Tavish?" No answer. "Please, Doctor Tavish, my baby's sick. She's burning with fever."

Still no answer. Dafydd took Lisbeth in his arms. Now Kate was yelling and pounding on the door. It felt like a very long time before the door opened to a yawning older woman in a dressing gown, her face lined with irritation.

"Why are ye wakin' me in th' middle o' th' night?"

Kate barely understood the woman's Scottish dialect, but the meaning was clear. "I'm sorry but please, we need the doctor. My baby's seriously ill."

"He's doon at th' pub ev'ry night."

Doon at th' pub, that much Kate understood. She saw a doctor's bag by the woman's bare feet at the door.

"May I just take his bag to him at the pub, would you mind?"

"God be wi' ye, lass." The woman's look had softened as she handed Kate the doctor's bag. "Hope he's nae had tae many pints."

Kate threw a thank-you over her shoulder as she hurried back to the Tilly, where Dafydd, Lisbeth crooked in one arm, had already started the ignition.

"We're almost there, Lisbeth," Kate said, taking her back in her arms. Her heart pounded as she rocked her daughter, bracing herself against the door in the bare-bones two-seater. Dafydd hurtled through Rinnigill's dark countryside, shifting into fourth gear and accelerating toward the pier.

In the distance a loud explosion sounded from the middle of the dark harbor where the HMS *Royal Oak* warship anchored.

"Is that an attack?"

Before Dafydd could answer, a ship burst into flames, lighting the sky and the surrounding water.

"Bloody hell, either the ship's cordite exploded or a submarine got through the nets and torpedoed it."

Sirens wailed as they neared the pub on the pier. Kate trembled, feeling Lisbeth's blanket damp with sweat against her chest. Searchlights were scanning the cold sky. A Red Cross truck flashed its headlights for them to get out of the way and shot ahead of them, then promptly stopped, blocking further progress down the narrow street to the pub. Rescue workers were unloading equipment and shouting instructions.

"I can't get any closer," said Dafydd, pulling over in front of the post office. "It's too cold outside for Lisbeth and the pub will be rowdy. Go fetch the doctor, we'll wait here for you." He opened his arms, collecting Lisbeth from Kate. His face was tearstained as he rocked her. Stricken, she realized he was right. Still she hated to leave them. But what else could she do?

She kissed him hard.

"Hurry, Kate."

She ran, passing the Red Cross truck, the rescue workers streaming to the pier—*what a disaster*—and pulled the pub door open.

She squinted through a smoky haze. The pub resounded with raucous laughter and singing. Peaty smells emanated from the beamed fireplace.

"Lookin' fur a pint, missus?"

"Where's the doctor?"

"What's 'at ye say?"

The place was so noisy she could hardly hear herself talk. "The doctor! It's an emergency!" she shouted.

"Over thar." The barkeep pointed to the bearded man singing by the fire, a beer in his hand.

She pushed by the laughing patrons, ignoring the invitations for a drink, if that's what they were even saying to her. As she took the beer from the doctor's hand and replaced it with his bag, the blacked-out windows in the pub shattered. Bottles fell, spraying whiskey on the bar. The crowd had quieted enough now to hear the wailing sirens.

"We're under attack," someone shouted. Men stood and reached for their jackets.

"Hurry, Doctor Tavish, come with me." He stank of beer but she pulled the doctor's hand and he stumbled out of the pub door. Behind them men were rushing out to the pier. "Please, it's this way. My baby's sick. She's with my husband—they're waiting around the corner."

Suddenly she heard the sickening crash of metal. Then a

thundering explosion ricocheted down the chilly street. The ground rumbled, throwing them against a stone wall.

She heard screams. Behind a low row of houses she watched the jagged roofline of the post office blush red. Flames.

Kate pulled herself up, her pulse racing, and yelled over the shouting for the doctor to follow her. She ran forward into a cloud of powdery dust that shimmered white in the heat, choking her. Flames crackled, their combustion sucking the air like a hot wind tunnel.

Had a bomb gone off?

Turning the corner, she found the street was a blast furnace. Cries and the yelping of a dog echoed from somewhere in the smoking haze.

"Dafydd! Lisbeth!"

Terror stricken, she saw a gaping hole where the post office had been. Now it was a flaming heap of collapsing stone. A figure writhed in the burning driver's seat of the Red Cross truck. Horrific. The doctor was trying to open the truck's door. Kate kept moving, she had to find her family. "Dafydd, where are you?"

She tried to see through the smoke, inching her way along a wall that was hot to the touch. Finally she could see through the smoke enough to make out a burning petrol supply truck, its front end crumpled and smashed into—no, no, it couldn't be. The truck had crashed into the Tilly, creating a fireball.

Screaming and stumbling toward the burning Tilly, she inhaled acrid smoke. The wall sparked into flame and began to crumble. She heard a baby's cry. Lisbeth. The last thing she remembered was a rush of raining soot.

KATE BLINKED AWAKE TO BRIGHT lights, a burnt hair smell in her nose. She felt a cold disk against her chest.

"Where am I?"

"You're in the naval hospital. I'm the duty doctor."

Kate's eyes focused on an older woman with short gray hair, a stethoscope hanging from her neck, who was feeling for her pulse.

"You've been treated for burns and smoke inhalation," the doctor was saying. "And for shock. All your vital signs are stable."

"I want to see Dafydd," Kate said, trying to sit up. "My baby."

The doctor sat down next to Kate on the bed, taking Kate's bandaged hand. "Miss—"

"It's Missus," she said. "Mrs. Rees."

"Mrs. Rees, we've had a terrible tragedy—"

"What happened?" Kate's foggy mind struggled to remember.

"There was an attack," the doctor said, fury in her voice. "The Germans torpedoed a ship—the *Royal Oak.* There were twelve hundred men and boys aboard."

"But—" Kate's memory was coming back—the glittering white heat, the Red Cross vehicle in flames. "There was a petrol truck," she said suddenly.

"Yes," the doctor said softly. "In the confusion of the attack there was a horrific accident. Three vehicles, including a petrol truck. It caused a huge fire. There were many casualties."

"You don't understand," Kate said, as *she* tried not to understand. "My husband was with my sick baby, waiting for me by the post office. They must have been taken to safety."

"They're gone. I'm so sorry."

"Gone?" She grabbed the doctor's arm and pulled herself up, startled by the sudden pain in her burned legs. "Gone where?"

"They didn't make it."

"No, that's not true."

"I'm afraid no one survived."

That's when she felt the searing pain in her gut. "Then how did I?"

"You were lucky."

"Lucky?" She threw the covers aside. "I don't believe you." Struggled as the doctor held her down. "We have to find them." She was screaming as a nurse came toward her with a hypodermic needle. "Don't you understand?" And then she felt the jab.

June 16, 1940

Hoy, Orkney

More than half a year had passed since the crash and Kate still woke up sick every day. This morning she'd gone to where the post office had stood, now an empty sore of a fire site, the whole place fenced off up to the pier it bordered. Scapa Flow's oily water churned below. Only a buoy in the harbor marked the watery grave of the sunken warship HMS *Royal Oak.* Her mind returned to its fiery sinking, lurching like a wounded whale. She climbed through the wire fence and combed through the rubble and burnt wood, up to her knees in soot. Always looking for a trace of Lisbeth, Dafydd. To find something for the hole in her heart.

She tossed charred bricks aside, finding chunks of mortar, shards of glass. Dug deep and felt a piece of smooth metal. Under it something jagged—a scorched wooden baby rattle, the handle blackened. Her heart fractured. Lisbeth's favorite. How had it survived the flames? It was as if fate were being especially brutal. Sobbing, she brushed the soot off, kissed it. Held it close to her chest.

Flapping in the rubble was a torn and crinkled newspaper page—a photo of a candlelit rally, Hitler standing before a giant swastika. The man who had taken her family away. And for what?

An aching split her insides. Nothing could fill the emptiness.

Below her foot a shard of glass sparkled in the morning sun. She thought about how easy it would be to pick it up and slice her wrist, put the emptiness behind her forever.

The wind blowing over the treeless fields carried the bleating of sheep. She thought of her pa back in Oregon. When she was a little girl and her stupid brother had tripped her, Pa had told her to get up. Get up and get even.

She stared at Hitler's picture and wiped her tears, letting her anger fill her.

You'll pay.

"I'M STILL SHOCKED YE CAME back ta work," said Greer, grinding out a cigarette with her toe in the brick factory yard.

Kate shrugged. "What else would I do with myself, Greer?"

Without work to distract her, she'd find herself on the roof, ready to jump.

Greer was local, the only good friend she'd made working in munitions assembly. Today, as usual, they ate lunch together perched on wood boxes of ammunition stacked in the factory yard under a metal canopied supply lean-to that protected them from the weather. Across from them at the other end of the dirt yard was the warhead examination room, beyond that the hurriedly built torpedo depot. In the adjoining building was the recreation center, where Greer's gran worked. The recreation center was a vital part of the military complex, hosting activities to boost morale on this remote island.

Troops marched past, headed toward the power station on the freshly tarmacked road, as Greer divided her doughy pasty, which was wrapped in a creased, much-folded piece of newspaper, and shared half with Kate. Kate had little appetite. Everything tasted like cardboard after her loss. She hated this dried-up pasty. Yet the doctor had warned her she'd get sick again if she didn't eat, and then she wouldn't be able to work.

"Don't ye want ta go back home ta Oregon?" asked Greer.

"Nothing makes it across the Atlantic anymore with the U-boats, Greer. Not even letters."

The last letter from her father had arrived three months ago saying her brother Jed had jumped the gun and enlisted in the army. He'd written how sorry he'd been not to meet his son-in-law and granddaughter. Touchingly, he had requested a lock of Lisbeth's hair to keep alongside her mother's.

She didn't even have that.

"Mah brother's bin evacuated," said Greer. He had been sent to France and Kate knew Greer had been desperately worried about him since the fighting began at Dunkirk. He was only sixteen—Greer had confided that he had lied to join the army. Just a kid.

"Hope he's home soon, Greer." Kate had listened to the BBC broadcast last week, when the recently appointed prime minister Winston Churchill had described the British soldiers evacuating the Dunkirk beaches on every kind of fishing boat, a flotilla bobbing in the Channel. Churchill had warned of the impending German invasion, his words still ringing in her mind: "We shall fight on the beaches, we shall fight on the landing grounds, we shall fight in the fields and in the streets, we shall fight in the hills; we shall never surrender."

"Have a wee sip." Greer poured steaming milky tea from a thermos into a chipped mug and offered it to Kate. "Mah gran found sugar on th' black market."

The tea was hot, sweet and strong as nails. "You're a real pal to share, Greer." Kate squeezed Greer's hand. Rationed sugar was like gold on the island. "Lovely, haven't tasted anything sweet since I don't know when."

Several of the maintenance crew were emerging from the torpedo depot, wiping their hands. As they passed Kate and Greer, one was saying, "What's that noise?"

Kate heard it, too. It came from the sky.

A propeller plane droned out of the clouds, followed by a second, then a third one.

A Royal Navy lieutenant was pointing. "Call control. We need to identify these aircraft."

The whole island of Hoy was a restricted security area. Special permits and security clearance were required to travel in or out. Planes brought supplies and equipment only at scheduled times due to the difficulty of moving the hydrogen-filled barrage balloons that camouflaged the pier, the anchored fleet and naval stores. A shipment had come in several days ago; there wouldn't be another today. But Kate knew yesterday's storm had grounded all but one of the barrage balloons; normally hostile aircraft would have been forced to higher, less accurate bombing altitudes.

"Sound the alert!" The team of servicemen playing hockey in the next field were beating a path off their pitch, shouting and pointing at the sky. As the planes approached from the east, the plane fuselages came into view—unmistakable swastikas. The Luftwaffe.

Startled, Kate choked on the tea.

"Bloody 'ell." Greer chewed faster.

Confusion set it. People were running for cover. Why hadn't the alert sounded? Kate saw the gunners at the newly installed Vickers Mk VIII light antiaircraft guns trying to fire, but the guns seemed to be jammed. So much for thinking this place was impregnable.

The planes made a lazy dip, then the droning faded away. Gone. Had the Luftwaffe strayed too far from their Norway base? Why hadn't the radar system warned the two frontline RAF fighter squadrons stationed over at Wick to intercept the planes?

The English officer was chiding servicemen to return to duty. "Back to positions," he said in that let's-be-sensible-and-not-cause-a-big-fuss way Kate had still not gotten used to during the time she had been living among English officers. "Control is looking into what's going on."

Greer stood, wiping crumbs from her work smock. "Gotta tell mah gran ta get home. She shouldna finish out her shift."

"See you later, Greer."

Kate put the half-eaten pasty in her pocket and drifted across the yard to join some coworkers. There was general excited discussion of the Luftwaffe planes as they trudged back to work, filing along the factory's blacked-out windows, their sills gray with clots of pigeon droppings.

They hadn't made it into the factory when Kate heard the drone of planes again. Her stomach clenched. Everyone looked up. The Luftwaffe were taking another pass now that the clouds had parted. Only two this time, their swastikas glinting on the fuselage.

Then a thundering explosion. A bomb. Dark black billows mushroomed from the naval barracks beyond the factory. The ground trembled.

"Attack," someone yelled.

The nightmare of the fiery explosion that had taken Dafydd and Lisbeth was happening all over again. Frozen in the horror of her memories, Kate watched as a plane broke out of formation, picked up speed and swooped down, flying low along the pier, not three hundred yards away beyond the factory wall.

Why were only the Territorial Army unit overlooking Lyness responding with their eight 4.5 heavy antiaircraft guns? Why wasn't an alert sounding?

The plane executed a loop. Showing off, the cocky bastard. Sun sparkled on the cockpit window. The plane dipped, heading straight toward the factory, the armament stores, the torpedo depot and the recreation center.

The place would explode, taking the wharf and the base with it.

She looked around at the shocked faces of her coworkers.

"Gas masks, everyone!" yelled the factory foreman. "To the shelter at the foundry!"

Sirens blared. Assembly line and munitions workers streamed past her now, jostling and shoving toward the shelter on the other side of the yard.

Over the fence she saw a plume of charcoal smoke rise from the black hull of the half-sunk shipwreck used to block submarines from the harbor. Everyone was running for cover, into nearby barracks, the canteen, any place to escape the plane's machine gun strafing. She saw a stream of bullets scattering people coming out of the recreation center. A screaming woman pulled her child down to the ground. An older woman ran terrorized only to be mowed down by machine gun fire, dropping like a doll.

Kate felt her heart seize. She thought of Greer's grandmother—could that woman have been her? But where was Greer? She searched the crowd.

"You there, get going."

Her heart thumped in her chest, fear icing through her veins. The plane's constant droning got closer. "Greer!" Her shout was swallowed by all the other shouts in the yard.

"Hurry inside, the shelter's filling up," said one of the older men from the ammo supply. He grabbed her arm, pulling her into the throng.

When they were inside, standing crowded together, she wiped the perspiration from her forehead with her sleeve. One of the English home guard wardens blew a whistle. "All inside, door closing." The metal door grunted and scraped over the stone as the other warden started to pull it shut.

More tat-tat-tat sprayed the brick wall. In the narrowing patch of daylight on the other side of the door, Kate saw a woman running toward the shelter. Her torn dress trailed in the oil puddles in the dirt yard and a gas mask was bouncing from her belt. Greer!

"Don't close the door, let her in!" Kate shouted.

The home guard warden was still pulling hard on the scraping door. "It's too late. We're responsible for everyone's safety—"

In the last inch of daylight coming through the door, Kate watched a trail of bullets raise dust puffs in the yard. Kate choked back a scream as Greer pounded on the door. Any second the gunner would pick her off.

With all her might, Kate shoved the guard aside and threw her body weight against the heavy door.

"Quick, Greer!"

Panting, she yanked her friend inside.

Greer huddled in the shelter, trembling. Kate rubbed her back, steeling herself against the dirty looks of the home guard wardens.

"You put a lot of lives at risk, Yank," said the one she'd shoved. "I'm going to have to report this."

There wouldn't be a report at all if the shelter was bombed to smithereens.

Kate hated feeling so helpless. And now here she was stuck in the shelter trembling in fear like everyone else. She tried to ignore the angry mutterings of her coworkers, but they carried loudly in the stale air of the shelter.

Greer's chin quivered. "I owe ye, Kate."

"You would have done the same."

After ten minutes, a fog horn sounded the all-clear.

"About time," Greer said. "Gotta find mah gran." Kate heard false bravado in her voice.

As people exited the shelter, the home guard warden took Kate's elbow. "You're a civilian subject to His Majesty's naval base regulations," he said, his tone officious. "In this military facility your security clearance depends on your adhering to the rules and regulations. I'm reporting you for disciplinary action. We're going to the head home guard warden's office right now."

"I understand," Kate said, trying to look apologetic. "But no one got hurt."

"She saved mah life, ye eejit," Greer said, dusting off her dress.

"She risked the lives of a hundred people!" said the home guard. "As a foreigner—"

"A foreigner?" said Kate. Would she lose her job? But this was ridiculous. "I am the widow of a Welsh naval officer."

"As a *non–British citizen*," the warden said, spittle flying from his lips, "you've been allowed to work here on sufferance because of your husband. You've gone too far now. Let's go."

KATE PACED THE LINOLEUM FLOOR in the home guard warden's empty office. Her blouse collar stuck to her damp neck. Outside the window naval cadets marched in unison; work was resuming on the wharf.

The base Red Cross ambulances had arrived after the all-clear; the nurses were moving among the injured in front of the recreation center. Kate watched as medics lifted the lifeless older woman onto a gurney. She recognized the face as they pulled a sheet over it. Greer's gran.

Heartbroken, Kate watched Greer, sobbing, follow the medics to the ambulance. *Mah feisty gran,* Kate could hear her friend saying with a grin, *always takin' the piss out of someone who deserves it.* This warm-hearted woman who'd always been so kind. Kate could still taste the black-market sugar she'd scrounged for that sweet milky tea.

An innocent victim of the Luftwaffe. A pointless death.

She sat on the floor, wrapped her arms around her bent knees. No tears left, she rocked back and forth, rocked and rocked until her back was tired and her rear end was sore.

After half an hour, Kate realized she'd been forgotten.

Now what?

Kate couldn't face returning to work. Or the cottage, filled with memories of what she'd never have again. Dafydd's warm arms. Lisbeth's soft cooing.

She had to do something with herself. For eight months she'd been treading water, wallowing in grief, mindlessly testing rifles and completing her factory work. She couldn't stand it anymore.

She arrived at a decision.

Time to fight back.

She reached for the warden's phone on his desk, asked for an outside line and repeated from memory the number the man with the cane had written on the card he'd given her at the firing range.

AN HOUR LATER, KATE WAS standing downstairs in the factory yard, waiting. She watched the cloud-puffed sky and the harbor shining with a scum of oil slick. The air reeked of oil mixed with a fishy tang. Black and white puffins took wing in the vanilla midafternoon, light spread over the rolling green fields dotted by sheep and the Nissen huts at the naval base. Somewhere a wooden shutter banged.

An olive-green staff car from the Hatston air base pulled up at the factory yard. Several of the munitions inspectors and the home guard warden had appeared to meet it. As the passengers disembarked, Kate recognized the man with the cane. He'd gotten her message.

"That's her. That's the one." The home guard warden pointed an accusing finger at her as she approached them. "I told you to wait, you're to be court martialed."

"Court martialed? That's for the military."

"During wartime court martials extend to civilians," he said.

"Why bother?" Kate turned to the man with the cane. Fine lines radiated from his eyes, whose irises were a mottled green with brown specks. He wore no uniform, in contrast to the military dress of his scowling assistant. "Thank you for responding to my message, sir. I'm interested in that job. Birmingham, you said."

A muscle in the home guard warden's cheek twitched. "What's this? Some kind of fairy tale? You're under disciplinary action."

"Thank you, warden, I'll handle it from here," the man said. "Ah yes, the job offer stands."

Kate looked him in the eye. "I can take the afternoon ferry and get the train to Birmingham tomorrow morning."

"Well, Miss—"

"Mrs. Rees," she corrected.

"Mrs. Rees, the job I have for you now is not in Birmingham." He looked at his watch, then indicated for his assistant to open the staff car door. "We'll give you a ride."

After a military flight from Hatston to somewhere on the mainland, Kate was bundled into a mud-splattered staff car for a short drive through the countryside. They pulled up to a grilled gate that opened into the driveway of a manor house. Peacocks strutted on the rolling grass in the twilight. It was like a scene out of *Rebecca,* the movie Greer had taken her to see at the recreation center a few months earlier. Only the emerging stars provided any light.

Once they were inside, Alfred Stepney, as he'd introduced

himself, ushered her into a high-ceilinged drawing room with a flagstone fireplace and dark wood-paneled walls. No one had told Kate where they were going. She tried to tamp down her apprehension.

She wondered if she'd made the right choice in calling this man.

The bookshelves were full and a large globe perched on a stand. She caught sight of herself in a gilt mirror over the sofa and looked down at her greasy hands and stained factory pants. Well, what did Stepney expect? Not that she cared.

"Mrs. Rees, are you prepared to sign the Official Secrets Act?"

This sounded serious. "What exactly would I be signing?"

"You'll be agreeing to never disclose any information regarding security and the intelligence services under the Crown. Basically, you will never speak of anything we ask you to do from this moment forward."

"I assume it's a condition of the job?"

"I'm afraid we have nothing more to discuss unless you do." The piercing gaze from his keen mottled green eyes turned to a look of amusement. The expression reminded Kate of the poker players in Sands Flats. "And I believe you're the right candidate."

What did she have to lose? The pen scratched on the fibrous paper as Kate wrote her name. "You brought me here because I can shoot, right?"

"There's a mission for you. You'll go through an accelerated training, since unfortunately we don't have much time."

For the first time she noticed the bald patch he'd carefully combed over, just visible under the overhead light. How he favored his left leg. "What kind of mission?"

"War work for your special skills." He tapped his walking stick. "I wouldn't ask if I didn't believe you could do it."

Kate looked around the drawing room, out the tall windows to the sloping lawn. She'd entered another world. Sensed there were different rules. She still didn't know what she was getting into.

"As long as I have a chance to get back at the Germans, fine," she said, realizing it sounded like a line from a dime novel. But it was true. "But does this mean I'm joining the military?"

"We're only accountable to the prime minister," said Stepney. "My group, Section D, doesn't exist officially."

Not just another world, a covert world. "So—you're spies?"

He considered her for a moment, then said, "All our operations are deniable. But I never told you that."

Deniable. She turned the word over in her mind. It meant that if she failed at whatever they wanted her to do, her life would most likely be forfeit. That no one would ever know what had happened to her.

She was in over her head.

Had that ever stopped her?

"Still interested?"

"When do we start?"

In the next room, which was even larger, a deal table was covered with maps. Stepney indicated a chair and they sat down. Kate spotted a much-thumbed street map of Paris by the foot of yet another large globe.

Stepney cleared his throat to get her attention. "We have limited time, Mrs. Rees. Please, listen closely and try to remember everything I say. If nothing else, remember these letters: RADA." He gave her a half-smile. "No, it's not the Royal Academy of Dramatic Arts, but that will help you remember. Burn the letters in your brain, make them second nature. RADA: Read, Assess, Decide, Act. This stands for: read the situation; assess possible outcomes; decide on options; act on your decision. Can you repeat that?"

She did.

"You'll have practice examples later. Think those letters, RADA, to yourself constantly, every moment of every hour; wherever you are, walking on the street, in the shop, boarding the Métro. Any moment a German soldier might stop and demand your papers. It's impossible to avoid them so you need to be prepared. Always have a story ready, but be flexible according to the situation. Use your intuition. Your instinct."

Kate shifted in the hardback chair. "So you're sending me behind enemy lines."

"That depends on how well you do in training," he said. "But I believe you're more than capable based on what I've seen. You've got what you Americans call moxie, Mrs. Rees."

"In Oregon we call it hellfire."

"Thinking on the fly is essential," he said. "Improvising. Wherever you go, a shop, a café, you'll need to always look for the back way out. Know the closest bus stop, and always have a *carnet* of tickets, one ready in your pocket. Mingle in crowds, blend in, never do anything to draw attention to yourself. The minute you open your mouth—well, it's not a good idea."

Stepney stood and went to the door, then turned around.

"Do you have any friends or acquaintances in Paris you still correspond with?"

She nodded. "One or two, but . . ."

"Who?" Stepney's voice rose. For the first time she saw wariness on his thin face.

"Actually, they were Dafydd's friends," she said. "My classmates in the Sorbonne were international—Polish, Swedish, German, Austrian. I have no clue if they're still in Paris now. With the war, I doubt it."

Stepney blew air from his mouth. "Avoid the temptation to look them up," he said. "Don't go anywhere near your old lodging, the bakery you used to visit. Do not say hello if you see your old concierge. You don't want to contact or compromise anyone."

"What do you mean by compromise?"

"Paris has changed under the occupation," said Stepney. "So has everyone you once knew. Some may have German sympathies, or need a job with the occupiers, or just need to keep their apartment, protect their family—there are a million reasons a former friend might turn you over to the Germans. Money, of course, is the simplest. Trust no one."

At his words, the reality of the situation began to sink in.

"Would anyone remember you?" Stepney was saying. "A teacher at the Sorbonne perhaps?"

"There were tons of students, but I don't think anyone would remember me. Haven't even kept in touch with my old tutor." She'd been oblivious to everything else after she'd met Dafydd. She'd spent every day at their café sipping wine while Dafydd sketched. "Why?"

Irritated, Stepney stared at her with those flecked green eyes. "Anyone you knew could point you out. Things have changed, you must understand that. We've lost two agents in the last few days."

Lost two agents . . . maybe that was why there was a job opening for her.

"Don't trust anyone," he said again. "I can't stress this enough. It's lonely, I know, I've done this myself. One friendly face from the past and the mission is ruined. Speak to no one. It's safer for you and for them. Never return to the same place twice. Wherever you go, think about a place you can hide. A bolt-hole."

"Bolt-hole?"

Stepney grinned for the first time. "Like this." He walked past her, slid open a wooden wall panel disguised to look like the others. Inside was a dark space, musty and full of dust. "It's a priest's hidey-hole. All the old manors had them to foil Henry the Eighth's henchman. This manor belonged to a Papist."

Kate ran her finger over France on the large globe. "Who exactly are you, Stepney?"

Just then, a gray mouse darted along the skirting board and disappeared behind a bookcase, and Stepney gave her a small smile. "I'm a little mouse like him. Part of the woodwork." He handed her a manual. "This contains the basics. Usually there are six weeks of training. There's much to teach you but we have so little time."

Her tongue felt too big for her mouth, which had gone dry, so she nodded.

She opened the manual, scanned the headings in the index: *Dead-Letter Boxes, Disguises, Escape, Surveillance.* A spy manual. "But you know what, Stepney, I think you're a big mouse."

He glanced at his watch. "And I think you need time for your coursework. Memorize chapter three. You'll recite it to me when I return. I'll leave you to it."

STEPNEY RETURNED AN HOUR LATER. After she'd repeated chapter three, "Escape," to him, he nodded. "Some people want to meet you," he said, brisk and businesslike.

Stepney led Kate down a long hallway and into a narrow sitting room, its walls hung with oil paintings. A moment later a woman, her white hair in a chignon, joined them. She was wearing a simple black dress, pearls, and bright red lipstick. *"Ça va, Madame Rees. Vous êtes bien méchante, eh?"*

"Moi? Pourquoi, madame?"

"No good," said the woman in perfect English to Stepney. "Her accent's too strong. She'd be picked out in a minute. I'd need a month of intensive work with her."

"Can't she be from the north, say Lille? Or Belgian?"

"She could say she grew up in Canada, that that's the source of her funny accent," the woman said. "Even better would be to keep her mouth shut, talk only when she had to."

Stepney shrugged. "Unfortunately, the Gestapo have cottoned on to the deaf-mute ploy."

He motioned Kate to sit down on a worn leather chair. Then he and the woman disappeared.

Curiouser and curiouser, Kate thought, like Alice down the rabbit hole. If he was sending her behind enemy lines to France, why not just tell her? She wondered who owned this big drafty house with its unlived-in smell and secret hidey-holes. Not for the first time she thought the English more than strange. Dafydd had always said the same thing.

June 16, 1940

Somewhere in the English Countryside | Evening

"A big-boned Yank. Her features and mannerisms are so obviously American. Good God, Stepney, they'd shoot her on sight." Thomas Cathcart, Stepney's counterpart in the Secret Intelligence Service, let his gruff voice ring out across Prime Minister Churchill's study. "The language issue would never even have a chance to come up!"

The prime minister's secretary entered. "Here's her file, Prime Minister."

Cigar smoke trailed from Churchill's large worn leather chair. The PM waved it away and took the file.

"The girl's a rifle champion. Gold medals from 1934, Butte Falls, 1934, Clackamas County, 1936, Deschutes County." Churchill looked up as he read. "I'm half-American but have no idea where these are."

"Oregon state, sir."

"Aah, I see." He puffed on his cigar. "What do you say, Stepney? It's your bloody idea."

Stepney met Cathcart's expressionless gaze. Cathcart, the new SIS head, looked like a middle-aged accountant. Cathcart was far more familiar with the inner sanctum than Stepney, as was his lackey, a public school twit who had never seen a day of combat in his life. Rival intelligence services with their onerous old boy factions looked down on Section D. Not to mention the damn military.

"With respect, sir. The woman's got spirit. And a woman can . . ." He paused. "Well, use her wiles."

"She is hardly an exotic dancer," said Cathcart. "A bizarre choice. Amateurish even for your Irregulars."

Stepney's Irregulars, who were both Brits and foreign nationals, did dirty jobs: clandestine operations involving Stepney's contacts in the Deuxième Bureau, France's internal intelligence branch. No one in the British government wanted to be seen interfering with other countries' internal affairs. Yet after the humiliation of Dunkirk, the new prime minister needed a success. He'd tasked Stepney to come up with a plan. Something bold. A shock tactic.

Cathcart closed his folder. "There are just too many risks."

"Our Paris network was compromised two days ago." Stepney stood up, stifled a wince at the pain shooting through his hip, and paused to look each person sitting around the table in the eye in turn. "Our boys who have been stranded in France since Dunkirk are getting picked off in their hiding places. There's a leak."

Stepney let the silence hang. A log sparked and crackled in the fireplace.

"We lost our two top snipers in the last airdrop. Our third sniper unit is engaged in a desert mission outside of Tripoli. It will be at least seventy-two hours, if not more, before they're in contact. There's no time with the given deadline. We need someone now. You want the list of suitable candidates?"

He pulled a piece of paper from his pocket, unfolded it and held it up for effect. Blank.

"No one's denying that, Stepney," Cathcart said. "But even if she's a crack shot, as I said, there's just too much risk that she'd compromise our entire network."

"She'll only know the information she's given. But yes, there's the language problem, and her appearance." Stepney lifted his arms as if in concession. "But no one knows her. We use only one contact, Mercier."

"What if Mercier's the leak?" the SIS lackey asked. Red-haired, a graduate of Harrow, going by his double striped old school tie. The type of Englishman who wore his pedigree around his neck.

Stepney cleared his throat. "I flew twelve joint-force combat missions with Colonel Mercier in 1917, until we were shot down. I vouch for the man."

A nervous cough. "No disrespect intended, sir."

"Gentlemen, you raise well-founded objections," Stepney said. "Allow me to make two important points." He laid the shot-up target on the table next to the burning cigar. "We've proof of her ability to hit consecutive targets at three hundred yards. A marksman, er, markswoman. And this is personal for her."

His finger ran over the holes made by the bullets.

"She's the only faint chance in hell we have to make this work."

Silence.

"Of course, if you have other candidates for this mission I don't know about . . ."

The cigar smoke drifted in lazy spirals under the carved ceiling arches. Cathcart and his lackey looked to Churchill.

"Hmm." The whiskey splashed in the heavy tumbler as the prime minister shifted it. He struck a match and took another puff from the cigar. "So you think I should meet her, Stepney?"

Let him think it's his idea. "Sir, my job is to furnish information. It's up to your discretion, of course. I just thought . . ."

"You just thought, Stepney?" A laugh.

The black phone by the whiskey decanter trilled. The prime minister answered. Grunted. He hung up and stood. "Midnight meeting for everyone in this room. Come up with a precise plan. I want it detailed down to which French-label silk blouse she'd wear. Get the weather projections and the latest decoded Abwehr rosters from Bletchley Park. I mean up-to-the-minute. Get a plane down there if you have to."

A few raised eyebrows. But each of the four nodded.

"Reserve your judgment until tonight," he said. "Treat this as Level One, highest priority. This doesn't leave the room, I might add." He gave a chuckle. "After all, we haven't even asked the lady."

An hour later, after a hot meal of rabbit stew at a scarred wood counter in a cavernous basement kitchen, Kate was escorted into what looked like a parlor and asked to sit down on another stiff-backed chair. It was hard to believe all this had happened since her lunch today with Greer. A radiator sputtered, emitting dribbles of heat. The high-ceilinged room was lined with blackout curtains and the only light came from a dim chandelier, which was missing several crystals, and an Anglepoise desk lamp. Three men in uniform stood surveying her. They began to ask questions, taking turns, impersonal and cold.

Are you a Democrat or Republican? Would you join a workers' union? Have you ever been, or are you, a member of the Communist Party? Have you supported the German American Bund?

So this was what an interrogation was like. Were they testing her to see if she could hold up under pressure?

She shifted on the chair, keeping her answers simple and truthful. Faltered once when asked about how she met Dafydd in Paris. She found her courage and replied, "Those memories are private, gentlemen, because that's all I have. Memories."

They grilled her about her childhood, the ranches her father had worked at, her student time in Paris, did she get along better with her mother-in-law now?

"How do you know all this?" Kate asked, nervous.

Had Stepney dug into her background since their brief meeting at the shooting range?

"We know all about you, Mrs. Rees. The only thing we don't know is whether you can shoot as well under more difficult conditions."

"I've hunted in blizzards and in the rain," she said. "I would have qualified for the Olympic sharpshooting team but there's no female division. Yet."

"Have you ever killed a person, Kate?"

So they wanted her to assassinate someone. Her throat went dry.

"Shot wolves when times got tough on the ranch. They brought in a twenty-five-dollar bounty. But mostly just deer, elk, and rabbits to feed us all winter long."

"Why don't you give us a demonstration?"

The men ushered her across the lawn to a shooting gallery in an empty stable. She hit the target bull's-eye at three hundred yards, ten out of ten attempts, at which point she put the rifle down.

"I'm tired of bruising my shoulder," she said. "This recoil needs adjustment before I continue."

One of the men, who sported a row of medals on his chest, nodded. "I hated that on the Lee-Enfield myself. Not bad, Mrs. Rees."

Coming from a Brit, and a high-ranking military man at that, she figured that was praise.

He handed her a rifle, another Lee-Enfield No. 4, Mk. I (T), mounted with a telescopic sight and cheek pads. "Try this. It's a prototype—not in full production yet."

She gripped it. About ten pounds, she figured. She looked through the telescopic sight, ran her hand along the wood fore-stock, pulled back the bolt. "Interesting."

"It's efficient. Little muzzle flash, credible accuracy. We've made modifications for faster disassembly. Care to try for the 'mad minute'?"

She'd faced that challenge in the '36 championship.

"You mean fifteen targets in sixty seconds?"

"Let's make it thirty." He set six charger clips on a ledge. Looked at his watch. "Ready? Go."

Kate grabbed a charger, lined it up vertically into the slot, pushed down hard with her right thumb to load the clip into the magazine, tossed the clip, and repeated this with a second charger to fully load the rifle. Aimed and fired. The rifle shot cracked and a soft *wuft* traveled through the air. She ejected the cartridge and reloaded, firing a round of ten, reloading each time. Each shot hit the target bull's-eye. She repeated a second round of ten and then a third.

"Time," he said.

She slid the safety on, turned and handed the rifle back to the bemedaled military man. "Not bad."

He smiled. "This one might have your name on it."

June 21, 1940

Somewhere in the Scottish Countryside | Five Days Later

Kate yawned as she trudged up the staircase to the trainees' rooms. Her brain ached from memorizing details, her legs from practicing parachute jumps. The air mechanic's jumpsuit, the smallest the trainer could find, hung from her shoulders. Completing her ensemble was an oversized gray cardigan and army boots.

After an RAF plane ride at dawn to God knew where, they'd driven an hour through a countryside of gorse and steep crags. Somewhere in the Highlands, she figured. Startled blackbirds erupted from the roadside brush as the camouflaged military truck shot past. Crystalline air scented with wild heather and coarse grasses rushed in the window.

They'd reached an old hunting lodge in a deep ravine dotted with bushes and stunted trees. The sunlight on the jagged peaks was familiar, reminding her of the wild way the crags of the Klamath Mountains caught the light.

For the last five days, the intensive training had lasted from dawn to late at night.

There were three other trainees stationed out here with her, under the constant monitoring of the instructors. Failure to follow any rule, they were told, meant dismissal. Talking among the trainees was forbidden. Mealtimes at the long refectory table were taken in silence. The only other woman, Margo, read magazines; Lewis, a small, rail-thin man, played solitaire; and George, ruddy-cheeked and stocky, did the *Times* crosswords.

In her room, Kate brushed her teeth at the porcelain sink, then padded across the bedroom's wood floor. Her roommate, Margo, lay asleep.

It was cold as hell, so she grabbed another blanket from the old chest. With heating, this place would be bearable. She fell asleep, exhausted, for how long she didn't know. And then she was back in the white-hot dust, flames licking her legs . . . *Lisbeth.* Her nostrils filled with the smell of burning hair. The doctor was grabbing her arms.

She woke up shaking, perspiring in damp sheets.

A candle flickered, casting dim light on the high arching ceiling. She heard sobbing from Margo's corner. Should she see what was the matter? Rules were no talking. This could be a test.

She'd never get back to sleep with her roommate sobbing.

To hell with rules. She pulled the blanket around her shoulders against the cold and knelt by Margo's bed.

"You all right?" Dumb question, but she'd never spoken to the woman. She had no idea where she came from or why she was here.

"Do I sound like it?" A British accent tinged by something European. It was the first time Kate had heard her speak. "Course I'm not."

Kate poured water into a glass from the pitcher on the bedside table. "Drink this."

In the licks of candlelight Margo's tear-stained face emerged from under the pillow. Her chestnut hair was matted to her wet cheeks. She took the glass and drank.

"What's the matter?"

"My fiancé died at Dunkirk," Margo said.

"That's terrible. I'm sorry." Kate pulled the blanket tighter in the chill room.

"Sweet man." Margo pushed back her hair, wiped her face with the sheet. "It's awful. I didn't love him."

"That happens. You shouldn't feel guilty."

"Hard not to. I love someone else. The wrong someone." Margo was looking for Kate's reaction.

Kate shrugged. "Don't we all at one time or another?"

"Sorry if I woke you," Margo said.

Kate's bare feet were like ice. "If you did, it saved me from the rest of my nightmare."

Margo nodded. "Every night you toss and turn, cry out."

"My turn to apologize."

"Did you lose someone, too?"

Kate's hands clenched. "An accident," she said, the words sticking in her throat. "A petrol supply truck, it crashed into our car . . . My baby and husband, they . . ."

Margo's arms were around her. "I'm so sorry. I can't imagine your pain. If you don't want to talk about it . . ."

But she did. The story gushed out of her, the first time she'd said it out loud to anyone.

"No wonder you have bad dreams every night." It was Margo's turn to pour a glass of water from the pitcher for Kate. "So do I."

An orange band of dawn glowed over the dark treetops.

"Do you dream about your fiancé, or . . . ?" Kate hesitated.

"It's complicated."

Was her lover a married man?

"He's my mission . . ." Margo's words dried up.

No one knew their mission, as far as Kate knew. She didn't know hers. Was Margo referring to some kind of personal mission?

"What do you mean?"

Knocking sounded on the door. "Rise and shine. Breakfast in ten."

Margo put her finger to her lips.

Saturday, June 22, 1940

Over the Forest of Fontainebleau, France | 1:00 a.m.

Unstable June weather, just like at home—cloud cover and fog. Martins hated fog jumps. He prayed for luck and hoped he wouldn't land in a henhouse, dangling from a tree or in a river. With the radio set's extra weight, he'd sink like a stone before he could swim.

He couldn't see a bloody thing.

The woman huddling in the back of the converted Whitley bomber wore a jumpsuit and parachute pack. They'd bundled her onto the plane last minute before takeoff. He had enough to worry about on his own, wasn't here to hold the woman's hand. But he wondered. Was she his contact? A spy?

Martins avoided her gaze.

The flight had veered into trouble two hundred and fifty kilometers beyond the Channel, where low-lying fog over the drop at Rambouillet had made for zero visibility despite the full moon. Now they were behind schedule. The RAF pilot kept on to Fontainebleau, destination drop two. There were no landmarks and no signal lights to guide the pilot to the drop zone, just the radioed coordinates and guesswork.

"I'm only going in once!" shouted the pilot. "Out you go. Now."

Martins straddled the exit hole in the floor of the fuselage, buffeted by the wind as the plane shuddered under the weight of the petrol. He looked down at the gray blanket of clouds below him. The woman glanced up at him, then away. He kissed the Saint Christopher medal around his neck, scissored his legs and let himself drop.

He plummeted for long moments in the slipstream until his chute billowed and led him on a crazy dance through the fog below. Blots of darkness, then a green space. Perfect. The marshy ground rushed up, meeting his feet, and he rolled several times. Gathering his chute, he peered into the night, trying to distinguish objects in the degrees of darkness, listening to the flutter of night birds.

He'd landed where the field joined the forest. To his right, a darkened French village; to the left, his contact was waiting—he hoped.

He dug a hole in the mud with a hand shovel, shucked off his jumpsuit, and buried it and the chute. A rapid succession of crow caws erupted from the forest. The signal. Thank God.

Buttoning his brown French-label jacket and smoothing down his trousers, he headed toward the signal. Damn mud made a sucking sound each time he took a step. The radio set in his rucksack weighed heavy.

The orange glow of a cigarette appeared between the trees, and he made his way toward it.

"You're late."

Lucky he'd made it at all with the fog, he almost said. Instead he said, "Guts for garters." He paused, waiting for the response to his password phrase. A moment passed. The dark figure threw the cigarette and Martins saw the arc of its orange tip disappear.

Uneasy, Martins reached for the Webley pistol in his pocket. A bright light blinded him. Shouts in German. It was too late.

Blood filmed Martins's eyes; all he knew was a haze of pain—searing, shooting flames in his arms, his chest. The voice, seductive and soft; the German saying, "Thirsty, Englander?" The cool wet cloth touched his blistered lips and then went away. "Come, come, drink all you want. It was your friend who told us where to find you."

Mercier, the French contact Stepney had vouched for, had turned Martins over.

". . . not my friend. Don't know anyone here."

"Your friend, your contact. Semantics. But we don't care about him. What's your mission, who are your other contacts?"

His aching arms were strung to a blackened wood beam. His feet dangled just above the dirt barn floor.

Martins gathered his saliva and spit toward the German.

A languid sigh. "Aaah, but you're thirsty, I know. It's so easy, just tell me. So much simpler if you do now. Take him down again."

The rope loosened and he landed in a heap on the dirt. Strong arms gripped his shoulders and his head was plunged again in the trough of tepid water already tinged with his blood. He'd had no chance to take a breath; he sputtered, water filling his mouth, his nose, struggling against the hands holding him down. Involuntarily, he inhaled a mouthful of water, choked. This was it: he was drowning in a horse trough, the Gestapo's torture of choice.

And then he was pulled up. Water gushing from his nose, his stomach heaved and he threw up more water and spittle.

"Who's your contact?"

"No . . . no one knows."

"But your radio—that, you know. You can help us, just cooperate."

Martins shook in terror. All agents were trained in techniques to withstand the pain and last forty-eight hours under torture. Could he? "I don't know anything about a radio."

His skull cracked against the wood trough. Pain shot through him. Pinpricks of light danced over the blood-smeared walls of the barn. He brought his vision back into focus on the black uniform, the SS insignia on the collar, those kindly eyes looking at him.

"When's your meeting?" When Martins didn't answer, the man gestured to a makeshift farm table. "This isn't what you want, is it?" Surgical instruments gleaming in the dim light of the barn. "I'm a veterinarian by training. But the anatomies and nerve impulse conductivity in animals and humans differ very little." He picked up a scalpel gently and stroked it. "We descend from primates. Shall we confirm that?"

Part II

Sunday, June 23, 1940 | 8:45 A.M.

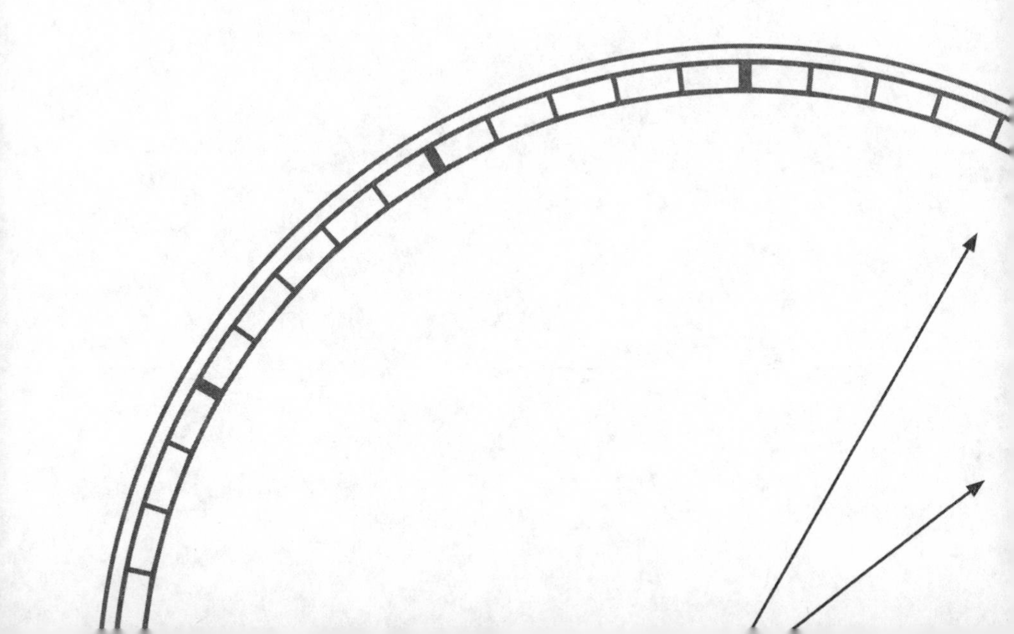

Sunday, June 23, 1940

Montmartre, Paris | 8:45 a.m.

Kate forced herself to remember the plan. To not let herself wonder what was going on outside. To ignore the Nazis scrambling Hitler down to the car.

Breathe, think, don't give in to panic, Stepney had said.

RADA.

The next thing she had to do: partially disassemble the rifle, enough to fit it in the bag. She'd practiced this a hundred times.

Focus.

She removed the magazine, flipped up the latch, lifted the rear sight and slipped out the bolt, removed the rear handguard and put the sight back down. Using the small flat-head screwdriver from the chain around her neck, she unscrewed the foresight protector and removed the upper band, continuing methodically, forcing her hands not to shake, going as quickly as she could without rushing, until finally removing the buttstock. How much time had this just cost her? She cleared the thought from her mind—there was no alternative.

Perspiring, she collected the shells into her canvas bag, then fit all the rifle's pieces in. She checked the room once more—she'd left no trace of herself that she could see. Then she was padding barefoot down the stairway.

On the third floor, a little face peered at her from behind the open door of the apartment. A face like a cherub. Kate noticed the little girl's pink socks on the wood floor. So sweet, so innocent. For a moment she felt an overwhelming desire to scoop her up and hold her close.

She turned her face away, hurried on.

At the rear door of the building, she slipped on the shoes she'd stashed. She stuck the canvas bag into the straw market bag she'd prepared and put the still-fresh bouquet of daisies, bought yesterday, on top. Ready as she'd ever be, she stepped out from behind the dustbins and onto a road that was really no more than a steep set of stairs lined with teardrop lampposts leading down the hill from Sacré-Cœur. Not far below, where rue Maurice Utrillo's stairs met flat rue Muller, she noticed the same melon seller she'd seen before, now stacking melons in his barrow.

Behind her at the top of the stairs came a flurry of horns, shouts, and the thump of boots. An uncontrollable shaking spread from her neck to her shoulders. Refusing to let herself sneak a glance behind her, she gripped the warm metal railing, head down, making her feet move, willing her shaking to stop. She forced herself to remember her instructions.

Don't stop, don't pay attention to any disturbance.

"*Achtung!*"

Kate's silk blouse stuck to her back and her breath came in pants as she kept walking. Only a few more stairs until she reached rue Muller. She felt warm air rush past her ears, raise the hair on her neck as footsteps thudded on the stairs behind her. Any moment she expected her arm would be seized.

Then German soldiers were rushing up from behind and past her.

"Halt!"

Just ahead on rue Muller the melon seller looked up, terror in his eyes.

A moment later he was surrounded. Soldiers were sticking bayonets into his barrow and tossing out melons, which split open on the cobblestones. One soldier held his arms while another roughly searched his person.

Kate averted her gaze and kept to the wall. Bile rose from her stomach. She tried to block out the man's yells, which raked like nails across her skin. She wanted to reassemble the rifle and pick the brutes off one by one. A car bearing small swastika flags mounted on either side of the hood squealed to a stop on rue Muller. The doors opened and the old man was pulled inside.

Too late.

Keep moving.

She rounded the corner, walking faster now, head down. Every bit of her itched to run. She forced herself to maintain an even pace, moving calmly among the few other people on the street: an old man walking his dog, a girl skipping rope, a woman beating dust from a carpet on her balcony. *Don't stand out.*

Three minutes later she reached the small storefront of Loulet among the clustered shops of Marché Saint Pierre, the fabric market. Since this was Sunday, the shops were closed, the place deserted apart from street cleaners sweeping the gutters. The sun beat down; leaves on the linden trees shimmered below Sacré-Cœur. Not a whisper of wind.

She licked sweat off her lip.

In Loulet's side alley, under the cracked wall covered in peeling circus posters, she found the second black bicycle on the rack, just where Stepney had said it would be. Focused on remembering the bike lock's combination: turn right to 4, back to 3, right again to 5. The lock clicked open.

The blue canvas bag, with a change of clothes and accessories, was waiting for her behind the garbage bin. Following the fallback plan instructions, she crouched behind the bin. Her hands were shaking again. She stripped off the plain blue skirt and blouse she'd worn under the parachute suit and pulled on the floral cotton dress, buttoned the collar. She buckled on the ankle strap sandals, put on the straw hat. Stood slowly and looked around. No one.

She searched the dress pockets and found her next destination written on a thin cigarette paper.

Boulangerie chez 64 rue des Batignolles.

She'd memorized the street map, hadn't she? Why was she coming up blank?

Think.

Finally it came back. She put her bag in the bike basket, clutched the handlebars and started pedaling.

Her heart was beating so fast she thought it would jump out of her chest.

THE WARM MORNING FELT ODDLY beautiful as she cycled down side streets, avoiding Pigalle. Linden blossoms in full heady bloom perfumed the air, taking her back to that summer in 1937—frequenting a Sorbonne café where Dafydd, the brooding, romantic Welshman, had caught her off guard with his smile. He'd been sketching the owner's cat when he looked up and she got lost in his amber eyes. They'd talked for hours. She'd loved his laugh. The way he joked around with her, the awkward, big-boned American bumpkin.

A *coup de foudre*, her concierge described it when she'd told her about meeting Dafydd. Love at first sight.

And now she found herself back in a Paris that had changed completely. Dafydd was dead, her mission ruined. The sirens behind her were growing fainter, and suddenly she was bone-tired. Every part of her wanted to lie down on a bench and rest her legs, despite her instructions. Just for a minute—or maybe forever. No one would have to know; she'd leave the rifle in a dustbin. She would find her way back to . . . where? Home in Deschutes County, where her father eked out a living as a migrant foreman on various cattle ranches? No ships were crossing the Atlantic. There was no place for her at her prissy mother-in-law's Welsh home now, not without Dafydd and Lisbeth. She wondered if she'd even be welcome back in Orkney, a widowed non-British civilian who had recently faced court martial at a military facility. She had nowhere to go.

She'd accepted a mission and failed.

Right now, she should be thinking about nothing but reaching the destination written on the cigarette paper.

As she cycled toward Batignolles, she was startled to notice she was passing horse-drawn carts, push barrows piled high with mattresses and household belongings, many old people and children. Parisians who had fled the city in fear a few weeks earlier were dribbling back in, returning to enemy occupation. Kate scanned the faces on the boulevard as her bicycle flew past. Defeat, anger and exhaustion were plain on their faces. A people licking their wounds.

At the traffic roundabout, she spotted German signs where she remembered there having been flowers. A couple was embracing on the open platform at the back of a passing bus. *Our Paris balcony*, Dafydd had told her once when they had stood at the back of a bus just like that couple, watching the spreading view of the city below as the bus climbed up to Montmartre. Inside, the deep ache opened, her longing for Dafydd seizing her, blurring her vision.

Jingling bicycle bells brought her back to the present.

Pay attention.

She took a side street and familiar scents assailed her: the tangy odor from a green metal pissoir, a whiff of a woman's perfume, the acrid smoke of a hand-rolled cigarette. Rapid-fire Parisian argot spilled out of a shop, now bearing signs of future rationing regulations, and onto the sidewalk. The conversation was punctuated by the snort of an ice wagon horse, the clatter of the wagon's wheels and the clip-clop of hooves on the cobbles, the flower seller's shouts. The Paris she knew, if more subdued.

"*Achtung, mademoiselle!*" Two Wehrmacht soldiers, white gloves tucked into their belts next to hanging daggers, stood in the crossing directly in her path. Her stomach lurched. She squeezed the handlebars, braked hard on the pedals. Her bike squealed to a halt inches away from the soldiers, the force throwing her straw market bag from the bike basket onto the street at the foot of the surprised Wehrmacht soldier.

"*Entschuldigen Sie, mademoiselle,*" said the taller Wehrmacht soldier, picking up the strewn daisy bouquet, then Kate's bag. The bag containing the disassembled rifle.

His well-fed face grimaced at the weight. Panic filled her as she stared at the Luger clipped to his belt. Scenarios flashed through her mind. Should she grab the bag . . . and get shot? Act helpless, faint on the street and hope for sympathy from the enemy? Flirt and distract him?

Her mind raced, searching for what to do, to say.

All of a sudden, she was alone on the street with the soldiers. The passersby had melted away.

This was it. She was dead.

Sunday, June 23, 1940

Montmartre, Paris | 9:45 a.m.

"Sir, we've got the suspect at rue des Saussaies ready for your interrogation," said the Wehrmacht soldier.

"The melon seller?" Gunter Hoffman crouched at the Montmartre apartment's open window, sweating in the sun. He eyed the shutter slats, imagining how the sniper had aligned the gun's sight. It was the perfect vantage point. "Have you found a rifle in his barrow? Or in a trash bin, the bushes, or by the staircase?"

"Not yet, sir."

And they wouldn't. He fingered the bullet that had been recovered from Sacré-Cœur's limestone pillar. This had been a trained sniper, military grade, who wouldn't make mistakes like that. Gunter had rechecked the apartment, empty except for the sheeted furniture, searching for a sense of the sniper, anything at all left behind.

Nothing. A professional.

He got down on his hands and knees by the window where the sniper had lain in wait to fire those two shots. He rubbed his fingers over the wooden floor. Stopped, feeling a faint damp spot, almost imperceptible and evaporating in the sunlight.

A faint aroma lingered in the hot air.

He sniffed his fingers, then stooped to sniff the floor. It wasn't rifle oil—it wasn't metallic or greasy. He licked his finger, searching for a taste. Water? The sniper's perspiration from waiting in a closed hot apartment? What was the elusive scent?

Just a nuance, then it was gone, lost in the pong of male sweat of the four officers turning the apartment over. En route he'd briefed these four on what to look for and questions he wanted answered.

"Sir, we've assembled the churchgoers in the crypt," said an arriving solider. As the Führer had ordered, the churchgoers had been kept locked in the church while SD and arriving troops searched the area. "They're ready for questioning."

Gunter knew that would lead nowhere. "*Danke.* Take their statements and names and addresses, then let them go." A formality.

"We're holding the building concierge downstairs. She's already half-drunk and moaning about how her feet hurt and she needs to lie down."

"Did she see anyone go upstairs?"

"She says the building is vacant except for an old woman and her grandchild on the third floor."

Gunter rose and pulled out his notebook. "I want to speak with both of them."

Just then a young lieutenant, dark eyed and tall, came into the apartment. "I've got an update from Munich for Gunter Hoffman."

Gunter waved. "Over here." He took the report from the young lieutenant's hand and scanned the pages. "Why wasn't this report given to me earlier?"

"Control just received this, sir. I was told to find you right away."

Mein Gott. A British radio operator had been captured. Gunter knew successful clandestine operations depended on wireless communication. Was this radio man related to the parachute drops mentioned in the decoded British messages he'd seen in Munich? Or was the radio man linked to the shooter? Had the Führer been right, this was part of a British plot?

His orders were to follow up.

"You, sergeant." Gunter pointed to the short-statured first soldier, the one who had been the most attentive during Gunter's briefing en route. "Conduct the questioning of the concierge and the grandmother. Write down everything they say. Everything. Have your report ready in an hour." He turned to the lieutenant. "You have a car?"

"Waiting, sir."

GUNTER SET HIS FAT ATTACHÉ case beside him on the leather seat of the Mercedes on rue Lamarck. The smudged car windows were partially open to the humid air. Lilac branches flowered, spilling down the Sacré-Cœur hill. Picture perfect, like a postcard. A world away from war.

Upset over the update he'd just received, he set his case loaded with reports on the seat and leaned forward as the car took off. "Lieutenant . . . ?"

"Rolf Niels, sir," said his driver, a young officer in a field gray-green uniform.

"Lieutenant Niels, does this mean they're already interrogating the British radio operator? Who ordered this?"

"My instructions to pick you up came from Roschmann, at SD. That's all I know."

Gottverdammt. There were already too many things going on he didn't know about. How had that SD lout Roschmann gotten involved? Gunter couldn't lose control. Jäger had made it clear this case was his; so had the Führer.

What more could go wrong?

SUNDAY, JUNE 23, 1940

Near Place de Clichy, Paris | 9:15 A.M.

Kate held her breath, expecting to be shot on the spot. But the Wehrmacht soldier set Kate's bag in her basket, doffing his cap.

"*Bonne journée, mademoiselle,*" he said with a wide grin, gesturing for her to pass. "*Allez-y.*"

Her fingers trembling on the handlebars, she gave him a thin smile and pedaled ahead, turning the corner and not looking back. She made herself take deep breaths.

Clouded by emotion, she hadn't stayed alert. She hadn't been on the streets of Paris ten minutes and she'd almost run down a German soldier. She'd practically handed the rifle to the enemy, revealing herself as a foreign spy. She would have faced interrogation. Then the firing squad.

Idiot.

Sweat trickled down her back. She had papers, an identity card, but would they have held up? She'd gotten so lucky. That wouldn't happen a second time; life didn't work like that.

Buck up, girl, her father would say.

Concentrate.

Stick to the plan. She pedaled by the Gaumont movie palace, now bearing a banner that read SOLDATENKINO, and the soldiers lining up for an early movie. Continued toward le square de Batignolles down a cobbled side street, where a man fed rabbits in a hutch outside a café. Beyond that lay a street market. On the steps of Sainte-Marie de Batignolles, a black-robed priest was welcoming parishioners. She could have sworn he nodded to her. She set her bike against the wall by the bakery, went inside, waited in line and asked for Jean-Marie.

"Jean-Marie's at church," said the curly haired woman clad in an apron. She gazed levelly at Kate. "Like always, mademoiselle." The woman held out a receipt and coin. "You forgot your change this morning."

Kate palmed it without a glance at what she'd received. "*Merci beaucoup, madame.*" The meet was on; this handoff would indicate the next location to go to.

Kate exited the bakery and walked her bike to a tree beside the church. Under the shady branches she pretended to be looking for something in her basket. There was a message written on the receipt. She stuck it in her pocket and walked the bike toward 59 rue Legendre, her destination, a few buildings over from the iron bridge that ran over the train tracks.

As instructed, Kate left her bike at the doorway of the recessed *porte cochère*—the signal. Behind her lay a deserted concierge loge, mailboxes on the wall, a baby buggy covered with a film of dust standing to one side of a locked glass double door to the courtyard. She crouched in the deep doorway's corner behind the bike, with a vantage of the street and nearby rail bridge. Her only way out would be to make a straight dash to the street then shimmy down the bridge's metal struts and drop to the rail lines. A long way down.

She struck a match and burned the cigarette paper and receipt, ground out the ash with her foot. Now she was to wait for instructions.

Her stomach churned. She'd shot the wrong person, botched the assassination, escaped while soldiers arrested an innocent melon seller. Now she was still putting others at risk, all for a mission that had already gone sour.

She tried to clear her mind by silently repeating her new instructions: *Stay in place. Jean-Marie will be wearing a blue railroad cap.*

But she didn't know her own escape route. What if Jean-Marie didn't show up? What if by failing at her mission she'd gotten herself abandoned?

She should fully disassemble the rifle to camouflage it better. But here? Risk ten minutes now but make it more likely she wouldn't get caught later?

The loose rifle screws and bolts were rolling around inside the basket. The barrel tip was making a hole.

She was stuck here waiting. She had to keep her mind occupied instead of looping in fear. But if someone stumbled on her . . .

She peered over the bike, saw no one and sat down. With the bike for cover, she removed her scarf with shaking hands, laid it out on the cracked mosaic tile and set the rifle pieces on top of it. She'd already removed the forestock from the buttstock. Now she got to work, rising to check the street every other minute. Finally, she'd screwed all the screws back on the rifle parts she'd removed in her hurry, then stowed the rifle pieces in the bottom of the bag after tying them together with her scarf. Now it was ready to reassemble, nothing loose or missing. Her gamble had paid off.

Ten minutes turned to half an hour. Kate waited, peering out periodically to see the light glinting on the metal bridge railings spanning the tracks. She heard the rumbling of trains below, the long whistle signaling approach, the pealing of the Batignolles church bells. Families who hadn't evacuated the city during the exodus were walking home from Mass on the narrow cobbled street, some with children, some couples arm in arm. In this residential pocket it seemed like a typical Parisian Sunday—on the surface, at least. But Kate's nerves jangled.

More than an hour passed. A young woman, swinging a basket, held a little boy's hand. The boy was asking her to buy MarieLu biscuits *s'il te plaît, Maman.* On their way to the street market, Kate figured. Preparing for the midday meal. German occupation or not, the Sunday midday meal, when extended families gathered together, was religiously observed.

Her shoulders ached. Hunger pangs and nausea warred in her stomach. As she waited obediently for her contact, she wondered if she should instead be climbing down from the pedestrian bridge to the railroad embankment to jump aboard a passing train.

But this was a working-class neighborhood; there was nowhere she would blend in better on a sleepy Sunday. She suppressed her fears, her urge to run. She waited.

Still no sign of her contact.

Kate arranged her bag with the disassembled rifle behind her and sat back against the shadowed wall. She'd barely slept in thirty-six hours. First the bumpy midnight flight Friday, then parachuting into a barnyard full of cows—she'd missed Stepney's contact who'd been supposed to take her to Paris. She'd stumbled through the dark countryside, her mission on the line, then somehow convinced a surprised dairy farmer to take her on his milk run. She'd lucked out and caught the early Saturday morning milk train to Paris. Found the apartment Stepney had showed her on the map. She'd bought the flowers, reconnoitered the target spot at Sacré-Cœur, then hid out in the apartment all day and night, nervous and unable to sleep. Waiting.

The heat emanating from the pavement, the insistent chug of train engines and the dull patter of footsteps on the cobbles lulled her to sleep.

Her dreams were laced with sirens, the ground shuddering from the explosion, the flames, an inferno, the sucking heat, tripping over the scattered hot bricks, the flying sparks catching fire on her skirt, burning her knees.

That wrenching in her chest, the pounding growing to a roar.

She sat up with a cry, soaked in sweat. Always that nightmare. But the pounding hadn't ceased now that she was awake. She heard the roar of engines, shouts. Flashes of khaki canvas-covered trucks passed—troops. The street rumbled.

She wiped the stinging sweat from her eyes. Disoriented, the rifle tip sharp in her back, she struggled to stand. Had she missed her contact by falling asleep?

Peering from the doorway, she saw a man with a blue railroad cap walking toward her on the opposite side of the street. With an unhurried pace he kept to the wall, smoking a cigarette, a magazine under his arm. At the doorway directly across he caught her gaze, then turned away and leaned against the doorway, taking a drag before flicking his cigarette into the gutter. He surveyed the street, looking up and down with maddening slowness.

Her palms itched. She wanted him to hurry, to get this over with. But he just stood there, staring nonchalantly down the street. She'd been told he would introduce himself as Jean-Marie, but was he waiting for her to approach him so he'd know who she was? She was about to take a step toward him when a black car pulled up in front of him, blocking her view. A moment later two helmeted soldiers jumped out.

"*Halt!*"

Her heart caught. The helmeted soldiers turned him around and put his arms up against the building, searching him, knocking his cap off to expose his thick black hair. Panicked, she stepped back in the shadowed recess. Remembered that the glass door behind her was locked. Nowhere to go. Despair filled her. Would he give her away?

She made herself small against the door, crouching, holding her breath. The black car's engine revved, and there was a shout in German. One soldier grabbed Jean-Marie's arms from behind and shoved him toward the car. He looked up and blinked in her direction before his head was pushed down. She heard the car doors slam. Then the car took off.

She was on her own.

She had to get out of this doorway, this quartier crawling with troop trucks. Had to figure they'd be on the alert for a woman wearing a straw hat on a bicycle. It would be suicide to return to the *boulangerie* for help.

Kate ditched the hat into a mailbox, wrapped the scarf she'd found folded in the dress's other pocket around her head, dusted off the baby buggy with her sticky hand, and stuck her straw bag with the disassembled rifle inside. Her explicit instructions had been to keep the rifle.

She hesitated. What if she were searched?

Common sense told her to ditch the rifle. Hadn't Stepney said to improvise and think on her feet? Her gut was telling her she'd be safer without it. Yet right now this was all the defense she had. Firearms were scarce and this was top notch, valuable. She might have to use it to shoot her way out or barter it for escape.

A second later she was pushing the buggy along the pavement, her knees shaking. She wanted to run. But she remembered the magazine Jean-Marie had carried under his arm, and how his arms had been empty when he raised them in surrender.

She pushed the buggy across the cobbled street and into the doorway he'd stood in. Shallow, no *porte cochère*, just a locked glass door. There was a shopping cart folded against the wall, one wheel broken. She rooted inside. Nothing. But in the side pocket she felt something and pulled it out. A folded French-language copy of *Signal*, the German propaganda magazine. Her lip quivered. Inside she found a blank sealed envelope. Quickly she slit it open. A cigarette paper with penciled words on it containing instructions to meet at 1 P.M.

More trucks pounded against the street. She'd read it more closely later. She stuck the envelope back in the magazine, which she dropped into the buggy. Her spine tingled with fear. Moving as casually as possible, she pushed the buggy out into the sunlight and toward the railroad bridge.

SUNDAY, JUNE 23, 1940

Outside Paris | 9:30 A.M. Paris Time

"We've got close to a half hour's drive, sir," said Lieutenant Niels.

Nervous over losing valuable time, Gunter sat back against the leather seat. He was still wearing last night's shirt. He should reread each report and make notes. No. Better to catnap so he'd be fresh to interrogate the radio man. The Steiff teddy bear poked from his bulging attaché case. Propping the bear under his head as a pillow, he leaned back and closed his eyes.

Sometime later a jolt bounced him awake. They were driving on a potholed dirt road, the smells coming in through the driver's open window familiar, wild strawberries and manure. The bright sunlight revealed flat green fields and an open barn door.

A soldier stood guarding the door. "Papers, *bitte*."

"RSD." Gunter showed his badge. "We've been informed of a captured English parachutist. I'm here to question him."

The soldier shrugged.

A gruesome scene awaited Gunter under the barn's blackened beams. Blood-speckled hay, red-tinged water overflowing the horse trough, a set of steel instruments on a milking stool.

A body sprawled on the floor. Gunter knelt down and felt for a pulse. None. The body was cold, the clothing damp. He fingered the Saint Christopher medal still on a chain around the blood-streaked neck.

Idiots. Gunter motioned for his driver, took the camera out of his attaché case and handed it to Niels to photograph the scene. "I want every angle documented."

"Caught the Bayern tailwind, eh? You're such alarmists at RSD." A man approached, wiping his bare arms with a towel. Gunter recognized Roschmann from SD, the intelligence service of the SS. Roschmann was the man they called the Vet. Why hadn't someone put a muzzle on him?

"We needed him alive," said Gunter. "From now on we need every one of them alive. Do you understand?"

Roschmann nodded. "The Englander talked. They all do when they spend time with me."

Gunter heard rhythmic strokes of a shovel outside, then a metallic ting as it hit stone. "*Scheisse,*" someone swore in German.

"Give me a full report," said Gunter. "*Schnell.* Too much time has been lost already."

Roschmann recounted his interrogation as Gunter examined the English radio set and its case.

"But where's his cipher code?" All radio operators carried a code transmission template. A manual, or sometimes just a paper.

"What you see is what we found." Roschmann was pulling on his shirt.

Gunter chose his words carefully so as not to reveal the assassination attempt on the Führer. "The report suggested this radio man might have been connected with a gunman. What do you know about that?"

"Gunman? No idea. We picked him up near his parachute drop."

"Show me the exact location where he landed. I want to go over every step. Meanwhile send a car back to the morgue . . ." Gunter paused to consult his notebook for the address. "The morgue at the Hôpital Lariboisière in Paris. Send the man's body, clothing, and all his belongings."

"Why create more paperwork? We bury him. Simple."

Roschmann pursed his pale thin lips. The SD didn't care

much for the Reich Security Service. And this brute Roschmann oozed ambition.

"My orders come from the Führer so we'll do it my way. Understood?" Gunter told him, annoyed by the cavalier attitude. "The body will be autopsied. This man could have stuck the code in his ear, in a suppository, or in a capsule he swallowed." Roschmann was not the first lout he'd had to work with, nor would he be the last. Munich abounded with henchmen like Roschmann, backstreet thugs all out for sanctioned violence. Gunter reined in his frustration. He needed allies, not foes—any policeman knew that you needed eyes you could trust in the field.

"The English put their eggs in more than one basket," said Roschmann. "My men have it under control. They'll report from the drop when they find something."

Under control? Gunter's adrenalin coursed. These imbeciles' actions had already wasted valuable time. Again he studied the interrogation log. "Who took these notes?"

With a shout Roschmann summoned the soldier who had been shoveling outside. In the light from the dusty window, Gunter showed him a page from the log notes.

"Can you explain these phrases?" Gunter's English was passable but this looked like gibberish.

"He was crying," said the soldier.

Gunter could imagine. He suppressed a shiver. A skilled interrogator obtained the information in other ways.

It took five minutes of the soldier sounding out the letters and words phonetically in German-accented English before Gunter grasped the radio operator's last words.

A woman. Lipstick. 1 P.M. Café Littéraire. Sorbonne.

Was this related? He remembered that fleeting fragrance in the Montmartre apartment.

A woman sniper?

SUNDAY, JUNE 23, 1940

Coordination Control Somewhere outside London
9:30 A.M. Paris Time

Stepney looked up from his charts as Brigadier Teague, the military Secret Intelligence Service liaison, entered the statistics room, a converted glass-walled conservatory in the Victorian manor house. Outside a fox crept across the rolling lawn, leaving a paw print trail on the dewed grass. Warm morning sunlight spread over the dark green horizon of forest.

Stepney tilted his cap over his receding hairline. "Any more news, Teague?"

His colleague held a clipboard under his arm. "Your man Martins overshot the landing site, Stepney."

As if that was Martins's fault? The fog had been unfortunate, but Stepney felt good about the plan.

"Blame the pilot and cloud cover. But overshot or not—"

"No word from him yet," interrupted Teague. "Bad news, that. And using that American woman was a mistake."

"Did you come up with a better idea, Teague?" Stepney wiped his brow. The heat and damn humidity in this place was stifling. Much better suited to growing orchids than war planning.

"I still don't understand what the point of sending her in was."

"Creating different levels of deception is a proven tactic."

"That's what you call your harebrained and scattershot missions, old man?"

"My missions have succeeded," Stepney said mildly. "Diversion is a military strategy as old as the Greeks. Remember the Trojan horse."

Kate was skilled, trained and credible—the perfect decoy assassin to distract from the primary four-man sniper team who had parachuted in this morning. These snipers were now in place outside the airfield at le Bourget. Their targets were Stossel, Lammers and von Duering of the German High Command, who were arriving to assume their posts in Paris.

Of course, Kate had the skill but there was no chance she would have been able to assassinate the Führer. Her drop point contact would have told her Hitler's travel plans had changed and that she should go to the fallback plan. Kate would be directed to a café at the Sorbonne, where her contact would reveal her to the Germans—Stepney had planted enough information in his compromised network about the rendezvous that he had no doubt the mole would report it back to German command. With any luck, Kate would weather interrogation long enough to distract them from the four-man team, giving them time to complete their mission and escape. She was tough; Stepney thought she just might hold out. But if she cracked, anything she might confess about her supposed mission would ring as true as it possibly could. When she was arrested, she would have a rifle on her.

Meanwhile Martins, installed in the attic room overlooking the café where Kate was to be apprehended, would see who betrayed Kate at the café—who had already betrayed Stepney's other operatives—and would transmit back the contact's identity to London. Stepney knew it had to be one of two men. Using Kate as his expendable would kill two birds—as they said—with one stone.

The best diversions, Stepney had learned from the last war, were credible operatives. Expendable credible operatives.

"Well, there are too many moving parts in this scheme," Teague said. "And Rees is the biggest one."

"The plan only works if the Germans believe she's an assassin."

"A ranch girl from backwoods Oregon to assassinate the Führer? I don't buy it and never have. They won't either."

Stepney leaned on his cane. "Quit complaining. Churchill signed off on it, for God's sake. We'll know more when Martins makes his scheduled transmission."

Crows cawed from the fenced lawn.

"Never liked the idea of a woman in the field," said Teague. "How can they withstand interrogation? What if she falls apart too early?"

What a waste of time, this whole conversation, considering the mission was already underway. Too late for cold feet now. "Rees's been trained. And trained well." He'd trained her himself, to the highest standards, as he did every agent in Section D.

"I give her one chance in ten of having even made it to Paris," said Teague. The medals on his lapel caught the light as he set down his clipboard and took out his pipe. "How much time do we need her to survive?"

Stepney checked the flight maps. "Until thirteen hundred hours. So if she lasts four more hours, we're fine."

Sunday, June 23, 1940

Near Parc Monceau, Paris | 11:00 A.M. Paris Time

Stepney's words pounded in Kate's head: *no one lasts long under interrogation.* If Jean-Marie hadn't given her up yet, how long could he resist under torture? His group was compromised. And for what? She'd botched her mission.

Guilt wracked her. She was worthless, and a liability now. Any chance to salvage her failure was gone.

Maybe she should have thrown herself out that window. Given up, like she wanted to. Forget trying to cross a whole city on a hot Sunday morning while troop trucks hunted for an assassin.

For her.

Sweating and ready to abandon the heavy baby buggy, she stopped, paralyzed, at rue de Lévis. A cordon of gray-green uniforms blocked the pedestrian market street, checking identification. Fear pulsed through her; perspiration dripped down her shoulder blades.

"*Bonjour, madame,*" said the tallest one. He reached down to peer inside the baby buggy. She'd be shot when he discovered the rifle under the flowers. By a damn Kraut with a whisker spot he'd missed shaving. Adrenalin filled her.

Think. Improvise.

"*Mais, monsieur, mon bébé dort.*" She smiled, cocked her head and mimed sleep with her hands together.

He nodded. "*Moi aussi, je suis papa.*"

Her insides curdled. Lisbeth's face flashed in front of her, her fringe of blond eyelashes, her perfect O of a pink mouth. *Stop thinking about Lisbeth.* She needed to survive, to make them pay.

She gripped his big meaty hand before he reached into the buggy. Smiling, she slid herself in between him and the buggy. "*Votre bébé, fille ou garçon, monsieur?*" The sharp bulge of his magazine belt dug into her hip. Startled, he grinned.

"*Sie liebt dich, Ulrich.*" Sniggering came from his partners.

The smell of his stale breath was nauseating in the heat. There was shoving and jostling behind her. She pouted, full-on flirt. "*S'il vous plaît, monsieur?*" An old woman beside her gave a disgusted sigh.

He shrugged. "*Lassen Sie das bitte.*"

And she was through the control. Past the disapproving eye of the aproned housewives. Forget going this way again.

At a shadowed passage she huddled against a church wall until the tremors in her shoulders subsided. Until her pounding heart slowed down to match her breathing. Pigeon feathers spiraled above her through a slant of light piercing the dark passage. She felt like those feathers—floating on the current buffeted by forces beyond her control.

She thought about hunting with her father, miles from anywhere, with only the big open sky, the snowcapped Klamath Mountains and blue all around. Not another person until the next county, and yet she'd never felt this alone.

A thunderclap of bells pealed above her and she almost jumped out of her skin.

She couldn't count on her papers holding up. *Think.* She had to decide what to do next.

Concentrate.

She tried to steady her breathing in the turgid warm air.

Her father's words came back to her: *When you're hunting a wolf, Katie, better you track him than him sniffing after you.*

She left the buggy in the passage, shouldered her bag and left the narrow corkscrew of a street, keeping her head down.

Farther on, beyond the sign for Galleries Lafayette, a German soldier stood sentry by the grilled fence, his rifle pointing up. She kept moving.

FIVE MINUTES OF WALKING DOWN side streets in the broiling heat brought her to a tree-filled square—a few carts and horses parked nearby but otherwise deserted on this hot Sunday. She sat on a bench and pretended to read the magazine. She looked around. No one. Then, shielded by the magazine, she opened the envelope again, unfolded the cigarette paper. As she read the instructions her hand shook. Less than two hours to a café meeting at 1 P.M.

To a meeting where she might get instructions for escape.

Here she'd been pitying herself—stuck in a foreign country, alone, a failure. Pathetic. Hadn't growing up on ranches with five brothers taught her anything? During the bitter bone-chilling winters no one shirked their chores; they were necessary to survive. No one complained, not even her work-worn mother, who had died giving birth to Kate's little brother.

There was always a way, she remembered her mother saying, you just had to find it.

She'd missed her contact after the drop, yet she'd gotten herself to Paris—only to blow her mission. The weatherworn bench slat bit into her back. What if Jean-Marie, or whatever his name really was, gave up her rendezvous at the café?

Breathe.

Her mind returned to the meeting instructions inside the sealed envelope. It was different from the messages written on the other cigarette paper and bakery receipt. Had Jean-Marie been a cutout, as Stepney would have said? Cutouts only knew the information source and destination—a messenger from point A to B, Stepney had explained, but no other points, no identities revealed. What if Jean-Marie had only relayed the message, hadn't even known what it said?

Her choices were to go to the rendezvous or not. She had to take that risk.

Sunday, June 23, 1940

Hôpital Lariboisière, Morgue Section, Paris | 11:15 A.M.

Gunter shoved open Hôpital Lariboisière's morgue doors, stepping into dank, cold basement air tinted by acrid formaldehyde. He noted the standard fixtures: scales for weighing organs, bone saws and partially sheeted bodies on slabs, drains in the concrete floors. He'd lost count of the autopsies he'd attended as a policeman, yet they still made his scalp tingle.

"Ready with the findings, Dr. Breisach?"

"A preliminary report." Dr. Breisach looked up from the porcelain autopsy table, his round spectacles slipping down his nose. He had hooded, heavy-lidded eyes and a tight mouth. "Here you've got an Englishman whose organs show good health apart from water filling the lungs, a concussed brain and ruptured kidneys." He pointed with his scalpel to the man's blue-tinged face and open, vacant eyes. "Cause of death? I'd say suffocation, indicated by the petechial spots in the eyes." Dr. Breisach shook his head. Whether in disgust at the torture or that Gunter had woken him up for a rush job after a twenty-four-hour shift, it was hard to tell.

Gunter's eyes smarted from the chemicals. How anyone could do this job was beyond him. "I'm more interested in what was hidden in his body receptacles."

"All clean, as we say."

That would have been too easy. "Then I need the analysis of the contents of his intestinal tract."

"Ask for the lab report tomorrow."

"This man was a saboteur, an enemy agent," said Gunter, pulling out his RSD badge. "I need you to go through the contents right now."

His white lab coat lifted in a shrug. "Suit yourself. It's all there in the green bucket." Dr. Breisach set down his scalpel, straightened up. "I recommend gloves, Herr Hoffman."

Accustomed to autopsies but never the smell, Gunter slipped on a mask and donned rubber gloves. Dr. Breisach adjusted a light over the bucket and took an aluminum-handled sieve.

"Whatever you're looking for could have already been digested."

"I understand, Doctor. Please go ahead."

As Dr. Breisach strained the mustard-brown stew of half-digested food, Gunter fought the urge to throw up. After straining several scoops, the doctor paused. "Seen enough to put you off their fish and chips?"

"Keep going." Gunter trained his eyes on a lump. "What's that?"

Gingerly now, using pincers, the doctor removed an inch-long grayish capsule and set it on a dry sheet. Inside the capsule Gunter found a paper pellet. Upon smoothing out, it revealed the British cipher code and transmission template.

Tension ribbed his shoulders. He'd salvaged something from Roschmann's botched interrogation. If he could just do what he did best without all the oversight and interference . . . but fat chance of that in the Third Reich.

A yawning attendant hosed down the dissection table, spattering blood-pink droplets on the tiled wall. About to yawn himself, Gunter debated taking one of those uppers in his pocket. He could really use one right now. He removed the gloves, threw them in the alcohol bucket. Then he used the phone behind the glass partition to call Jäger in Berlin.

"You let Roschmann, that vet, interrogate the English radio operator?" said Jäger. "Weren't my instructions clear?"

"Gruppenführer, this interrogation was reported to me after the fact." Gunter kept his tone steady. "The Englishman was dead when I arrived."

"Of course, Roschmann obtained a confession?" The normally brisk authority in Jäger's voice wavered.

"More important, sir, are my findings from the autopsy."

"Autopsy? Wasted on an enemy spy?"

"The man swallowed what appears to be his radio cipher code. I retrieved it from his stomach contents."

A grunt from Jäger. "Smart, Gunter. Thorough." He heard a slight thaw in Jäger's voice.

"Gruppenführer, if I'm allowed to investigate my way—"

Jäger cut him off. "Telex the cipher to Karst in decryptions. You can trust him."

Another minion of his chief, whose reach stretched far and wide. Gunter's nose tickled. "Just a moment, sir." He put the phone down. Sneezed. Sneezed again.

"Karst will make the decryption a priority. Gunter, did you hear me?" he could hear Jäger saying.

Gunter pulled out a handkerchief, blew his nose, then picked the phone back up. He thought back to that elusive smell in the apartment. "Yes, sir. When the Englishman was interrogated, he said there was a woman involved. He knew details about a meeting near the Sorbonne." Gunter lowered his voice. He didn't like communicating details where it could be overheard on either end. "What if it's an Englishwoman sniper?"

"Possible. The Russians use them. Have a whole trained regiment. But from the British that surprises me."

"How's that, sir?"

"Where would the English get a woman that skilled?" A bark of laughter. "From the ranks of fox hunting aristocrats? Find out, Gunter. Their goal could be to scatter our attention to several venues, diluting our manpower."

It wouldn't be the first time.

"Get the decryptions, then report to me from the drop site near le Bourget."

Le Bourget . . . again? That drive used up valuable time. "Sir, the radio operator's last words indicated a rendezvous at Café Littéraire at one o'clock. Near the Sorbonne. That's in less than two hours."

"Don't worry about that. I'll get that covered."

Wasn't Gunter supposed to be running this investigation? Or would Jäger order Roschmann and his SD strong arms to flood the café and drag this woman away?

"Finding a possible second assassin, that's your priority now. We deciphered a new message about parachutists dropped near le Bourget and telexed the report to you at the Kommandantur. Go with your driver right now. Make the Führer happy and find them, Gunter."

Gottverdammt. He'd been working on that report before he'd left Munich.

"Be prepared, Gunter. The Führer might return to Paris." He had intimated he'd return for the reprisal and for his good luck charm, the little girl.

"Today, sir?"

"Imminent."

Gunter knew "imminent" meant the Führer's plans were in flux. He imagined the back-and-forth telegrams from the Führer bunker at Brûly-de-Pesch; first the Führer's visit scheduled in forty-eight hours, then it's tonight, no, in two days, then tomorrow. Dithering like always, Hitler's astrologer dictating his schedule by the planets.

"Keep me informed, Gunter."

The phone clicked. Gunter sneezed again. *Ach*, a summer cold on top of it. All this rushing around in the humidity, then into a dank underground morgue.

"*Danke*, Doctor." He beckoned to Niels, his green-faced lieutenant driver, that it was time to go.

"Did you want coffee, sir?"

Coffee? No, he needed his wife's homemade onion juice to stave off his cold. But he had a sniper on the loose and less than thirty-four hours and counting to get the Führer the results he demanded. And now there was a second set of possible assassins.

Minutes later, in the requisitioned hospital office, he telexed the code found in the British radio operator's stomach contents to Karst in decryptions.

Then popped a pill dry. "Get the car."

Sunday, June 23, 1940

Near Place Saint-Augustin, Paris | Noon Paris Time

Kate walked up the street, knowing any hesitation would look suspicious. Heat traveled up her spine. Damned if she went to the meet, damned if she didn't. She passed ornate buildings with tall green doors, looking for a spot to think.

She needed a moment to regroup, to visualize the Paris streets she'd memorized. She'd known them like the back of her palm yesterday. But her mind was coming up blank.

Beyond the covered entryway of a belle epoque townhouse she saw a bakery. Alongside it lay a passage. She turned and walked over the cobbles. Here the bakery shop's side door stood propped open for air. She inhaled the crisp baked bread smell, listening to brakes grinding on the street, an engine. Then she heard voices in German. Fear crept up her arm.

Had they found her already? Were they conducting house-to-house searches?

Quick as a wink she stepped into the *boulangerie*'s side door, pulled a few franc pieces from her coin purse. A thousand francs in small denominations, so roughly sixty-seven bucks, were sewn into her jacket lining for later. If she had a later.

She bought a baguette and hurried out, keeping her eye on the street. A black Citroën was parked before the doorway, and by it stood several men in black uniforms. One wore a suit that looked too heavy for the warm weather, his jacket sleeves rolled up.

Two blocks away, she paid for two ripe nectarines from a fruit vendor's cart. Catching her breath, she leaned against a wall. Her legs ached, and her shoulders were sore from the hours of crouching with the rifle. From a pocket in her bag she took another little pink pill Stepney had promised would keep her awake and swallowed it.

Focus.

Near the small tree-sheltered Place Louis XVI, Kate saw several bicycles leaned against the iron filigree fence. By the time anyone noticed their bike was missing, she'd be long gone.

She selected the bike with a canvas basket and a book inside, pulled it off the kickstand, put her bag and food in the basket and headed toward a street she hoped led to the Left Bank.

Sunday, June 23, 1940

Le Bourget Village Near le Bourget Airfield outside Paris
11:45 A.M. Paris Time

Lieutenant Niels pulled up in front of the village *gendarmerie.* "We're here, sir."

Gunter scanned the small square: a fountain, a few cats sunning on the cobbles, the village church, a *boulangerie* bordering a side lane. His pistol rested in his jacket pocket.

Jäger had instructed him to enlist their friends *les gendarmes* for help at this drop site. His boss said he'd be surprised at how helpful they'd become since Marshal Pétain had motivated them. Gunter imagined the *gendarmes* found the threat of conscription and forced labor in Germany plenty of reason to cooperate, but he knew it was problematic to trust an occupied people whose resentment lay just below the surface.

Gunter spoke only halting French. During holidays in France before the war he'd depended on his wife, Frieda, an Alsacienne, but now he wished he'd tried harder to learn. Thank God Niels turned out to speak passable French.

Inside, an old woman in a long skirt and shawl was demanding the *gendarme* on duty help find her dog, Didine. She glared at Gunter. "Boche. *Encore les Boches.*"

The *gendarme*'s brow creased in worry. "Madame Marie, we'll sort this later," he said, shooing her to the door.

"Soldiers everywhere, falling from the sky," old Madame

Marie said. "Like big flowers. One of them took my Didine, as God is my witness."

"*Les parachutistes? Les Anglais?*" said Gunter, searching for words. He nodded to Niels, who jumped in.

"Where did you see the *Anglais, madame*?"

A frown creased her nut-brown forehead. "You Boches killed my husband in the trenches at the Somme."

In 1916, different soldiers in a different war. Not that that would make a difference to her.

"Tell her we need to know about the soldiers."

After some back-and-forth, Niels turned to Gunter. "She says to ask Lebel."

Gunter noticed the station's directory on the wall, scanned it for the name of the officer in charge. He turned to the *gendarme.* "Where's Commissaire Lebel?"

"Lebel?" The *gendarme* shrugged.

Gunter's collar was soaked in sweat. This *gendarmerie* was like an oven. With snipers on the loose and a deadline, his patience eroded. "I can make your life miserable," he said turning to Niels to translate this to the *gendarme.* "Even make it shorter if you don't help me find *les Anglais.*"

The *gendarme* tapped his finger on his head, raised his eyebrow toward the old lady. He was telling Gunter she was crazy, hadn't seen flowers falling from the sky.

"*Nein.*" He turned again to Niels. "Tell him I know they're here. We've got proof of the airdrop."

A Gallic shrug. "I just came on duty," said the *gendarme.*

"There were soldiers jumping from the sky. Tell him, you imbecile," said Madame Marie. "They took my dog."

"Took her dog why?"

Niels translated.

"He's a puppy and wanted to play."

Or caused a fracas and the soldiers needed him out of the way. Gunter nodded. "Better that you talk to me than to the people who will come to talk to you if you don't. *Comprenez?*"

Gunter noticed the old woman's gaze flicked over to the

small square. "Lebel is rotten like the rest of you. His wife runs the *boulangerie.*" She pointed to a poster of Marshal Pétain. "No fool like an old fool. After *la Grande Guerre,* now it's happening again. I lost my man for your war."

Rewarded by another shrug from the *gendarme,* Gunter nodded to Niels. More than one grandmother in his country had lost her man, too.

Gunter and Niels left the *gendarmerie,* crossing the square to the *boulangerie.* As he stepped into the suffocating heat, he shivered. Felt the chills.

Gottverdammt. He couldn't get sick. Now of all times.

"I'll go inside," he said to Niels at the *boulangerie* door. "You go around, watch the back door."

Niels pulled out his Luger.

The bell on the door jingled. Inside, the buttery scent made Gunter's stomach growl. He hadn't eaten since he couldn't remember when. He walked behind the counter, parted the beaded curtains between the shop and the kitchen.

"*C'est interdit.*" A woman in an apron rushed up to the curtain, blocking his view with her body, but not before Gunter spotted a man using the wall telephone. "*Un moment,* I'll serve you at the shop counter."

Gunter stepped past her into the kitchen. He noticed the two coffees on the table, served in those soup bowls the French used. There were dirt marks on the tile floor. In the sink, he touched two more coffee bowls. Hot.

Lebel, who was in his mid-fifties with sparse gray hair, took his blue police jacket from a peg and pulled it on over his shirt. "I just got word of your arrival." Lebel spoke a kind of German probably acquired in the last war.

"Which means that you have been holding . . ." Gunter lifted the upside-down tablecloth—someone had thrown it over the table in haste—to reveal muddy boots. "*This Anglais* until I arrived, *ja?*" He pointed his pistol at the gangling man, all legs and elbows. "Where's the other one?"

Lebel shot a wild-eyed look at his wife.

"Whatever your feelings may be, monsieur, Marshal Pétain has ordered you to cooperate with us. Madame, I suggest you close your shop before we confiscate it."

As the man, a tawny-haired Englishman in too-small farmer pants, crawled out from under the table, Gunter pointed to the sink. "There are two coffee bowls over there. I asked you where the other Englishman is." He took handcuffs from his back pocket and cuffed the Englishman to the ancient oven's door handle.

Lebel stuck out his jaw, shrugged. "He left this morning."

Gunter was unimpressed with this policeman. "You can do better than that, Lebel. Harboring enemies of the Third Reich carries a sentence."

The back door opened, revealing Niels on the other side. He shot a meaningful glance at the shed in the garden. A German shepherd puppy with a gnawed muzzle hanging from its collar yelped at the shed door, clawing the wood. Madame Marie's Didine, Gunter figured. The soldiers had probably taken the dog who'd followed them and hurriedly muzzled it to keep it quiet. The tactic had backfired when the puppy chewed the muzzle off and he and Niels showed up.

"We need a rope," said Gunter.

Niels untied the clothesline, murmuring Didine's name until he was close enough to loop the dog's neck. Once he'd tied him to the water pump, he slid the water bucket within the puppy's reach.

"Impressive," said Gunter. "You're a dog handler?"

"I grew up with dogs, sir."

Gunter entered the dark shed, Niels with the Luger covering his back. There was a mound of displaced earth and a cart that only partially hid a pair of boots.

Outside the shed, the dog's growl spiked into a frenzy of barking. Niels kicked the cart aside to reveal a tall brown-haired man. The dog's teeth marks showed on the broken skin of his bleeding arm. Niels grabbed the man by the shoulders before he could lunge.

"Let's see what you're hiding," said Gunter, thrusting a spade at him. "Dig."

A few minutes' digging brought up a cloth sack. Inside were two disassembled rifles and cartridge boxes. Gunter looked at his watch. Had enough time passed since the incident at Sacré-Cœur for this assassin and his spotter to have returned from Paris? It would have been easy for a British plane to pick them up in the woods here behind le Bourget.

He'd found them. Nice and tidy, for once.

Gunther felt a moment of relief—he'd be able to go home to his wife and bring his daughter her belated birthday gift. Get a good night's sleep before these chills . . .

Nein. It couldn't be this easy. He'd force himself to be thorough. Conduct the investigation properly and to the end.

He sniffed the rifle's firing chamber. Stuck his finger inside. It came back oily but without bullet residue or the telltale smell of firing. The second rifle was the same. The box of cartridges was full.

Gottverdammt.

Gunter used Lebel's phone to request a truck and manpower from le Bourget. Both Englishmen now sat cuffed in Lebel's hot kitchen. They had each given their name, rank and serial number. Nothing else.

"Hiding any more, Commissaire Lebel?"

"You're going to shoot me? Take reprisals out on the villagers?"

His wife started sobbing.

"Should I? I'm arresting you for hiding English spies. But my report could show that you cooperated."

A lot of good that would do Lebel if Roschmann, the Vet, got hold of him.

"You think I invited them here?" Lebel scowled at the men in his kitchen chairs.

"No, but you hid them. Are there any more?"

Lebel's eyes wobbled back and forth. He shook his head.

Gone were the days when anyone would offer you a traditional courtesy coffee. Gunter poured himself some from the still-warm chipped yellow enamel pot. It only took him a few minutes to persuade Lebel that he needed to cooperate if his wife ever wanted to reopen the *boulangerie*. Then the French policeman began to bad-mouth the butcher, who was hiding two other parachutists in his cellar. Not very patriotic, these French.

Gunter looked again at his watch. Thirty-three hours left.

He downed another pill with the last sip of coffee, then pulled out his handkerchief to wipe his runny nose. "What about a woman?"

"Eh?"

Lebel's wife nudged him. "Tell him."

"Never saw her."

"But you heard something."

Silence apart from the dripping sink faucet. "Listen to your wife. Tell me."

Not a word.

"If you don't talk, my boss will make sure that you do."

Only the dripping faucet answered him.

Gunter nodded to Niels. "Handcuff Madame, take her to the car." He pulled out his Luger.

Lebel's eyes batted in fear. "Someone saw a woman on the milkman's cart yesterday."

"Here?"

"Near Noisy-le-Grand."

"Where's that?"

"Twenty-five kilometers away."

"Then how do you know?"

"My brother-in-law works at the dairy cooperative," said Lebel. "People were talking. He heard . . . a foreign woman took the early milk train to Paris. That's all."

Gunter nodded to Niels, who tucked the handcuffs back in his pocket. Gunter put his gun away. "Commissaire Lebel, my report's going to reflect how the local commissariat assisted in the capture of British snipers. You're still going to the station."

"You expect me to thank you?" said Lebel.

"Not at all."

"What about the dog?"

Gunter wiped his forehead with his handkerchief. "Return Didine to Madame Marie. *Guten Tag.*"

SUNDAY, JUNE 23, 1940

Right Bank, Paris | Noon Paris Time

Kate's anxiety mounted as she bicycled through the Place de l'Opéra. The outdoor tables at Café de la Paix were jammed, the crowd speckled with German uniforms. Women with elaborately curled hair smoked, drank and laughed with the enemy. Disgusted, Kate scanned the side street, noting camouflage-painted troop trucks parked by a former bank that bore a bold German banner proclaiming PLATZKOMMANDANTUR. Cordons and troop trucks were set up on the wide boulevard. Striped wooden sentry houses manned by bayonet-rifle-bearing soldiers stood on the corners of Place de l'Opéra. She slowed as a trio of soldiers strode into the crossing, their rifles over their shoulders glinting in the sun.

A horn tooted and she took off past the arrow signs pointing to Lille, Metz, Brussels.

Stepney had underestimated the damned German efficiency—such a pervasive military presence in place after only two weeks of occupation. Like a plague of locusts, the victors mowed down and sampled everything in their path.

At least the Germans appeared on their best behavior. They looked like tourists with their cameras and maps. She wondered if somewhere they were carrying out reprisals for her botched mission.

Now she knew where she was. She needed to concentrate on meeting the contact. Pray that the café rendezvous hadn't been compromised. What if the meeting proved impossible? That was her only connection to her escape route. Would she ever get out of Paris?

She'd worry about that later.

Concentrate.

First: How could she stow the rifle? The train station's left luggage counters would be watched. Lockers in the public bath, she remembered, were scrutinized by bathhouse attendants.

She parked her bike near the Palais-Royal and wiped her brow with the back of her hand. Under the arcade ringing the garden, shaded by rows of leafy plane trees, a frizzy-haired old woman bent feeding stray cats. Kate spied a full garbage bin. Among the household items discarded during the exodus from Paris, she found a wicker picnic basket with a lid and dusted it off. Perfect for the rifle. She left the straw bag and fitted the wicker basket into the blue canvas bag that had held her change of clothes at the fabric market. It only just fit.

Back on her bicycle, Kate wove through traffic consisting of *vélo-taxis,* bikes, buses and the occasional Mercedes. The light breeze ruffled the black flags with red swastikas that stood at every block along rue de Rivoli. Notices in French and German were plastered on the walls. Her legs still ached but she was making up time.

She crossed the Pont Royal with her picnic basket. The green-gray of the Seine was the exact shade of the Wehrmacht's feldgrau uniforms. Her skin crawled. The pain welled up fresh as she remembered how she, very much in love, had spent a summer afternoon strolling with Dafydd below on the quai. How Dafydd had uncorked a bottle of wine and they'd celebrated his selling a drawing.

A lifetime ago.

Ten minutes later she entered le Bon Marché, the chic department store at Sèvres-Babylone, for the second time in her life. She found the cloakroom in the same place where it had been when she'd come here to shop for a birthday present for Dafydd three years earlier. She smiled at the attendant, a bored young woman, who gave her a blue claim check for her wicker basket.

Sunday, June 23, 1940

The Kommandantur, Place de l'Opéra, Paris
12:30 P.M. Paris Time

After rounding up the two other parachutists, Gunter herded them all into a troop truck from le Bourget and had them transported to Paris for questioning. He'd let them stew in holding cells. The murdered radio man's last words rolled in his mind. Something told him the woman at the rendezvous at Café Littéraire would be the missing piece to this puzzle. Was she the assassin targeting the Führer?

But the Sorbonne would have to wait—a radioed message relayed to him at le Bourget had ordered him to the Kommandantur. Niels gunned the Mercedes and made it in record time to the building on Place de l'Opéra that the Reich had commandeered for the Kommandantur. Gunter would have to keep this appointment short if he was going to make it to that café at 1 P.M.

Kostoff, the *Militärbefehlshaber* of the French Reich, was barking into the phone. It was Gunter's boss, Jäger, on the other line.

"Himmler's livid," Kostoff was saying.

More like frightened out of the few wits he had left, Gunter thought. He stood at less than attention in Kostoff's half-unpacked office.

Kostoff's polished black boots creaked as he rose to his feet behind his desk. "We uphold order and security here. I refuse to let your branch short-circuit our authority—" Kostoff paused, listening and flicking his fingernail over the blotter on his desk.

As usual, the Führer played favorites and kept his elite off balance.

"*Jawohl*," Kostoff said, his voice steady now into the phone, "May I remind you we had less than two hours' advance notice of the Führer's visit? It took us by complete surprise."

Exactly what the Führer had wanted.

". . . round up civilians?" he said into the phone. "I've got a city to control. It's only been two weeks; we don't want to make the natives restless."

Gunter, his dilemma mounting as the minutes ticked away, stared out the window at the sun-drenched boulevard below. He dreaded confrontation. He wondered how he would manage to withhold his findings from Kostoff once he'd interrogated the four English snipers.

Kostoff slammed the phone down. "Don't you have the latest report on the sniper for me, Hoffman?"

Gunter snapped to attention. Now he knew Kostoff had been informed about the sniper and Gunter's assignment. No wonder the *Kommandant* wanted to stick his finger in the investigation.

"In progress, of course, sir," he lied. He had to tread carefully. First and foremost he reported to Jäger and the Führer. "However, the investigation's progressing minute by minute." Gunter was desperate to leave.

"*Ach ja*, Hoffman," said Kostoff. He opened a dossier on his desk. "This sniper incident has happened on my watch, my first week in charge, as the Führer reminds me, so I'll need you to keep me informed."

Jäger had demanded Gunter report only to him, then had informed Kostoff of the incident himself, leaving Gunter in an awkward position of either disobeying his boss's explicit orders or looking uncooperative to the Parisian head *Kommandant*. Was Jäger hedging his bets, or was the Führer demanding more immediate action?

Gunter could get dizzy wondering who played whom these

days. Still, he couldn't ignore Kostoff, and had to give him something. "You'll have my report this afternoon, sir."

He glanced at his watch. Thirty-two and a half hours.

"*Gut.* This is your case; you're the lead investigator," Kostoff said. "That's understood. But from now on you'll collaborate on the report with Roschmann's Feldgendarmerie unit. *Verstehen Sie?*"

Bad to worse.

SUNDAY, JUNE 23, 1940

Left Bank, Paris | 12:30 P.M. Paris Time

Stepney's script ran through Kate's head: *always scout an exit strategy before a rendezvous.* She took a bite of the nectarine. Its warm, sweet juice dribbled down her chin.

She'd arrive at the café early, prop herself behind the old book that had been in the bike's basket and use it to observe what she could about the patrons and staff, their movements and mannerisms, get a sense of the atmosphere. When it felt safe, she would go downstairs to check for the message confirming the contact meet was on. She tried to banish the notion that she was gambling with her life. If it felt wrong, she'd get up and leave.

She pedaled past the Jardin du Luxembourg's gold-tipped gates, over the cobbles by the blackened stone portico framing the Sorbonne's tall wood doors, which she'd walked through countless times in the summer of '37.

Her Paris trip had been the fault of Auntie Mae, her mother's older sister, *the old maid,* as her pa called her. Kate's father, like many Americans of his generation, had moved from job to job during the Depression, taking his five boys and Kate with him from one ranch to another. The year she spent in Medford was the longest she'd lived any one place until Orkney. Auntie Mae had insisted Kate needed some female influence in her life, and when Kate turned ten, Mae'd invited her to spend *lady-like* time at the boarding house she ran in Eugene. Kate's pa had surprisingly agreed, and from then on Kate spent a whole month with Auntie Mae every summer. Kate loved the boarding house, and loved Martine, Auntie Mae's lodger, a Parisian war bride who had ended up in Oregon after the Great War. Martine taught French, drank strong coffee and taught Kate how to apply lipstick. Inspired, Kate studied French from Martine's old textbooks. She got good enough to win a Portland French competition, then the Oregon state final. That was how she won a scholarship from the Alliance Française to study at the Sorbonne in 1937. Her conversational French—rudimentary and old-fashioned, according to Max, her Sorbonne group tutor—had blossomed into something approaching what Parisians spoke at the café.

Down the hill she turned left on rue des Écoles and continued up to the wide boulevard Saint-Michel, detouring around le Pam Pam, the *art moderne* café where she and her classmates had spent afternoons over tiny cups of espresso, smoking and discussing everything. They had all been international misfits, exiles from Franco's Spain, starving Polish artists, a Swedish cellist, an Austrian linguist—even a migrant rancher's daughter from Oregon.

That heady summer anything had seemed possible in Paris. Even peace. Hooked, she'd thought she'd never want to leave—until she met Dafydd.

On the bustling boulevard Saint-Michel, the women wore summer dresses that floated at the slightest breeze. Lipstick, round sunglasses, their hair wrapped in turbans or waved and shoulder-length. À la mode, as usual. The Luftwaffe officers in blue uniforms with bronze gull-wing pins strolled in groups and soldiers rumbled by on motorcycles with sidecars. Paris was reawakening, but the nightmare remained. Posters displayed a photo of white-haired Marshal Pétain entreating his *citoyens* to cooperate. From outward appearances they obliged. Kate saw shops with hand-lettered reopening signs and notices of future ration coupon requirements in their windows. In England rationing had been in effect since January. She noticed a woman wearing silk stockings, and remembered how Greer had drawn a seam up her legs with eyebrow pencil.

The kiosk vendor sold German newspapers and magazines—*Signal, Tagblatt*—and the *Bulletin Municipal Officiel de la Ville de Paris,* as well as a single copy of *Paris-Soir,* reduced to a double-sided sheet. The right-wing daily's front page announced that Mussolini threatened the French borders. She noticed the movie poster advertising a German film at the Soldatenkino. By the lamppost, German signs shaped like arrows pointed the route to the Kommandantur, the Deutsches Rotes Kruez, the Kriegsmarine.

Left Bank, Right Bank—they'd moved right in and set up shop.

Quite a few Parisians, focused on their journeys, ignored the soldiers. Kate simmered in anger at their laissez-faire attitude.

By the time she returned to Place de la Sorbonne, she'd located two escape routes that would loop back to the Jardin du Luxembourg, where she could get lost in the gardens. Now she was back at her old stomping grounds. A feeling of familiarity spread over her, lit by a flicker of hope. She'd gotten this far, hadn't she?

At Place de la Sorbonne, her eye caught the *Buchhandlung* banner over the corner bookstore. The windows displayed German books instead of textbooks now. Sickened, she parked her bike near the potted hedgerow bordering the café, took a breath and shouldered her bag.

Café Littéraire's outdoor tables opened onto the narrow rectangular Place de la Sorbonne. It was quieter than she remembered it being in '37, when conversation had buzzed at the teeming tables. She remembered how Sorbonne students had clustered by the outside fountain, smoking and talking on the street. Now the café's few occupants were a mix of bourgeois matrons and a professor or two.

Nothing unusual jumped out at her, but she heard Stepney's voice warning her to be vigilant. *Always vigilant.* And even more so at this rendezvous, she thought, in an area she knew from her student days. There was a chance of running into someone from her past, although a remote one—the war had probably changed everything.

Looking into the café now, Kate recognized the sullen fish-eyed waiter behind the zinc counter. She doubted he'd remember her. She hadn't spent much time in this café; her interest had always been the Latin bookstore on the other side of the square. It was still in business. She hoped the old woman who ran the musty, piled-high bookshop continued to hold court.

Kate's heart fell as she noticed several Wehrmacht approaching the *terrasse*. They sat down at an outdoor table, set down their guidebooks and pointed to menus, "*S'il vous plaît.*" No chance they'd leave soon.

Her instructions were to sit at the third outside table, left of the entrance under the awning. The table the Wehrmacht had claimed. Just her luck.

Her hands trembled.

Breathe.

RADA. Read the situation, assess options, decide, act.

She sat down at the table nearest the window, ignoring the now smiling and polite Germans, who were attempting to order. Did they think smiling and speaking broken French made them more palatable to the occupied? How could the French stand it?

Kate had to stop letting her thoughts run wild. Too much was at stake to let emotions get in the way. She had to control her fear. And her anger. She needed to get a hold of herself. Follow the instructions—it was her only chance now. Her contact would appear when she signaled at 1 P.M. but she didn't know if it would be someone at the café, didn't know if it would be a man or a woman. Unease enveloped her. She couldn't dismiss the possibility that Jean-Marie had revealed the meeting under torture. Or that whomever she was to meet had been caught.

Stay aware, she thought. *Alert.*

The waiter took the Wehrmacht order amid laughter and requests for beer.

She ignored them as the other patrons did and took the biography of Madame de Maintenon, mistress then morganatic queen of Louis XIV, from her bag. She looked up at the unsmiling waiter. "*Un café, s'il vous plaît,*" she said quickly, keeping her voice low. She'd practiced the Parisian intonation for hours yesterday on the milk train through the countryside, to the strange looks from the conductor.

The waiter nodded curtly and gave the round marble-topped table a quick swipe with his almost-white towel. He went inside, tucking the towel back over his arm.

Now the next part of her plan. She set her book on the table and entered the dark, cool café. A workman in overalls perched at the zinc counter drinking a beer. One table was occupied by a young couple holding hands, the other by a student writing in a notebook.

Quiet reigned. Most people in these times ate lunch at home, Kate imagined.

At the rear of the café she descended the steps to the tiled lavatory composed of a public sink and a warped wooden door painted with the letters WC. A telephone cabin stood to the right of the passage leading to a back exit. All just as her instructions had described.

To the left lay a low, coved door. She tried the hook-shaped handle and it turned. She opened the door to a damp, chill mildew, the underground smell of Paris. Here she found the café wine cellar, the sewer manhole and storage. An old ring of large keys hung from a nail on the wall. From the shank of the hollowed last key, she slid out a rolled piece of paper. Blank—which meant the meet was on. Kate stuffed it in her pocket. Something skittered. Rats.

She shivered.

At the sink, she rubbed the soap-spattered mirror with her sleeve to check her face. She could almost see the bacteria on the dirty gray bar of soap stuck to a rod in the tile. Forget it.

She splashed water on her face, opened her compact to discover the mirror had cracked; the flaking powder granules shimmered over the sink. Seven years bad luck, her Auntie Mae would say.

Sunday, June 23, 1940

Requisitioned Kommandantur Office, Paris
12:45 P.M. Paris Time

Gunter set down his case on the desk, so recently vacated by a French official that it still held a desk calendar agenda with appointments dated yesterday on the ink-stained blotter. He had barely caught his breath before he had to answer the ringing phone.

"The Führer is pleased," said Jäger. "Report back to me immediately after you interrogate the parachutists."

How could Gunter tell his boss that he doubted any of the parachutists were the assassin? Enlisting the arriving troop sergeant's assistance, Gunter had dismantled the four found rifles in a room at the village *gendarmerie.* They'd found no residue fouling in the barrel, no traces of powder on the breech face, no fresh scraping on the ejector. Gunter was certain none of the rifles had been fired since the last time they had been thoroughly cleaned.

Following his policeman's training, he'd sent them to the ballistics lab. But he knew what the technicians would find.

"Of course, Gruppenführer." That at least was the truth. His mind went back to that faint garden whiff he had picked up from the Montmartre apartment's wood floor. The familiar scent had been nagging at him. And now, suddenly, he put his finger on it: a childhood memory, a school hiking trip in the Bavarian Alps—he must have been eleven or twelve. There had been a group of British women bird watchers staying in the lodge, and they had been annoyed by the noisy schoolboys. It was the first time he'd ever seen binoculars; he'd thought they looked like little telescopes. One lady complained to the teacher that Gunter and his mates stole her Pears soap, insisting their teacher search their bunks in their dormitory. The soap was *for women only*, she declared. The boys made fun of the Englishwoman until the landlady confessed.

One of the British women said, "Let her keep it; we won the war and they don't even have soap." But the landlady was so ashamed she'd tossed it in the garbage. Gunter and his mates recovered the soap and kept it like a treasure, dividing it into slivers.

Gunter dredged that fragrance from his memory, the translucent amber bar. Pears soap, for women only. The lipstick signal the dead radio man had alerted them to reinforced Gunter's suspicion: he had a hunch he was looking for an English female assassin.

He had to get to that 1 P.M. meeting.

Gunter checked his watch, anxious to end this call.

"No one will ever know about the assassination attempt, Gunter," Jäger was saying. "Goebbels informed me the official cameraman destroyed that section of film."

Gunter had expected no less. All newsreels were doctored. The last thing Goebbels, Minister of Propaganda, wanted was for the world to see that not all the French citizens welcomed the Reich. If the Parisians knew, it could signal a call to arms. The footage of the attempted assassination no doubt was already nothing more than celluloid bits on the editing room floor.

"Of course, Gruppenführer. But how will we explain Admiral Lindau's . . . ah, untimely death?"

Jäger snorted. "Lindau had angina and suffered a crippling heart attack in the company of his beloved Führer," he said. "The Führer's very upset about the admiral's passing. Lindau's invasion campaign has had to be handed over to a U-boat captain.

And of course, his plans for Lindau's birthday party at Berchtesgaden have been ruined."

So Hitler still planned on invading Britain by sea when he already had troops across Poland, Holland, Belgium and half of France?

Gunter checked his watch again. He cradled the phone receiver between his neck and shoulder, stuffing files inside his case.

"Keep me informed, Gunter." Jäger hung up.

Gunter raced out of the office and beckoned Niels.

SUNDAY, JUNE 23, 1940

South Coast of England
1:00 P.M. Greenwich Mean Time

Posted signs on the shale beach and abandoned pier read KEEP OUT. MILITARY AREA. OFF LIMITS.

"Grandma," said nine-year-old Robbie, standing in the shallow surf, "look at what I found."

"More cockles, I hope." His grandmother, skirt rolled up, stood by the old pier in the low tide, stuffing cockles into her hip basket. The sand around the pilings was thick with them. Beige striped whelks, too.

Robbie was holding a dark green buoy. Blue blinks came from what looked like an eye in its metal casing. Fizzing bubbles trailed from it, disappearing in the sea foam.

It looked like a machine from one of his Flash Gordon comic books. Or that picture in that book *Voyage to the Bottom of the Sea* that Grandad read to him.

"Grandad should see this," he said.

"What's that you're holding?"

He lifted it up. It was heavy.

And his grandmother was splashing toward him. "Never you mind about Grandad," she said, panting. "Put that down." She took his hand, seeing the military trucks approaching the old pier. This was a restricted area patrolled by the Home Guard.

Still Grandma and the villagers would sneak in to fish and collect cockles as they always had. "Time to go."

"Will we get in trouble?"

"You let me do the talking, Robbie."

That she did.

Ten minutes later, the Home Guard squad commander in charge had conferred with his squad, who'd stowed the buoy-like thing in the back of a jeep. "Mrs. Whately, we need Robbie to answer some questions," he told Robbie's grandmother.

Robbie's eyes brightened. "To help the war effort, sir?"

His grandmother's work-worn fingers twisted on her basket. "Robbie, keep quiet."

"You'll sign the Official Secrets Act. And this never happened."

"Can we tell Grandad?"

"You'll need to speak with the group commander."

She sighed. "Understood."

In the truck Robbie looked at his worried grandma.

Sunday, June 23, 1940

Café Littéraire, Place de la Sorbonne, Paris
12:50 p.m. Paris Time

Seven years bad luck? Kate hoped not, staring in dismay at the cracked mirror in her compact. On the bright side, she wouldn't mind knowing she had another seven years to live, bad luck or not. At the moment she couldn't even guess whether she'd survive the next ten minutes.

She dipped her finger in the rouge, which had melted then caked in the heat. She ran a comb through her dirty dark blonde hair, parting it on the side, clipped it back with a tortoiseshell comb. Not too different from how she'd looked when she'd sat down, but primped enough for the waiter to sense *un rendez-vous amoureux.*

"The trick is to blend in, not stand out," Stepney had told her, over and over. "That is crucial."

On the morning of what had been her last day of training, she'd been taken to another mansion, this time on the outskirts of London. One of those places royalty lived with servants, drafty and unheated. Stepney ushered her up a grand staircase to a suite of rooms and into a long rectangular dressing room with closets, a full-length mirror and a vanity dresser lined with perfume bottles and lotions. Uneasy, she wondered why Stepney brought her into a woman's intimate boudoir. She felt like more of an outsider than ever, wondering how this fit in with her mission.

Peter, a Shakespearean actor, sat at the vanity with a stage makeup kit compact. "We call it our palette, like an artist's." Peter appeared to be in his thirties. He had a craggy face, prominent chin. He studied her thoughtfully. "As I illustrate and explain I'll be assembling your palette to use on the spot. Your own kit."

Stepney had lingered at the door. "You've got two hours, Peter. See that she passes this postgraduate course with honors."

Peter began by taking a thin makeup brush and dipping it in alcohol. "An agent's cover involves the use of quick disguises. But a disguise doesn't mean a false beard."

Kate smiled. "So a mustache in my case?"

Peter took her hand and squeezed it. Smiled. "Avoid thinking theatrically. Instead make small changes to your appearance." He put a brown-framed pair of glasses on the vanity. "Try this. Now part your hair differently—on the left."

She did. She could be a librarian, a shop clerk, a teacher.

Amazing what a little change could do.

"Now stand up." Peter had her turn around in front of the mirror, all fingernail-bitten five foot six inches of her. "You're a big-boned girl."

Did he mean her looks doomed her mission? All of a sudden dread overwhelmed her. "You're saying I'll stand out. It's hopeless."

His brown eyes danced. "I'm saying use it. Actors plays many roles by changing appearance to alter audience perceptions. We do it all the time." He lifted a photo of a bent old man from his case. "That's me in *The Merchant of Venice*." He showed her another of a young straight-backed warrior. "As Banquo in *Macbeth*. In repertory especially, actors play all kinds of roles, young and old." He squeezed her hand again. Reassuring. "Remember, it's how you play with what you've got to alter perceptions. So use it."

Peter handed her a blue cardigan from the wardrobe. "Try a different gait. Walk with a slouch to the door and watch yourself in the mirror."

Kate fit her arms in the sweater, buttoned it, hunched her shoulders and slouched. It felt so awkward. So false.

"Now inhabit this woman wearing this sweater whose back gives her trouble. *Be* her. *Believe* it."

Kate remembered how her back ached after a long day standing at the munitions factory. That long trudge home on the rutted dirt road to the cottage. Then her world brightening as she picked up Lisbeth at Mrs. McLeod's, twirling the little girl through the air despite the twinge in her back. She let her mind go there and crossed the carpet.

"Good." Peter smiled in encouragement. "Walking is one thing you can change right away. Putting a pebble in your shoe is guaranteed to make you walk differently. Height is harder to disguise, although you can make yourself even taller with heels."

He waved the thin makeup brush. "Don't rely on one of these. Use your fingers. And never use perfume. Or nail polish, ever. And file those jagged nails."

He demonstrated how to use liquid collodion that dried into a wax-like substance to create scars. A simple scarf could be worn several ways, creating a new look each time.

"A stub of charcoal or soot darkens hair. Or you can give yourself shadows under your eyes. Try it with me."

Beside him at the mirror, she brushed the charcoal stub into the laugh lines around her eyes as Peter did. Blended it in with her fingers, watching him and following his lead. Smudged it under her eyes.

"I look ancient," she said. "So do you."

"See." He grinned. "A haggard, tired appearance in less than a minute. Remember, if you want to be invisible go old. No one notices old people."

In two hours he'd shown her how to use lip outlining pencils to thicken brows and change the shape of her mouth, rouge for cheeks and lips, saltwater drops to make her eyes bloodshot and watery, and an array of other subtle tricks.

"Minimalist and effective. We use these on stage every night, several times during a single performance if you're playing more than one part. Changing your appearance and your walk helps you get into character." Peter lifted her chin. Stared straight in her eyes. "Most important, believe and be the character. If you do, others will."

A knock on the door and Stepney came in. "Ready?"

"Remember—in the field, a quick and simple disguise works best." Peter handed her a Gauloise Caporal tobacco tin, inside a tiny palette arranged with a piece of charcoal, rouge, lip pencil stub, a vial of drops, collodion, hair combs and coiled blue ribbon. "Your kit. *Believe.* Best of luck."

Back upstairs in the café, Kate scanned the crowd again, then sat down at the outdoor table just at the moment the waiter brought her coffee. He gave her an approving smile and she handed him three francs from the money prepared in her jacket pocket. When he left, she set a few *sous*—about ten cents, the customary *pourboire* the French refused to call a tip—on the table.

Now she rested her canvas bag under the rattan chair between her feet. Checked the time. The distant church bell of Saint-Séverin in the Latin Quarter chimed the three-quarter hour. To her left on boulevard Saint-Michel was the bus stop where, if all went well and according to the instructions, she'd meet her contact.

She opened the book she had pulled from the bike basket—tough going in classical French. She concentrated on her breathing. She kept her eyes half-lidded so her gaze appeared focused on the page to anyone who was watching her; meanwhile she continuously scanned the area—for trouble or for her contact, whoever that was.

Welcome mist from the fountain hung in the dense heat. The laughter of the red-faced beer-drinking Wehrmacht filled the *terrasse.* Which of the waiters had left the door unlocked and message in the hollow key, she wondered? Which one could she trust?

According to the Maquet wristwatch Stepney had given her, eight minutes had passed when a new patron, a mustached man reading *Signal,* claimed a table. The Wehrmacht's voices had grown even louder. A good blind—protection, unless they scared her contact off. But she couldn't control that.

She glanced inside the café. The young couple nestled against each other; the student bent over his notebook; the workman nursed another beer at the counter. She turned the page as if engrossed in the book.

RADA, she could hear Stepney's voice in her head; *read* the *terrasse* activity—normal; continue to closely *assess* the patrons; *decide* if it felt right and according to plan; prepare to *act* at the scheduled time.

The fish-eyed waiter was washing glasses; the other waiter stood at the chalkboard by the window, adding today's menu. Her contact could be any of the patrons inside, or either of the two professors sitting outdoors on the *terrasse.* The young one's face rarely looked up from his wine glass and the older one intently rolled his cigarette with shaky hands. All she knew for sure was that it wasn't one of the loud Germans in front of her.

Sunlight glinted on the window of the Latin bookstore under the striped awning directly across from her. She yearned to visit the dusty aisles piled high with books, inhale the smell of old paper the way she had done so many times during her Sorbonne days, talk with Madame and . . . what? Exchange pleasantries?

Sweat formed on her brow. Not a hundred yards away she spotted Max, the French tutor she had spent so many hours with in '37, pausing at the Latin bookstore window. Wispy brown hair, full cheeks, those rimless spectacles and jacket with elbow patches—he hadn't changed.

She caught herself just before she raised her arm to wave to him. If Max recognized her, her cover was blown. She tipped her head down, her heart pounding, wishing she could make herself invisible. Why did he have to show up here now? What were the chances? But Max had always haunted the bookstores during the lunch hour. For God's sake, he'd been the one who had first introduced her to this one.

He entered the store now. No time to worry over him.

Two girls speaking what sounded like Swedish were smoking by the fountain. A young woman walked by with a shopping bag full of leeks hanging from a baby carriage. Leeks? The nearest market was at Maubert, downhill and six or seven blocks away. How many times had Kate shopped there before class?

Head down, Kate turned the book's page and followed the woman's progress from the corner of her eye. Could that be her contact? The woman slowed in the heat, stopping at the fountain and patting the back of her neck with a handkerchief. She draped her sweater over the buggy, then sat on the fountain's edge, fanned herself with the handkerchief and rocked the carriage. Nothing unusual in taking a break in the heat. A perfect cover.

Reassured, Kate flicked her gaze over to the professors, then the Latin bookstore where Max had gone inside. It was 12:59. Time for one last check before giving the signal.

Her fingers shook as she set down the book and reached into her canvas bag for the compact. She opened it, checked her face in the cracked mirror, then tilted it to see the waiter behind her through the open window. He was still washing glasses. The couple seemed engrossed in each other; the student sipped a *limonade*. She shut her compact. Almost one o'clock.

Kate took a deep breath. It was time to take out her lipstick, apply it and blot her lips. The signal. Hyperalert to her surroundings, Kate tried to focus on the task at hand. But she was filled with unease. Her arm tingled, a shiver in the heat.

The woman leaned down toward the carriage. If she was the contact, shouldn't she have started to walk in Kate's direction by now? The plan had been that Kate would apply lipstick to signal her contact, who would then meet her at the bus stop.

But the woman wasn't standing. A warning jolt shot up Kate's spine. If the woman had just come from shopping at the Maubert market, she would have come from rue de la Sorbonne, not as she had from boulevard Saint-Michel, the opposite street. A Parisian wouldn't have taken any other route; neither would an agent with a good cover.

Her gut told her something was wrong.

Had Jean-Marie given her away?

What should she do? Give in to fear and jump ship? Sabotage her only escape route?

She needed to signal now or the whole rendezvous would be off. She made up her mind and reached for the lipstick tube in her bag. And her hand froze.

The woman at the fountain took a makeup compact out of the baby carriage, a makeup compact just like Kate's. She angled the mirror and it flashed in the sun, not once but twice.

A signal, but not for Kate.

For whom?

Kate's heart pounded. This only made sense if she'd been set up.

Footsteps sounded behind her in the café. The young couple were now standing in front of the door.

RADA.

All her instincts were telling her the same thing.

Leave. Get up and leave.

Instead of taking out her lipstick, she scooped up her bag, stood and beat it back down to the café's loo.

Sunday, June 23, 1940

The War Rooms under London | 12:40 A.M. Paris Time

Running a live mission with agents, when everything depended on split-second coordination, was enough to give anyone ulcers, Stepney thought. Never mind exacerbate the one he already suffered from. Now he had to endure this meeting with the Secret Intelligence Service crew, who felt Stepney's section should concentrate on the imminent German sea invasion.

"We know they're planning it, sir," said the prime minister's SIS advisor, a wet-behind-the-ears thirty-year-old with thick-lensed glasses. "You've seen the aerial photos of bunker and jetty construction along the Brittany coast. You were the one who told us about the decoded naval messages."

Stepney's tea tasted sour as he reiterated that of course he would keep on top of the invasion, but in the meantime he needed to rebuild his Paris intelligence-gathering network. As the meeting adjourned, an aide arrived and handed him a decoded report.

"What's this?"

"An update, sir. You said you wished to be informed on the latest from Y sector in Paris."

Y sector submitted, via a diplomatic pouch to Lisbon, weekly reports only; this was off schedule. Stepney read the decoded telex quickly and his throat caught. Kate hadn't met her contact at the drop site. However, Y sector reported contact with her this morning, and reported passing her the message. They'd thought it important enough to report this to the British embassy in Lisbon.

He tried to think how they'd have this information. His only conclusion being that the Y sector, a Portuguese priest and his sister working in a bakery, were in contact with other cells.

"How's the American's diversion going?" asked the PM's SIS advisor.

Worried she was running loose, Stepney wondered for a moment if Kate could have actually been capable of pulling off the impossible. Not that it mattered now.

"No word from the link at her drop site," he said, recovering. "However, there's a report she's made contact in Paris."

"Please back up, sir. Are you saying Rees got to Paris on her own?"

"It looks that way. She's most likely on her way to the café meeting."

"Odd, that, for her to go off plan." The SIS advisor adjusted his glasses. "Wouldn't you say?"

Stepney needed time to find out. "Not really. She's trained to think on her feet. The important thing is she made contact." Stepney glanced at the clock. "I'll know more when Martins radios after the one o'clock meet. Any chatter from Berlin?"

"Nothing new from Bletchley, sir."

Stepney hobbled as quickly as he could through the underground passage to the listening station below King Charles Street. Men ran back and forth along the warren of hallways. The gas mask hanging from Stepney's belt scraped the walls as he made his way to the radio operator's desk. Damn cramped down here for a military intelligence hub.

Billy, the operator, headphones clamped over his brown curly hair, looked up as Stepney approached. "One minute forty-five seconds until Martins makes contact, sir."

Stepney consulted the latest report to verify that the Germans had not made yet another time zone change—Fritz had made

Paris run on Berlin time after the occupation, an hour ahead, wreaking havoc with the train system. "Good. Upon authentication follow standard procedure."

"Of course, sir."

Martins was a good radio operator, with six missions under his belt. Stepney hoped this radio transmission would be the end of his compromised Paris network.

"Sir?" Billy's eyes twinkled as he handed Stepney the spare set of headphones.

Right on schedule, Stepney heard long and short taps of Morse code. In pencil Billy inscribed them on the keypad, then aligned the dots and dashes to the code tablet and noted the time. When Billy looked up, the light was gone from his eyes.

"What's he say, Billy?"

"Meeting imminent. Advise details." Billy swallowed. "But it's not Martins's key touch, sir."

Alarm flooded Stepney. Each radio operator used a distinctive keypad touch—a lighter or heavier tap, a longer or shorter pause, a particular rhythm. His own signature, or fist, as operators called it. This was a built-in security step to confirm identification.

Martins had been compromised. Did they have him?

Stepney clenched his cane. "You're sure?"

"Afraid so, sir. It's not Martins's finger pressure." Billy pointed with his pencil to a series of bold and light marks. "As I listen I bold the heavier taps. There's too many heavy taps for Martins's usual signature. What do I do, sir?"

Stepney tamped down his panic. Before he cut the transmission and shelved the whole operation, he needed more verification. Rules be damned. He wanted this to succeed too much.

"Respond asking for double authentication."

Billy dashed the message. Stepney leaned on his cane in the cubicle, trying to maintain calm. Martins was a valuable radio operator, the only link to his operatives for this operation in France.

"Martins says he sprained his wrist in the drop, sir. Injured his arm."

"Did he give the double authentication, Billy?"

"Yes, sir. See for yourself."

Stepney cast his eyes over the code verification. If it was indeed Martins, he had given the proper authentication, and an injured hand was a plausible enough reason for the discrepancy in touch. But it was a little too convenient.

"What do you think, Billy?"

"Me, sir?"

"Could German intelligence have cracked our authentication codes?"

"Not for me to venture an opinion, sir," Billy said, like the weasel he was. No responsibility for him. Like all the young ones, he wanted the glory but had no guts.

Stepney took a moment to think. He had a bad feeling. "We delay. In the meantime, we compare this message and Martins's previous messages to other examples of compromised touches the department has discovered." He would meet with the code experts before he killed the whole operation and stranded his snipers.

Stepney felt a black ache in the back of his head. The harbinger of a migraine. He'd be lucky if that was the extent of it, he thought, hurrying to the SIS head's office.

Sunday, June 23, 1940

Place de la Sorbonne, Paris | 1:01 P.M. Paris Time

Kate smiled at the waiter, passing the café counter as if it were the most normal thing in the world for her to be making a second trip to the bathroom. Tension crackled in her brain. In the café's mirror she saw the young couple at the door turn. Would they follow her? In several steps she was down the staircase, heading toward the WC and beyond to the exit.

At the coved door, a man wearing a worker's cap and duster coat stood in her way. Was he her contact or had he been sent to intercept her? She froze. Despite all her training she couldn't move.

"It's important," he whispered, palming something into her hand. With his cap pulled low she couldn't make out his face in the shadows but his accent was French.

Just like that—what about procedure? Could she trust him?

Read, Assess, Decide, Act.

"*Pardonnez-moi, monsieur.* I need to apply my lipstick."

He didn't move. Worse, he smelled like the sewer. "This meeting's been compromised," he said. "The eagle got away."

Code for the Führer. But she already knew that. Could she believe him?

"Answer my question first. Why should I trust you?"

He flashed a dirty index and middle finger in a V.

That was what her contact was supposed to do when they met at the bus stop. Still wary, she stood back in the low-ceilinged walkway.

"What's this you've given me?" she whispered.

"Get out of here. Go to that address. Our group's been infiltrated. There's a traitor."

Her breath came fast. Uneasy, she asked, "How did you know I'd come to the café today?"

In the dim light she saw how his large blue worker shirt hung on him, disguising a smaller frame.

"I was told an agent would come here yesterday or today. So I checked. Then today the paper was gone from the hollow key," he said. "Signaling the meet was on. You brought the rifle?"

She realized she must have been meant to hand it over to him. She trusted him a little more now.

"*Non*, it's safe, but . . ."

"Later. There's Boches everywhere. You need to leave; the radio contact's blown."

This café rendezvous had been her only hope of learning an escape plan. Her stomach clenched. She finally noticed the Paris sewer insignia on the man's jacket. No wonder he smelled so fragrant. One of the lenses in his glasses was cracked.

"How do I escape?"

He moved toward the service door behind her in the hallway. "Take the back exit."

"Yes, but I mean to England."

"We'll make contact later."

He'd disappeared the way he must have come—through the sewers.

She stooped and stuck whatever he'd slipped her in her shoe, then hurried to the exit door and turned the bronze knob. Stuck. Should she go through that coved service door as he had, try the sewer?

No damn way.

Chairs scraped above her; she heard arguing voices approaching the stairs. She reached for the lockpick set safety-pinned to her panties. Her hands trembled, slippery with perspiration. *Get with it, girl. Concentrate.* She played her lock-picking lesson in her head, hearing the instructions in her teacher Tony's East End accent. *Toggle ever so gently, massaging the lower pick down until it connects.*

Tony, the cat burglar on Stepney's training roster, could charm birds from the trees. Not that she'd thought so at first when he'd locked her in a dark room. He'd told her to listen to his voice and let the feel of the lock mechanism guide her. *Like you would with a lover, darling.* Thirty minutes later, sweaty and furious, she'd opened the door. Tony, a rakish salt-and-pepper-haired sprite of a man, beamed and handed her a glass of fizzing champagne. *Bravo! Celebrate, darling.* He toasted her, clinked her glass. *Now again, darling. Again and again until you open her in less than sixty seconds.* And she'd done it again and again.

The voices were getting closer. Echoes of a scuffle on the stairs. Her heart pounded.

Click.

She turned the knob and didn't look back.

Sunday, June 23, 1940

Communications Center under King Charles Street, London
1:10 p.m. Paris Time

Stepney's outward demeanor radiated, he hoped, controlled calm. Inside, he fumed. "Coubert's body was found yesterday in the Fontainebleau forest," he said. "And you're only telling me now?" Coubert was the French contact who was supposed to have met Martins on his drop.

Fleming, a member of the Joint Intelligence Committee, avoided answering the question. "He never met Martins." Fleming had served with Stepney in the first war, a former officer who'd been mothballed out and now appeared decidedly rotund in a brown suit. "One of the Chantilly network agents waited for Martins at the second meet to take him to Paris. Martins never showed. You know what this means?"

"Why didn't I know earlier?" Good God, the implications.

"Ask Teague," said Fleming. "He's waiting for you in the Tactical room."

The Tactical room was swarming with activity. Teague summoned Stepney to a table stacked with a sheaf of reports from the teleprinter. Bright spotlights illuminated the maps covering the wall, colored pins indicating troop locations. The place was so damned hot, full of scurrying staff and stale odors of tea.

"Bletchley Park decrypted this ten minutes ago, that's why none of us knew." Teague, his khaki shirtsleeves rolled up, shook his head. "We suspect the code's been compromised. As we speak, Bletchley's changing the cipher codes, but the Germans already have an hour's start on us. More, probably. We don't know anything, Stepney. It's a fiasco."

More like a tragedy. Martins, their best radio operator, dead; his code key in the Germans' possession. He didn't want to think of the torture Martins must have endured before cracking. They all cracked; it just took some longer than others.

As he'd feared, the message Billy had received from Martins hadn't been from Martins at all.

"Don't tell me the whole Alpha network's compromised, too?"

"Unknown at this point," Stepney said. "Y sector reported Rees made contact."

"Good. We need that Yank alive to provide diversion more than ever now," said Teague. "You've assured me they won't get anything useful from her, correct?"

Stepney winced inside. Kate Rees would be caught, interrogated, tortured. He hoped that cowgirl moxie came to her aid. America wasn't at war with Germany yet; at least there was a chance the Germans would honor the Geneva Convention regarding prisoners.

Stepney let out a sigh. "She knew the risks when she signed on."

How many times had he trained agents and signed their death warrants?

Always in the service of King and country.

Sunday, June 23, 1940

Near the Sorbonne, Paris | 1:07 p.m.

Kate emerged in a rectangular courtyard by trash bins smelling of fish. Shafts of bright sunlight cut though the shadows cast by the backs of buildings. Runner beans climbed a trellised wall beside a chicken pen. Laundry hung from windowsills; the sound of a violin drifted from somewhere.

Run. Escape. Hide.

She lugged a trash bin to the back door, blocking the exit.

Sweat broke out on her upper lip. She forced herself to breathe, think and keep moving as she'd been trained. She'd go to the Jardin du Luxembourg, as she'd planned.

In the portico across the cobbled courtyard a concierge was sweeping and talking with the postman, whose yellow postbag hung from his shoulder as he paused in the tall open doorway. They'd both remember her if they were questioned.

Head down, she walked at a steady pace. No break in their conversation. Good.

A church bell rang. Pigeons scattered as she passed.

"*Mademoiselle, mademoiselle!*" a man called.

She didn't turn around. Footsteps were coming toward her, were coming faster.

Sunday, June 23, 1940

Near the Sorbonne, Paris | 1:06 p.m.

"*Oui, monsieur?*" a woman's voice rang across the courtyard behind Kate.

The approaching footsteps stopped. "You forgot your mother-in-law's mail."

It must have been the concierge he was calling. Phew. Kate kept walking.

Before she turned into the street, she heard a German-accented voice behind her.

"*Entschuldigen Sie, bitte, excusez-moi, madame.* Did you see a woman . . . ?"

Not out of the woods yet. Kate hurried out onto the street and into a swarm of young schoolchildren.

"*Attention, les infants!*" their teacher was saying and pointing to a statue across the street.

Not now. She couldn't get stuck like a sitting duck! Spying a doorway, which opened to another courtyard, she beelined inside to the wooden outhouse under the eaves. The toilet was a hole in a wood plank, ripe with the odor of *pipi* and damp leaves. Like outhouses back home, only here the torn-up newspaper squares that served as toilet paper were in French. Her hands were shaking as she removed her blue sweater and folded it into her bag. They shook so much she almost poked out her eye putting on the brown-framed glasses.

Breathe.

The message in her shoe was written on a rolled-up caramel bonbon wrapping. She memorized the information about the next meeting and tossed the paper in the stinking hole.

She removed the tortoiseshell comb and gathered up her hair into a ponytail. Tied a blue ribbon around it and got the hell out of there.

Back on the street, Kate focused on keeping her knees close together as she walked, pointing her toes outward to change her naturally pronated gait. Clutched her basket like a woman going shopping.

Believe.

At the first shop, a *quincaillerie*, she went inside to catch her breath. She was surprised to see crochet needles among the hardware offerings. Perfect for self-defense. Back home in Yreka the hardware stores only sold things like feed and shovels. She bought a beige canvas shopping bag, exchanged the contents and ditched the blue one.

Her heart was still pounding from her close shave.

"If you're trying to lose a tail, change tactics at a moment's notice," Stepney had told her. "If you're going north, turn south."

So ten minutes later, instead of strolling under the shadowed allée of trees in the Jardin du Luxembourg as she had planned, she was riding the bus toward the Right Bank. She couldn't recall ever having been to this neighborhood before. She found the address the sewer man had given her at 224 rue du Faubourg Saint-Martin near a canal by a closed music store. The shop's windows, like many she'd noticed, were crosshatched by tape to prevent glass shattering in case of bombing.

Inside the sun-drenched courtyard both of the third-floor shutters were closed—the all-clear, according to the message. But she debated—the sewer man had mentioned a traitor. Was she walking into another trap?

Damn Stepney, why hadn't he given a lesson on traitors?

Sunday, June 23, 1940

Place de la Sorbonne, Paris | 1:15 P.M.

Stuck behind the troop-truck traffic on the leafy tree-lined boulevard Saint-Michel, Gunter wiped his damp neck with his handkerchief. It was past one o'clock. He felt sick with frustration as Niels pulled the car up near the Sorbonne café.

Too late. Roschmann was already there, strutting across the *terrasse,* pointing and barking orders to his Feldgendarmerie unit.

Gottverdammt.

"Took your time, eh, Hoffman?"

"This isn't a pissing contest, Roschmann." This was his investigation, not the SD's. Roschmann reported to him. "Give me an update."

"We've spread a cordon for accomplices."

Gunter controlled his surprise. "So she was a no-show."

"Oh, we picked her up."

"An Englishwoman, here at the café?" He saw the Feldgendarmerie under Roschmann's command fanning out across the *terrasse.* "You saw her signal with lipstick?"

"*Nein,* a mirror, right here, sitting at the fountain."

Gunter eyed the abandoned baby buggy. The fountain's cool spray misted his cheek. Why would the signal have changed? That didn't add up. "Who was she here to meet?"

Roschmann gave a dismissive wave. "If you remember, I was

the one who obtained the Englander's confession. The rest of the story will come out after this woman's interrogation, *nein?*"

No doubt this idiotic raid had frightened off the real contact, and any network of accomplices. Roschmann's tactics were derailing Gunter's investigation. That was most likely intentional—jockeying for power at any cost. Typical SD.

His head pounding, Gunter took off his jacket, undid the collar buttons of his sweat-soaked shirt and hurried to the back of a troop truck guarded by a Wehrmacht solider. Inside sat a petite brunette in her early twenties, one wrist cuffed to the metal rod behind the wood bench. He saw blood dripping from her split lower lip and a sullen look in her eyes.

Jäger, his boss, had demanded Gunter find the sniper and report only to him; Kostoff, the *Kommandant* of Occupied Paris, insisted Gunter work with Roschmann. Meanwhile four British parachutists awaited questioning and the Führer's thirty-six deadline hours dwindled. With little to go on, he needed to get results.

"Show me her bag. Her things."

The soldier handed him a string shopping bag containing leeks, a key ring, and a *carte d'identité—Jeanne Albrecht, 49 rue Cujas.* A nearby address. Not a pro.

"What was in there?" He pointed to the baby buggy. A perfect size to hide a rifle.

"Nothing. That's everything she had."

"Where's the baby?"

"The buggy was empty, sir."

"Go find my adjutant."

"My orders were—"

Gunter flashed his RSD card. "To do what I say. Ask my adjutant to get ice from the café. *Schnell.*"

He sat down on the bench next to the woman. Dripping blood had stained her collar. He pulled out his handkerchief.

"*Excusez-moi,*" he said, dabbing her lip. "I'm the one you talk to, not him," he said in his broken French. He gestured toward Roschmann, who huddled with several Feldgendarmerie outside the open doors. "Speak English?"

She looked away. Wet spots flowered on her print dress. Despite his runny nose, he caught that familiar sweetish scent of breast milk he remembered from his daughter's infancy.

Niels leaned into the troop truck and handed him a dirty ice chunk wrapped in a cloth café napkin. "All they had, sir."

"Permit me?" Gunter lifted the ice and held it to her lip. Her shoulders trembled. "This should help the swelling. Where's your baby, Jeanne?"

She blinked. Hesitated, then answered in German with an Alsatian accent. "What's that to you?"

She wasn't English, nor was she the sniper, not with leaking breasts and no scent of Pears soap. "Don't you want to feed your baby?"

A nod. "He's with my concierge. Let me explain."

Good. A talker. "I'm listening."

"My husband is—he's in Germany. A volunteer soldier with the Reich. So you can't put me in jail." Her swollen lip trembled.

"That depends. Help me and I'll help you, *verstehen Sie?*"

She winced. "This morning a note with fifty francs and a compact was slipped under my door. Look, I'm surviving as best I can. My baby's hungry."

He watched her eyes. "Go on."

"The note said to come sit by the fountain at five to one and flash the compact's mirror when a woman sitting on Café Littéraire's *terrasse* applied lipstick." Her bony shoulders shook. "It looked like she was about to apply lipstick, so I flashed the mirror. I don't know who she was or what this was about. The note said I'd get another fifty francs when I got home. Now I'll never get it."

"Who gave you the message?"

"I don't know."

"But you have an idea."

She squirmed on the bench. "There's no real names. They use Latin words as code. That's all I know." Her voice choked. "They could kill me for admitting this."

"Not if you help me, Jeanne." He motioned to Niels. "Call the sketch artist."

As the Werhmacht sketch artist, a thin art-college type, joined them, Gunter motioned for the soldier on guard to unlock her handcuffs. Time for the carrot-and-stick approach.

"You're from Alsace, Jeanne?"

A nod.

"Why are you in Paris with your baby?"

"My mother-in-law works here at the Renault factory. Cars. On the assembly line. My husband thought it best we stay with her but she got injured at work. She's in hospital and I'm stuck." Jeanne accepted the wrapped ice and held it to her chin. "So my accent gave me away?" She had spirit.

"It's like my wife's. She's from Mulhouse. She never tires of reminding me she's Alsatian."

A little unguarded smile appeared. She was a child herself, only nineteen.

"So tell me what happened from the beginning. You saw the message under your door, then what?"

He listened as she walked him through her afternoon. "There were a group of Wehrmacht sitting over there," she said. "There were a few other people, too. But then at one table, just one woman. She took out her lipstick tube, like I said, so I flashed the mirror."

Gunter nodded to the sketch artist, who had already started drawing the café scene on his pad. Outside, Roschmann was barking orders. A troop truck engine whined.

"Describe her."

"Head down in a book." Jeanne rubbed her wrist. "That's what I remember."

"Her hair, her clothes, her height?"

Jeanne fanned herself with the edge of the damp napkin. Thought. "Not old. Young."

"How young?" Gunter shifted his legs. The metal ribs of the troop truck dug into his back.

"Maybe early twenties?

"What else?"

"Dirty blonde hair with a tortoiseshell comb. She was wearing a blue sweater, I think . . ."

"Did you hear her speak?"

"Speak? No."

Jeanne was cooperating but this wasn't enough information. He needed details.

"Which table?" Gunter opened the truck's back doors wider. "Point it out. Picture her sitting there and that will help you remember more."

She pointed and the sketch artist looked up then down again, busily drawing as Jeanne described what she'd seen.

"Try to remember, Jeanne. Did she have a scar, a birthmark, or wear makeup?"

"Rosy cheeks. From the heat . . . or maybe makeup? Oh, wait, I remember—there was a canvas bag under the table."

The artist's quick sketch was surprisingly skillful. A real Rembrandt, if he lived through the war.

"Does this look like her?"

Jeanne shook her head. "Bigger. I mean, wider shoulders. She was tall, I think. And her eyes . . . well, it was only a few seconds, but . . ."

The sketch artist flipped to a fresh page and redrew as Jeanne tried to remember the woman in more detail. Minutes passed. Sweat dripped down Gunter's back in the stifling heat of the truck.

"That's more like her."

Staring back at Gunter was a deft portrait of a big-boned young woman with wide-set eyes, arched brows, prominent cheekbones, and a pouty mouth.

Got you, he thought.

Gunter nodded and the sketch artist commenced drawing a second copy on his pad. Jeanne ran her tongue over her swollen lip. She rocked on the stiff wood bench, as he'd seen suspects do when they were holding back. "Go on, Jeanne. Something's bothering you. Tell me."

Her pinhole brown eyes blinked. Clearly she was afraid.

"Someone has been watching me. I just . . . felt it."

Gunter nodded. "Who?"

"I was supposed to be getting fifty francs out of this. Under my door, the note said, if I did what it said. Maybe they have been watching to see if I did what they told me to and now it's all gone."

Gunter reached in his pocket. Handed her a hundred francs.

"You'll find out if you want to stay with your baby." Gunter gestured to Niels. "Pull the car up." He wrote down the name *Café Midi*, which he'd seen around the corner. "My driver will drop you a block from your place. No one will see. You'll wait until your watcher slides your money under your door, and then you stop that person and bring him to the Café Midi in one hour. Say there's money in it for him."

"What if I can't find him?" Her voice rose. "Or he doesn't show up to leave me money?"

He slipped her another hundred francs. Held her ID card up for her to see before tucking it into his pocket. She'd get nowhere without her ID. No rations or train tickets.

"I'm sure you'll figure it out."

GUNTER BLINKED IN THE BRIGHT sunshine as he stepped out of the café's cellar. He sneezed and wiped his nose with his damp handkerchief, only to be assaulted by a fishy odor coming from the upended garbage bins. She'd escaped this way.

He doubted the English radio man had lied under torture. The spy had either been tipped off that the meeting was compromised or had figured it out on her own. Thanks to that idiot Roschmann she was on the run—again.

Gunter led a search of the courtyard and café himself. No rifle turned up. Roschmann had been threatening to arrest the staff until Gunter ordered searches of all baggage storage in the nearby train stations and museums to keep him busy.

Who would be in the crosshairs next if he didn't find the rifle—or the woman?

He looked at his watch. Thirty-one hours and thirty minutes.

Back inside the café, Gunter picked up a box of matches. Took one out, played with it while the pop-eyed waiter, who reminded him of his uncle who suffered a thyroid condition, looked at the sketch.

"He says she spoke French," Niels translated for Gunter. "She ordered coffee. He remembers her bike, sir."

"Is her bike still here?"

The waiter gestured to follow him. Outside the café several bikes were parked by a planter spilling with ivy.

"He says she got off this old one—he noticed because she parked it beside his. She took a book from the basket, then sat on the *terrasse*."

The bike was a beat-up affair with rusted spokes. A stained canvas basket was clipped to the handlebars. Gunter felt inside the basket. Crumbs? His fingers closed on a torn paper scrap, then a sharp sliver of what he recognized as a piece of thick brown wicker. Odd. This bike basket was old canvas, not wicker.

Two theories formed in his mind. She'd either brought the sniper rifle here to the aborted rendezvous to hand off, or she'd stored the rifle elsewhere. Roschmann was searching the train station lockers but a pro would pick another site. Something convenient and accessible.

Gunter studied the sliver of paper: torn blue with a trace of perforation on the corner.

"Ask the waiter what this looks like to him," he told Niels.

The waiter shrugged. Thought. Then spoke.

"He says maybe a receipt, a claim check?"

A claim check for a parcel.

The spray from the fountain misted Gunter's arms. "It's blue. Does that have any significance? Like a laundry receipt?"

The waiter shook his head.

"Those receipts are pink, he says. Maybe from a shop? A big store."

"Ask the waiter what's open today besides the museums."

The waiter listened and shook his head.

"Churches. Bakeries in the morning but no shops on Sunday afternoon."

"Wait, the department store we passed—that big one. It was open."

Of course, the French knew how to make a mark with German troops eager to shop.

Niels nodded. "You mean le Bon Marché?"

"Get the car, Niels."

Sunday, June 23, 1940

Near Canal Saint-Martin, Paris | 2:00 p.m.

Kate sucked in her breath, looked around. No one, from what she could tell, had followed her. Summoning her courage, she headed through the courtyard of 224 rue du Faubourg Saint-Martin—the contact's address that the sewer man had given her.

"*Oui?*" The stout concierge's hoarse voice stopped Kate in her tracks. She had a gravy stain on her apron. "Visiting someone?"

The last person Kate wanted to have seen her. Concierges were notorious for noticing and informing. Kate willed herself to smile, act casual.

"Mademoiselle Gilberte," Kate said.

"I'm not sure she's in."

A dead end so soon?

"She's expecting me," she lied, peering up the narrow dark winding stairs.

"Suit yourself." The concierge loge door slammed.

Kate climbed three winding flights. The air was redolent of old cooking oil and cheap perfume. At the third floor she knocked on the left door. No answer. She tried the handle. Locked.

Kate reached under the mat—only dust. The geranium pot was swathed in a cobweb, but scrabbling her fingers in the dirt, she came back with a key.

So much for security. The watchdog concierge wasn't much of a cattle guard, as her pa would have said.

She unlocked the door, slipped the key back under the geranium and stepped into a surprisingly light and airy flat covered in pink and apricot wall hangings. Feminine. Several rooms opened off the hall.

"*Allô?* Gilberte?"

Only the sound of rattling water pipes in the walls.

A Siamese cat with turquoise eyes brushed her legs. Its fur was like velvet. Narrow strips of light fell on the wood floor through the half-closed shutters. A check of the front room revealed no one. Her breath lingered in the warm air. The air of a closed room. A setup?

She had nowhere else to go, no other contact except the sewer man. No weapon.

But there was a kitchen down the hallway. Kate figured it would hold utensils, like knives.

Kate slung her bag higher on her shoulder and padded to the old-fashioned kitchen. No knife rack, but by the sink in a cutlery drawer, she found a carving knife. She slipped it in her pocket.

She splashed her face with water at the sink, which was filled with dishes. No housekeeper, Gilberte. Kate washed a glass and drank down a tall one of cool water. Then another.

Kate set down the empty glass. After two days she needed a bath. Desperately. She hoped this place had a bathroom and not just a smelly shared squat hole between the landings.

The first door she opened was to a bedroom where a naked man was sitting up in bed, sheets tumbled on the floor. His musky odor was like a punch in the stomach—the smell reminded her viscerally of Dafydd.

She backed up, embarrassed. "*Pardonnez-moi.*" She looked away, but not before getting an eyeful of his tangled black hair, his muscled shoulders. And the nose of a single action revolver poking out from under the pillow.

Her heart skipped a beat. A trap, and she'd walked right

into it. *Stay alert,* Stepney had warned—*every minute, every moment.*

"Look, I'm a friend of Gilberte's cousin."

He watched her. The vein in his tanned neck pulsed. "They all say that."

Sunday, June 23, 1940

Le Bon Marché Department Store, Paris
1:45 p.m. Paris Time

"Do you recognize this person?" Gunter asked, holding up the sketch.

"Should I?" asked the saleswoman behind the counter in the wood-paneled vestibule.

Gunter flashed his badge. The mascaraed woman didn't look impressed. Shook her head. "This is lost and found, monsieur. Did you lose her?"

What was the French for "cloakroom"? He mimed taking off a coat, hanging it up.

"*Le vestiaire.*" She pointed a lacquered red nail toward the opposite side of the sprawling department store main floor.

Gunter headed past the fragrant perfume counters. The glass roof dome filtered light over a tiled floor and sumptuous deco staircase. Nothing here he could afford on a Reich Security Service investigator's salary. His wife would drool.

He and Niels made their way among officers thronging the counters and speaking German to the sales staff, who replied in kind.

At *le vestiaire,* he aimed for diplomacy. "Can you help us, please?"

The young woman in a tailored Bon Marché navy blue frock managed to look diffident and inviting at the same time. These Parisians. "You checked a coat, monsieur?"

"A young woman left something with you," he said. "Does this look like part of a claim check?"

A brief nod. "But we require the client furnish the complete claim check."

He had to admire her.

"Does she look familiar?" he said as he held out the sketch.

She considered the drawing. Shrugged.

"Why don't you give me a hand here. Have a look for something like a wicker basket."

"I don't make the rules, monsieur."

The usual bureaucratic response. In Munich it would have been "I'm only following orders."

"Then you won't mind if I look around."

"I'm afraid that's forbidden, monsieur." She'd blocked his way to the dark wood cloakroom.

Gunter shoved her aside. He didn't have time for this.

She reached for a phone. "I'm calling the manager."

"Not a good idea."

"Monsieur?" An alert man in a dark blue suit was striding across the tiled floor. The manager, Gunter guessed. "May I help you?"

"I need access here."

"But our job's to assist you and—"

"You'll do that by giving me access to the cloakroom. Now. Or do you want me to close the store and do a proper search?"

GUNTER'S EYES ADJUSTED TO THE dimness of the cloakroom, a dark wood-paneled wardrobe affair with spacious shelves and coatracks. Among the hanging jackets and shopping bags he spied something out of place. He lifted a heavy wicker basket from the shelf. Took the wicker piece he'd taken from the bike basket and fitted it to a loose end.

A match.

He shook it, producing a metallic rattle. He lifted out a bouquet of wilted flowers. Beneath it was an oblong object wrapped in a scarf.

Gunter contained his excitement.

He took note of the check-in time on the torn half of the claim check.

He reached for the Café Literraire matches in his pocket. Circled the café's phone number, removed the scarf full of disassembled rifle parts and left the matchbox. He replaced the wicker basket on its shelf and stowed the rifle in his now bulging attaché case.

"My mistake, mademoiselle. *Danke.*"

Niels behind him, he strode through the clouds of heady fragrance to the door.

"Where to, sir?"

"Quick stop back to the café, where you're going to chat again with your friend the waiter. Then all speed to the ballistics lab."

In the back seat of the car, he pulled out the package. Studied the knotted scarf. Buried his face in it, searching for the smell. Pears soap.

His neck tingled. She'd left this at 12:30, just before going to the café. *Close. So close.*

When she came back for it, he would be ready for her.

He sneezed. This damn summer cold.

Sunday, June 23, 1940

Near Canal Saint-Martin, Paris | 2:15 p.m.

"Hands up."

Kate's hand froze midway to her pocket.

She scanned the dresser for something she could reach and throw at the man on the bed. Nothing but a bottle of Guerlain L'Heure Bleu. By the time she'd grabbed it he'd have shot her.

"The piano tuner sent me," she said. "He said to ask for Gilberte."

Either he'd recognize the sewer worker's code or she'd have to move fast. In either case, he couldn't be alone. If there was a naked man in bed in the middle of the afternoon, there had to be a lover around.

He put the revolver down.

"Trust me now?" she said. The sweat was running down her neck.

"Like I trust a snake," he said in British-accented English. "You're late."

Late? Instinct told her to play along until she figured out what was going on.

"Things got complicated," she said, keeping it vague.

"They're in the fishmonger's basement. Round the corner."

Who the hell was he talking about?

"I need to talk to Gilberte," she said. "Those were my instructions. She's here, right?"

"Mais non. And you woke me up. And I'm tired of, how do you say . . . holding your soldiers' hands. It's been three weeks. The fishmonger wants them out of there today."

Your soldiers. He must have thought she was British. She'd heard there were pockets of stranded British soldiers trapped in France after Dunkirk. But what could she do?

Prioritize, Stepney would say.

She'd deflect him for now.

"Talk to Gilberte," she said, eyeing a pink lace robe hanging from the door. Were those two a couple?

From the apartment's entry came the sound of a lock turning. Kate froze.

The black-haired man hissed, gestured for her to come. Put his finger to his lips.

The hallway's wood floor creaked. A man's voice.

Then a woman's laugh. "Hans, you're silly."

A German.

Hide. But where?

The man in bed had been reaching for his trousers, but he hesitated, then got back under the sheets.

Read the situation. Assess the options. Decide. Act.

She pushed aside the lace curtain of the window. No balcony and three floors down to an alley blocked by a black car. A soldier in gray-green uniform stood smoking, booted leg on the running board. A raid?

She wondered if Gilberte had turned in the man in the bed. Led the Germans here to find out where the Brits were hiding?

"Here's your corsage for tonight," said the male voice she'd heard. Now she caught the heavy German accent.

Kate tiptoed to the bedroom door and looked out. The woman wore a paisley dress, her hair upswept. Over her padded shoulder Kate saw the gold braid of an officer's hat. Her German lover?

Terrified, she tried to think what to do. She couldn't fall apart.

Assess options.

Kate closed the door quietly. The man was holding his revolver aloft, his eyes narrowed. She shook her head and pointed under the bed.

But he didn't move.

"*Un moment*," the woman was saying. "Let me—"

Panicked, Kate threw her bag down, dove into bed and pulled the sheets over them. Felt for the knife in her pocket—gone. Fallen on the floor? The man's hot breath was in her ear, the cold revolver he gripped scratching her thigh. His musky scent pervaded the sheets; his perspiring skin rubbed hers. Giddy, she couldn't breathe. "Keep the gun down," she whispered.

"*D'accord*," said the woman, "I'll get my scarf."

"*Vas?*" Boots stomped on the floor, following her.

Terror rippled down Kate's spine. She heard the door open, the wood floorboards creak.

"But you promised us a little privacy this afternoon, Gilberte," said the German.

Black Hair had popped up and stuck his head out from the sheets. She felt him sliding the revolver up her rib cage. He coughed, covering up the sound as he cocked the hammer.

Kate's heart pounded as she waited for the sound of the revolver shot. If the German didn't shoot first. She pictured the driver running up the stairs, a gunfight, troops descending on the apartment.

Act. Believe.

Kate stuck her head out from the sheets. Gave a loud yawn. Stretched, keeping her fully clothed self covered by the sheet.

"*Scheisse*." The German's brow crinkled and his hand went to his holster.

The woman stepped in front of the German. "This is Philippe, my cousin. Silly me, I forgot he'd . . . be visiting." Gilberte gave a nervous laugh.

Philippe played along. "Gilberte, you promised I could bring my fiancée here," he said, sounding annoyed.

"Fiancée." The German snorted. "You French rut like rabbits."

Hadn't he been planning on doing that himself?

Black pinhole eyes scrutinized them. Kate wasn't sure if the German was upset because this woman's "cousin" had foiled his romantic plans or whether he suspected something more. He wiped the sweat from his brow and stepped toward the bed.

Kate felt the revolver cold against her shoulder under the sheets. The vein in Philippe's neck pulsed. His arms tensed.

"*Mon cher,*" Kate murmured, low and smoky, and nuzzled his ear. Her pulse raced. Would their charade work?

"I'm sorry, Hans." Gilberte shrugged and gave an exaggerated sigh. "*L'amour.*" She nestled her arm in his. "Time for that cognac."

Sunday, June 23, 1940

Near Jardin du Luxembourg, Paris | 2:00 P.M. Paris Time

Once the waiter understood his café would be closed down if he didn't cooperate with the plan Gunter outlined, the German investigator softened the blow with several hundred francs.

Now they were on their way to the ballistics lab. Detouring around incoming troop trucks, Niels sped instead along the Seine, a ribbon of sluggish green blue in the sweltering heat. Gunter stuck his forefinger in the rifle's barrel. It came back greasy with residue. He sniffed. Even through his stuffy nose he could tell it had been fired recently.

In the Lycée Montaigne, now the Luftwaffe *Kaserne,* Gunter made his way through the labyrinthine school halls to the lab, mentally debating whether to call Jäger with an update now or to wait until he had questioned the Brits.

In the ballistics lab, the radio played classical music, the orchestral strains punctuated by the cracks of gunshots from the test shooting gallery. Greenish light filtered through the leafy branches into what had been a large classroom.

Volke, the ballistics expert whom he'd trained with in Munich, looked up from a microscope. A Prussian aristocrat with a dueling scar on his cheek to prove it, Volke was a wary man who refused to relay any kind of findings over the phone. He rose to converse a moment with an assistant, then shooed Gunter through a side door and into another lab.

"About time," Volke said, shutting the lab door behind them. "Jäger's called every half hour. Your neck's on the line, Gunter. Now mine is, too."

As if Gunter needed any additional pressure right now. Why couldn't Jäger leave him to do his job instead of hounding him? The Führer must be demanding hourly reports on the investigation's progress in finding the sniper.

"What's going on, Gunter?"

He and Volke went way back. They'd formed an unlikely duo during police training—an aristocrat's son and the working-class nephew of a Munich policeman. When a drunken Volke had challenged a Brownshirt thug to a duel outside a Munich beer hall, Gunter had managed to hustle him away. They'd looked out for each other ever since.

"First, Volke, tell me your progress with the English rifles."

"Two were clean and showed no evidence of recent firing. Even a cursory examination reveals that, Gunter." Volke shot him a *you knew that* look. "Still, we're testing the other two. My report will be complete."

Typical Prussian. He was glad he'd sent Volke the rifles even though he'd known what the outcome would be. He needed it done right. But besides that, he needed the excuse to drop by so he could leave the rifle he'd found with Volke, one of the very few people he knew he could trust. Volke would pull fingerprints, fibers, maybe even hair to put a nail in her coffin. Wary of Roschmann, he needed evidence to cover his back. His uncle had raised him to *do something the right way or not at all.*

"Thank you. Put that on hold for now."

"I need explanations, Gunter."

"I'm reporting to the Führer, Volke," he said to galvanize him into action. "Now test this Lee-Enfield rifle. I believe it was fired this morning."

Volke frowned, but spread out a sheet of waxed paper to begin the analysis.

Gunter reached for rubber gloves as he ran down the events for Volke. "Then I found this under a bouquet of wilted flowers." From his attaché case he took the rifle wrapped in the simple blue floral cotton print scarf and placed it on the paper. "Recognize this knot, Volke?"

Interested, Volke stared at the knot tying the fabric into a thin X.

"A clove hitch," he said. "We learned to tie knots like this in the Hitlerjugend. My sister learned it, too, in the Bund Deutscher Mädel."

Gunter nodded. "So did my cousin. No doubt they've got the equivalent in England."

He untied the scarf and spread out the disassembled parts and shank. Volke leaned over the laboratory counter, studying the pieces. "Interesting. I've never seen this particular Enfield model before. But it's a specially modified sniper rifle. It was recently fired."

Gunter watched as Volke examined each of the dismantled rifle parts. Only a marksman would have disassembled the rifle in this fashion. A professional. He took off his gloves. Sticky and sweaty, he turned on the sink's water faucet, cupped his hands and splashed water on his temples. Refreshed, he glanced at the clock.

"How long will this take, Volke?"

"Fingerprint, fiber, and bullet analysis, plus all the usual tests?" Volke smiled, giving his scarred face a lopsided look. "You know I hate to be rushed."

"I'll be back in two hours," said Gunter. "And we keep this to ourselves."

Sunday, June 23, 1940

Tactical Center under King Charles Street, London
1:30 P.M. Greenwich Mean Time

Stepney stood at the teleprinter, rubbing his aching hip. The printer churned out the coastal report. Churning butter would have been faster.

There was not only the deadly fiasco in his Paris network to worry about but now this report of the strange buoy discovered by a little boy. Whitehall was convinced the buoy was German technology, a harbinger of the sea invasion.

"We know the invasion is imminent, Stepney," Teague had taken him aside to say. "We need you to contact your operative through the reactivated Alpha circuit."

"Why, Teague?"

Teague showed him a photo of a stocky man wearing graduation robes.

"Who's this?"

"Our operative Nigel Swanson. Code name Swan."

Not very original. Teague kept this mission from him and now wanted his help?

"You're running a separate operation and didn't inform me?"

Teague lowered his voice. "Swanson is an engineer who was contacted by his former colleague from Paris—the colleague who he'd worked with on a special project when they were both at the University of Birmingham."

"By special project you mean something to do with this buoy?"

Teague gave a brief nod. "That colleague is working in Paris now, and the Kriegsmarine have taken over his project. He reached out to Swanson and offered him information to sabotage the project, but made it clear he would only pass along what he knew directly to Nigel Swanson himself—"

"Teague, before you go on," interrupted Stepney, "have you thought the Germans could be manipulating this colleague to hook Swanson?"

"It is a risk. But the two men worked together at the University of Birmingham developing the damn thing. The Frenchman has more loyalty to his old partner than he does to the Germans who want to use his invention to wage war on his friends."

Stepney knew what friendship was worth in the world of secret intelligence. "What's in it for the colleague to put himself on the line? What does he want?"

"A way to leave France."

"That means money, right? Safe passage?"

Teague shrugged. "Of course. But it had to be Swanson making the pickup. No one else. And now he's incommunicado."

"Had Swanson been trained for the field?"

"Plans to drop him were last minute. We only had a six-hour window."

In other words no. He pitied the poor engineer, who had to be dead. "It's certain death to send in a novice."

Teague took his arm. "It's critical we salvage his mission. I'll fill you in on the way to the code room."

Sunday, June 23, 1940

11 rue des Saussaies, Paris | 2:30 P.M. Paris Time

The tang of urine and fear pervaded the chilly limestone interrogation rooms overlooking the Sûreté's courtyard in a former mansion the Gestapo had requisitioned for this purpose. A token force of three French policeman nodded as Gunter flashed his RSD badge. Cries followed him as he walked down a hallway lined by scuffed metal-grated cells, formerly used by the Sûreté, behind which prisoners were chained to thick metal rings in the walls.

In the interrogation room, he pulled his half-finished report out of his attaché case. "Bring the first prisoner to me."

The guard, one of the Feldgendarmerie who manned the detention area, looked nervous. "There's been a development, sir."

"Development? Send in the commander. Meanwhile, sergeant, bring the first prisoner."

"But sir . . ."

Roschmann, the Vet, had appeared outside the door in the hallway. One step ahead of him everywhere he went.

Gottverdammt.

"The cowards beat us to it, Gunter." Roschmann stood feet apart, arms crossed, unhappy.

The cold from the stone floor rose up Gunter's legs.

There were holes in the plastered walls sprouting mold and the limestone arches showed mildew. The sun never entered this damp hellhole with its lone hanging light bulb.

"First, Roschmann, explain how you managed to get here before the officer in charge of the investigation." Gunter plunked himself down on a metal chair. He was angry but kept his voice calm. "My boss, who reports directly to the Führer, wants to know, and so do I."

Roschmann didn't miss his weighted words, and adjusted his left jacket cuff with thick fingers. "I'm obeying orders."

"Orders? I instructed you to check the luggage and baggage counters at the train station."

"And officers continue to search. So far no rifle's been discovered."

And it wouldn't be until he'd had it thoroughly examined for evidence.

"Again, why are you here, Roschmann?"

"Kostoff ordered me to join you in questioning the parachutists. Your delay caused—"

"I'm here now," he interrupted. So Kostoff wanted to keep his finger in the investigation. Gunter waved for Roschmann to leave. "Given the delicacy of the situation, I'll handle the questioning." And discover the link between the British parachutists and the woman at the café, he hoped.

He couldn't read Roschmann's face in the shadow.

"Whatever held you up, I hope it was worth it. They chewed suicide pills."

He was too late.

"Where are they?"

"We put the bodies in the last interrogation room."

Gunter shot up out of the chair and hurried down the damp corridor, past the peeling paint and the screams. Roschmann's boots echoed as he followed.

Four bodies lay on stretchers covered by stained sheets. The ceiling lamp cast a wan yellow glow. A smell of voided bowels filled the room. Two Feldgendarmerie officers stood guard.

Based on the orange mess in the corner, the officer with the pale face must have vomited. Gunter opened the small window to let out some of the stench.

"Why weren't these men searched completely?"

Roschmann pointed to the first officer. "Answer him."

"Of course we did cavity searches, sir," one said.

Gunter took a pair of rubber gloves from a shelf on the wall. Handed a pair to Roschmann, who was covering his nose.

Gunter knelt and removed the first sheet. The young man's face was contorted with the rictus of death. Leaning close, he caught a faint whiff of bitter almonds. Cyanide. Death might have taken only seconds. The smell disappeared, overpowered by the reek of urine. Gunter removed the sheet from each one, checked their stained uniform pockets. Nothing. Then their hands.

"Fingerprint the corpses before taking them to Hôpital Lariboisière, Roschmann."

"Going to check the prints against a rap sheet?" Roschmann laughed, recovering his bravado.

No, against the Lee-Enfield he'd found at le Bon Marché. "I follow procedure."

Gunter ordered the Feldgendarmerie to remove the British men's dog tags, log in their numbers. Then he pried open the mouth of the corpse he recognized by the dog's tooth marks in its arm.

He found tiny white shards under the stiff tongue.

"Next time, check their back molars for false caps. Like this one."

He lifted up a sliver of false tooth.

The Feldgendarmerie officers exchanged a look. Ashamed, Gunter hoped.

"So you'll be heading back with another feather in your cap, eh, Gunter?" said Roschmann, a tinge of jealousy in his voice. The man breathed ambition. "Case closed, eh? Nice and neat."

As if any of this would make Gunter look good. But Roschmann was ignorant of the assassination attempt; he couldn't guess all the implications.

"The investigation's ongoing, Roschmann."

He wouldn't be able to keep this from Jäger long. The clock was ticking and he had to catch the sniper. He stood, pulled an evidence bag from his pocket and dropped in the bit of false tooth.

"Done, as far as I see. You've got their corpses, the rifles . . ."

For once Roschmann was right. Within Gunter's grasp lay another way out. He could make it easy on himself. Apart from Volke, only he knew about the fired rifle. He could substitute that rifle for one of the four from the dead men. Pick one as the "sniper" and submit the findings in his report. He'd accomplish his mission ahead of the deadline, get Jäger off his back and satisfy the Führer. His family would be safe.

Yet the easy way out stood against everything his uncle had taught him. Against the very reason he'd joined the police, against what he worked for every day—an honest investigation. It was the reason he could sleep at night, why he kept at it despite all the Roschmanns who brutalized and followed no law. Someone needed to do the right thing. Despite his dislike for the Führer, a crime had been committed. He would uphold his own integrity. He would not take the easy way out.

And what if she struck again?

Whatever it took, he'd find her.

And face it—he relished the hunt.

"As you know, I'm investigating on the Führer's orders," said Gunter. "The case is closed when the Führer says it's closed. Remember that."

"You wouldn't be threatening me, Gunter, would you? That's not a smart idea."

Tiresome and dangerous, this big lout. Nothing penetrated his thick Aryan head.

"Let me spell it out. We're not in a pissing contest. But if we were, you'd be on the Polish front."

He hurried out of the reeking room, down the stairs and into the car where Niels waited.

Thirty-one hours and thirty minutes.

Sunday, June 23, 1940

Near Canal Saint-Martin, Paris | 2:30 P.M. Paris Time

Hans strode out of the bedroom, following Gilberte, who was murmuring something about a café. The last thing Kate saw of him were his knee-high black boots. The front door shut behind them with a loud bang.

Philippe put his finger to her lips. Listening. Footsteps faded down the stairway. From outside the window a car engine started up.

How much time had Kate bought herself? Maybe half an hour—time to clean up, change into one of Gilberte's dresses and leave?

"You can get off me now," said Kate.

But he didn't move. Or put the pistol down. Yellow cream light filtered through the lace curtain. "Why should I?"

Pinned down in his arms, his eyes inches from hers, she tried not to blink. Or respond to the shiver of fear, the heat of sudden wanting. "I smell like a barnyard." His hot skin burned through the thin cotton dress clinging to her thighs. She needed to focus.

"You're not a country girl."

"But I am." Caught herself before she said ranch fed and bred—one of the last things she'd joked about with Dafydd. "To the core. And you?"

"As provincial as they come," he said. He grinned. He stroked her hair. His fingers came back with her ponytail band. For a moment she didn't want him to stop. "They won't be back for a while."

"Seduction with a gun in my thigh?"

He propped himself on his elbow. "Need a formal introduction?" Amusement glittered in his amber eyes. Amber with a sparkle, like fool's gold in the rocky foothills of the Cascades. She wouldn't trust him a second.

"Let's keep it simple," she said. "No names."

"But you know mine."

"Okay, Jane Doe," she said, doubting Gilberte had used his real name.

"*Enchanté,* Jane Doe." He pronounced it *Chanedough.*

"How many lovers does Gilberte have besides you and the German?" She was no prude but she couldn't help wondering what Gilberte's neighbors would think if they knew who she consorted with.

"Never say that. She'd be offended," he said, his voice turning serious. He sat up, set the gun on the nightstand and pulled his trousers on. "Her husband, François, got shot in our escape from the POW camp." His eyes darkened. "François didn't make it. But I will."

A moving story. Could she believe him?

"Gilberte's got a big heart. Too big."

She guessed he meant helping spies and refugees. Kate had been given Gilberte's address, after all. Maybe Philippe had, too.

"What's your plan?"

"Plan? Get to London, of course." Philippe threaded a belt through his trouser loops. "She's putting me up until I can join the Free French Forces."

So he was on the run, along with a fishmonger's basement full of stranded Brits. *Don't get involved.* She was reminded of Stepney's words.

Another thought swirled in her mind—she couldn't count on Stepney's knowing she'd survived. She needed to relay word to him.

"I need radio contact with London."

Philippe's shoulders jerked. "Why?"

To get the hell out. But she kept that to herself. She'd be lower priority than the stranded Brits. "Long story." Her sweat-dampened hair stuck to her neck. "Look, Gilberte's contact understands. He gave me her address. Indicated there's a way to send a message."

The last part she'd made up.

He shrugged. "Then you know each contact only knows the next."

What Stepney called a cutout. Or did he know more than he let on?

The Bakelite clock on the nightstand ticked. He pulled on a shirt, buttoned it. "I've got to go."

"Where?"

He grinned. "See, known me five minutes and already you'll miss me."

The way he teased her reminded her of her older brother. "You wish." She averted her eyes as he unzipped his trousers and tucked his shirt in.

"You're on your own, *chérie.*" And with that he'd gone. The door shut, and again, she heard footsteps fading down the stairs. Only his muskiness remained.

She didn't have much time. And she reeked.

She entered the *salle de bain* and gasped. A real tub, bath salts, a pink towel. Heaven.

A quick bath, that's all.

She turned on the chrome faucets, dumped in bath salts and lavender oil and lowered herself in the warm luxury. As the steam rose, she checked her stomach. No more stretch marks. Flat as a pancake. Her thoughts wandered—she could almost feel Lisbeth rubbing her tummy, splashing in their Saturday night bubble bath. Playing peekaboo, those sweet slippery chubby fingers, Lisbeth squealing in delight.

The aching loss lanced her heart.

She scrubbed until her whole body felt raw. Clean for the first time in weeks—those English country houses during training had offered nothing but lukewarm water in hip-high tin baths.

A scum floated on the water. Worse than a cattle trough back home. She unplugged the stopper, reached for the used towel lying on the tiles to clean the dirty bathtub ring. She tugged but the towel was caught on something protruding under the tub.

Getting out dripping wet, she got on her hands and knees. Strapped with tape under the claw-foot tub was a dark green handgun.

A knock on the door.

Fear nested in the back of her throat. Idiot. She'd let her guard down. Daydreaming about Lisbeth when she should have been escaping. That silly luxury of a bath when she was on the run. Hunted. Why hadn't she left when she had the chance, stinky or not?

She was ashamed, too, of the attraction, that shivering heat, that had gripped her at Philippe's touch. It was the first time she had remembered that feeling since Dafydd. Guilt flooded her.

The knocking on the door was loud now.

How could she really trust Gilberte or Philippe?

She couldn't. She could trust no one. Stepney had pounded that into her head.

Philippe might have been lying; Gilberte might sell her out to the Nazi. They might be on their way to arrest her even now.

The draining water masked the scratching sound the tape made as she tore it off the bathtub.

"I don't care if you're decent, open up." Gilberte's voice.

The door opened just as she put the gun under the towel.

"The sewer worker gave me your address," Kate said, looking up at Gilberte from where she crouched on the floor, naked.

"My other stupid cousin," said Gilberte. "You can't stay here."

Goose pimples popped on Kate's wet skin. She stood up and wrapped the towel around herself, keeping the pistol tucked away under the towel. "Is your German here?" she whispered.

"Hans? He's not my German and he got called to some emergency investigation."

Emergency investigation? Looking for an escaped assassin? Kate covered up her nervousness. "What kind of emergency?"

Bold as brass, she stared at Kate. "Everything's important to the Boche. How do I know?"

"I know about the hidden RAF pilots," said Kate.

"Big mouth, that's Philippe."

"But I think you're responsible for moving them on. That you can help me move on, too. I need your help."

"They're not my problem. Not anymore. Nor are you."

A heaviness beat on her chest. She'd turned them in and now she'd turn Kate in.

But Gilberte was saying, "The pilots got moved. If the sewer worker gave you this address . . . Well, be thankful I owe him. But you can't stay here. We keep separate, for everyone's safety."

If Gilberte had betrayed her, they wouldn't be having this conversation. She had to go with her gut feeling and trust the woman. For now.

"Please, just give me something decent to wear."

"Like anything would fit?" came Gilberte's tart reply. She leaned close to the mirror, opened a pot of rouge and, with a few deft brushstrokes, now resembled a magazine cover. Wary yet fascinated, Kate examined slim and chic Gilberte. Soft curves encased in a rustle of silk, a flash of leg—she had it all.

Next to Gilberte, Kate felt fat and dumb. She'd grown up wearing overalls and her brothers' shirts. Her one best dress was kept for church and funerals.

Still, they were close enough in body size. Gilberte was just being obnoxious because she resented Kate's intrusion. Right? Kate had gotten this far; she wouldn't give up. Somehow she had to gain the woman's sympathy, get her to want to help.

Water gurgled down the drain.

"That man Philippe told me about your husband. I'm sorry."

"Sorry?" Gilberte's gaze met hers in the mirror.

Kate felt her calculating, deciding whether to believe her. "I lost my husband. My child, too." Her breath caught. For a moment, that firestorm slashed through her mind. The smell of burnt flesh. "Do you have children?"

Gilberte's hand quivered as she held a lip pencil. "I promised my husband to keep our children safe. And I will."

Was that guilt in Gilberte's voice? Kate met her eyes again. "Not for me to judge you, Gilberte."

"Aren't you judging me? But I'll do what I need to. We'll survive."

Gilberte rolled with the punches. A bit like Kate. Didn't she run a safe house, hide guns, smuggle stranded RAF soldiers?

Trust no one, Stepney said.

Kate noticed photos of Hollywood film stars pinned up over the lace lingerie filling the bathroom shelves. "You've got lovely things."

"I'm a *corsetière*," Gilberte said, with a hint of pride. "Josephine Baker, Arletty, Mistinguette, you name it. Cabaret, theater, film actresses come to me. Now it's the Fritz buying lingerie for their *Frauen* in Stuttgart. Or whoever."

"Sounds like a booming business."

"Even the *haute bourgeoise*, they all come to get fitted." Gilberte paused to pluck a stray eyebrow with a tweezer. "I'll keep Monsieur Claverie's shop going any way I can. But my children need to eat."

Kate pulled the towel higher up around her.

Gilberte pulled out a thin wand brush and moistened a black cake of mascara. Didn't she have more to do than worry about her makeup?

Gilberte noticed Kate's expression. "I doubt you Anglo-Saxons understand," she said. "Keeping up your appearance is a form of resistance. Why look dowdy to these uncouth men who secretly admire us? So jealous of our culture." She brushed her lashes, lengthening and darkening them. "Always better to show we're occupied, not vanquished, and make them burn inside. *C'est simple.* Every Parisienne knows. *Respirez.* Breathe."

"Can you help me?"

"I could alter something," said Gilberte standing back and

looking at her. "Something apricot to suit your coloring. But you've got to go."

"Where?" Kate said desperately.

"*Ecoute,* I pass people on, that's all. Ask for Dédé at le Mouton below Pigalle. Wait fifteen minutes and someone will give you an address. One night only."

"*Merci,* Gilberte," she said. "It's vital I get a message to London."

Gilberte shrugged. "Don't tell me any more."

Before Kate could press her, she took a champagne colored silk slip from a drawer.

"Here. And if you took something from under the tub, I don't want to know that either."

Kate lifted the revolver from under the towel. Handled it and pulled the safety. Checked the barrel, cocked it.

Gilberte was staring at her wide-eyed.

"I'm taking this."

On the run, a step ahead of the Gestapo, getting caught with this would be death. Then again, it would come in handy.

She handed Gilberte the blue Bon Marché cloakroom tag. "I'll swap you for it. Bring this to le Bon Marché's *vestiaire.* There's a rifle checked there. Pass it to the sewer worker; he'll know what to do with it."

Sunday, June 23, 1940

The Latin Quarter, Paris | 3:00 p.m. Paris Time

Gunter's fingers drummed on the leather seat in the staff Mercedes. He watched Jeanne Albrecht pushing the baby buggy down rue Cujas. She was alone.

He glanced down at the latest reports. Then at his watch. He didn't like to think what would happen if his plan backfired.

Gunter joined her in the café, his sleeves rolled up and jacket over his arm. He peered into the buggy. A pink cheeked infant blew whistles of sleep.

"Where's your contact, Jeanne?"

"Going to order me a coffee?"

Gunter signaled to the waiter, who was wiping his brow in the heat.

"My contact's sitting on the third bench from the Medici Fountain in Jardin du Luxembourg. He's reading. You'll ask, 'What book are you reading?' He'll answer, 'Plutarch's *Lives.*'"

"What did you tell him?"

"He supports the Reich. Can I have my ID back?"

Her spirit had returned.

"Answer me, Jeanne."

"I said you'll pay him. Then he agreed."

As a policeman in Munich he'd had varying results with paid informants.

The coffees arrived. Gunter paid. He slipped two more hundred-franc notes under Jeanne's saucer.

"I need your eyes, Jeanne. You're going shopping at le Bon Marché."

"Like that's enough for anything in *that* department store?"

"You're going to watch for a woman who picks up a wicker basket from the cloakroom."

He didn't know if she'd return to pick up the rifle. But sniper rifles were precious—someone would. That was all he had to go on right now.

He put the Café Littéraire matchbox in her hand.

"Will I get my ID back then?"

"Follow whoever picks up the basket and call this number. If you lose her, call that number immediately. Then I'll return your identity card."

She'd cooperate. No one got ration coupons without an ID.

"*Je dois y aller.* That fancy Bon Marché closes soon."

"Then you better drink up." He stood up and signaled Niels.

Sunday, June 23, 1940

Map Room, Tactical Center under King Charles Street, London
2:00 P.M. Greenwich Mean Time

Stepney passed the Map Room, its raftered ceiling braced for bombardment, its walls covered with maps and colored stick-pins. Two mice in signature drab Wren uniforms scurried past him, arms laden with files. The PM, puffing on his cigar, spent hours here in the middle of the night, studying those little pins, rearranging notepapers vertically and diagonally over the Continent indicating troop emplacement and Atlantic convoy routes.

At the moment, though, Stepney's only concern was his summons to the Cabinet War Room. He was late.

As he made his way down the narrow corridors, his mind turned over the problem of Nigel Swanson. He passed rooms where stenographers in cubicles transcribed notes and typists pounded on their soundless typewriters—the PM couldn't stomach the clacking keys. Stepney gauged the quiet tension and single-mindedness of each component: here the war was planned, plotted and strategized. From outward appearances, it was a well-oiled operational headquarters. Stepney knew better.

Just as Napoleon had, Hitler stood just across the Channel, only a body of water between England and the Reich-dominated Continent.

In the Cabinet War Room two men waited. Cathcart, with his thick brows, sat by his SIS lackey, who gave a nervous tug on his Etonian tie. And to think these types, who'd never seen combat, conducted a war. On the table sat a Secraphone, the scrambler telephone with a green Bakelite handset and black body.

Cathcart indicated a leather chair.

Stepney almost declined, his damned arthritis was so inflamed from sitting too long. Cathcart knew bugger all. If Stepney kept score he'd mark one up on the old-boy public school network.

"What's your progress on that buoy, Stepney? Any idea what Admiral Lindau was planning?"

Stepney caught Cathcart's verb tense. "Was? You mean Admiral Lindau's been reassigned?"

"Permanently reassigned, according to chatter we intercepted from Berlin. Lindau suffered a heart attack while visiting Paris's Sacré-Cœur with his beloved Führer. The Paris visit was cut short after three hours."

Stepney controlled his surprise. Could it be the Yank had actually . . . No, it was extremely unlikely. He brushed that thought aside. At last report his parachuted sniper team had landed on schedule. But no, they wouldn't have jeopardized their own mission—taking out Stossel, Lammers, and von Duering—with a different high-profile attack.

"What exactly do we know?"

"By zero nine hundred hours, air traffic monitors believe, Lindau's body was aboard a plane following the Führer's Focke-Wulf." Cathcart thrust a telex at him. "This just came in from Bletchley. As soon as we received it we called you here."

And here he'd been stuck in a meeting.

"We have other, even more pressing issues, Stepney," Cathcart said. "We need you to contact an operative named Nigel Swanson."

"Already working on it, Cathcart," said Stepney.

Sunday, June 23, 1940

Jardin du Luxembourg, Paris | 3:15 P.M. Paris Time

Gunter crossed his legs, fanning himself in the hovering heat. Laughter and splashing drifted through the Jardin du Luxembourg as children pushed small colored boats with sticks in the round pond. Gunter's daughter, Anna, would love this place.

Right now she was most delighted by soft cuddly things. How he wished that Steiff teddy bear wasn't sitting in his temporary office.

Next to him on the bench sat a matron, next to her a young man with rolled-up shirtsleeves reading a book. Finally the matron spotted a friend, waved and left, and the young man laid the book on his lap. A book in Latin, Gunter noticed.

Gunter felt the perspiration on his neck. The chills.

"What book are you reading?" he asked in broken French.

"Plutarch's *Lives.*"

Gunter nodded.

"What did you want to talk with me about?" the young man asked him in *Hochdeutsch,* formal High German. Gunter figured him for an academic.

He shuffled the artist's sketch across on the bench to him. Then casually left his hand on the bench. "This woman."

"Her?"

From the way he said this, it sounded like he knew her.

"Who is she and where?"

"I deal through my connections with people I trust," said the young man.

"*Gut.* Now you're dealing with me. Lift up the sketch."

A pile of German marks.

"I don't like to disrupt my connections."

Of course not. Gunter glanced at his watch. "So you leave me no choice but to bring you in for questioning."

"I'm protected by someone at the Kommandantur."

"Tell me the *Kommandant*'s name."

"Kommandant Kostoff, military head of Paris."

"I'll give the *Kommandant* your regards when I see him today." Dappled leaf shadows patterned his shoes. "But now you're working with me. See him." Gunter pointed to Niels walking by, as prearranged, crunching gravel. "He's not as polite as I am."

The young man's eyes darted. In his moment of distraction, Gunter slid his hand into the jacket that was folded on the bench.

"Think of us as added protection. The highest."

The young man nodded. Put the sketch and bills in his canvas bag.

"Cowgirl. A code name."

Gunter stretched and shifted closer. "Where's she hiding?"

"Not sure."

"You can do better than that."

The young Frenchman took an empty cigarette packet from his pants pocket. Turned and wrote something inside it. "My best guess."

"That's not good enough."

"No one in the group will talk. But there's a meeting tonight at this place."

"Why would she go there?"

"Contacts, to try to find a way to escape . . . I don't know." He took a sunglass clip-on and clipped it over his glasses. "Look, my mother's German; she raised me properly."

All this *Hochdeutsch* and academic posturing made Gunter wonder if he was just a poser climbing up the ladder.

"It's important in my family to be loyal to the Reich. I've managed to infiltrate an underground group, but these days everyone's suspicious of everyone. I have to keep my cover with them. You'll need to arrest me at the meeting, too."

With pleasure, Gunter thought. "I want her."

The young man reached for his corduroy jacket on the bench, about to stand. "Understood. I heard she's been informed of the meeting. She'll show."

"*Gut.* Because if you want this back later." Gunter flashed the wallet that he'd lifted from the young man's jacket pocket. He scanned the contents, then slid it into his own jacket pocket. "You better be right, Monsieur Verdou."

Part III

Sunday, June 23, 1940 | 4:00 p.m.

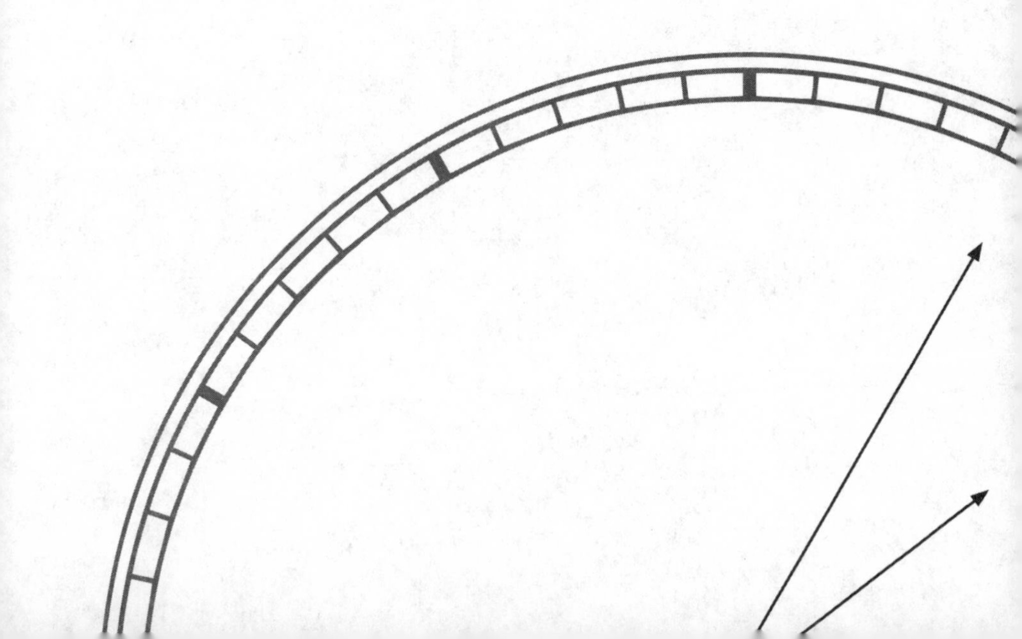

Sunday, June 23, 1940

Place Pigalle, Paris | 4:00 p.m. Paris Time

As Kate walked the peach frock rustled over her champagne silk chemise. Her new look, styled by Gilberte, earned her glances from the café terrace at Place Pigalle. Her hair was swept back in a crocheted snood topped with a bow like Ginger Rogers, and she wore round sunglasses and red lipstick. She almost felt French—the Guerlain Gilberte had dabbed behind her ears helped.

Believe. As long as she didn't open her mouth, she'd pass.

Blend in, don't stand out, Stepney had told her.

In the red-light district of Pigalle, she fit right in.

Alert, she walked into le Mouton and approached the zinc counter. On the walls were framed photos of prizefighters and a map of Corsica.

"What can I get you, mademoiselle?" asked the barman, thick black hair oiled back and gold crucifix around his neck.

Gilberte had told her most in the nightlife milieu were part of the Guerini brothers' gang, that the Corsican gangs from Marseilles infested Pigalle.

Keep it simple.

She smiled. "Dédé."

The barman eyed her. His gaze rested on her hips. "Who's asking?"

"Gilberte sent me."

The barman slapped a card on the counter: *Club le Select.*

Hadn't Gilbette said she was supposed to wait fifteen minutes?

"But I thought . . ."

"Plans change."

She felt a knot form in her stomach. Had something gone wrong already? Keep moving, something told her. "*Merci.*"

Club le Select turned out to be two doors down, and Dédé in the cellar.

"This better be good." Dédé, a short squat man, was heaving beer barrels down the steps into the dim cellar. Curly chest hair peeked from under his sweat-stained undershirt. "Got something for me?"

She showed him Gilberte's pistol. Leaned close enough to whisper in his ear. "I need radio contact with London. Consider this a trade."

He sucked in his breath. "That's hard. Takes time."

"Dédé," someone called. "Hurry up."

"No guns here. Take it with you."

"Gilberte said you knew a place to stay."

He shrugged. "The cheese shop on rue des Martyrs. Tell Lily I sent you."

"Look, I need to get a message to London."

"Someone might know how, I'll ask around. Now leave." He gestured her up the beer-reeking stone steps and out the open back door.

"Why would Dédé send you here?"

Lily, if that was her real name, shook her head. In the closed cheese shop she leaned over the counter under a map of France with all its cheeses by region. A cheese for each day of the year, Dafydd would have said, and more.

"I've got kids. My parents. A sergeant's billeted on the top floor. You can't stay here."

Dejected, Kate didn't feel any sense of surprise—it was too

dangerous for her to stay in Paris, dangerous to anyone who helped her. Through the window she saw a soldier in a feldgrau uniform walk by, then knock on the door.

"He lives upstairs," said Lily. "Go." She shoved a wedge of Gruyère into Kate's hand and saw her to the door.

"*Merci, madame,*" said Kate, controlling her nerves as she ducked past the sergeant standing in the door.

A close call, but what now? A sense of foreboding filled her. She had begun to wonder about Stepney's mission, how it possibly could have gone well, where she would have ended up if it had worked out. If she was nothing but bait for a bigger fish.

Breathe.

Every moment she risked exposure. But she paused at the cheese shop window to study the map.

Improvise, Stepney had said, *think on your feet.*

Why not take a train down south? From there work her way to the Pyrénées and cross to Spain? She'd do better in the wilderness, hiking through the mountains, than here, where any word she spoke could get her killed.

Kate waited in the hot, crowded ticket line in Gare Saint-Lazare, the nearest train station. She waited with women and children who sat on their suitcases, old men fanning themselves in the heat. She still had many people in front of her when the ticket window was shut. Sold out.

What now?

She followed the others as they ran to another window. A local train—it would take hours. As the crowd parted she noticed German soldiers and French police at the platform entrances checking passengers' papers. They were picking out women to question.

A shudder ran through her. She couldn't count on her papers holding up. Jean-Marie could have given her away under torture.

Forget the train. She shouldered her bag, got in step with the disembarking passengers and headed for the station exit.

The only option was to press Dédé for another hiding place.

In the steep and otherwise deserted cobbled alley behind Club le Select's cellar, Dédé was still rolling beer barrels from a cart. The cart was hitched to a thick-legged draft horse, a dappled chocolate and white reminding her of Rosie, the mare she'd hitched up for crop furrowing on the ranch outside Klamath Falls.

Her eye caught the horse's sweating flanks, which were encrusted with matted hair and an oozing sore. A crying shame to treat a horse that way, and no water or feed in sight. Pa always said the disposition of an owner could be told in the way he treated his stock.

Dédé had disappeared. She'd chew him out when he returned.

Wild yellow roses trailed up the lichen-scabbed wall, perfuming a woody sweetness over the sour odor of beer. Kate filled an empty bucket with water at the nearby green metal faucet that serviced the alley. The horse neighed as she offered it to him. He was afraid.

She knew the feeling.

"Good boy," she murmured, "good boy," patting his damp flank. He snorted, his nostrils flaring. Kate kept stroking him until he calmed down. "That's right, boy." She grabbed a rag, rubbed down his damp flanks, then stroked his neck as he lapped up the water.

She liked Dédé less and less.

In the alley's nearby lean-to shed, she found a feed bag. As she was lifting it, she heard groaning.

Startled, she dropped the bag, spilling feed. A man, white faced, huddled under burlap sacks. She gasped as he grabbed her ankle in a viselike grip.

"*Aidez-moi,*" he rasped. "*S'il vous plaît,* you've got to get me to . . . bloody hell." His thick British accent was tinged in pain.

A stranded British soldier?

"First let go of my ankle," she said.

He did.

"You . . . a Yank?"

"Got it in one. Who are you?"

"Can you . . . help me to . . . ?"

Concerned, she knelt down by the burlap sacks. Saw his sweating brow in the dim light. "Help you do what?"

The man's eyes creased in pain.

"You're hurt. What happened?"

He shook his head. Spittle trailed from the edge of his mouth. Flushed cheeks. She felt his brow. He was burning up.

Like Lisbeth.

" . . . the plans . . . invasion . . ."

She heard footsteps coming from the beer cellar across the alley, whispering from the shed's door.

". . . have to tell Gilberte."

She peered outside to see the Corsican barman running across the alley. Then Dédé grabbed her wrists. Caught off guard she stumbled against the flimsy wood. A big mistake.

"What are you doing in here?" Dédé had kicked the shed door closed and pushed her against the wall.

"It's a crime to work a thirsty horse like this, Dédé." Light filtered through the cracks over the blood-smeared hay.

"That's none of your business. There's Boches everywhere. You need to get out of here."

He let go of her wrists. The man lying on the ground let out a long moan.

"This man needs a doctor."

"Not here," Dédé said. "He needs to leave. Since you know horses, you drive this Englishman where he's going on the cart."

"Changed your mind awful quick. Who is he?"

"All I know, he's got something. He's important."

"He said something about the invasion . . ."

"Then you know more than me."

An idea was forming. She'd failed her mission, but if she helped this wounded man, maybe Dédé's network would help her. If he was so important, maybe he would be able to help her make radio contact . . . or even escape. "Okay, but I need your help."

"*Tant pis.* The Boches will be here any minute for beer."

"Didn't you have a plan to hide this man? Somewhere for him to go?"

"I know someone," Dedé said. "You take him to the address I give you. We're all dead if the Germans find him."

Her insides twisted. But she nodded.

She couldn't go out driving a horse cart dressed like this. While Dédé backed up the cart, she wiped off her lipstick and rooted around the shed for something to put over her dress. Among the feed sacks, bushels of hay and empty barrels, she found a *bleu de travail* and a cap. The work coat was none too clean but it would do for now.

The man moaned. With the burlap covering him, she couldn't see his injury, but blood streaked the dirty straw on the floor.

"Don't worry, I'm taking you to a doctor," she said.

Dédé had backed up the cart to the shed's door. He bent down, grunted and heaved the man up, struggling and stumbling under the man's weight. Cries of pain filled the shed as dust motes swirled in the fractured light.

"He's not a barrel of beer," said Kate, rushing to lift the injured man's legs. "Go gentle."

Dédé got him into the cart with Kate's help.

"Shhhh," he said, settling the whimpering man and covering him with more burlap sacks. He stowed a grain bag by the horse's reins and pointed to a bell. "Ring that as you go to muffle his cries."

Worried, she knew she had to hurry. Would this man make it?

"Don't forget about the radio contact."

Dédé wiped perspiration from his brow with the back of his hand and nodded. "I'll work on it and send you a message." He led the horse and cart down the alley.

"How?"

"I don't know. That's how it works. Safer for everyone." Dédé glanced back to where he'd been unloading the beer barrels. "Hurry. You'll turn right before the abattoirs in la Villette. The stable's at eighteen rue des Ardennes. Dr. Ramou will expect you."

Kate offered the horse a handful of hay and stroked its neck. She mounted the trap, checked the handbrake—a worn black iron knob—and took the reins.

Dédé slapped the horse's rear. She held the reins tight in her right fist, her left hand poised on the handbrake, as the horse lurched forward.

Just as a Mercedes pulled up at the end of the alley, cutting her off.

Sunday, June 23, 1940

Near the Sorbonne, Paris | 3:45 P.M. *Paris Time*

Gunter took the call from his lieutenant in Café Littéraire's phone cabin. "Le Bon Marché's closed now," said Niels. "No one showed up, sir."

That would have been too easy. The woman might show up tomorrow, or perhaps the rifle had been written off.

"What should I do about the girl, sir?"

"Drop her off a block from her place," he said. "Then pick me up."

He called Volke at the lab.

"I said I needed two hours," Volke said. "It's going to be more like three if you keep calling me like this."

Gunter caught the warning in Volke's voice. "Who's there?"

But Volke had hung up.

Gunter made notes in the back seat as they sped toward the lab. On a fresh page he drew a diagram. By the time Niels parked at the requisitioned Lycée Montaigne he'd put more of the puzzle pieces together.

Birds chirped in the courtyard. A sheen of sun lingered, glossing the leaves of the climbing ivy.

As Gunter got out, he showed Niels his sketch. "Tell me, Niels, how long does it take to get from Montmartre to le Bourget Airfield?"

Niels pulled a Michelin map from the glove compartment. Spread it on the warm hood of the Mercedes. "It's thirteen kilometers." Using the tip of a pencil, he traced the route. "Took us thirty minutes driving."

Gunter studied it. "What about these smaller roads?"

"It makes me think of the 1938 Tour de France, when our champion Willi Oberbeck won the Paris-to-Caen stage."

Gunter shook his head. "You think the sniper might have been on a bicycle?"

"Sir, I'd have to ask a real cyclist, but for someone in shape, trained, a route like this could take twenty-five to thirty-five minutes. To be safe, forty-five."

Barely enough time. "So in theory a sniper dropped by parachute at le Bourget early morning cycles in, attempts the assassination, hands over the rifle to an accomplice and cycles back in time for us to find him?"

Niels shrugged.

"I don't like it," said Gunter. Thinking out loud helped him. And standing out here in the fresh air, in a garden fragrant with blooming wisteria, away from the cells and miasma of death, the clatter of typewriters and barked orders. "Plus, there are checkpoints, which would add extra time."

He thumbed open the latest reports. A noontime telex stated the cancellation of the High Command's visit.

Canceled after the attempt on the Führer.

"This could make sense if we're dealing with two assassination attempts. Maybe they're unrelated, or maybe one is a smoke screen."

He wiped his brow. Now to get the lab results from Volke. And convince Jäger of his theory.

Sunday, June 23, 1940

Off Place Pigalle, Paris | 4:15 P.M. Paris Time

"*Nicht so schnell.*"

An SS officer in a black uniform stepped out of a Mercedes.

Kate's heart skidded. Caught already?

Keep calm. Get him to move the car. Unblock the alley.

Kate nodded, pulled the cap low and pointed. "*Bier?*" But the SS officer didn't move his car.

Where the hell was Dédé?

She jumped off the wagon and grabbed the horse's reins. Made clucking noises, praying the horse would cooperate and back up to let the car by.

Only a loud neighing. She'd lost her touch.

She had to get hold of herself. She calmed the skittish horse, his yellow teeth bared, as he munched the hay in her hand. She kept her back to the soldier and rubbed the horse's mane. Sweat beaded her lip.

What could she do?

He was saying something in German. Coming closer.

Of all times.

"*Bier,*" she said again, pointing toward the beer cellar's stairs.

Just then Dédé appeared, wiping his face with a handkerchief and beckoning the German.

Finally the man got back in the Mercedes and pulled over to let the cart pass.

It made her sick with fear but she gritted her teeth in a smile—smiling yet again at a German—and waved thanks. She climbed back up, clucked to the horse, and drove the cart through Place Pigalle. The cart wheels produced a spine-shaking rumble over the cobbles as the horse dragged the cart uphill on narrow winding streets. She passed silent, shuttered *boîtes à nuit* and strip joints, as if everyone was napping before the life of the evening.

Another close call. She needed to be more careful.

Kate urged the trotting horse to gain speed as the cart crossed over the train lines shooting from Gare du Nord. They reached the canal. Apprehension thrummed through her body from her head to her tingling toes. She had been on the run since dawn, since failing her mission. But now she felt a flicker of hope that Dédé might come through.

Along the stretch of the canal toward la Villette, barge oil glistened on the metal boat rings. She passed the twin warehouses on either side of the arched drawbridge where the wide Bassin de la Villette thinned into canal de l'Ourcq. Late-afternoon sun filtered through leafy tree branches, casting a lazy greenish haze. From somewhere ahead droned the dull roar of military vehicles, trucks and tanks on the road from Germany.

The huge glass-roofed Grande halle de la Villette, supported by metal arches, stood on the dockside horizon. The livestock market and abattoir, so close to the train tracks, took her back to the slaughter yards outside Medford—those rail yards at the depot where cattle cars were unloaded. She remembered the glimmer of yellow-tongued flames, the bearded, tattered hobos hunched over trash bin fires, rubbing their hands to keep warm in the cold afternoon drizzle.

It had been the day of her mother's funeral during the Depression. That morning her father bought a pine box for her burial. After the funeral, he'd taken them to the rail yard to hop a train back to the ranch; he'd had no money left for train tickets or food. Kate and her brothers huddled under a blanket amid the frightened moans of the cattle, the clatter of their hooves on the metal ramps, until they jumped a freight car.

She pulled herself from the memory. The bleating sheep that were being herded from the cattle cars drowned out the horse's clopping hooves. Where the hell was rue des Ardennes?

Bone-tired, she forced herself to pay attention. She couldn't afford to overshoot the street, waste a vital moment with an overworked horse and a wounded man. He'd made no sound since they'd been on the road, or none she could hear over the horse's clip-clop.

At last. On rue des Ardennes, she pulled back on the right rein and slacked the left to turn into the narrow street. The horse neighed, as if he knew where he was. Finally.

Too late she saw the dark red slick sheen of clotted cattle blood staining the cobbles. The wagon's back wheels slipped, causing a gut-wrenching wobble. The cart was sliding out of control, swaying and scraping against the wall.

Her heart jumped. She pulled at the brake, tightening the reins. Feared the tired horse would fight her, break away. "Whoa, boy."

A man riding by on a bicycle looked up at her.

He'd heard her blurt that out in English.

Idiot.

The bike passed.

Somehow, she regained control, the force pulling them through.

Too many close calls.

Near the stable entrance a woman in a long blue apron dispensed fresh milk from a dairy cart to a group of barefoot children. Kate had seen services like these provided by the local Assistance Publique volunteers in poor districts. The long sleeves and full skirt the woman wore under the apron looked hot. But the woman was doing a better job controlling the street urchins than Kate had done the cart.

The rundown street was lined with assorted barn-like sheds and warehouses. She turned into the stable, which smelled of fresh hay. Two men were playing cards at a table bearing a wine bottle and glasses.

"Please, where's Dr. Ramou?" She dismounted, her legs shaking.

"Doctor?" one said, irritated at the interruption of his card game.

"He's expecting . . . me."

"Ramou, you've got a customer," the man said, raising his voice.

In the back stable doorway, a barrel-chested man loomed, wearing an apron stained with blood. She noticed his drooping mustache, and small feet that surprisingly supported his girth. Dédé called this a doctor? More like a butcher.

He jerked his thumb. "*Louchébem.*"

What did that mean?

The man at the table put down his cards, grabbed the reins and led the horse and cart to the back.

Alarm bells jangled in her head. "Look, I think there's a mistake."

Sunday, June 23, 1940

Kaserne near Jardin du Luxembourg, Paris
4:30 p.m. Paris Time

In the lab, Volke turned the radio's volume knob down and handed Gunter the phone, a tight look on his face. Gunter braced himself.

"The Führer's displeased, Gunter," said Jäger. "The Englanders are all dead? You questioned none of them? This looks extremely careless of you."

Gunter tried to quell the sense of dread bubbling in his gut. "Herr Gruppenführer, I'd take full responsibility. However, the SD were in charge of the prisoners. You wouldn't find four men hiding a cyanide pill in their molars on my watch, sir."

"For God's sake, you've got a force at your disposal."

He wished that were true. Jäger didn't seem to want to remember that he'd instructed Gunter to report only to him and to work alone.

He looked at the clock in the lab.

Twenty-eight and a half hours.

"Herr Gruppenführer, the ballistics lab is testing a modified Lee-Enfield rifle I believe was fired this morning."

"Another one? What are you saying, Gunter?"

Gunter shot at look at Volke. "So far, the evidence I've collected points to two separate assassination attempts."

Silence, then the sound of a door closing. Gunter imagined

Jäger in his office, his hawk eyes narrowing over his long nose. "Explain, Gunter." He sounded interested.

"One moment, sir." Gunter put his hand over the mouthpiece. "I need privacy. Is this line secure, Volke?"

"Should be, but who knows?" Volke took the hint and left.

Gunter took out his notebook. "Sir, in my notes . . ."

"You alone, Gunter?"

"Yes, sir. I believe logistically it's unlikely the British snipers we arrested at le Bourget were involved in the assassination attempt at Sacré-Cœur."

"If that's so, Gunter, why would they commit suicide?"

"Most agent provocateurs have orders to bite a cyanide pill if caught," said Gunter, "to avoid revealing information. As you so wisely pointed out, sir, a woman's involved."

"I did, *ja* . . . But how? Give me a rundown. The Führer wants an update. Quickly."

Gunter thumbed through the pages, rustling them in his haste. "We know the English radio operator had a rendezvous at thirteen hundred hours in Café Littéraire by the Sorbonne—that would have been approximately four and a half hours after the assassination attempt. A woman in the café would signal with a lipstick. But the rendezvous never happened. I've questioned an Alsatian girl who was at the scene because she'd been hired to help trap this woman."

"Hired by whom?"

"A man named Verdou, a Reich sympathizer, who has infiltrated the underground group I believe may be involved in the attempt on the Führer's life. Now we have the woman's description and a sketch of her, sir."

"A likeness? Excellent, Gunter. Go on."

He could hear Jäger's pen scratching as he wrote this down.

Gunter wiped the sweat from his forehead with the back of his hand. "After questioning the café staff, I managed to track down the woman's bike, which contained evidence that brought me to le Bon Marché, where she'd checked a recently fired Lee-Enfield rifle in the cloakroom. Volke's examining the rifle now."

Gunter knew Verdou had hired Jeanne to do his dirty work outing the female spy so he could lay low and keep his cover. It made sense Verdou acted alone to claim the bounty.

Loud knocks came over the line.

"So is she the shooter? Or an accomplice?"

The shooter, but he'd keep that to himself until he got proof. "To be determined, sir. The group is meeting tonight, according to the informer, Verdou." Gunter paused, leaving out that he distrusted his source. From his attaché case he took out the report he'd skimmed on the way over. "Call it my policeman's nose, but what if the High Command visit that was scheduled for noon today was the focus of the British snipers? The attempt on the Führer was separate. Maybe even a smoke screen."

"How do you know about the High Command?"

"I read the latest report, sir. I'm a policeman. That's why you put me in this job."

Pause. "We discovered radio codes were compromised, Gunter. The Brits knew the High Command were meeting the Führer concerning the sea invasion."

Jäger was telling him now?

"You need to find her."

"When was the message detailing the High Command's visit transmitted, sir?"

"The first on Friday evening. The final confirmation went out this morning at zero six hundred hours."

This morning the old woman had seen parachutists falling from the sky. The British had known about the High Command's visit and had sent the snipers to le Bourget. Hadn't he been working on a similar scenario based on decoded British messages in Munich?

"Find out, Gunter. And inform me of the ballistics results. The Führer wants an up-to-the-minute report. Now."

Jäger hung up.

Gunter turned the faucets on the lab's sink. Cupped his hands, drank, then splashed his face. Wetted his handkerchief and dabbed his neck. Refreshed, he dried off, making a mental note to question Verdou thoroughly.

Through the glass partition he motioned to Volke.

"Anyone you trust here?"

Volke shook his head.

How could he mount the surveillance team he would need for tonight with damned SD idiots like Roschmann? He grabbed his attaché case.

"I'll check in with you later."

Volke wrote a name on a lab slip. Set it in Gunter's pocket and put a finger to his lips.

Sunday, June 23, 1940

Communications Center under King Charles Street, London
4:00 p.m. Paris Time

Worried, Stepney read the latest decryption from the Alpha network. He saw no mention of his agents or the snipers' mission. He should have heard something by now.

"You've double authenticated this message, Billy?"

"Per your instructions, sir. Comes up viable. Alpha's window for response ends in two minutes."

This decoded message contained an urgent request for agent extraction with the code name Swan. Good, the SIS mission problem solved.

Yet he'd heard nothing from Kate Rees via Y sector. He'd given her up for dead since Martins's body was found. Still . . . he'd inquire.

"Respond agreeable. Extraction tomorrow. Details coming. Request an update on Cowgirl."

By the time Stepney tracked down Cathcart in this warren of tunnels, he had a plan.

"Alpha's asking for urgent removal of Nigel Swanson."

Cathcart's neck craned looking over Stepney's shoulder, then behind him. No one. "Correct. We'll arrange a Channel extraction."

"Why not send a Lysander?" said Stepney. "Tomorrow night should be perfect flight conditions."

"We want him taken to the coast. Any word from your agent, Rees?"

Stepney doubted there ever would be word of her, but Cathcart didn't need to know that.

"Not yet. But why use a Channel extraction with the rough seas forecasted?"

Cathcart hesitated.

Never back down, the first rule in the game. If Cathcart wanted Stepney's deniable Section D to coordinate this operation, he wouldn't accept a brush-off. "Spit it out, Cathcart. What aren't you saying?"

Cathcart scanned the empty corridor. "Stepney, all I can say is that the ship captain set sail equipped with the S-Phone."

Stepney contained his surprise. All this subterfuge over a piece of equipment? Was that it?

The device, in early development, was designed to fulfill three functions at the same time: radiotelephone, homing beacon and parachute drop spot indicator. He had requested this prototype, which they were calling an S-Phone and which could transmit ultrashort waves between a plane cockpit and a mobile set on the ground, to equip his group on their drops and extractions. Several were in field test use and the device was still in experimental stages. Flawed or not, quiet as it was it would have been ten times more secure than the ground fires built by underground agents to light the landing zone for agent drops and extractions. His request had yet to be processed. Meanwhile he had lost how many good men in the last few weeks?

It more than rankled that Cathcart already had one.

A Wren scurried around them with a clipboard in her hand. The men waited until she left the corridor.

"The S-Phone would have been of great use for our drop pilots," Stepney said, fighting to keep his voice neutral.

"They're equally useful ship to shore," Cathcart said. "We are starting to employ the S-phones on submarines and fast patrol boats during clandestine landing and removal operations."

He hated being so low on the SIS totem pole they hadn't thought to inform him.

"I'm late for a meeting," said Cathcart.

Dismissed.

Cathcart wouldn't get away so scot-free. Stepney had to get something in return. "My new radio operator gets a ride over on your ship. I need trusted radio signalmen for ground communication."

"You're asking a lot, Stepney."

A lot?

Cathcart was gone.

SUNDAY, JUNE 23, 1940

Canal de l'Ourcq, Paris | 5:00 P.M. Paris Time

Kate didn't know how much she could trust this butcher Ramou, a burly man with a bloodstained apron and expressionless black eyes. The two card players were lifting the wounded man up a rickety ladder to a hay loft in the stable's rear. The familiar aromas of sweet hay and dried blood filled her nose.

"This man needs a doctor," she said. "Dédé said—"

"No names."

She figured Dédé was an alias, but nodded. "Fine, but he wanted me to bring this man here. He's important."

"What do you mean?" said the butcher in stilted English.

Was he playing dumb or safe? But the truth was she didn't know, either. Instead of answering she said, "Why would he send us here if he didn't think you'd help?"

The butcher lifted a basket down from a nail on the wall and handed it to her. It contained a bottle of wine, a baguette, a jar of confiture and a half-open packet of pills.

"This isn't enough. He's badly hurt—fevered—"

The butcher cut her off. "Best I can do."

"He needs medical attention."

"*Zut!* Who is he?"

"He's important, that's all I know."

He could have internal injuries. She swallowed hard. Wondered if the man would last.

"*Bon,* you take care of him."

"Me?" she said. "That's not my job."

The sewer man had told her to make contact with the underground, that they'd be able to help her. So far nothing had panned out.

"It's your job now," said the butcher. "Nothing to do with me."

"Nothing to do with you?" Her frustration boiled into anger. "Look, call the bar, he'll verify."

"We don't have a telephone."

"So how do messages get through?"

"Messages? I'm a butcher, not a doctor."

Hooves clopped on the cobbles, signaling an arrival in the stable. The two men descended the ladder, conferred with the butcher in what sounded like convoluted French. Kate couldn't understand a word.

"What's the matter? What were they saying, some code?"

He raised an eyebrow. "Butcher's slang, *louchébem.* You're on your own," he said. "I've got to work."

She eyed the injured Brit and weighed her options. Zero. The butcher had to be more connected than he let on. Stepney's words came back to her: *Change plans at a moment's notice. Improvise.* "Look, find a doctor. Meanwhile I'll do what I can."

The wounded man lay among the bales of hay in the loft, his sandy blond hair matted with sweat, eyes closed. Now that the burlap sacks were off him, she took note of his appearance: a leather jacket and ripped leather headgear, a single boot. His right leg was splinted to a stick of wood. Midway between his knee and thigh was a dirty dressing over the pants. A knapsack was still slung over one shoulder despite all he'd been through.

A downed pilot.

She set down the basket and knelt beside him. His forehead burned. But his well-fed figure filled out the flight suit.

His eyes blinked open and he grabbed her shoulder. His teeth chattered. "I'm so c-c-cold."

She found a horse blanket, covered him with it. "Thirsty?" He shook his head. "Try a little." She took the red wine, put the bottle to his lips. He sipped, a trickle running down the side of his mouth. She dabbed the wine away with the end of the blanket. He gave off a fevered smell of dried sweat. "Now some bread."

He shook his head. Clutched his leg.

Kate couldn't fight off the memory of Lisbeth's fevered little body and her febrile convulsion. Lanced by pain, Kate struggled to focus, to help this man before it was too late.

"Were you shot down?"

"Ambushed . . . others gone . . . only winged me," he gasped, then let out an awful moan.

She pulled the blanket off to see blood gushing from the dressing. There was a bullet wound in addition to the fracture, she finally realized. She should have checked the wound first, damn it. *Idiot.*

She had to focus. Put everything else out of her mind.

She remembered the hired hand who'd gotten gored by a bull on the ranch. Pa had said it bled bright like that when a vein got punctured. Or was it an artery? She couldn't remember.

Good God, she prayed, *help me.*

Her pa's voice rang in her head. *You're not a ranch girl for nothing, Kate. You've patched up plenty of injured cattle in the ranch yard. Get to work.*

She unsnapped his flight suit. Took off the blood-soaked dressing, ripped his pant leg down to mid-thigh to expose a small dark red hole now spurting blood. Tried not to gasp. The man was losing so much blood.

She pressed the blanket over his wound. Was she doing the right thing? She had to sustain pressure. With her other hand, she took the torn pant leg in her teeth and ripped off a strip. She attempted to lift his heavy thigh to slide the strip under it. "Try to help me and turn your leg."

Groans answered her.

She had to stop the blood flow above the wound. Hating to do it, she rocked his thigh back and forth while he cried out in pain. Finally, sweat beading her brow, she managed to tie the strip tourniquet-style at his groin above the bullet hole. That done, she applied pressure to the wound.

The blood flow had lessened.

Taking a deep breath, she rolled him on his side. Didn't know if this was right or wrong medically. She saw a large jagged exit wound, the shredded flesh spotted with dirt, leaves and tiny bone fragments. His leg had swollen due to the fracture and no doubt the exit wound was infected. Christ, he'd be lucky to keep his leg.

She summoned her courage, dipped her fingers in wine and swabbed the edges of the dirty exit wound. Whiskey would have been better. She'd seen her pa remove buckshot spatter from his own leg with his pinkie and a bottle of whiskey. Holding her breath, she picked out the dirt and leaves.

The pilot shrieked.

"Sorry, sorry, this will only hurt a minute." She had no idea if that was true. She had to find the bullet.

He was screaming now, flailing his arms.

"Shhh. Please try to stay still."

Sweat trickled down her neck. Her fingers came back with clotted blood and yellowish bits of tissue stuck in her cuticles. No bullet. Bile rose in her throat. Her nerves vibrated.

The man's screams had died, giving way to shallow breathing. Anxious, she wiped her hands off on the straw and blanket. She took a pill from the basket, opened his mouth and let it dissolve on this tongue. She hoped it was an analgesic or a fever reducer. At this point, she figured, it was crueler not to try it than to misuse it.

Kate dabbed his forehead with a strip wetted in wine since there was no water. Banked prickly hay around him to keep in his body heat. He closed his eyes.

An eternity passed in the stifling barn loft. She listened to the man's fevered moans, dabbed his fevered brow. Medical help, if that's what the butcher had gone for, wouldn't take this long, would it? Hiding out with the British pilot in this suffocating heat, she felt like a sitting duck. The butcher could have turned them into the Germans, claimed a reward.

Stupid to get herself in this mess. She needed a plan. Tried to think things through. *RADA*. But here she was with a seriously wounded man; she couldn't leave him.

She felt his forehead again. The pilot's temperature crept higher. The tight tourniquet had stanched the blood, but his condition had gone from bad to worse.

The time stretched. Anxious, she dabbed his forehead again. Then looked down into the barn. No one.

In this hot, silent barn, all her fear and anger came crashing down on her. She'd failed her mission. This pilot needed a doctor and, despite her efforts, seemed to be dying on her watch. She'd tried, like she had tried to save Lisbeth, and was failing again. Not only couldn't she save this man, she didn't see how she could save herself. Any chance of escaping to England looked remote. Tired, so tired, she battled to stay awake, but her eyes were heavy with fatigue.

Kate couldn't fall asleep now. This man's life depended on her. She had to figure something out. An image of black-haired, musky-smelling Philippe, if that even was his name, flickered in her mind, and for a moment she indulged in a daydream of curling up in his arms and shutting her eyes.

"Get ready." The butcher had appeared at the top of the ladder. The suggestion of a summer evening hovered outside the barn window. She remembered how late it got dark. She must have dozed off.

He thrust a blue apron and a long-sleeved blouse and skirt like the one she had seen the dairy cart volunteer wearing at her. "Put this on."

"Ready for what?"

"We have to move him."

"You're kidding, right? He needs medical help. This man's in no shape to be moved. Infection has set in and his leg's fractured."

"You're a doctor now?" The butcher glanced at the passed-out pilot. "Look, our doctor's been arrested. And the veterinarian, well, he's a collabo. It's too dangerous for him to stay here. We could all be killed." He nodded to the garments he'd handed her. "Put that on. We need to get moving. We grease the canal watchman's palms, but for who knows how long."

"Wait—where are you moving him?"

"To a boat, that's all you need to know. In the meantime, whatever you're doing, keep it up."

Kate had no choice.

Sunday, June 23, 1940

Near Canal Saint-Martin, Paris | 7:00 p.m. Paris Time

After more than two hours wasted writing a detailed report for the Führer, finding Kostoff at the Kommandantur to sign off on it, then finally relaying it to Jäger, Gunter met Niels in the Mercedes. Gunter hoped he would catch the Englishwoman at the address the informer Verdou had given him—privately he had come to think of her as the Englishwoman, for no reason besides his childhood memory of the English ladies with their Pears soap.

If Verdou wanted his wallet back, he would have to deliver. Gunter wanted to sew this up, appease the Führer and be on the evening plane back to Munich.

Niels downshifted, pulled the brake and kept the engine purring. Next to Gunter sat a lab tech named Karl dressed in drab green. It was Karl's name Volke had written down for Gunter—he had turned out to be Volke's cousin. Gunter needed an extra pair of hands for this and Volke trusted him.

"Seems like a dodgy area, sir," Niels said. "Reminds me of Wedding."

The neighborhood did indeed look like the Berlin slum. Gunter peered out the car window at a string of dilapidated bars, an old one-legged beggar on crutches, medal on his lapel, holding a tin cup. He reminded Gunter of the maimed war veterans he still saw back home.

Mid-block, one door down from a shuttered music shop, was a nineteenth-century sign lettered CLAVERIE. Beside it, numbered 224, were light blue double doors framed by art nouveau plaster curlicues. The shop window displayed no old-fashioned whalebone contraptions but lacy peach satin lingerie.

"Sure about this address, sir? It's a corset shop."

"Yes. We're in Paris, Niels. Home of the Moulin Rouge, the Folies Bergère."

Gunter eyed a lace garter belt—would his wife like it? Two hundred francs. Not on a RSD investigator's salary. A salary dependent on catching this sniper.

Not just his salary—his post and family's safety hung in the balance.

Gunter outlined his surveillance plan. "You know how to use a gun, don't you, Karl?"

Karl frowned. "Of course. I work in the rifle testing range. But I've never killed anyone."

"Your job's to wait in the courtyard out of sight and write down the descriptions of people coming into the building. *Verstehen Sie?*"

"*Jawohl,*" Karl said. "How detailed should this be?"

Karl's question irritated Gunter. He needed him to play his part. "Note their weight, height, hair color, age."

Karl's sallow face looked unconvinced. "Is this operation sanctioned? I mean, who are we reporting to?"

Had he asked this kid's opinion? Sweat prickled his neck.

"I report to the Führer."

Sunday, June 23, 1940

Canal de l'Ourcq, Paris | 7:30 p.m. Paris Time

Kate donned the heavy cotton clothing over Gilberte's dress, then tied the apron on top. She hated the heavy starched skirt. Why couldn't they wear summer uniforms? The sweat on her neck stuck to the stiff collar. Jittery, she shooed away the bluebottle fly buzzing near the confiture in the basket. Hunger pangs hit her. She dipped the bread knife inside and licked the jam off. Raspberry. Sweet, fragrant and delicious.

Where had Ramou gone? After the hurry up it was all wait.

A breeze drifted from the stable's open door up into the stifling hay loft. She flapped the skirts up to feel the cool air on her legs. The pilot's eyes blinked open.

"What kind of nurse are you?"

"The worst kind."

He shook his head. Winced. He'd slept a good two hours.

"Feeling better?" She smiled encouragement.

Instead of smiling back he glared at her. Good, maybe he was rallying. Now he could tell her what mission he'd been on and maybe how they could get out.

"Who are you?"

"Swan. I'm just a . . . This is . . . this is . . ." He reached out, his arm flailing at the hay. "So thirsty . . ."

He wanted the wine. She lifted his head and put the bottle

to his lips. His labored breathing came in gasps. "Antoine," he managed. "Meeting him Grand Palais."

She put the wine bottle again to his lips. "Antoine who?"

"We studied together . . . Birmingham. My best man . . . must give him . . ." He trailed off.

She needed more from him or there was nothing for her to go on. "Give Antoine what?"

"Damned cauliflower . . . I hate vegetables."

He was babbling.

"What about Antoine? Your best man from Birmingham?"

Exhausted by the effort of speaking, the man's jaw slackened. "Where . . . am I?"

Oh no, it felt like she was losing him to delirium.

"C'mon. The wine will make you lucid." A gulp. Then another. No answering smile. "Buck up, pilot."

Again, he shook his head. Winced.

"You're not an RAF pilot?"

"B-b-bloody hell, I'm . . . an engineer."

The more he spoke the more agitated he became. And the more flushed.

"An engineer? What are you doing here?"

She heard a low rattle from his chest. "Listen, can't you?" His flushed face tightened with exertion. Sweat beaded his upper lip.

"I'm listening."

". . . our project . . ." He closed his eyes.

"Before you said something about invasion plans. What do you mean by that?"

Horses neighed below. The gate scraped.

"Engineer! Can you hear me?" She dabbed his forehead.

"Bloody . . . Kriegsmarine . . ." His jaw slackened.

He was talking in circles. He looked too near death for a haul across Paris. He struggled to sit up and she pressed his shoulders down. A new red stain spread from his wound.

"Don't move, please," she said. "You're bleeding."

His drawn face appeared more haggard than before. Weakened from the exertion, he reached out again, his hand flapping in the hay. "Must . . . get this to Grand Palais . . . Antoine. There's a conference. At the Grand Palais."

Then his eyes rolled up in his head.

As clear as day she saw Lisbeth's little eyes roll up until only white remained. No, no, not again . . .

She felt his fluttering pulse and shook him. No response. "Wake up, engineer."

A moan. She slapped him.

His eyes opened. "D-d-don't you understand, you cow?"

The most lucid he'd sounded yet. "I understand you won't make it anywhere if you won't lie still," she said.

Desperate for him to pull through, she applied pressure again to the wound and noticed the wedding band on his fourth finger. With her other hand she felt around in his leather jacket. All she found in the pocket was a black-and-white photo. In it a light-haired woman perched on a horse, squinting in the sun.

"Is this your wife?"

"My . . . darling Pippa." A weak smile broke over his face.

"See, you're almost nice when you smile," she said. "Tell me why you have to go to the Grand Palais."

"Antoine . . . the plans."

His eyes fluttered closed. His breath came in shallow beats. The pallor in his cheeks had a gray tinge. His forehead felt hot again.

Where was the damn butcher?

Mumbled conversations drifted from an adjoining courtyard. Horses neighed below.

A deep hooting sound startled her. She sat up and locked eyes with a pair of unblinking yellow ones in the rafters. It took a moment before she realized they belonged to a barn owl.

Her father had always said owls took care of the barn mice. But here in Paris?

She heard the wooden ladder creaking. The butcher's head appeared above a clump of hay. The look on his face was unreadable.

"My son's saddling up the cart." He glanced at the man. "How is he?"

"Fever's still high."

"We need to move him. There's patrols."

Before she could argue he was gone again.

"Hear that, engineer?" she said. "We've got to get you out of here."

She put her shoulder under his arm.

"The buoy locations," he said, a strange lucidity in his eyes. "The invasion plans. Antoine's . . . arranged my escape. A barge."

Blood bubbles streamed in a thin line from his mouth.

"What about buoy locations?" Her heart hammered. He had to tell her. He had to survive. "Swan?" She felt his pulse—thin and reedy.

"Look, I need a little more information here if I'm going to get us out of this. Does Antoine have the plans?" She stroked his face as his eyes slid closed. "Don't leave me, engineer. Not yet, engineer, please." She felt the life ebbing from him. "You hear me, engineer?" She slapped him again. "Swan. Swan! Goddamn it, answer me."

His eyes blinked open. "Directive 17."

His body went limp, his mouth falling open. The fly alighted on his pupil but he didn't blink.

Terrified, she shooed away the fly. She remembered what her father had done the time her brother fell off the roof, straddling him and pumping his chest until his heart started again on its own. It worked magic—it had seemed to Kate that her brother lurched awake from the dead. Kate folded her hands together, prayed and thrust hard into his chest, then again.

But he was gone.

Gasping, she fell back.

The owl hooted again. There was a whooshing of wings as it flew across the barn and out the door.

The butcher had appeared and shook his head. "We say a hooting owl bids *adieu* to a departing soul."

Shuddering, she blinked away tears. Was the owl an omen? Was she cursed? Her mother, Dafydd and Lisbeth, and now this engineer, whom she desperately needed to have kept alive.

"There are new German patrols," the butcher said, closing the engineer's eyes. "You have to hurry."

"Why?" she asked, her voice hollow.

"We must bury him before they find him here."

"You want me to bury him?"

The butcher's rough hand gripped her shoulders. "Not you. You must go, mademoiselle. Get yourself out of here. Escape."

She stared in shock at the man's blood on her hands. *Escape* . . .

"How?"

The butcher took her by the shoulders and shook her. "Now. We don't have much time." His gaze bore into hers.

Galvanized, she wiped her hands on the blanket. Watching the butcher gather the engineer's few things and stick them in the small rucksack, Kate wondered how important Swan and his mission could be. What could he have meant about buoys? All she knew was that he was meeting someone named Antoine, whom he'd known in Birmingham, at the Grand Palais. She didn't know when, or why, or what information was being passed.

But she did know that there was a barge waiting to take him away after. If she completed his mission for him, would they let her make use of his escape route?

Down in the stable, she washed her hands, then stuck her head under the water pump and washed off the sweat, the blood. Toweled her hair with the hem of the skirt. The butcher's son was helping his father load the body into the cart.

She climbed in the horse cart behind the butcher and his son, a gangling teenager in overalls. Next to her lay the engineer's covered body and his bag. The canal's expanse reflected the sun's orange evening glow. A time when it wasn't day or night, reminding her it wouldn't get dark for about another two hours. She breathed in the algae-scented air.

Guilt and sorrow nagged at her. There'd been no way she could have saved him—even if she'd had better medical knowledge, she was almost certain he'd already been too far gone. The cart lumbered along the bank amid the chirps of crickets. The cart's hay scents mingled with the reek of ship oil. She checked the engineer's bag: a compass, a pack of cigarettes, a lighter—all regulation items. His wife's photo. But where were his papers? She didn't even know his name. Would "Swan" be enough for her to fake her way through this?

She remembered his agitated disjointed words, how he wanted her to understand.

Invasion . . . buoy locations . . . plans . . . Grand Palais . . . Antoine . . . barge . . . escape.

And his last words*: Directive 17.*

She needed something else to go on—some clue as to what she should do next. She replayed every word and interaction that had passed between them, remembered how every time she'd tried to get him to lie still his arms had flailed in the hay, reaching. She'd assumed he was thirsty, that he was reaching for the wine. *Never assume*, Stepney had drilled into her.

What if he'd been reaching for something else in the hay? But what? There was nothing in his bag. She checked his leather headgear. Nothing. She took the leather jacket from the bag, fished around in the empty pockets, then squeezed the lining in case there was anything hidden inside. She felt an unusual thickness in the collar band, stiff with whatever had been tightly stitched inside. Something was encased inside. Using her fingernails, she tried picking the stitches, then when that failed, biting the threads open.

"Shhh, the patrol's nearby," said the butcher, looking over his shoulder. "Keep low."

She nodded. Picking away quietly at the threads with her teeth, she finally tore them and was able to rip apart the leather jacket's collar.

She threw a blanket over herself, took the lighter from his bag. In the flickering flame, she saw a folded piece of silk with uneven contours. She unfolded the silk, what appeared to be a neck scarf stitched with old-fashioned beading, like one of her aunt's old scarves. It was hard to believe this much silk had been wadded into such a narrow collar. Peering closer, she realized it was one of those tourist scarves imprinted with a large Eiffel tower. The beads were tightly stitched along the edges. Tacky.

She raised the blanket for air. A barge was passing. In the summer evening light, the scarf looked even more tacky, its cheap glass beads glittering.

Then again, they were catching significant sparkle. Glass didn't sparkle like that.

Her jaw dropped. How dumb could she be?

Diamonds.

The scarf was stitched with diamonds. This was what the engineer must have been reaching for. Was this what he had to get to Antoine? Her mind scrambled. It must be a bribe, or a payment of some kind—it must have been for information. Information about the German invasion? Something about buoy locations? If she could salvage his mission, make the exchange, this could be her way out.

Directive 17.

She folded the scarf and wedged it deep inside the apron's pocket, then pulled the blanket off. About to stuff the pocket compass back into the engineer's bag, she noticed the compass was heavier than the one her pa used tracking and hunting. She remembered Stepney had a similar one on his desk.

She fiddled with the casing. The bumpy cart jolted on the cobblestones, making her hand slip. She kept pressing and scraping at the compass's contours until her thumb hit a button. The compass's face popped off. Inside was a tiny Minox Riga camera, like one she'd seen in training. A spy camera—lightweight aluminum, only the length of her index finger. The Minox Riga's tiny window showed the number one. Ready to take a picture.

The cart was slowing down. She slipped the Minox back into the compass and into her pocket.

The butcher gave her a hand down from the cart. "You're on your own from here. We're taking the body to bury. Curfew's at ten." He pointed to a beat-up bike leaning on the quai's fence. "Use that." He stuck a note in her pocket. "Read it later. Not now. *Bonne chance.*"

He sounded almost friendly. Maybe death drew people together.

Her mind clicked into action. Somehow she'd track down Antoine, whoever he was. This time she wouldn't fail. The engineer had died for this mission. She prayed she wouldn't, too.

Sunday, June 23, 1940

Near Canal Saint-Martin, Paris | 7:30 p.m. Paris Time

Gunter's eyes accustomed themselves to the dim light in the concierge loge to the right of the apartment's courtyard. It contained only a bed, table and one gas burner, a rack on the wall with a row of keys hanging under corresponding tenant names. This place felt like a dark stone cave and exuded the smell of cooking oil.

The concierge, a fifty-something woman, short and rotund in a shapeless smock, eyed him, expressionless. Her left eye had a milky cast. Hair straggled from her bun.

"Papers," said Gunter, reaching out his hand.

The concierge pulled a *carte d'identité* from her grease-stained pocket. Gunter glanced at the papers.

"Madelaine Tremont?"

A nod.

"Where were you born?"

"Around the corner. Forty-two quai de Valmy."

Her gaze darted to Niels, then Karl out in the courtyard sizing up the situation. She knew something.

Gunter slid fifty francs and the drawing of the Englishwoman into her hands. "Seen this woman?"

The fifty francs disappeared into her pocket. Another nod.

"When?"

A shrug. "This afternoon. Asking about Madame Masson. She's second floor on the right."

Gunter reached for the keys of a Gilberte Masson. "This apartment?"

Another nod. "And I never saw her leave."

Sunday, June 23, 1940

Grand Palais, Paris | 8:10 P.M. Paris Time

Kate cycled down side streets on the butcher's beat-up bike. The quiet of the warm evening was punctuated by bells from passing bicycles and the occasional bark of a dog. In the distance, though, she heard the engine of a troop truck.

It stayed light late in summer; she'd once thought it almost enchanted, as if the sun hadn't wanted to sleep. Wispy clouds patterned the indigo sky. Dafydd had once explained how these clouds would turn noctilucent illuminated by the sun when it had set and gone below the horizon.

She inhaled the linden trees' scent and cursed as the long apron caught on the tire spokes. With unsteady nerves she tried to focus and formulate a plan. First, find Antoine; second, figure out how to complete whatever Swan's spy mission had been so she could escape.

But she wasn't a spy, whatever her training. She was a sharpshooter.

She parked the bike and walked along the gravel path toward the Grand Palais. Its arched humpback roofs were fretted by iron, joining thousands of glass panes, their dark green surfaces reflecting a furred sunlight from the sky. She wished for nightfall, for a more complete cover of darkness to hide in.

"We're closed," said the guard, gesturing toward the sign. He gave her a dismissive nod, taking her for a domestic.

Play the part, she thought.

Men underestimate women, Stepney said. *Use it.*

"Monsieur, I'm sorry to bother you. But my cousin's attending the conference here; can you show me where it's being held?" she said, hoping her slow inflection marked her as provincial.

Believe.

"What conference?" He wanted to shoo her away.

Stricken for a moment, she wondered if she'd remembered Swan's words all wrong. Or maybe the conference had ended. Or hadn't begun yet—he'd said nothing about when.

Or maybe the lazy guard was just giving her a hard time.

"A group of engineers," she persisted. "Here for a conference."

Wouldn't it be this guard's job to know?

How stupid of her, she realized. A conference didn't run at night. Unless there were evening lectures. She stared at the guard, hoping he could give her some clue. The day's heat hovered.

"Aah, you probably mean at the university observatory. The astronomers," he sniffed. "In back."

Was that what engineers did? But she nodded. "*Merci.*"

Kate spied several men smoking as she wound along an evergreen hedge toward the rear entrance. In a large foyer, stucco peeled from the arched walls. The whole place smelled of damp and mold. Several students mounted a wrought iron balustraded staircase. Her gaze caught on the conference sign: UNIVERSITÉ COLLOQUIUM DES SCIENCES.

Not exactly what she'd been expecting. But close enough.

She followed the students upstairs. Paused at the open door on the second floor. Looked around and, seeing no one, slipped inside and stood at the back.

A group of fifty or sixty men and a few women sat in a small amphitheater, listening attentively to a white-haired man standing at a podium in front of a diagram labeled FUSION PROCESS.

Her heart sank. Not one of the distinguished attendees looked under fifty. How could any of them have gone to university in Birmingham with the thirtysomething man she'd met?

The white-haired speaker droned on about *les particules* and *des électrons* and she understood nothing.

Apprehensive, she watched the black-uniformed Germans clumped in the front row. Worried, she slunk back into the woodwork.

RADA. Read, Assess, Decide, Act.

An old man poured the long-winded speaker a glass of water. Took the water pitcher to refill and passed her in the doorway. She followed him to the stairway landing across from the amphitheater's door. Smiled.

"*Excusez-moi, monsieur,* would you be the conference registrar?"

"*Moi?*" The white-bearded man stared at her outfit. "The conference began yesterday, everyone's registered," he said. Suspicion showed under his thick black eyebrows. Did she look too young or odd? "The area's off limits to the public."

Act helpless.

"You're right, monsieur." Kate faltered and leaned on his arm. "But I'm on a mission of mercy and with this heat, you know—and my anemia." She sighed. "My brain's already turned to mush."

"Sit down." Concerned now, he guided her to a small spindle-back chair in the landing's corner.

"I've got a message for an attendee. His name's Antoine. I've never met him, monsieur." She gave a big sigh. "Very sad. This comes from Rafael Santos, Professor Neliad's assistant at the Polytechnic," she said, ready to launch into the story she'd fabricated on the long ride. Rafael, an actual Spanish engineering student Kate had known in '37, had become the assistant to his advisor, Professor Neliad, a short squat perfectionist Raphael had mimicked incessantly. "I hate to trouble you, monsieur, but it's important I speak with Antoine. Please."

The man set down his folder, which was labeled ÉCOLE POLYTECHNIQUE.

"But what's so important?"

She had to make this credible. Make him believe her.

She sniffled and shook her head. "There's horrible news. Antoine's mother . . ." She paused for effect. "A terrible accident in front of her apartment. The bus . . . and Rafael saw the whole thing." To make herself cry, she thought of the dead Swan and how the fly had settled on his sightless eye. Tears brimmed in her eyes. "Terrible."

"Calm yourself, I'll fetch you some water."

He returned with a pitcher and poured water in a glass.

She drank, relishing the cold liquid on her parched throat. "*Merci, monsieur,* you are very kind."

Kate's ankles were swollen in the heat after all the running and biking. She'd forgotten how hot it got in Paris in the summer. A mildew smell wafted.

"He's gone to the hospital with her and sent me to fetch Antoine."

"But not everyone's here right now," the man said. "The reception's later. Do you know his last name?"

"Absurd, but no, Rafael forgot to tell me. Antoine's in his late twenties, early thirties. He studied in Birmingham. Can't you help me find him?"

"*Regardez,* we're the academics, the old crust." He shook his head. "If you mean the research engineers, they're upstairs with the Germans. It's a closed session."

"Cooperating with the Germans?" she asked before she could bite her tongue.

"Like anyone has a choice, mademoiselle? The day the Germans marched in they began regulating our research. They're in the process of taking over select projects. Soon they'll control them all. If we want to keep running our programs, we report to them." The old man snorted in disgust. "To think I survived the trenches in 1918 to work for the Boches."

The old man left her to go back to the lecture in the amphitheater. She swallowed the rest of the water. So welcome, so cold.

She had to reach this Antoine. Now. Kate didn't know how long she could keep us this charade.

She continued along the landing to a side corridor. Here a metal staircase wound up like a snail shell. Voices of students reached her ears. Men in white lab coats directed them as they climbed on ladders toward the glass panes of the roof. She wondered what they were going to do.

To the right in a side corridor were double doors, a red velvet rope strung across it to prevent entry.

A whiskered porter blocked her way to the side corridor. "*Interdit, désolé.*"

The blue cape of a French policeman hung from the hook in the hallway. In a glass reception area, she spotted the policeman speaking on the phone. Careful—she needed to watch every move.

"But, monsieur, I must get word to someone." She put her head down. "There's been an accident."

"Closed session, mademoiselle," he said. "Try at the reception."

Should she put the scarf of diamonds in the envelope she'd prepared, hand it to the porter and trust him to give it to a man whose last name she didn't even know? If anything went wrong, she'd have no bargaining chip left. No escape on that barge.

"Understood, monsieur."

She thought of the poor engineer. His pain. Her throat caught.

Believe.

A sob escaped her. "Please, it's important."

The porter hesitated.

"May I leave a message, monsieur?"

"Be quick about it, then," he said.

"*Merci.*"

Instead of leaving the scarf, she borrowed a pen and paper and wrote a note: *Important message from Swan, meet outside.*

If this was intercepted, it shouldn't compromise him, she hoped. She folded that paper, stuck it in the envelope the porter furnished and addressed it *to Antoine who studied at Birmingham.*

"Give him this, monsieur, please."

"*Mais alors,* there's only his *prénom* and there's a roomful of men in there."

She reached in her bag and handed him ten francs. "You'll find him."

The porter shook his head.

"It's life or death, monsieur." She sniffled and pretended to wipe a tear from her eye. "That's all I have."

The policeman hung up the phone.

"Please, monsieur."

The porter nodded. Kate melted behind a pillar, then flew down the narrow metal stairway.

Sunday, June 23, 1940

Near Canal Saint-Martin, Paris | 8:15 P.M. Paris Time

Gunter had surveilled Gilberte Masson's apartment for more than half an hour and had seen no one go in or out. He hadn't wanted to tip Gilberte off or frighten the Englishwoman away. Yet he couldn't twiddle his thumbs any longer.

Gunter motioned Karl to stand guard by the apartment's service stairs in back. He gripped his Luger. With Niels following, he padded up stone stairs grooved with age.

Gunter paused, listening at the faded maroon door. Low, indistinguishable conversation. He peered at the shuttered windows facing the courtyard, the wilting potted plants on the landing, and hesitated. A trap?

How many dicey situations had he walked into in his rookie days? He and his first partner had followed an informant's tip into a back-alley shoot-out. They'd been set up. He'd survived, but his partner hadn't. He'd learned the hard way to stay wary, keep his eyes open and head down.

With a loud click, Gunter turned the key.

In the apartment a portly man in SS jackboots, suspenders over his undershirt, stood uncorking a bottle of champagne. He looked up in irritation. The whole place—wallpaper, furniture—was a riot of pink, red and gilt. Some high-class bordello?

"What's the meaning of this?" the SS officer said.

Flustered, Gunter took in a woman in a peignoir. The pink silk slid off her shoulder, revealing alabaster skin. She smiled, holding an empty waiting flute in her hand.

"It's good manners to knock first, monsieur," she said.

A private flophouse?

"Who gave you the right to burst in here?" said the German—a colonel, by the stripes on the uniform jacket thrown over a chair.

Gunter showed his RSD badge, pointed Niels down the hallway to check the bedrooms. "The Führer."

Fear puddled in the colonel's eyes.

"We're looking for this Englishwoman, who was seen entering this apartment."

The colonel stared at the drawing Gunter brandished. "Her? No idea."

Gunter quickly searched the front room, checking behind the recamier, under the table, for anyone hiding. "Put your shirt on, colonel. The party's over."

"I don't know what you're talking about," he sputtered.

"There's a mix-up, some confusion," said the woman. She looked amused, gave a little laugh. "This apartment's—well, we rent it by the hour, if you know what I mean."

Hookers who used plush apartments instead of hotels for their business. Or so she wanted him to believe.

"Who knows who was here before us," she was saying

Niels returned from the hallway. Shook his head.

"You're lying, Gilberte Masson. The apartment's in your name. I'm afraid you'll need to clear it all up for us at headquarters."

As the woman set down her flute, it tinkled on the glass-topped table. Her hands were shaking.

Nerves.

While they dressed, Gunter searched the bathroom. A fogged-up mirror, makeup, photos of film stars, the scent of perfume. In a bedroom, he noticed several empty hangers in the armoire.

In the kitchen, he searched the trash bin. Raked through the potato peelings and empty wine bottles.

A blue sweater.

He brushed off the potato peels, lifted the sweater to his stuffy nose.

Sweat and that faint fragrance of Pears soap.

SUNDAY, JUNE 23, 1940

Grand Palais, Paris | 8:30 P.M.

Kate waited by the evergreen shrubs at the Grand Palais side exit, half-hidden in the lengthening shadows. A crowd of men had come out and several of them stopped to smoke under the dim blue globe lights. One man was speaking to a guard, who pointed at her.

Antoine, wiry black hair like a bristle brush, reminded Kate of a hedgehog: short, round and prickly. He wore small round brown glasses and continually picked at his cuticles.

They walked farther into the cypress shadows. Nervous, he looked around. He lit a cigarette before his manners kicked in. "*Excusez-moi, mais* . . . I don't understand this message."

"Are you Antoine, who studied in Birmingham?" she whispered in English.

He lifted his palm. "I'm one of many engineers and researchers who studied in Birmingham . . . but I'm French."

Kate looked around, registering a group of Nazis waiting for Antoine. Sweat pooled in the small of her back. *Think.*

RADA.

She had a chance and needed to act fast. Antoine was in the company of Nazis, but Swan had specifically said he was meeting Antoine at the Grand Palais. Antoine hadn't ignored the message, which told her he knew Swan's name.

She'd persist. Stay alert. Reassess if it went to hell.

She made a sign of the cross as if she were pious and about to pray. Hopefully it would allay suspicion for enough time to learn something. She leaned toward him. "Swan had a message for you."

"Swan . . ." More picking at his cuticles. "You mean . . . ?" He caught himself.

"You were the best man at his wedding."

"But I h-h-haven't seen him since B-b-birmingham . . . That's a while ago. S-s-several years."

A nervous stutter.

"He was meeting you here tonight, right?"

Antoine moved the gravel with his toe. Exhaled smoke. "So w-why are you here?"

The engineer had been right, even in his fevered state.

"Swan died en route and insisted I meet you . . . about your project."

His eyes, small behind the glasses, flickered. "Died . . . h-how?"

"Shot down trying to get here."

"I d-d-don't know if I sh-should believe you." He was scared. "How do you know . . . h-h-him?"

"Long story. He was seriously wounded so I helped and took him to a doctor . . ." She caught his arm before he stepped away. "But before it was too late he told me about the plans." Hoping he hadn't been delusional, she went ahead and added, "The buoys." The man was still listening fearfully. Sweat trickled behind her knees. "He asked me to bring you something. You know what I'm talking about, right?"

Antoine nodded.

The diamonds.

"We need to talk, Antoine."

He glanced back at the Germans who were waiting for him. The tall one ground out his cigarette, appearing annoyed. Looked like Antoine was collaborating with the Germans—out of choice or necessity, it didn't matter.

Everyone had a price, right?

Kate's heart raced as one of the Nazis cast a curious look in her direction. She was placing her life in the hands of a collaborator. Trusting that Swan hadn't died for nothing.

She pulled him deeper behind the evergreen bushes, out of their direct view.

"Swan said you'd arranged his escape on a barge."

"He s-s-said that?"

"He died in my arms," she said. Her voice quavered, she couldn't help it. "He had this for you. Please believe me, Antoine."

She'd torn off a scrap of scarf with several diamonds and she pressed it into his palm.

He blinked at the piece of the silk scarf, rolled it between his thumb and forefinger. "Only this . . . what about the rest?"

Trust no one. If he knew the diamonds were in her pocket, he could take them and turn her into the Nazis. "They're in a safe place."

Antoine picked his cuticles. It drove her crazy. "Who are you?"

This was taking too long.

"That's not important, Antoine." She needed to find out how to escape on the boat.

"Your friend's dying words were your name, Grand Palais, buoy, plans, a barge, Directive 17."

Antoine glanced back at the Germans. Would he blow the whistle on her? Tension knotted her stomach.

"Look, Antoine, I need to get on the barge."

He'd made a decision—she could see it in his eyes.

"Swan is . . . w-was supposed to take the plans to England. Directive 17." He glanced back again. "Now you'll have to do it."

"Me?" Her throat went dry.

"I can't steal the plans themselves or they'll know. Swan was bringing me something."

"You mean this?" She slipped the compass concealing the Minox camera into his jacket pocket. The pieces fit together. "So you'd photograph this project plan and he'd get the plans back to England? In return for the diamonds, right?"

Antoine nodded. Tossed his cigarette and stubbed it out with his foot.

"The camera's in there. Take the photos and I'll bring them on the barge."

A brief nod.

He'd agreed. Relief spread through her.

"They're sticking to me like g-glue. Meeting after m-meeting, I don't know when I c-c-can get away." The Germans were beckoning him. He waved back. Kate moved farther into the shadows.

Any moment they might come this way.

"My g-g-group was counting on Swan." He took a step back. "Bring the diamonds."

"And the barge . . . ?"

"Call me at École Polytechnique t-t-tomorrow. Ask for the engineering lab."

Boots clomped in the shrubbery.

"Now make the sign of the cross with me," she said. "As if we've been praying over tragic news."

"I'm an atheist."

"Do it."

Together they each made the sign of the cross.

A second later she'd ducked behind the cypress tree.

Kate felt as if encased in a straitjacket in the heavy skirt, long apron and long sleeves of the volunteer uniform. The collar felt damp enough to ring out. She'd ditched the bag and crammed her few things, along with Swan's diamond-studded scarf, in the deep pockets.

But her outfit did provide anonymity. She hoped no one would pay her any attention. While she'd been waiting for Antoine in the shadows, she'd used her cracked mirror and applied collodion, given herself a scarred upper lip, darkened her eyebrows and shaded under her eyes to change her look. She now walked with a limp courtesy of the pebble in her shoe.

The Nazis would recall a limping older servant with a scar.

And for a moment she wondered when Stepney would find

out that there was a traitor in the underground network. That she'd survived.

But Swan hadn't.

She'd been set up at the café. With Germans hunting her, everything happening so fast, she hadn't had time to figure out why.

What would Stepney tell her to do?

Improvise—well, she had. *Get creative*—she'd done that, too, but maybe not creative enough.

Keep your goal front and center, he'd said.

Swan's mission. She'd agreed to take what the nervous Antoine photographed to get herself on the barge. Tomorrow was a long way off.

Why hadn't Stepney trusted her with her own escape plan?

Had he in fact been the one who set her up?

Her shoulders ached; the sore muscles in her calves protested. About to pop another pink pill from the packet in her bra, she realized her supply was almost out. She'd need more later, so she bit off a quarter of a pill, downed it and hiked up the skirt and apron, ready to mount the beat-up bike. Jittery, she saw a shadow move behind a tree. She leaned the bike against a bench and slowly crept toward it. It was nothing. A twig cracked. She whirled around and saw a squirrel.

She listened and only heard the sound of the leaves playing in the wind. But every fiber told her someone was watching her.

Sunday, June 23, 1940

Near Canal Saint-Martin, Paris | 8:30 p.m.

Gunter showed the colonel out, motioned for Gilberte to sit back down and closed the door.

A knowing look painted Gilberte's face. "All you had to do was ask for a rendezvous."

Nice try.

"The building's surrounded."

Gilberte's creamy white shoulders shuddered but she tamped down her reaction so quickly that if Gunter hadn't been looking for it he would have missed it.

"Be helpful, Gilberte, or I arrest your friends, family and everyone you know." Gunter sat down next to her. "I'm only interested in her. This woman." He showed the drawing. "I know she was here."

"No doubt. But as I said, monsieur," she said, tugging at her bra strap, "people come here on an hourly basis."

"Not according to my investigation," he said, lying. He hadn't asked the concierge what time she'd seen the woman. He would.

If he had rattled her, the only evidence was a tightening of her lipsticked mouth.

Gunter flashed the photograph he'd found wedged in the bottom of the drawer. A family scene of a younger Gilberte, fresh faced, a man with his arm around her shoulder holding a baby. A dog and toddler at their feet. Happy and smiling. A cake on a picnic blanket. Mountains behind them.

"My daughter just turned two," said Gunter. "I missed her birthday."

No response.

"That's because I was ordered here to find this woman, Gilberte. And at any price I will. That's my job."

"I don't know why you're asking me."

"Is that what you will say after we find your children?"

Her eyes glittered. "You think I trust you Germans? My husband died two weeks ago in a POW camp. He's gone and I'm alone."

Did she think she'd elicit his sympathy?

"All the more reason to protect your children."

Gunter saw no evidence children lived here. His instinct told him she'd sent them away to family or the countryside. Did she "work" to feed them?

He tried a hunch. "The concierge says you send money to the countryside. For them, eh?"

Anger flashed in her eyes.

Niels, whom Gunter had sent to retrieve Gilberte's mail from the concierge, returned and handed him a postcard.

Gunter nodded. "Why don't you read it out loud, Niels."

"'Paul and Lisette send Maman hugs and warm wishes. They're so happy Auntie got them a kitten.' Sir, it's postmarked in the Savoie. See."

Gilberte's mouth quivered. Her eyes never left the postcard in his hands.

"All I need to do is call the *préfecture* in Savoie—"

Gilberte slammed the table. "You can't prove anything."

Gunter held up the damp blue sweater. "We know she was here. Start talking or Auntie goes to prison and your children to an orphanage. You don't want that, do you?"

"Leave my children out of this."

"Cooperate, Gilberte, and I will. That's the price."

A knock sounded on the door. Niels answered and returned

in a few moments motioning Gunter to the hall. "Karl reports people entering through the back of a shop in the courtyard, lots of activity going on."

Gunter mulled that over. "Activity as in workers stocking merchandise?"

"He managed to see through a slit in the blackout curtain. People talking in low voices and no work was going on. He thinks it's a meeting."

"Stand by." Gunter strode to the window. "Is she down there at the meeting, Gilberte?"

Stricken, Gilberte looked up. Then at the postcard Gunter had set on the table.

"You'll leave my children alone?"

"It will be left out of my report. Never mentioned. I want the woman."

A sigh escaped her. "No idea if she's there. I sent her to Dédé's."

Gunter took out his notebook. "The address?"

Five minutes later Gilberte had revealed it was Dédé's group who met downstairs. He'd be there.

And Gilberte was the front. Her clientele's comings and goings were a perfect screen for the underground's meeting downstairs.

Gunter sensed the assassin was close—so close he could feel it. She'd been here, she'd return. Verdou's info had led him to this apartment; now he needed the right outcome to wind up this operation

Gunter noticed Niels's still-crisp uniform. He took off his jacket. "Put this on like you're a civilian and go meet our friend outside."

"Friend, sir?"

"Strongly remind our Monsieur Verdou that we expect her," he said under his breath. "He needs to deliver."

Gunter motioned for the shaking Gilberte to sit back down.

"Now tell me about her."

Sunday, June 23, 1940

Grand Palais Garden, Paris | 8:45 p.m.

Kate crept away from her bike. She searched behind the hedge for cover. The Grand Palais garden was a maze of shrubbery, trees, the odd statue, and she could hardly see in the growing shadows. The damn blackout didn't help.

A guard lugged a pedestrian barrier between her and the bike. She needed a place to hide, quick. She tucked herself up into a wall niche and tried hiding behind a winged statue of a nymph. If she could just blend into the shadows for now and figure out her next move . . . She pulled herself around the nymph using the handy wing, squeezed her chest against the marble and—

"You again?"

Fear shafted through her.

"You'll never fit in there." Speaking English, too.

She turned to see the guard wagging his finger at her. Not the guard she'd queried for the conference location—Philippe, the man she'd met in Gilberte's apartment, in a guard's uniform and a cap. At first she hadn't recognize him because of the uniform; after all, she'd only seen him naked.

"Such a genius for finding a tight spot," he said.

"You were the one following me?" she snapped. Wary, she looked around. Only the canopy of dark branches.

"You should be so lucky."

Nice. "I wouldn't call that luck. What are you doing here?"

Under his cap, she saw he wasn't smiling. Gilberte's sweat-soaked dress weighed heavy under the apron.

"I'm here to meet someone—someone who was meeting someone," he said. "A man. Not you."

"Who sent you?"

Philippe shook his head at her ruefully. Of course he wouldn't say.

"Was it Ramou?" she blurted out before she could think it through.

He narrowed his eyes at her and nodded once.

Philippe was here to meet up with the engineer who was supposed to meet Antoine. He must be part of the same network; he might have access to an escape channel. Sly Ramou had kept it all from her—all he'd done was give her a crummy bike and itchy clothing. It made sense now—Dédé, Ramou, Philippe and Antoine were in the same underground group. But how was Philippe involved in the rendezvous with Antoine? Something wasn't adding up.

And wait—it didn't make sense. Ramou knew the engineer was dead.

She couldn't trust Philippe.

Controlling her fear, she said, "How long ago did Ramou set this up?"

"Got word this afternoon. Why?" said Philippe, irritation in his voice.

Swan had been alive then.

"Why are you involved, Philippe?"

Her toehold in the niche was slipping. She grabbed the broken wing.

He studied her, then decided to answer her question. "Not that it's your business, but the man needs a bolt-hole. My job's to provide it. That's all you need to know."

"The engineer's dead. I've taken his place."

A snort. "Impossible."

"Get it though your head, I'm his replacement, understand?"

"No replacements," he said, more stern than irritated.

Such gall, arguing with her.

Infuriated, she said, "Why not? I'm taking the information and leaving on the barge."

"Didn't you hear me?" Anger vibrated in his low voice. "The barge escape's only for the engineer; the plans were organized this way. You think it was easy to arrange false papers? That's not how it works."

Her hand slipped from the wing and she fell to the gravel with a loud thump. Like an idiot she'd landed flat on her belly, arms sprawled.

The bright beam of a flashlight shone through the bushes.

"What's going on here?" said a loud German voice. "Papers."

Philippe had stepped in front of Kate shield-like. He quickly kicked her with his heel, then again, so hard she twitched in pain.

"*Mon Dieu,* I could use some help, please," said Philippe. "This old woman's suffering some kind of seizure. I just found her."

Kate moaned. Not hard to do—it hurt.

"*Quoi?*"

The flashlight beam played over the bushes and blinded her. Trembling, she knew she was caught. Next stop a German prison.

"Can't you see, she needs a doctor." Philippe raised his voice. "We must get her to a *clinique.*"

Terrified, she played along, jerking her body, rolling her head back and forth. Spitting and drooling. The actor's instruction played in her mind: *Believe.*

"It's close to curfew," said Philippe. "Please, Officers, I need your assistance. It's not far."

"Is she contagious?" one of the Germans asked, taking a step back. They didn't want to get involved.

"*Mais non,* she's *épileptique.* My boss, the director, has told us we can count on the German soldiers." His voice was commanding. "That as French people we can trust you. Please, it's an emergency."

Some murmurings in German.

"*Jawohl.*"

Suddenly the two men in black uniforms were in her face,

the flashlight's beam blinding her. She yelled, writhing on the gravel, until Philippe and one of the soldiers, grunting, lifted her up by their strong arms. The other German was ushering them through the bushes toward the street, into the back seat of a Mercedes.

One took the wheel; the other, his superior by the look of his medals, handed him the keys. "*Schnell.*"

The car lurched ahead.

In the seat next to her, Philippe leaned forward, directing the nervous driver, who ground the clutch, past the Pont Alexandre III, the dark Seine rippling below, then along narrow dark streets. Meanwhile, Kate writhed and moaned in the back seat. Desperate and terrified, she was pretty sure she would have been able to play-act just as well without Philippe's incessant pinching. If she survived this car ride, she would be completely black-and-blue.

Will this work?

It felt like an hour before the car stopped but couldn't have been more than ten minutes. Above them a darkened sign read CLINIQUE NICOT. Philippe pounded on the massive wood door until a light went on above. Shutters banged open revealing an open window on the upper floor.

"An emergency, please open up, Doctor."

A yawn. "*J'arrive.*"

Five minutes later, Kate rubbed her bruised arm on an examining table. She sat alone in the sheeted cubicle while Philippe and the doctor spoke in the front office with the black-uniformed German soldier, who insisted on writing up a report.

Tense, she looked around her for an exit. Only the curtains divided the cubicle from the front office. What would happen if the German demanded to observe the examination?

As she gripped the thick skirt to stop her hands from shaking, something crinkled in her pocket. She pulled out a cigarette pack containing only a single cigarette paper. She unrolled it, revealing a message. *Idiot.* Ramou had slipped this in her pocket on the quai, told her to read it later, and she'd forgotten with everything that happened.

The message said:

Meet before curfew

224 rue du Faubourg Saint-Martin

That was Gilberte's address. And curfew was at 10 P.M.

If she'd managed to leave directly after meeting Antoine, she'd have made it there by now. Not possibly dug her own grave.

She tore the cigarette paper into tiny pieces, dropped it in the bin and hopped back on the examining table. She needed to hurry.

In the office, she heard the German asking for her papers. If he examined her *carte d'identité*, he'd find the photo was that of a young woman without a scar.

Prickles ran up her scalp. The conversation in the doctor's office receded as she descended into panic. She was dead. This was the end of her line. She fought to make herself breathe.

She heard the clicking of heels departing from the front office and the closing of the door. Outside in the street the car's engine started up. There was a grinding of gears that faded in the night.

Could it be? She had escaped again?

Kate pulled off the apron, blouse and skirt, careful to transfer the contents to the pocket in Gilberte's dress, which she was still wearing underneath. The cubicle curtains slid open to reveal Philippe and the puffy-eyed middle-aged doctor, glasses perched on his nose. The doctor lit a cigarette.

"Need a doctor's note to get out of class?"

Just what she didn't need—a joker.

"I'm fine," she said, throwing a dirty look at Philippe, "apart from the bruising."

The doctor shrugged and took a small brown bottle from the shelf. "Arnica. Apply several times in the next twenty-four hours."

If she lived that long.

"*Merci, docteur,*" said Philippe, "didn't mean to drop you in the *merde.*"

"He asked for your papers," said the doctor. "I told him I wouldn't know anything until after I examined you, but who can say if he bought my excuses. If the Boche check back, they'll hear I referred you to a hospital in the suburbs."

Philippe whispered in his ear.

"Impossible," the doctor said. "You can't stay here. A German commandant requisitioned the top floor apartment." From his pocket the doctor withdrew a key and handed it to Philippe. "But you can stay at 124 rue de Provence. Second floor, the name's Chaumiere. Tonight only. Leave this under the mat in the morning."

The doctor showed them out the clinic's rear door without even a goodbye.

They kept to the shadows in case the German had circled back, but the narrow street lay deserted. Tomblike. "Fill me in on the man you were talking to," said Philippe.

Philippe had saved her. He had ties in London, as well as with Gilberte and Ramou, who had each helped Kate stay alive. Still she held back. What did she really know about him? She couldn't discount the fact that he might have ulterior motives.

Stepney said trust no one.

Did she even trust Stepney, the man who'd sent her here?

"Why should I?"

"Stubborn, eh?" he said. "You're thinking of your own skin."

"And you're not?"

"*Tant pis*, you're upset that the barge won't work out . . ."

Upset?

"Thank you for saving me, Philippe," she said instead with unconcealed sarcasm, "or whatever your name is."

She still didn't trust him. Without the barge she was on her own. Her best bet was to learn something at the meeting and find somewhere to hide. Beg Gilberte, if she had to, for help until she figured out what to do. Ahead of them, a red and white Métro sign shone at Solférino, but, following her gut instinct, she took off in the opposite direction toward the bus that was pulling up at the stop on the corner.

Threw back over her shoulder, "*Adieu*, Philippe."

Sunday, June 23, 1940

Near Canal Saint-Martin, Paris | 9:15 P.M.

Kate used the bus ticket she had ready and changed twice to get to Gilberte's apartment near the canal on the Right Bank. From the mountain of material Stepney had given her to read, she knew the occupation meant no gasoline rations except for those in reserved professions like doctors. With traffic limited to *vélo-taxis*, buses, an infrequent horse cart and the occasional Mercedes, the bus made good time.

She could see bands of color layering the sky; dark blue, light azure melting to burnt orange.

Concentrate.

She hurried off the bus and reached Gilberte's street a half hour before curfew and just in time for the meeting in Ramou's note. Catching her breath by the art nouveau Métro sign across the street from the corset shop, Kate spied a familiar loping walk. She recognized the man wearing the corduroy jacket with elbow patches passing the shuttered music store. Could it be? Her heart thumped in her chest.

Max, her tutor.

She'd caught sight of Max this afternoon going into the Latin bookstore. Like he'd always done at lunchtime.

But here, now, on the Right Bank?

She remembered he'd had a room near the Sorbonne. His

stomping grounds were the Latin Quarter. Coming here so close to curfew?

There was no reason, unless Max was headed to Ramou's underground meeting.

And despite Stepney's advice to never return to the same place, here she was returning to Gilberte's building, where she'd been sent by the sewer worker she didn't know if she could trust in the first place. She wondered how safe any of these connections were—as Stepney had said, it only took one person to talk. And they all seemed connected. Hadn't the sewer worker said there was a traitor? She wondered if this had been a good idea.

She stepped behind the thick trunk of a leafy linden tree, watching.

Max had paused at the faded aqua double doors at the side of Gilberte's corset shop. He pulled out a blue pack of cigarettes—Gitanes, if she remembered right. She had once taken a sharp, woody drag off of one of his. Never again.

She watched Max light up. Her thoughts raced. The quarter pill had made her jumpy. There was a traitor, she knew. But Max? Would their old friendship at the Sorbonne mean anything now?

She remembered Stepney's warning against contacting anyone from the past: "Don't trust anyone. I can't stress this enough. It's lonely, I know, I've done this myself. One friendly face from the past and the mission is ruined. Speak to no one. It's safer for you and for them."

If Max belonged to the cell, he'd help her. Wouldn't he? Or was she a fool not to believe he was the one who had set her up at the café?

Before she could decide which risk to take, a figure appeared out of the shadows. It was difficult to make out much in the low light from where she stood behind the linden tree. She could see the flame of a match, the brief illumination of the young man's face and dark hair as he bent toward Max to light a cigarette, pausing to exchange some conversation.

Her mind flickered to that summer of '37, the hot and stifling nights like this. Max sitting across from Kate after the Sorbonne class, in the café with that ragtag cast of international misfits: Jews, Poles, the radical Spaniard who'd gone to fight Franco. Max was always witty, patient with her slaughter of the French language. Before her *coup de foudre*, when she fell so hard for Dafydd, Max had been her best friend in Paris.

A radio blared jazz from an open window. Then the window slammed shut, slamming her back into the here and now, with Max sharing a cigarette with a man outside a building where an underground meeting was being held. Was Max a lookout? Or the traitor?

She tried to put together everything she knew. From the café *terasse* she'd seen Max enter the Latin bookstore like usual during his lunch. And not ten minutes later she'd been running away desperate to avoid capture. Yet how could Max have even known she'd be at the café?

Then again, if he hadn't known she'd be there, if he hadn't been the one to set her up, why hadn't he come over to say hello? Could she believe he hadn't noticed her? Or that he'd guessed the danger she was in?

The back of her throat was dry with fear.

Think.

Hadn't Dédé intimated he'd get her a message when contact with London was made? After helping the engineer she hoped he'd make good on that and somehow let Stepney know. She might find out here.

Or not.

She was frozen with doubt. She needed to make a choice.

Maybe she didn't want to believe Max could have betrayed her.

She thought of the engineer—ambushed, probably betrayed and shot. How the whole cell stood at risk. What were the odds she'd make it out of France even if Antoine came through? Tired and frustrated, she was invaded by a sense of hopelessness. Face it, this whole thing was suicide.

But her father's words echoed in her mind: *Katie, if you hit the ground, get up. And get even.*

She felt the pistol in her pocket. Traitors deserved to die.

She hardened her resolve. She'd go to the meeting.

She had to know.

The man he'd smoked with had gone back inside the blue double doors.

All her senses went to high alert as she watched Max stub out the cigarette with his toe. Then he was pushing one of the blue double doors open.

Her nerves jangled. As calmly as she could, trying to look like she belonged, she walked the fifty feet to the door. The street lay deserted.

She pushed the blue door open a crack, slid inside. The geranium smell she remembered from the concierge's loge filled her nose.

She kept to the wall by the concierge's door. In the building's covered *porte cochère,* Max stood in front of her; his silhouette showed against the dimly lit courtyard entryway ahead.

He was so close she could smell the cigarette smoke on him.

"Max?"

He turned.

"Fancy meeting you here, Kate," said Max.

But she heard no surprise in his voice.

Her hopes crashed. She had made the wrong choice. "And you, Max, tutoring the Nazis now?" She reached for the pistol in her pocket.

He grabbed her arm. Held her close. "It's not how you think, Kate."

Her skin crawled. "Max, you're the last person I'd have thought would set me up."

"Who said I set *you* up, Kate?"

Process of elimination.

He hit the light-timer switch on the wall, that started clicking and the *porte cochère* was bathed in blue.

Her eyes darted, looking for a dark corner. "Don't lie to me."

"Kate, I had no idea it would be *you.* Believe me."

He let go.

She read his eyes. He hadn't known. Emotion clouded her mind. Now that she faced him, did she really think she could shoot someone who'd been her best friend? Her fingers froze. Where had her resolve gone? A crushing despair threatened to take her over.

"Why, Max?" she said, her mind racing through possibilities. "How can you betray your own people?"

"My people?" He tightened his grip on her arm. His dark eyes glinted. "I'm half-German, Kate. It's not betrayal." His words came out rushed and tense. "We're still friends and I can help you."

Like she believed that? But she played along. "I don't know if I could work with the Germans," she said. Her fingers flexed, reaching for her pocket.

He didn't protest anymore. "In your shoes it's a good idea."

Her insides cramped with fear.

"Max, what do you know that I don't know?"

In the passageway, Max cupped her shoulder. The light went off with a click. With his other hand he hit the timed light switch, which started ticking again, sending the bluish glow over the walls, shadowing his face.

"Quit being naive, Kate. The Brits set you up." He put his mouth close to her ear. "A Brit parachutist gave you up. A saboteur radio operator, captured and questioned by the Germans."

She remembered the parachutist who had been on her drop plane with her on Friday night, a nervous man with a large backpack who'd kissed his Saint Christopher medal before he jumped. He must have been caught.

"How do you know?" Her voice caught.

"You're a good shot, aren't you, Kate?" whispered Max. "I remember all those stories you told us about hunting in the mountains. I know what you're here for. So do the Gestapo." Max gave a low laugh. "Did you know they have your description? They're hunting you."

She had to get away. "The others know you're a traitor, Max," she lied.

"*Non*, they only suspect me," he said. "Meanwhile they do

know you're only here as a decoy. A sacrificial lamb. I don't know what exactly the Brits sent you over here for except that our group's instructions were to let you get caught."

Was he making this up to shake her resolve? It was true Stepney had omitted giving her an escape plan.

"They're using you, Kate. Use them back. Come upstairs."

Doubt hit her. Was there any chance that if she followed him into the meeting he would actually help her get out of this?

No. Once she entered the meeting she'd never leave.

Max played dirty; well, so could she. Success depended on speed and surprise.

She wouldn't hesitate as before. Be weak; fail again. She'd turn him in to the group and let them exact revenge.

Now or never.

She shoved him away hard, kicking out at his leg. He tripped, surprised, and caught himself on the wall, spinning back to take a swing at her. She turned, but not in time, and it caught her on the side of the jaw. She felt a dribble of blood from her mouth. Her head ringing from the whack, she kneed him in the groin.

Grunting in anger and pain, he aimed another blow at her. She ducked and turned, as she'd learned to from her brothers, and kicked his backside.

"You're coming upstairs," he rasped. The blade of a knife caught the blue light. Kate tensed. Suddenly the timed light clicked off, plunging everything into shadow.

Her fingers found the trigger of the pistol. The air trembled as he lunged. She aimed into the dark and fired twice. The shots echoed across the courtyard and there was a thump as Max fell. His shoe scraped against the stone.

Gilberte's third-floor window shutters had creaked open. From the shadows where she stood she saw a man backlit at the open window. All of a sudden lights went on in Gilberte's apartment. The light shone full on the man and she saw his face.

Those gray eyes. The man in Hitler's entourage who'd looked

up from Sacré-Cœur's steps. She recognized a fellow hunter after a target.

Somehow Max had already betrayed her to the Nazis. This meeting, too, was a trap.

It was as if the gray-eyed man smelled her presence. Sensed her like a wolf after its prey.

A shout. "*Da unten, schnell!*"

A gunshot cracked above her head. Stone dust powdered her face. The next bullet wouldn't miss.

She aimed, squeezed the trigger.

The gun jammed.

Sunday, June 23, 1940

Near Canal Saint-Martin, Paris | 9:40 P.M. Paris Time

Gunter hurtled down the winding stone steps and across the courtyard.

Niels, pistol drawn, ran after him.

Gottverdammt, where was Karl?

"Karl?"

"Right over here, sir, come to the shop's back door," Karl was saying. He was herding several protesting young men and women into the courtyard. They waved freshly printed sheets of anti-German propaganda and shouted, "*Brutalité!*"

Karl made them stand against the wall raising their ink stained hands. Gunter shouted at Karl, "Forget them, follow me." This was the underground meeting? He had bigger fish to fry than kids operating a clandestine printing press.

Gunter found the slumped form of Max Verdou against the porte cochère wall. Blood seeped from a bullet hole between his eyes, another shot to his chest. A professional hit. Impressive.

Karl shone his flashlight around the *porte cochère*. "Where is she? Where'd she go?"

She'd murdered him practically in front of his eyes.

And he'd missed her by mere seconds.

"Quickly, after her." Gunter ran from the *porte cochère* through the front door and into the street. Looked both ways.

"There. By the Métro."

SUNDAY, JUNE 23, 1940

The Louis Blanc Métro Station, Right Bank, Paris
9:50 P.M.

Terror coursed through Kate's veins. Just as she crossed the street to the Métro she recognized the sewer worker, who was emerging from the Métro stairs. She had to stop him before he walked into that trap.

"Turn around," she said, taking his arm. Sniffed. He was still fragrant. "Quickly."

He stiffened. "What's wrong?"

"The place is crawling with Germans. Walk slowly."

They descended the Métro steps.

"Max sold the group out." She caught her breath. "I shot him."

"That presents problems," he said. He snorted. "London liked him. Not me."

"So you're a real Sherlock," she said. "But I think your group's riddled with traitors." She was trying to work out how Max and the Germans had known about the café meeting.

"Like who?"

"Jean-Marie."

"Which Jean-Marie?"

She bottled her frustration. "The train worker who left me the message to meet in the café. The one who got picked up by the Germans."

"Him? He's a cutout. Knows nothing."

She thought back to the envelope hidden in the magazine.

"But he can read."

"His name, maybe. Never went to school, he's illiterate. That's why we used him."

"For all I know you're the traitor."

"I'm a lot of things but not that." He growled. "I was three when my father died in the Somme trenches. Haven't liked the Boches since. But Max Verdou's betrayal explains a lot."

The sewer worker lowered his head as they walked toward the wicket. So far Kate had avoided the Métro. She hated that claustrophobic feeling, that feeling of being stuck.

The Métro hadn't changed since 1937. A tired looking uniformed ticket taker still sat at a tired looking wooden wicket stall, the ticket signs indicating first and second class. The same Métro map was posted on the wall.

She liked it even less now. Her heart thudded. Signs indicated two different directions and two levels.

"Which way?"

"Keep going direction Ivry to central Paris. The last Métro usually runs at nine-thirty but this line runs late."

"Hold on," she said, "shield me."

Backtracking she huddled behind him in the tunnel's bend. She tugged off her collodion scar, wiped off the charcoal, quickly powdered her face and applied lipstick. Took the green paisley scarf she had folded in her pocket and draped it around her shoulders to disguise Gilberte's dress.

"Ready?" he asked. She nodded. "Go ahead of me."

Nervous, she handed her prepared second-class ticket to be punched at the wicket. Kept a few paces ahead of the sewer worker as they walked down the white tiled tunnel toward the *2ème classe* area near other waiting passengers at one end of the platform. The uniformed station master stood at the other consulting his pocket watch.

Posters of Salamander shoes à la mode and an upcoming *cirque d'été* were plastered on platform walls above wooden benches. The air was thick with the smell of trapped summer heat and the breath of hundreds who'd passed here before. To a ranch girl used to wide open spaces, it felt like a tomb.

He stood behind her now, holding a rustling newspaper. "We're making radio contact with London," he said, under his breath. "Tonight."

She put a hand to her mouth, pretending to rub something off her cheek. "The cell's blown. London needs to know."

"I figured that. They already know."

They did?

"Send an urgent message saying Swan's dead and Cowgirl needs out," she said, keeping to a whisper.

"No promises." Pause. "Your hand's shaking."

She dropped her hand from her face and kept her head down.

"How will I know if . . . ?"

"Can you remember this phone number?"

She gave a tiny nod, committing to memory the number he whispered. Repeated it. But he'd gone. She watched him out of the corner of her eye as he ascended the Métro's stairs and back out the exit.

She debated following him. But the Germans would be fanning out along the streets, setting up roadblocks. Better to take the Métro and not be caught on the streets.

Kate tried to blend in with the working-class crowd of the quartier waiting for the last Métro. It was late. Nervous, she wondered if something had happened. If it wouldn't come.

She did her best not to stand out among teenage boys wearing short pants and carrying fishing poles, middle-aged women yawning and fanning themselves on the platform. It struck Kate how there were so few men—Paris was populated by women, old people and children—and the conquerors.

The station master and crowd's attention gravitated toward the announcement indicating the last train was arriving. No one paid her any mind, concentrating on the arriving train. She had only a few more minutes to wait and board it.

Shouts came from the stairs leading to the platform.

Passengers were looking to the source of the commotion. German voices echoed. Could she risk their scrutiny, continue to stand here to board the train?

Forget waiting. She fluffed her hair, backing up to the rear edge of the platform where it narrowed to the dark tunnel. Gripped the thin railing. The train light loomed as the shouts grew louder. She backed down the service steps and crouched on the narrow workers' catwalk lining the tunnel. Ahead she could see an indentation—a place to hide. As the train slowed she ran hunch-backed down the tunnel, the coming-up light behind her. She made it into a tiled cove with a lit wired control panel. Behind her the train doors clanked open. German voices commanded the driver to wait.

Had the driver seen her? Would he rat her out?

Huddled low in the niche, she opened her compact, angling it up and smudging the powder off the small cracked mirror. She could make out Germans questioning the station master and passengers on the platform. One gestured to the exit stairs. She hoped they'd search for her up the stairs in the other direction. From what she could make out through the powdery cracks, it looked like only three men.

That wouldn't last long. Reinforcements would arrive soon. There was nowhere left to go. She'd face arrest, torture and execution.

She was so tired. Her mind turned through what the torture would be. How would she stand it to the end? What was the point in even trying to survive? There had never been any path out of France for Kate Rees. They had only sent her because she had nothing to lose. She saw that now.

She could at least spare herself the torture—throw herself on the electrified rail, end it herself now, on her own terms. Give up like she'd wanted to do so many times since Dafydd and Lisbeth had been taken from her.

But what would that get her? Only another failure, nothing to show for herself.

One of the Germans boarded the train. Signaled the driver in the front car to leave. Another took off up the stairs, his footsteps echoing. The third paused on the platform.

The one with the gray eyes.

Sunday, June 23, 1940

The War Rooms, London | 9:40 P.M. Greenwich Mean Time

"What do you know about this list, Stepney?"

On the war room table lay a telexed list labeled *Recovered.*

Stepney brushed his thinning hair back to cover his bald patch. Leaned on his cane. "First I've seen of it, Cathcart."

"Take a look."

It sounded like an accusation.

Stepney read the list of recovered items Cathcart handed him: Swan's airman's rucksack containing a leather jacket, binoculars, cigarettes, a lighter and a black-and-white photo of a woman.

"Bad form for an operative to carry a telling photograph," commented Stepney.

"We only had a six-hour window to drop him outside Paris. This was all last minute. Now the Dutch barge captain in Paris radioed to indicate he's waiting to transport an item."

Item meant a dead agent.

"So your Swan didn't make it. I gather this came via an S-Phone transmission, correct?"

The SIS lackey from the ministry adjusted his tie. Nodded. "And his mission's incomplete. Important items missing."

The SIS mission botched and now, too late, they wanted Stepney's help.

"Cut the shadow talk and put me in the picture, Cathcart," said Stepney. "Show me the transcript of the barge captain's dispatch. Was there a message?"

"Oh, there was a message all right." Cathcart handed it to him. "This was relayed from a Dutch barge captain's Morse code message to a coastal fishing trawler, forwarded by S-Phone to naval operations HQ, who alerted us. It arrived three minutes ago."

Swan's dead and Cowgirl needs out—urgent.

Stepney read the message. Reread it. Good God almighty, she was alive. Stepney's arm jerked, knocking his walking stick over.

By jove, that moxie had kicked in all right.

"That's your operative's call sign. What do you make of it, Stepney?"

"I'd venture to say my operative might have taken on Swan's mission. God knows how. Better fill me in on everything you know and I'll do the same."

Cowgirl.

Sunday, June 23, 1940

Louis Blanc Métro Station, Paris | 9:55 p.m.

Gunter knew she wasn't far. He sensed her presence nearby in this stifling hot Métro.

She wouldn't slip through his fingers again.

She'd be frightened, but she'd keep running, he knew. Not the type to freeze like a scared deer paralyzed in a car's head-lights.

Nein, not this woman. She had killed a man only minutes ago, but that wouldn't shake her. She had assassinated an admiral and barely missed the Führer then kept her head about her to escape his net of searchers. She was strategic and smart. He felt a flicker of admiration. Face it—she was a worthy opponent.

His uncle said a clever adversary deserved respect. Locking up a drunken lout on Friday night for slitting his wife's throat didn't exercise the gray cells. But outwitting this woman would be more than an exercise. It was a deadly game, and Gunter was ready to play.

After all the setbacks and obstructions of his investigation today, he was finally closing the net. The Führer's clock was ticking with twenty-three hours remaining and Gunter needed manpower.

He heard a noise from the tunnel, but Niels came running before he could peer past the platform's edge.

"Sir, there's a report of her sighting at the Grand Palais."

Had his hunch been wrong? "When?"

"I don't know. For your ears only. The Kommandantur's calling on the radio in the staff car. Says it's urgent, sir."

Gunter didn't want to leave the Métro station until he could summon a search party.

The Métro workers were arriving with pails and mops. The gates were creaking shut.

"They're closing the station, sir," said Niels. "The station master says they clean and shut down the line for work in the tunnel."

"Instruct them to hold off," he said.

Niels ran toward the workers.

Then Roschmann came flying down the stairs forcing the Métro workers aside with a contingent of soldiers. "The *Kommandant* sent orders for me to assist your search."

Glad, for once, to see the Vet, Gunter turned and stared into Roschmann's eyes. "Alive. I want her alive, *verstehen Sie?*"

Roschmann nodded.

"I hold you accountable, Roschmann. She's no use to us dead."

Gunter pointed down the Métro tunnel.

Sunday, June 23, 1940

In the Métro, Paris | 10:05 P.M. Paris Time

Kate clung to the Métro tunnel wall on the narrow catwalk with one shaking hand, her other yanking at the taut wires connected to the control box panel. Electrical outages occurred all the time in the Métro system—short circuits, power failures. How often in that summer of '37 had she sat in a dark train while the Métro crew fiddled with the fuses in the tunnel?

C'mon, something had to happen. Lights flickered in the tunnel. She yanked harder, ripped out one, then another, then pulled on a red switch. A flicker, then the tunnel and platform plunged into darkness.

Phew. She'd have a few minutes.

Knees trembling, she stumbled ahead on the catwalk flush with the tunnel's right wall. Her breath came in spurts. She tripped and fell down onto the greasy track, skinned her knee on the pebbled track bed. No doubt they heard her. Pulling herself up, scrambling and trying to avoiding the electrified third rail in the dark, she maneuvered back onto the catwalk. She squeezed herself against the wall, feeling her way, twisting her body to stay close and keep her balance. The catwalk was designed for workers repairing the tracks, not a getaway. She stumbled her way around a curve as best she could in darkness, her hands guiding her along the sooty wall. *Don't think, just move.*

The tramping of boots, shouts, then a buzzing and sizzling behind her. A zapping sound. A scream. Someone had stepped on the electrical rail, the death rail.

Keep going.

Sweat poured down her neck. Everywhere it was pitch black. Adrenalin coursed through her. There had to be a way out. That burnt metallic peanut-like smell from the heated oil for the wooden block used for braking layered the suffocating heat permeating the musty underground. Her pocket holding the diamond-encrusted scarf bounced against her hip as she hurried.

Don't let the bastards win. Run. Escape.

Flashlight beams bobbed on the soot-caked Métro tiles. More shouts. The tramping boots were getting closer.

Don't look back. Don't stop. Don't let the darkness and fear take over.

Her fingers doggedly raked the sooty wall and finally caught on metal. A ladder with iron rungs. Without a moment's hesitation she climbed, pulling herself up, no idea where it led. And then she was in another tunnel, a branch line lit by blinking red signals and a sign pointing in the direction ST-GERVAIS.

The swish of rat's tails on metal pipes overhead didn't faze her—they knew where to hide.

So did the rats behind her.

Run.

Now she was beside a single track and there was no more catwalk, just a narrow concrete strip alongside. Feeling her way through the dark, trailing her black soot-stained hands on the wall, she ran deeper and deeper along the track into the tunnel and more darkness. Then another branch opened and she followed that toward distorted echoes of metallic screeches. As she approached, she could make out white-yellow sparks from blowtorches. Under portable lights men in coveralls and protective face masks were repairing a rail line.

The close air tasted metallic and made her lightheaded. Afraid she'd pass out, she stumbled ahead. Climbed onto a short platform.

The crew bent over their work, but one had noticed her, set down his torch and pulled up his mask. "The Métro's closed. It's off limits here. Dangerous."

Sparks flew and he walked toward her, shooing her away.

"Please help me . . ."

"Go back the way you came."

"I can't."

"No one's allowed here. The boss has orders to call the *flics.*"

"So help me get out. I'm lost."

He ambled closer. "You're not French."

Tears brimmed in her eyes. A hard lump sat in her chest. At the end of her rope, she didn't know what to do.

"*Emigrée,* eh?" he said. "Afraid my duty's to report you."

"Please, no one has to know. Point me out of here."

One of the work crew shouted at him. "What's going on, Lefèvre?"

He turned. In that moment she hid herself behind the pillar. Saw the EXIT sign where the tunnel branched and forced her legs to move.

She didn't know how she made her burning legs climb the narrow metal staircase. The scent of fresh air had given her a second wind. Then she met locked metal gates.

She used her lockpick set, replaying the Cockney burglar's instructions in her head, fighting down her panic and impatience. Two minutes later, she stood on the street and breathed in the open air. Long breaths, again and again, until her mind cleared.

Where was she?

Sunday, June 23, 1940

Section D HQ Somewhere in London | 10:00 p.m. Paris Time

Stepney labored down the back stairs of the nondescript building, Section D's covert headquarters, with a bulging case of files to read. Not only was his ulcer bothering him again, but so was that sinking feeling he was too old for this job.

A wave of melancholy swept over him.

Everyone these days was young, sharper-than-sharp. He knew asset material when he saw it.

As he had with Kate Rees, the first moment he'd spotted her in the Orkney firing range.

Antiaircraft searchlights swept the dark London sky above him. Barrage balloons bobbed over Westminster, and sandbags shored up the other anonymous buildings, hubs of defense strategy.

Kate Rees hadn't been the first agent he'd sent on a condemned mission. He'd do the same again for King and country.

Yet he couldn't believe Kate had gotten this far. And without contacts in his network.

After the first war, Stepney's French military comrades had joined the Sûreté and Deuxième Bureau. Due to his war injuries, Stepney had instead gone into military intelligence. But he kept those relationships going during the interwar years, building a network of shared intelligence that benefited both countries.

He'd always been hands-on with his operatives, training and preparing them to be field ready. It would have been a crime not to. This fiasco with Swan illustrated what happened to a novice. No matter the mission's outcome, he'd never deployed an agent without the necessary skills and tools. He lost sleep over the spies he'd sent to their deaths, whose patriotism put him to shame. No glory for them after the bloody war ended—no mention in the history books.

He had promised his wife he'd retire, stay home. Angie, his childhood sweetheart, had deserved it after tolerating his schedule all those years. But in 1936 she'd been run over by a bus in front of his eyes as he went to meet her in Trafalgar Square. Too late.

Stepney reached the staff car. A Wren opened the door for him. "Sir, I've received orders to drive you to Communications. You're needed."

What had happened now? he wondered.

"Carry on, then," he said.

Weary, he settled in his seat, taking the flask from his hip pocket for a stiff drink. He offered Kate a silent toast as the car whisked him through the night.

Sunday, June 23, 1940

Rue du Faubourg Saint-Martin Near the Canal, Paris
10:15 p.m.

Inside the Mercedes, Gunter cupped the listening device over his ears. Nothing but clicks and garbled voices on the line from the Kommandantur. And the damn heat hadn't let up.

"Repeat that, *bitte*," he said, irritated.

"*Jawohl.*" More static.

"Can't you get the line clearer?"

A series of clicks. "The report filed five minutes ago . . . is that better? Can you hear, sir?"

"*Ja, ja*, go ahead."

"This incident report of a sick . . . cleaning woman . . . wearing an apron . . . odd as reported."

"Odd? How do you mean?"

More clicking.

"I've changed the line, is this better, sir?"

"*Ja*, much better."

"The report said she had no papers. A woman suffered an epileptic attack at the Grand Palais. She was driven by Oberleutnant Wiesen's adjutant to a *clinique*. Highly unusual but done as a gesture of goodwill. The adjutant's request for her papers brought no results. I thought you'd want to know after the all-out alert."

Moot point now.

Or was it?

"What time and location was this?"

He wrote it down.

What if . . . ? She would definitely have had time to make it here and shoot Max Verdou.

She would have gone to the Grand Palais for a reason. A contact?

Would she try to return?

He'd trust Roschmann and the hundred men at his disposal to find her if she was somewhere in that Métro. Roschmann had too much riding on this to screw up again.

"Where is Oberleutnant Wiesen's adjutant?"

"Unclear, sir."

"What does that mean?"

"His unit is on duty but his whereabouts are unclear."

Of all times.

"Search every brothel if you have to. Find him."

The real question was, if it had been her, what had she been doing at le Grand Palais?

Sunday, June 23, 1940

On the Right Bank, Paris | 10:30 p.m., Past Curfew

Curfew.

Kate had to get off the street. Out of sight. Away.

Could she hide in a courtyard for the night, to avoid roving patrols? Risky at best. Or chance 124 rue de Provence, the address the doctor had given Philippe, if she could even find it? A risk, too.

RADA.

She'd shot an informant, German troops hunted her, if she didn't get off the street she'd be dead, her only option was to go to the only address she knew.

Now.

She slipped off her torn sandals, ran while keeping to the shadows and studied the street names.

Her pulse raced. The surrounding streets could hold checkpoints. Maybe a description of her had already circulated.

Focus.

Do the one thing that made sense. Get out of here.

She dipped into an alley, the windows darkened with blackout curtains. Pigeons cooed from the rooftop. The pearlescent orb of the moon had risen in the cloudless, star-dusted sky. She knew the address was near the Opera and checked the compass. Better head south. Nothing for it but to steal the bike behind the potted plants.

Kate now tied the scarf around her head, put on the tortoise frame glasses. Feeling guilty, she left fifty francs by the potted plant and walked the bike over the cobbles. She'd keep to the small streets to avoid a checkpoint or patrol.

She scanned the dark street. Clear. Took a deep breath.

Then pedaled as fast as she could.

Twice she heard voices in German, checkpoints, and cycled away. She got lost. Terrified, she forced herself to read the street signs, orient herself. Somehow she made it to rue de Provence. She remembered this narrow street behind the *grands magasins* or department stores from 1937, when it had been filled with prostitutes. Even now, one or two peeped from doorways. No curfew for them.

Cars pulled up at 122 rue de Provence, discharging men in suits, women in evening dresses accompanied by men in German uniforms. They pressed a buzzer and disappeared inside. The cars drove away. What in the world?

Wary, she parked the bike next door. No. 124 was a glass and metal art deco door that yielded to her push. She crept up the staircase to the first-floor landing and saw CHAUMIERE, the name the doctor had given Philippe, on the door to the left. Something told her to stash the scarf. She tiptoed down to the mid-floor WC. It stank. But she put down the lid, stood and felt around to find a crevice above the window. After stuffing the scarf with the diamonds inside, she took a pee.

Back upstairs, she knocked softly and the apartment door drifted open.

"Philippe?" she whispered.

Blackout curtains shrouded the room. In the candlelight she made out a figure. A figure roped to a chair with a bandana in his mouth.

Philippe.

His eyes darted. He was trying to tell her something.

Then the tip of a pistol was nudging her in the ribs. A black-haired man appeared from behind the door.

To get this far and be caught like this.

Furious, she whipped her elbow back and up to connect with his ribs. *Crack.* As he lost his balance, she stomped on the man's feet. Hard. Again.

Just like she'd learned fighting with her brothers.

The man staggered back. Fell. She stomped the man's wrist and heard a yelp of pain. His pistol skittered over the faded Turkish carpet and she grabbed it. Moaning, he tried to get up.

She kicked his chin and threw him off balance.

Not wasting any time, Kate struggled with the rope knots binding Philippe. Once free he pulled the cloth out of his mouth.

"Nice reception committee," she said.

"For you, *chérie*," he said, "I do my best."

She leveled the pistol as Philippe tied the groaning man's wrists and ankles behind him, then stuffed the wet bandana in the man's mouth. He rifled through the pockets of the man's suit.

"Bonny Lafont, or so it says."

Her shoulders ached, her feet stung and weariness dragged her down. But she couldn't stay here. "Time to go," she said. "The doctor's a rat."

Philippe shook his head. "This *mec* followed me from the Métro."

"So we can't stay here."

"You don't understand. It's something else. Personal."

Like she'd believe that?

"This place isn't safe."

"Au contraire. We're right next to le 122, the fanciest bordello in Paris."

She'd seen the glittering crowd entering.

"How can this place be safe?"

"The Nazis and celebrities next door are otherwise occupied, you could say."

"Why's this personal? What's Lafont got on you?"

Philippe pulled the groaning man up by the collar. "Questions later."

He dragged the half-unconscious man down the hallway into

a closet. Locked it. Returned and parted the blackout curtain a crack. Seeming satisfied, he readjusted the curtain and walked over toward her.

"That man recognized me in the Métro."

"Recognized you as what? A spy, an escaped POW? Tell me what's going, Philippe."

A muscle in Philippe's cheek twitched. "He's my father's employee, a gangster working for the government, the Germans, anyone like my father who'll pay him enough."

The candle wax dripped. With the draperies and wall hangings the place felt like a museum. An ancient cocoon.

"That explains nothing. What are you?"

"It's not your business."

Bone-tired, she'd had enough. "Fine. I'm leaving and taking the pistol."

"Don't do that. It's safe here until the morning." Philippe rubbed his forehead. "My father's in the government. He wants me to join the military branch of puppet cowards." Philippe shook his head. "We don't get along. But I owe you."

And she believed him. Was too tired not to. "Call it even. Except for the bruises."

She saw a phone. "He might have called someone."

"He was about to before you came in."

"And I should trust you?"

"Face it, you like me." He grinned. "Don't you, *Chanedough.*"

She wanted to sock him. No denying his good looks, though, and he knew it.

Stop it.

He was trouble. With a capital *T*, like her Auntie Mae used to say.

"You'll have to get rid of your gangster."

"He'll go out with the morning trash," said Philippe. "Where he belongs."

"I'll feel better if you make sure he's tied up tight."

Philippe went back to check on the man in the closet.

Reckoning that he couldn't hear, she picked up the receiver.

Nervous, she hesitated before dialing the number she'd memorized from the sewer man.

RADA.

The sewer man had said he'd make radio contact with London, but should she believe him? He'd been at both compromised locations. If Philippe was right and there was no chance for her to get on the barge she needed a way out.

She dialed the number: PASSY 6014.

Several rings before a voice said, "*Oui?*"

She debated on how to identify herself. *Simple is best,* Stepney had said. "You gave me this number half an hour ago. Any news?"

"Delayed until morning."

The line went dead.

In the hallway, she saw Philippe pulling a table against the closet door where he'd stuck the gangster. Good thinking.

Discouraged and stuck here until tomorrow, she dragged a heavy chair to barricade the front door. If someone moved it, she'd wake up. Afraid she'd pass out with tiredness if she didn't sleep, she cradled the pistol, sat down on the Damascene embroidered gilt-edged recamier, kicked off her ragged sandals and put her dirty feet up.

"Where'd you learn to fight like that?"

Was that almost admiration in Philippe's voice?

"Five brothers. So don't get any ideas," she said, holding the pistol.

"Oh, but I have."

"Wake me in an hour."

She put her head down and was out.

Sunday, June 23, 1940

Grand Palais, Paris | 10:45 P.M.

Oberleutnant Wiesen's adjutant, Joachim Heller, stood at attention, sweat beading his forehead. His full cheeks were flushed and he held his cap under his arm. He looked about eighteen.

It had taken fifteen minutes to locate Heller on duty—he'd been accompanying Oberleutnant Wiesen's party at the Café de la Paix at la Place de l'Opéra. They called that *duty*? Gunter had also summoned Oberleutnant Wiesen.

"You followed procedure filing your report," said Gunter, consulting his notebook. He and Niels stood with the two soldiers on the gravel path beside Grand Palais. "Commendable. However, your report indicates she had no papers. Can you explain that?"

Heller's cheeks blushed even brighter red.

"Yes, sir. I mean, no, sir. The woman was suffering from an epileptic fit, sir. The doctor insisted she needed treatment and he'd deal with that later."

Convenient.

"You will follow up on that and inform me after we're finished, Heller," said Gunter. "Now please talk me through the events."

With a worried blink, Joachim did. The *Oberleutnant* corroborated.

"However, I didn't accompany my driver to the clinic," said Weisen with a clipped Hamburg accent. "I had an appointment."

An appointment at the Café de la Paix.

"Think back, both of you please, to what happened prior."

"What do you mean?" asked Wiesen.

"I mean before you heard noises and investigated. Had you seen the woman in the apron before? Around here, talking to someone?"

Joachim's brow furrowed as he concentrated. "I was waiting for the *Oberleutnant* by the door. He was in a meeting. I had a smoke."

He paused.

"Go on."

"I heard a woman, but I'm not sure it's who you mean, sir. Could have been a cleaning lady or part of the staff."

"Continue, Adjutant Heller."

"I just heard a woman's voice."

"How's that?"

"I don't speak French. Never saw her. But I remember *Antwann*."

Gunter rolled that in his mind. "Antoine?"

"Possibly, it sounded like that, I'm not sure. But she said it several times."

Oberleutnant Weisen took off his hat, revealing prematurely white hair over his young face. "Not Antoine Doisneau?"

"I don't know, sir."

"He's an engineer attending the conference here with École Polytechnique."

"Can you explain this participation? What it's concerning?"

"It's technical work. Classified," said Wiesen. "But now that I think about it, I recall Antoine was talking to someone."

Could this mean the woman was in contact with this Doisneau? Gunter took this idea down in his notebook.

"You mean the woman wearing an apron?"

"No idea," said Weisen. "They were somewhere over here by the trees. I couldn't see." Weisen, his face flushed from drink, seemed anxious to return to his party. "If that's all?"

"One more thing, *Oberleutnant.* What's this conference concerning?"

"As I said, it's classified."

Gunter took the *Oberleutnant* aside. "I appreciate that it's sensitive." He showed his RSD badge. "I'm investigating on the Führer's orders, *verstehen Sie*?"

They both knew the Führer's orders superseded any rank.

Weisen debated. Gunter recognized the nervous shift in his eyes. Then he glanced around and lowered his voice. "Directive 17. It'll be your neck, not mine, if this gets out."

"Doubtful. I have no idea what that means." Gunter smiled. "But I'll have to ask you to elaborate or I wouldn't be doing my job."

Weisen scowled. Then he leaned and spoke into Gunter's ear. "French scientists from the École Polytechnique attended and submitted classified material. That's all I will say."

"So Directive 17 involves material presented at this conference?"

"As I told you, it's classified. Pursue your enquiry with Kommandant Kostoff."

He'd follow up with Kostoff. For now his gaze took in the hedge, the cypress tree which would provide a screen. A scene always spoke to him if he listened and paid attention. His shoes crunched on the gravel and he surveyed the dimly lit ground. He bent down to pick up a cigarette butt with his handkerchief. "Does Antoine smoke?"

"A Frenchman? Of course. He was smoking and speaking with someone right here."

But neither could identify this person as the woman wearing an apron Joachim had driven to the clinic.

After the *Oberleutnant* and his helpful adjutant left, Gunter took one last look around, then joined Niels.

"Any luck, sir?"

"It makes me wonder, Niels. Let's say it was her." They headed back to the Mercedes under a star-studded sky. The Champs-Elysées where Niels had parked looked like a thick black velvet ribbon, empty and discarded. "Why would a sniper disguised in an apron appear at the classified meeting with top French scientists from the École Polytechnique?"

"Hard to say, sir."

Gunter opened the car door.

"She's got contacts, a network. And time's running out."

For both of them. He glanced at his watch.

Twenty-two hours.

"Drop me at le Meurice."

Sunday, June 23, 1940

Near Place de l'Opéra, Paris | 11:30 p.m.

Kate battled awake through a fog of fatigue. Her jaw hurt and her bones were achingly tired. A telephone was ringing somewhere.

Where was she?

Her feet wiggled, hitting the frame of an old-fashioned sleigh bed surrounded by threadbare tapestries in candlelight, ghostly wall hangings showing dead animals. The warm, wax-scented air felt tomb-like.

Then she remembered. Felt for the pistol. Her hand came back only with a rucked-up linen sheet.

Panicked, she bolted upright.

Where was the pistol?

She wobbled off the bed, still in Gilberte's dress, stiff with dried perspiration. Seconds later, she found the pistol under the blanket. Sighing in relief, she rubbed her eyes, then staggered, barefoot, pistol in hand, to the front of the apartment.

Philippe looked up from the chair where he sat reading by candlelight. He wore an old silk robe, his clothes hung over the back of a chair.

"I heard the phone ring," she said, suspicious. "Who was it?"

Philippe stood and parted the blackout curtain, glanced out, then replaced the curtain. "I'm leaving tomorrow."

"For where?"

"London, I hope. I can't risk staying in Paris."

"How are you getting out?"

"I don't know."

That put a new spin on everything. Or did it?

"Look, I need to get to London," she said. "It's dangerous for me here, too."

"You're not the only one. Bad news." Sadness filled his eyes. "Gilberte was arrested."

Kate shook her head. Didn't want to believe it. Was it her fault somehow? She thought of the Bon Marché claim check for the rifle, Max's appearance at Gilberte's building, the shoot-out she had caused.

Only a matter of time until they were all caught. Heartsick, her thoughts went to Ramou, Dédé, the sewer worker . . .

"Were others arrested, too?"

Philippe averted his eyes. "Probably. No details yet."

Her heart thumped. She'd let her guard down, gone to sleep and now was a sitting duck.

"Who's to say the doctor hasn't informed on you or me? He gave us this address. It's time to go."

Pause. "He's not a doctor."

"What do you mean? His office smelled like a *clinique,* I saw medicines in the cabinet and he wore a stethoscope."

Was this a trap?

Idiot. Again. "You've been lying to me." She raised the pistol at Philippe.

"Aim that somewhere else. Look, Luc's an actor. Comédie Française," said Philippe. "The real Dr. Nicot died in the exodus. *Alors,* the *clinique*'s been convenient for operations. But now Luc's left. We can't use that place for a while."

Philippe wasn't the man she'd first thought. At first he'd been a Casanova, a Gallic seducer; now he seemed more like . . . what? A spy? A patriot with personal convictions? There were layers upon layers she didn't understand.

"You're telling me about this Luc for a reason," she said. "Why?"

"He hid people. But he's gone and people in London want Antoine Doisneau's information. You've turned up, so I'm supposed to assist you."

"That's a different tune than you sang tonight. You told me there could be no replacement for the engineer. Why should I believe you?"

"The message said I'm supposed to say *cowgirl.*"

Her code name. Which meant Stepney had gotten her message from the sewer work. That was fast. What about her evacuation? How was Philippe in contact?

"Prove it."

"The less you know the better."

"Don't give me that. How are you in contact with Stepney?"

"I'm not and I don't know anyone in London," he said. "There was only one transmission. All the relayed messages go through several channels for security. The exit plan is still up in the air. Might not happen."

She desperately needed to sleep. To digest this. "I'm meeting Antoine tomorrow."

"*Bon.* Tomorrow we'll go our separate ways. You meet Antoine; I'll dispose of the gangster, then set up a letter drop at Place de la Concorde to communicate." Philippe set down his book—Rimbaud's verse. "I'm going to help you, okay? Right now you look awful." He blew out the candles. Took her shoulder.

She wanted to shake him off. But her legs wobbled and she grabbed the chair for support.

The next moment he'd picked her up in his arms.

He set her in the bed, then plopped down next to her. "Tomorrow's busy. Sleep while you can."

SUNDAY, JUNE 23, 1940

Le Meurice, rue de Rivoli, Paris | 11:30 P.M.

"Directive 17? That's an open secret, Gunter," said Kostoff.

Kostoff, the *Kommandant* of Gross-Paris, sat back in his striped pajamas in the hotel suite of le Meurice. "It's one of our imminent plans to invade Britain."

Plans to invade Britain?

"Britain's petrified," Kostoff said. "The little island's preparing. They've always had a fortress mentality. Read the paper, it's all there."

Kostoff pushed a British newspaper across the inlaid marquetry side table. A copy of the *Evening Telegraph* with bold typeface headlines FRANCE GIVES UP. Underneath this an article titled INVASION THIS MONTH OR THE NEXT BY SIR NEVILE HENDERSON.

Gunter wished his rudimentary English were better. But he understood.

Kostoff eyed him over a cup of warm milk. He smiled in amusement. "I'm surprised you didn't know this, Gunter."

Gunter's RSD job gave him little time to ponder the European war theater. His world was crime. Catching criminals was what he did best.

"I'm a policeman, sir."

Kostoff added a shot of brandy to his milk. Offered a shot to Gunter.

He shouldn't, but . . .

"Danke, Kommandant." He accepted and felt the liquid amber soothe his scratchy throat.

"The Englanders know we're going to invade. A matter of time. So they better start learning German, *ja*?" Kostoff poured them both another shot. "You're awfully quiet, Gunter."

"My investigation is ongoing, sir," he said. "Have you gotten an update on Roschmann's progress with the Métro search?"

Kostoff waved him off. "Don't worry about that," he said, his voice slurring.

"Worry, sir? This is my investigation."

"It's under control."

"Roschmann doesn't know about the assassination attempt, does he?"

"Course . . . not." Kostoff emitted a loud belch.

Drunk.

Before Gunter could press him for details, Kostoff's phone shrilled. He answered it and a lengthy conversation ensued. For the second time today Gunter sat listening to Kostoff drone away on the phone.

His mind began to wander. Maybe it was the brandy but this morning's scene on the steps replayed in bright color in his mind—the toddler's yellow dress, the bullet hole in Admiral Lindau's forehead, the rifle he caught glinting among the green leaves as he looked up to the sniper's window. Directive 17, a sea invasion—what if Lindau had been the intended target instead of the Führer?

Kostoff hung up, yawned. The next moment he was snoring.

Gunter poured himself another shot of brandy, downed it and left.

Outside in Kostoff's salon office, he saw reports and telexes in the in tray. He caught the attention of the aide standing at a file cabinet.

"Has the Feldgendarmerie report on the search at Métro Station Louis Blanc come in?"

"Half an hour ago, sir."

Why hadn't he been alerted? Frustrated he thought of the delay, time lost and the actions he would have taken,

Gunter showed his RSD badge. "Of course, a duplicate report has been sent to my office at the Kommandantur, correct?"

"I have no orders to that effect."

That damn Roschmann should have sent it there immediately.

Gunter nodded. "An oversight. I'll take this for now. Kommander Kostoff instructed me to bring this to the Kommandantur."

The aide sat down, swiveled in his chair and thumbed through the papers. Pulled several from near the top.

"Has any follow-up action been initiated from this report?"

"None that's come into the office, sir."

So Roschmann hadn't caught her.

The aide handed the report to Gunter. Pointed to a log.

On purpose Gunter scribbled something indecipherable. "*Danke.*"

A drunk Kostoff wouldn't remember and the aide would be off duty in an hour.

Gunter put his legs up on the desk in his temporary office in the Kommandantur at Place de l'Opéra. He pulled out the photo of Frieda he carried in his wallet, kissed it and propped it on the desk to keep him company. She'd be asleep; he wouldn't call her and disturb her.

He adjusted the Anglepoise lamp to read the message from Wiesen's adjutant, Heller. Heller reported returning to the clinic to follow up on the woman's missing papers. He'd searched the clinic and the living quarters but the doctor had gone.

Of course he had. Gunter doubted he'd even been a doctor.

He positioned the Steiff teddy bear between his shoulder and neck as a pillow and began reading Roschmann's report.

MONDAY, JUNE 24, 1940

124 rue de Provence, Paris | 2:00 A.M.

Kate snuggled into a familiar warmness, the cocoon of Dafydd's arms, nuzzling his bristly chin. A candle burned, suffusing the room in a yellow glow. Secured with Dafydd in a pillowy softness, her legs wrapped around his, that heat rose in her. He rubbed her nose against his, pulling her closer. Her breath quickened.

Her eyes blinked open.

It wasn't Dafydd she held, nor his scent, nor his warm legs sliding against hers. That old aching sliced through her. She doubled up, tight with pain.

She remembered the flames of the inferno. Her family gone.

The revenge in her heart.

Beside her in the bed, Philippe lay propped on his shoulder, watching her.

"Who is Dafydd?"

"Why?"

"You kept calling out to him. To a Lisbeth."

Her hands went cold.

"My husband and baby . . . They're dead. There was a terrible explosion. Because of the Germans . . ." Her throat caught. If today was the last day of her life, she'd make it worth it. "I will make them pay."

Philippe's legs still entangled with hers.

"So that's why you're fighting the Brits' war for them?"

"It's my war now."

The cold shell inside her cracked. For the first time since Margo, the woman she'd trained with, she'd told someone the truth.

She'd wanted to give up so many times, to die.

In Orkney, the constant reminders of Lisbeth and Dafydd had almost driven her to throw herself off the munitions factory roof. She'd wanted to slit her wrists the day she found Lisbeth's rattle in the burned rubble.

On the run here in Paris after her botched mission, she'd felt the urge to end the struggle. Last night she'd contemplated throwing herself on the Métro's third rail—a quick death. Yet she'd fought through the hurt, determined to get her revenge.

Her time was running out. She had to make it count.

Our last two agents didn't make it.

Philippe pushed her damp matted hair from her cheek.

"You're tough on the outside, *chérie*, and soft inside," said Philippe. "*Comme un bonbon.*"

"Bonbon?" She stared in his wondering eyes. "I learned from my father if you fall down, you've got to get up. You either die or you fight and get even."

Her hands ran over his chest. She felt a stirring of something that she thought had died with Dafydd.

She inhaled his scent. Couldn't believe how her hands were pulling him close. How she wanted him.

"I still love my husband. But I might die today." She stroked his bare arm. "Can you deal with that?"

Part IV

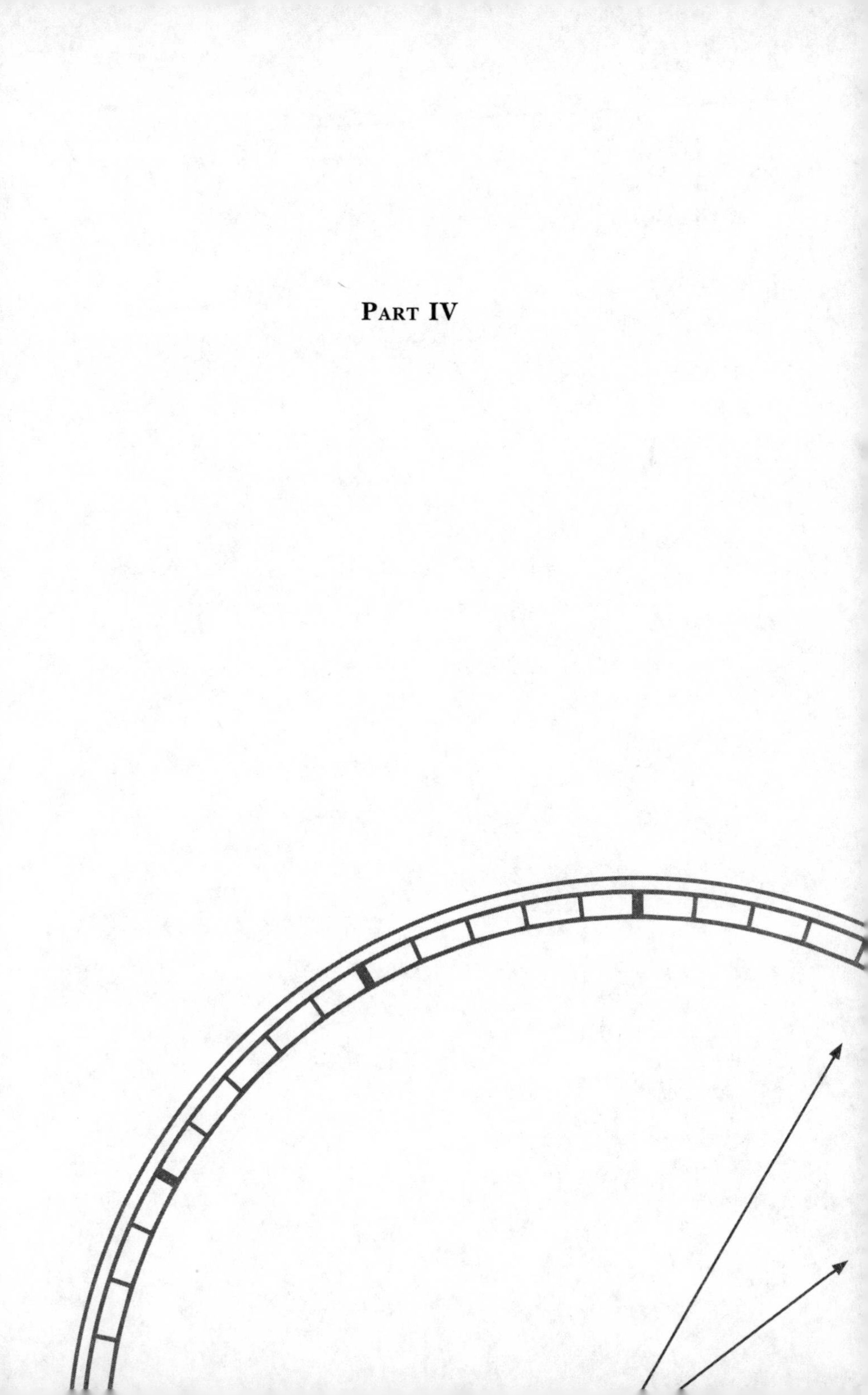

MONDAY, JUNE 24, 1940

On the Seine at Île de Puteaux | 5:30 A.M.

The Dutch barge captain strained to hear the radio message over the rumble of the engine.

"Location? We're on the Seine, outside Paris, anchored at the Île de Puteaux. Relay that we can't stay for much longer, it's almost sunrise."

Faint tappings came over from the other end—the coastal fishing trawler's signalman on the Channel. The captain waited as his radio operator tapped Morse code, which the trawler would relay to London. As part of the Alpha network, the Dutch barge captain rescued stranded RAF and British soldiers from pick-up points on the outskirts. He transported them to the trawler on the coast, who handled the extraction to Britain. It had worked for three weeks.

He got a thrill having one over on the potato head Krauts, and the money wasn't bad either. *So far, so good,* he thought, but they had increased river patrols on the Seine last night.

Lights blinked—a signal from the lockkeeper's house to proceed. Wary of an early morning German river patrol, he wanted to leave.

"Can't you hurry up?" said the barge captain to his radio operator.

"Instructions are to dislodge your fuel line," said the radio operator.

"Why would I do that?" The captain slammed his hat on the rudder.

"You'll say the fuel line's broken and you're in the middle of repairs," said the radio operator, reading from his decoded message. "Stall for time. Wait for the package."

MONDAY, JUNE 24, 1940

124 rue de Provence, Paris | 9:00 A.M.

Sleepily, Kate stretched in the cool bunched sheets. Her toes curled, bathed in sunlight. She rubbed the sleep from her eyes and felt the empty space beside her in the sleigh bed.

For a moment she wondered if she'd dreamed it—Philippe's arms, the way he made her feel. But his musky smell on the sheets was real. Her dreamy haze gave way to a wistfulness of how it might have felt to wake up with him. Then a twinge of guilt. Guilt for being selfish and hungry to live while she could.

So she'd slept with him. She let the guilt evaporate. It had happened and it was over.

A note with a diagram of Place de la Concorde was propped by the candleholder thick with dripped wax.

Taking out the garbage. Will see if I can find anything on the barge. Look for a msg at X marks the spot this AM.

Philippe had marked an X for the drop location. What Stepney called a dead letter drop to pass items or information between agents without a direct meet. This one looked like a flower box.

And at least she'd had a couple of hours' sleep. If she'd scared him off, or he was planning on betraying her, she'd be gone before he returned. She'd rethink the dead letter drop if it came to that.

Stepney had said, *Trust no one.*

And did she trust Stepney?

Max's words tunneled through her mind: the parachutist on the plane, the café, using her as a distraction for another mission.

It made a kind of sense. The idea that she'd been used infuriated her. Was it true?

Would this contact with London pan out?

So many balls in the air. She needed to catch one. Make the dead engineer's mission count.

She glanced at the time. She'd determined to meet Antoine no matter what and get those plans. Now she had to figure out a plan.

A smell of coffee came from somewhere. Real coffee, not the ersatz chicory blend that was all you could get these days. She draped a bedsheet around her, walked down the corridor to the closet where Philippe had put the attacker. Empty.

She left the apartment and crossed the deserted hallway to the WC. Found the scarf where she'd wedged it. *Good,* she thought in relief.

She wound the silk scarf into a headband, tied it around her head, tucking and hiding the diamonds, then realized she must look like an idiot draped in a sheet.

Never mind. She hurried back to the apartment, barricaded the door and quickly put on Gilberte's slip. She was going to follow the scent of coffee. She'd kill for it right now.

The aroma came from the open kitchen window overlooking a small courtyard lined with soapy washing tubs. Damp laundry hung from a clothesline. A laundress sat smoking and sipping from a cup. Kate tiptoed down the back service stairs from the small kitchen to the courtyard.

"*Bonjour,*" she said, waving the ten franc note she'd taken from the lining of her jacket. "Smells wonderful, can I buy a coffee?"

The laundress looked up. Slavic cheekbones, wide-set eyes. She'd be quite pretty if it weren't for her pockmarked complexion.

Kate mimed drinking and pointed to her cup.

The woman's French was nonexistent but between Kate's hand gestures and the proffered bill, she caught Kate's meaning. Lifted up her palm in a wait gesture, showing lobster-pink fingers puffy from washing. Patted a place to sit beside her.

Kate joined her. The laundress nodded, took the francs and disappeared into a courtyard door.

The hanging laundry caught her eye. A schoolgirl uniform, a nurse's outfit, a gold lame–trimmed brassiere with matching crotchless panties. A woman stood in the open window of the adjacent building overlooking the courtyard, wearing her hair in a bob and nothing else. She blew smoke in the air, saw Kate and smiled as she pinned up her hair. The next moment she was gone.

Laughter floated down.

Of course, this was the bordello. After a steaming cup of real coffee, her mind was jumping with ideas.

Back at the apartment's kitchen sink, she used a sliver of the laundress's Marseille soap, gave herself a quick sponge bath, lathered her hair, rinsed and pinned it up wet. She rinsed out Gilberte's dress and rolled it damp into a shopping bag by the sink. Now she put on the almost dry nurse's uniform, purchased with fifty francs from the laundress.

"Shhh, *la madame*," she'd said.

Kate folded the scarf into a small triangle, safety-pinned it to her bra strap and wore it under the nurse's uniform. Hardly even a bulge. She was ready.

She waved to the laundress, who was back to scrubbing, and crept across the courtyard. She turned the corner and bumped into the ample bosom of *la madame.*

"Where do you think you're going with my outfit, mademoiselle?"

Monday, June 24, 1940

The Kommandantur, Place de l'Opéra, Paris | 9:00 a.m.

Gunter moaned, clutching Frieda's back, feeling her arched spine under the silky lace slip he'd seen in Gilberte Masson's shop. He ran his hands over those freckles dusting her naked shoulder and shivered with want. He was home in Munich.

Outside the window a rifle tip glinted in the sun.

"Sir, sir?" A faraway voice coming closer. Loud knocking.

Mein Gott. His sleep crusted lashes blurred his vision. Instead of Frieda's warm body he was clutching the Steiff teddy bear. Drool dripped from his mouth. He was sprawled over a desk in an office chair, a report under his cheek.

It all flooded back now—Paris, on the trail of the female sniper . . .

His dream of Frieda had been interrupted, but at least it had been replaced by the intoxicating smell of coffee.

Niels had entered the office followed by a young woman in uniform. Gunter reached for the cup Niels offered him.

"*Danke,*" he said, sipping the scalding sweet coffee, letting the aroma wake him up.

"Sir, Roschmann wants you for a meeting in the *Kommandant*'s office," said the female *Feldkorps.*

Little gray mice, that's what they called them, suited in drab gray, even their neckties. All business, too.

Gunter sat up to disguise the bulge in his pants. "Noted, I'll join him shortly."

She headed out to the adjacent office, which was teeming with human activity. Until the door closed behind her the room resounded with the staccato chomping of a telex machine.

"We just got this off the telex," said Niels. "Antoine Doisneau's been located, sir."

"Good work, Niels. Get the car."

"But Roschmann's meeting—"

"Forget it. He didn't find her. We need to talk to Doisneau."

"Before that, sir, this needs your attention. The radio unit's ready to code your reply."

His eyes snapped to the message from the Führer. He was wide awake now.

Twelve hours.

What he wouldn't give to be back in that dream. In bed with Frieda, in that silky lace. Anyplace but here.

Monday, June 24, 1940

Bordello, 122 rue de Provence, Paris | 9:30 A.M.

Kate figured the madame of the bordello would be willing to negotiate; Libby, the Madame of the flophouse in Sand Flats, always had been.

As Kate expected, Madame was a businesswoman. A diamond covered her needs.

Kate used the tools from the tobacco-tin palette Peter had prepared for her to alter her look. A few quick charcoal touches darkened her hair and brows and shadows under her eyes aged her. She completed her outfit with a peaked cap, white shoulder cape and white socks under ankle strap sandals. After removing condoms from the "doctor" bag Madame had given her to complete the look, Kate surveyed herself in the bordello mirror. Different enough from the dirty blonde in a blue sweater at the café and the scarred servant wearing an apron. Old women were invisible, Stepney had said. Still, her disguise couldn't hide her height.

She'd called the sewer worker's number again. No answer.

No radio contact. No escape route.

She'd have to hope Antoine came through.

She needed to steady her nerves. Plan for possible outcomes. Antoine might have informed the Germans. There might be a welcome committee waiting for her.

But if he had, he'd never get the diamonds.

Maybe Antoine had photographed Directive 17 as promised and it would be a straight handoff—diamonds in exchange for the film and the escape route.

In the best-case scenario.

Never assume.

She wouldn't give him a chance to rethink. She'd show up without warning at the École Polytechnique.

Monday, June 24, 1940

École Polytechnique, Latin Quarter, Paris | 9:45 a.m.

"*Bonjour*, Professor," said Kate to Antoine in the corridor of École Polytechnique in the Latin Quarter. "*Un moment, s'il vous plaît.*"

She smiled, beckoning him to where she stood by the tall windows. Honey sunlight streamed over the scuffed wood floor.

Antoine did a double take and took a long moment to recognize her in her nurse's uniform. Nervous, he looked around the corridor, then shot her a look of annoyance.

"You were s-supposed to call first."

So he could tip off his Nazi cronies from last night, or his superiors in the lab? She didn't trust him. Yet he was what she had to work with.

He picked his cuticles.

"Get to the point, Antoine, give me the photographed plans and we keep to the deal."

"Deal?" Antoine took her elbow and pulled her into a doorway. "The deal was the diamonds first," he whispered. "I told you last night. Now I'm n-not so sure. I don't know who you really are. Or w-what you're doing. Last night several members were rounded up. Now they're being q-q-questioned by the Gestapo. My contacts don't t-trust you."

Did he mean Gilberte? It sickened her to think their capture might have been her fault.

Damn, she needed his help to escape.

"I understand, but it's Max Verdou who's the traitor. He sold out the group meeting at Gilberte's. He's the reason she was arrested."

Antoine snorted. "Think I'll f-fall for that."

"I shot him with this." She took the pistol from inside her waistband and handed it to Antoine. Nervous, he almost dropped it.

Voices echoed down the corridor.

Her hands trembled. She shouldn't have come. What if he turned her in?

"Where's your office, Antoine?"

"Over there. But the l-lab's quieter," he said.

After checking, he motioned her inside the laboratory. Panicked, he ushered her through the lab to a back sink. Stuck the pistol down a chemical waste chute.

"I'm an engineer, n-not a spy."

"And I'm a markswoman. Spying's not my game either."

The lab smelled of a sulphuric residue, soldered metal and chalk dust. Kate noted mathematical equations chalked on a blackboard. Gibberish to her, but it got her wondering.

"What's an engineer doing working with the Germans?"

"You must un-understand, my department project is closely watched by the Germans."

"I still don't get it, Antoine."

"Research I began in 1935 . . . It's g-government work."

"Why's it so important?"

"Back in Birmingham, Swan and I worked on a team d-developing a cavity magnetron. It's a device emitting high frequency r-radio waves."

She remembered Dédé saying Swan was a priority. She tried to put this together.

"Swan said buoys . . . How does that fit?"

"When I came back here, I got funding from the government . . . I c-c-continued the work."

Antoine picked his cuticles. It drove her crazy.

"Continued what work, Antoine?"

"Condensing emitters in buoys. The Germans have taken over everything and adapted it. For the military. There's charts and maps outlining r-routes of the naval forces assembling for Directive 17."

"What's Directive 17?"

In the sunlight, Antoine's Brillo-like hair haloed his head. She doubted a comb would make much headway.

"The invasion. I got word to Swan . . . I o-only trusted him." Antoine reached in his lab coat pocket. Took out a handkerchief and blew his nose. "And now he's dead. This was a m-mistake."

Hot air seeped through the open bubble glass windows.

"No, it's not," she said. "We'll make this work."

"You're a s-s-strange Yank."

"Because I'm in disguise?"

"Why involve yourself? It's not your war." His thick eyebrows arched. "You've got n-no stake in this."

So he distrusted her because he didn't know her angle?

She could have said her husband and baby were dead thanks to the Germans, or that the mission had been the only thing driving her to live. That she was thousands of miles from home and would do anything to survive, including risk herself further. But there wasn't time.

"It's my war now, personal reasons," she said. "Give me the film, Antoine."

Antoine took a step away from her, knocking into a table and rattling its glass beakers. His eyes were unreadable. He was hesitating.

Or stalling, waiting for the Gestapo to come and arrest her?

Part of her wanted to get the hell out of here before she was caught. The other part wanted to slap him and make him come to his senses.

But neither of those things would get her what she desperately needed. *Strategize.*

Maybe she could exploit his uncertainty, his nervous awkwardness.

"You're not the helpless type," Stepney had said, grinning.

"That's why we chose you. Flirt, charm, use your female arsenal. But think like a man."

Kate reached for Antoine's hand, held it before he could pull away. Put another small twist of diamond-studded scarf she'd cut out in his palm. "Swan died in my arms trying to reach you. He gave his life to get these plans to England. You're a patriot, Antoine." She pulled his elbow, drawing him close. "Help me get them to England. Help me make sure he hasn't died in vain."

He glanced at the diamonds, twisted the fabric into a knot and slipped it in his pocket. "The Polytechnique's relocating t-to Lyon. In the last week the G-Germans have appropriated much of our research. We've had to assist m-moving the materials."

Fear clamped her stomach. The Germans were about to invade.

"These materials aren't here, Antoine?"

A shake of his head.

All this and the materials were somewhere else.

"Everything's at the Ministère de la Marine, or the Kriegsmarine, they're calling it."

Kate had cycled past the building on rue de Rivoli where it met Place de la Concorde. It had sickened her hearing the German marching band parading in front like they owned it. How the German officers strutted in and out of nearby Hotel Meurice.

Why hadn't he told her that before?

"Do you want your research taken like this? Used by the Germans?"

"The Germans demanded my c-cooperation. They're like spiders taking over our department's work. It's not like I've had a choice . . ."

"But you do now. The Germans have no right to steal your work."

Consternation filled his round features. "*Peut-être, mais* the Kriegsmarine's guarded."

Antoine needed more backbone for this.

"You've been there officially, correct?" Of course, he had. "You should be able to walk right in."

"The place is so huge I'm not sure w-where to look . . . "

Break it down, Stepney would say when she'd been overwhelmed at the enormity of a task. *Break it into bite-sized pieces. Doable steps.*

"This is what you do, Antoine," she said. "Tell them you've returned to follow up on certain documents to make sure they've arrived. You need a receipt, you're cataloging the documents list at their location in case further action's needed." He was listening. "Let me see the official pass you used."

He showed her an entry pass stamped by the Kriegsmarine. It was written in German and French.

"Looks valid."

"I'm a scientist, not an a-actor. They'd s-s-see through me in a second." He bit his lip and looked away.

She wanted to seize his jacket lapels and shake him. So much was at stake.

At least she sensed that it was fear holding him back, not a double cross.

Hadn't Stepney said, *Make them want what you're selling*? Or was that her pa?

"Antoine, Swan meant these diamonds for you. His widow would believe you can do this. With them you can keep your family safe, help your group."

Muted voices came from across the hallway.

"That's my colleague. We've got a meeting."

She wouldn't let him weasel out on this.

"Postpone the meeting, Antoine."

She could feel every diamond in the scarf safety-pinned to her bra strap under the nurse's uniform.

He nodded. "Give me a minute."

"Hurry," she said, afraid he'd chicken out. "Then we'll go to the Kriegsmarine together."

Beads of sweat trickled down her neck. She reached to wipe them away but her hands shook. A long minute passed. Outside the window a green parakeet swooped through the tree branches—one of the growing flock who'd escaped their cages in the Parisian exodus from the Germans. She wished she could escape, too.

She rooted through the drawers of the lab desk but found nothing useful. In the adjoining cloakroom she found a lab coat with a badge: *A. Medan, assistant de laboratoire.* A good disguise change. She stuffed the lab coat in the case, the badge in her pocket, and took a deep breath.

A troop truck of soldiers idled in the courtyard.

Fear weighed like a brick on her chest. This was all taking too much time.

By the time Antoine returned, having furnished satisfactory excuses to his colleague, she'd taken the first aid kit off the lab wall. It was small and of red metal, a white cross painted on one side. Handy.

"We'll go out the b-back after the trucks leave."

She had to control her fear, keep her mind thinking. "How did the Germans prepare the invasion so quickly?"

"Quickly?" He snorted. "Over the last d-decade Germans collected postcards, English phone directories, employed c-c-cartographers and even consulted Swan's and my . . . our u-university proposal to map out the invasion. It m-makes me angry."

Good, angry enough to do something. He was getting back.

"The Germans p-planned this for years," said Antoine. "They're g-going to invade, it's only a matter of when."

"The when is . . . ?"

The troop truck engine rumbled.

"Ask the planets," Antoine said. Gestured to the photo of Hitler, black and white and with that pretentious mustache. "He does everything by astrology." Antoine opened a drawer. "But this is real."

Inside were booklets titled *Militärgeographische Angaben über England.*

"M-military geographical information about England," he translated for her. "These b-booklets are broken down into eight regions of Britain, incredibly detailed, highlighting strategic attack information, from the locations of train stations and industrial areas to soil composition."

Kate thumbed open the booklet with photos and diagrams.

"You speak German, Antoine?"

"One of seven languages I speak."

Wasn't he working for them? Selling out his bosses?

"But why contact Swan now?"

"I tr-trust-trusted him. My w-w-wife's pregnant." Antoine lowered his voice. "She's J-Jewish. There's wr-wr-writing on the wall."

"What do you mean?"

"She's not safe. Or my b-baby. I need to get her from Lyon out of France. C-can't wait any longer."

She believed at least some of what he'd said. Maybe she wanted to believe him and this clouded her thinking.

"You need to give me the diamonds," said Antoine. "Now. Or m-my comrades won't believe me."

Kate felt almost a physical punch in the gut. Playing hardball.

Well, so could she. Except she was in enemy territory, surrounded by black uniforms and jackboots that clicked with precision on the marble floors.

If she gave him the diamonds, he could disappear or have her arrested.

RADA. Use whatever you can and play dirty, her pa would have added.

"No dice."

"C'est quoi, ça?" asked Antoine.

"The deal is I get the film and a way out, then you get the diamonds." She turned, about to leave. "Decide, Antoine. Now."

He hesitated, then reached for the telephone and made a call. A few mumbled words she couldn't make out.

He hung up, handed her a gas mask. "Keep your m-mouth shut."

Relief took over. Then nerves. They'd be walking into the lions' den.

Monday, June 24, 1940

The Kommandantur, Place de l'Opéra, Paris | *9:15 A.M.*

Gunter washed himself up with Lanvin perfumed soap in the marble *salle de bain* adjoining his requisitioned office. He felt almost human despite his summer cold. And ten times fresher in the clean shirt Niels had scrounged up for him. His nose ran and his arms tingled. It was the feeling of expectation he got when a case started coming together.

Antoine Doisneau was the key to capturing the English assassin. Based on what Gilberte Masson had given up, he realized that this Englishwoman had never been connected to the British snipers. She'd been operating alone. Tonight, he could be home, having dinner with Frieda and giving his daughter her Steiff teddy bear, Papa's late birthday gift, with lots of kisses.

"Hoffman." Kommandant Kostoff appeared in the hallway, blocking his way. Roschmann stood beside him, arms folded. "We're waiting for your report."

Caught. He'd stall. Get them off his back.

"Of course, *Kommandant.* As soon as I collate the ballistic findings from the lab."

"Consider it a command that you attend the meeting," said Roschmann. "Now."

Commanding him? Was that a leer stretching his fat lips? Gunter's knuckles tightened on his attaché case.

"Roschmann, need I remind you again I'm on the Führer's express orders . . . "

"As we all are," said Kostoff, his tone stiff and formal. All traces of last night's overindulgence were gone. "And as the Führer reminded me in a phone call not two minutes ago."

Now these two had the Führer's ear. Gunter's blood boiled. The Führer interrupting again! He still had just under twelve hours to the deadline.

"There's a telegram for you, Gunter. Come to my office."

He smothered a sigh. "*Jawohl*, sir."

Gunter held back a moment in the hallway so he could motion to Niels, instruct him to find Doisneau and report back. Gunter would slip away at the first opportunity and follow his own agenda.

Trying to hide his irritation, Gunter joined Roschmann in the *Kommandant*'s office.

"You're off the active investigation, Gunter," said Kostoff.

This was the meeting? They couldn't take the case away from him. He kept his voice even with effort. "I'm following direct orders."

"As am I," said Kostoff. "You bungled a simple operation in the Métro last night. The saboteur got away. It's all in Roschmann's report. Now you'll furnish him with your current leads and hand over the investigation."

Roschmann had sabotaged him. Engineered a SD coup—neat and bloodless.

"My boss, Gruppenführer Jäger—"

A telegram from Jäger was thrust at him: *Roschmann now leading the investigation.*

Monday, June 24, 1940

The Kriegsmarine, Place de la Concorde, Paris | 10:30 A.M.

At the Concorde Métro station, Antoine handed her the pass labeled *Laboratoires École Polytechnique.* They had ridden over in a second-class Métro car, where Antoine had busied himself writing in a notebook—equations, it looked like. Maybe it had helped him calm his nerves.

Kate wished she knew how to calm her own nerves now. Her eye caught on two German navy officers flanking the tall entrance doors of the Kriegsmarine. They stood at attention, holding rifles. Fear prickled up her neck. A third guard greeted and checked the passes of two arriving officers ahead of them. Would her bordello-costume nurse's uniform and Antoine's pass get them through?

One of the officers, his naval trench coat slung over his arm in the warm morning, noticed Antoine.

"More problems, Doisneau?" he said, a frown under his pink cheeks. His French bore almost no German accent.

Antoine Doisneau's lips parted. *Don't freeze,* she prayed. *Remember the plan.*

"I hope not, Captain Hinzer," said Antoine, with no noticeable stutter. "My department asked me to check that our latest documents arrived in order."

Kate had been holding her breath. Relieved, she let it out.

Hinzer raised his gloved hand. "I'm teasing you, Doisneau." He swiveled his attention to Kate as if registering her for the first time. She didn't think he was, though. From his behavior, control was Hinzer's game. "Someone injured?"

They'd prepared the story. Yet Antoine hesitated. Her throat caught.

Why didn't he spit it out?

"Remember those boxes that got mixed up in transit, Captain Hinzer?" said Antoine. "Those contained first aid supplies from the École Polytechnique."

Antoine was in charge of the bomb shelter under École Polytechnique, including its first aid supplies, so if Hinzer checked, their ruse would hold up—although not under serious scrutiny.

"Was that on some list, Doisneau?"

"Exactly, sir. The discrepancy stood out on yesterday's log. It needs rectification and Sister Marie is going to help me sort the first aid supplies."

"Carry on," said Hinzer, his tone dismissive.

He strode ahead to join his colleague.

One hurdle crossed.

Hinzer turned back. "See me on your way out. Both of you."

Of course it wouldn't be that easy.

The naval guard handed back her pass. She wished her knees weren't trembling.

They entered the rectangular courtyard. The German-language building directory smelled freshly painted. At the far end sailors unloaded supply trucks. Cleaning women dusted the bannisters and mopped the staircases. The place buzzed like a well-organized beehive. No one paid attention to them.

For now.

Hurriedly, she noted the side exits, the front and rear staircases. Where was the service exit?

"We're going right, then upstairs to the first floor," said Antoine under his breath. "Stay with me. It's important we look like we know where we're going." Antoine stopped speaking to let two sailors hurry past with boxes. "We've got ten, fifteen minutes before Hinzer will check. Pokes his nose everywhere. That's the way he is."

"We can do this, Antoine," she said, steeling herself.

"Keep your eyes down."

Antoine was right. Best not to invite attention.

Despite his earlier protests, Antoine acted with purpose, moved quickly. Two hallways and a staircase later they stood in front of a door labeled KOMMUNIKATION.

Antoine rubbed at wiry wisps of hair that had stuck under his collar.

"Do as I say; k-keep your mouth shut."

His stutter had returned.

Nervous, she nodded as he opened the first double door into an anteroom choked with the haze of cigarette smoke. To the left a typewriter and teletype machine sat on an exquisite rococo desk of inlaid wood. On the right, beyond another open double door, she glimpsed the salon adjoining: the crystals from a dripping chandelier catching the morning light, blond wood panels lining high walls.

She heard intermittent conversations in German through the half-open door to the office next door. Antoine motioned for her to wait. Clutching the Red Cross case, she stepped out of view.

He spoke in German. A perfunctory conversation, from what she gathered. All she could make out were the spitting clicks of the telex. A phone rang.

"*Danke*," said Antoine, emerging with a black log book.

She trailed him to the salon. Her eyes popped seeing a wall covered with charts, a large map of the northern French coastline. The map was pierced by colored stickpins. She recognized labels with the insignia of the different branches of the German occupying forces, the Luftwaffe, Kriegsmarine, Abwehr. She felt glad Stepney had made her memorize them.

Kate followed Antoine to the side salon, looking at her watch. Already three minutes.

The army-green metal cabinets lining the salon's intricate woodwork wall spoiled the classic charm. What appeared to have once been a dining table had a large diagram spread across it. Rulers and magnifying glasses littered the surface. Reflections from the crystal chandelier created dancing prisms of light on the table.

None of the diagrams meant anything to her.

She glanced at the door, afraid someone would walk in.

"Where is everyone?"

"Gathering for some big shot's visit, I h-heard. But Hinzer will be here any moment."

Crazy, she'd been crazy to push Antoine, to even think they could—

Footsteps sounded in the outer office. Her heart jumped in her chest. She didn't know which would be more dangerous, to hide, which would out her immediately if she was caught, or to let herself be seen accompanying Antoine, which might raise questions.

She ducked behind the door, but the footsteps receded. A false alarm.

She joined Antoine at the table. He set down the log book and opened the metal cabinets. Inside were rolls of paper banded with numbered labels. He scanned the shelves, business-like. Looked back at the log book as if matching entries to the rolls of paper.

"Where is it, Antoine?"

"Here. It's the Channel map."

"Is that Directive 17? You're sure?"

"Shh, come closer."

She did and took the unwieldy roll from him while Antoine fiddled with the Minox camera.

"I'll spread it out," she said, "it's faster."

Kate unrolled the crinkling sheet. A grid overlaid a map recognizable as the northern coast of France, the Channel and the southern English coast. To her untrained eye, the red and blue lines and arrows showed routes, coastal landing sites and troop advances through Kent and Sussex.

"See," whispered Antoine. "Ship routes over the Channel,

land forces and troop emplacements." Antoine clicked the shutter, emitting a barely audible ratchet sound as he advanced the tiny Minox's film roll.

The pine furniture polish mingled with smoke and the odor of a half-eaten sausage left in a bin. The smell made her want to gag. Antoine methodically photographed the map's sections. It seemed like hours but it took only seconds. "Done."

Kate rolled up the sheet. Pointed to the table diagram. "Photograph this, too." Little bell-shaped figures—buoys?—dotted the British coastline. That had to be important.

"Why?"

"It's dated this morning. Could be an update. Just do it."

But Antoine was closing the log book. She took the Minox from the table, fumbled with the tiny shutter. Her damn nerves made her hands shake.

Voices came from the office. Antoine replaced the paper roll in the file cabinet. Kate focused on the curious diagram, taking photographs from top to bottom.

"H-Hinzer's coming."

Stuttering again. Not a good sign.

"Keep him occupied, Antoine."

"You c-can't be found in here." His voice vibrated with fear.

"I won't. I'll go out that side door." She paused, took the rest of the diamond-studded scarf and slipped it in his pocket. "Good job, Antoine. Now how do I escape?"

"You've had the d-diamonds all along?"

"I lied."

He met her gaze.

"So did I. Diamonds in exchange for the film. We're done."

Her heart cramped. "What?"

"The rest doesn't involve me. I'm a scientist . . . d-d-d-don't you understand?"

"But there has to be a barge, a way out—or you wouldn't have asked your friend and former colleague to risk his life, right?"

A quick nod. His lip quivered and he looked away. She grabbed his elbow. "Tell me so I can get this to England."

"The c-contact was supposed to handle all that—getting Nigel out safely. His job was to meet him last n-night."

"You mean at the Grand Palais?"

"T-talk to him."

She put it together. Philippe.

Then Antoine was hurrying out of the salon with the log book. Trying to control her shaking hands she snapped the last shot. She hoped the effort was worth it. It had to be.

But did she really trust Antoine? He had the diamonds, could turn her in and rise in Hinzer's estimation.

Kate closed the side door without making a sound. Seeing no one in the corridor, she ran.

MONDAY, JUNE 24, 1940

The Kommandantur, Place de l'Opéra, Paris | 10:30 A.M.

Back in his office, Gunter twisted the phone cord while he waited for Jäger to answer.

"Gruppenführer Jäger's in a meeting," said Jäger's secretary.

Avoiding him.

"Tell him it's urgent."

"Under no circumstances can he be disturbed. He'll return your call as soon as the meeting's over."

Click.

A mounting dread tingled his spine. Now he studied the report he'd taken from Kostoff's aide last night, the one Roschmann had submitted without sending a copy to Gunter's office. The rat hadn't found the Englishwoman and had skewed the report to make it sound like the whole debacle was the result of Gunter's incompetence. There was no mention of Gunter's having been called away from the search.

Fatigued to the bone, he'd fallen asleep reading it. He should have been on top this. *Gottverdammt.*

A setup. Roschmann, always ambitious, had found a way to take over a high-profile case and to make Gunter the fall man all at once. He wanted the glory and a medal from the Führer. And Jäger, never one to stay on a sinking ship, had jumped. Leaving Gunter accountable.

Gunter didn't want to think what would happen to him and his family.

Meanwhile Kostoff had bound him to his office to finish his report.

But it was Gunter's neck on the line, not Kostoff's. Gunter's neck and his family's safety. The Führer never forgot. He had to find this woman.

"Any word from Niels?" he asked the gray mouse in the outer office.

"He called and left a message, sir."

"Why wasn't I informed?"

"I was ordered not to disturb you."

So she was under the SD's thumb, too.

He mustered a small smile. "A miscommunication. The message please."

A phone number. He'd instructed Niels not to trust anyone here with information.

Downstairs, he found a driver. Had him stop at the first café he saw. Bought a phone token from the waiter and called the number.

"Where's Doisneau?"

"I'm at l'École Polytechnique, sir," said Niels. "He's already gone."

"Where to?"

"He left with a nurse."

So she'd given up cleaning and entered the medical field. Always one step ahead.

"Tell me what you see, Niels."

"Roschmann's just pulling up, sir, with a troop truck."

Gunter could just picture Roschmann trailed by his goons, officious and heavy handed. "Go talk to the concierge. Slip him that hundred francs I gave you. Find out where the scientist and the nurse might have gone. Then slip him the other bill to keep his mouth shut."

"Oh, he told me already, sir."

Gunter caught his breath.

"Doisneau's gone to the Kriegsmarine," said Niels. "According to the concierge, he's been taking documents there all week."

The Kriegsmarine was six blocks away. Gunter glanced at his watch.

"Good job, Niels. Meet you there."

Monday, June 24, 1940

The Kriegmarine, Place de la Concorde, Paris | 10:45 A.M.

Kate stuffed the Minox in her waistband and pulled the nurse's cape closer despite the heat. She passed the office where Antoine had returned the log book and heard a teletype clacking and conversation—Hinzer?

A phone slammed and she heard a chair scrape back in the other room. Cigarette smoke wafted accompanied by the creaking of footsteps over the hardwood floors. Holding her breath, she tiptoed past the door. Her heart pounded. How soon until her presence was discovered? If she was caught with . . .

A car horn interrupted her thoughts. No sign of Antoine. Sounds of car engines and German voices floated. Hunger gnawed at her. She reached the other end of the hallway that overlooked a side courtyard. Here, telephone wires hanging from fresh timber telephone poles and metal grids trailed overhead to the adjoining building, which had a gated garden that opened onto the street. A way out.

But how to get there without crossing the courtyard?

Footsteps and voices came down the hallway.

Her pulse pounding, she searched for a place to hide. Only offices. Under the stairway stood the WC door with the distinctive diamond-shaped window. She wrenched it open to find brooms, mops, a metal pail and boards covering the porcelain drain—a squat toilet. Closed herself in the smell of must and mildew. Smock-like aprons worn by cleaning staff hung from nails.

Her breath came in panicked gasps. There was not even the possibility of climbing out the barred, dust-filmed window. No escape.

Kate peered out the small diamond. Several Kriegsmarine officers stood in conversation at the door she'd just run past. One, pockmarked and with bristling red hair, had a cigarette hanging from the side of his mouth. He was shouting as he punched a paper. The tall one next to him turned and she recognized Hinzer's profile. Her spine stiffened.

She heard Stepney's voice in her head: *Concentrate and focus. Think and plan your next move. Forget the shaking in your hands. You don't want to sneeze in a hot cleaning closet reeking of disinfectant. Or forget the fact that the enemy throngs the building.*

RADA.

She couldn't worry about Antoine. Her escape with the film was all that mattered. She had to get the hell out of here. Any moment Hinzer could have the building searched for a nurse.

She advanced the film in the camera until it was completely wound. Tented her hands to protect the film from exposure, popped off the camera cover and slipped the tiny film roll into her bra. She removed the nurse's outfit, put the Minox back in the compass case, balled it all up and stuck it under some rags. Then she pulled a smock from the nail and slipped into it, buttoning a few buttons to keep it loose in the front and to avoid her pocket's bulge. She'd saved two diamonds from the scarf and pinned them to her panties. That done, she took a cleaning rag, tied it around her head and waited.

When she looked again, the hallway was empty. Now was her chance. She'd blend in with the cleaning women, get out and head to the letter drop Philippe picked in Place de la Concorde. She slid out of the stifling closet holding the mop and pail. Five seconds later she'd gone downstairs into a black-and-white-marble-tiled foyer.

It looked like the whole of the Kriegsmarine had swarmed

into the courtyard to greet an arriving Mercedes, swastika flags flying on the side of the hood. Shouts of "*Heil Hitler.*" Her shoulders tensed—had plans changed and Hitler returned?

But a quick look revealed a woman in a red cloche hat with a stylish net veiling her face, a matching red froth of a frock on the arm of a bemedaled, corpulent and chubby-faced man in a flamboyant white uniform with epaulets and gold braid trim. Murmurs of "Göring" came from the crowd.

The head of the Luftwaffe himself. Smiling and saluting to the cheering sailors, reveling in the glory. A known attention seeker, he was visiting the Kriegsmarine HQ. Concerning the invasion, she wondered?

This was the man who had commanded the Luftwaffe to bomb Orkney. His planes had strafed Hoy's naval base, killing Greer's grandmother. Her fingers gripped the mop. Automatically she imagined him in her crosshairs, mentally aligned a clear shot to his temple.

Wake up, girl.

She had no Lee-Enfield rifle, only a greasy damp mop.

Control yourself and move.

She hunched her shoulders, passed the supply trucks and kept along the walls. Her heart hammered in her chest. At last she joined a cleaning woman mopping the marble entryway under the glass awning. Kate kept her head low, set down her bucket and mopped.

"Quit making double work for me," the woman said. She had tired eyes and a scarf tied around her head.

Kate realized her bucket was empty. Suspicious.

"*Pwahh.*" Kate expelled air in a "silly me" gesture. Lifted her bucket and headed to the green metal water spigot. Nerves taut, she noticed a staff service door. More pails and buckets inside a stone-paved corridor. This must have been that service exit she couldn't spot before.

The woman with tired eyes was watching her. Pretending to exchange her mop, Kate slid into a group of cleaning women dumping their dirty rags into a basket for clean ones.

Act.

She hunched lower, trying not to stand out and shuffled ahead with the group.

At the first opportunity, when no one was looking, she broke off and ducked through the service door. Any moment she expected the Germans to notice a rogue cleaning woman out of line.

Head down and chest heaving, she kept going. She hurried into the discreet side garden, which was lined by manicured topiary trees in planters. She'd seen this from the landing—she remembered the garden had a back gate to the side street.

Ditching the mop, she kept on the gravel path past damp ivy-covered walls and blooming primroses. By the open grilled gate in the stone wall stood a lone sentry. Through the gate she could see a laundry truck parked in the side street. Drawing closer she saw straw baskets piled high with dirty rags near the sentry post.

Sweat trickled down her brow. Her body felt ten degrees hotter with the smock covering her clothes. The film stuck to her breastbone. Dizziness washed over her and she steadied herself against the wall. If she didn't hurry, she'd pass out.

A man was loading the laundry baskets into the truck.

She smiled at the sentry, who examined her pass with a bored expression. Would he notice that her pass came from École Polytechnique? Wonder why a cleaner would have such a pass? Pinpricks of fear ran down her damp spine, the heat overtaking her.

He was winking at her, an older woman, the flirt. Young, blue-eyed, a cornfed country boy, reminding her of Joss, her middle brother, a rogue-eyed charmer who set hearts fluttering in Beaverton. But this young German was not her brother; he was the enemy.

From the corner of her eye she saw three uniforms by the roses. One of them was Hinzer. Her heart jumped. She had to get out of here.

She felt a sharp pinch on her rear. Unbelievable. Kate swatted the guard's hand away from her behind.

The guard, now aware of the uniforms, stepped back at strict attention. Had Hinzer and the men noticed her? Without thinking, Kate lifted a laundry basket full of smelly rags. Then she was lugging it through the gate. Grunting and smiling at the surprised truck driver. She shoved the basket in the truck and put her finger to her lips.

And then she was walking fast, pulling the rag off her head. Down the side street, staying close to the wall toward rue de Rivoli. In a jewelry shop doorway, she unbuttoned the cleaning smock. Panting, she pulled on the long light blue lab coat from École Polytechnique. Took the glasses from her pocket and fluffed out her hair, hoping she looked like a lab assistant.

Without looking left or right, she stepped back out onto the pavement as if she belonged.

Act the part. Believe it.

She mingled with pedestrians, walked pigeon toed and didn't stop. Kept breathing, expecting a shout for her to stop any moment. Or Hinzer to pull up in a car. She kept her eye on the bright spark of red geranium at the Place de la Concorde station—the letter drop. A long block away.

Monday, June 24, 1940

The Defense Ministry Laboratory, London
11:00 A.M. Paris Time

Stepney was leaning on his cane but straightened up as the door opened.

"This way, sir," said a brisk lab coated technician. "We've got those results. Interesting."

Finally. Time was running out. This had to lead somewhere.

Stepney followed, struggling to keep up with the young man's stride. How he hated growing old.

"That's the first one a young boy discovered on the coast near Ramsgate." The dark green buoy with a blinking blue light sat on the stainless-steel lab table. "Here's the second one, which was found farther north. On ministry orders we partially disassembled it to see what makes it tick." The second lab table was covered in neatly sorted piles of wires and metal parts.

"Recovered where exactly?"

The young technician pointed to a spot on the map of the southeastern coast. "By the pier here, sir. It's a restricted area, off limits to civilians but the boy and his grandmother were collecting cockles. In dismantling the buoy we discovered this. Take a look through the microscope."

Stepney leaned down and saw a magnified series of letters printed in a dark casing. A telltale signifier of a German-designed product.

"Typical Siemens product." Stepney returned to the table with the buoy parts and picked up a piece of wire mesh. Held it in his hands, remembering the last war, the German airfields he'd flown over. The radio towers.

That was it. "The damn thing's emitting radio waves."

"We need the *how* of the how, sir."

"There's a whole department at the University of Birmingham developing this. They call it microwaves or some such. It's classified work," Stepney added belatedly.

He reached for the phone on the wall. "Now stop standing around and get working on the *how* of the how, young man."

Monday, June 24, 1940

The Kriegsmarine, Place de la Concorde, Paris | 11:15 a.m.

Gunter had avoided all the fanfare of Göring's entourage and instead took Niels to track down Antoine Doisneau. They stood in a high-ceilinged office where the adjutant made them wait while he tore off a telex. He read it, rolled it up and slid it into a pneumatic tube. The telex whizzed away to the upper regions of the Kriegsmarine and the adjutant sat back down. "Who did you say you've got an appointment with, sir?"

"Antoine Doisneau, where will I find him?"

"Doisneau's affiliated with us through the École Polytechnique."

"That's not what I asked."

"I don't know, sir. He doesn't work in this building, but he was here earlier. He signed out the log book and signed it back in."

"Show me."

Gunter scanned the entry. Scribbled numbers. "What's this for?"

"Several École Polytechnique documents."

"Was he accompanied by a woman?"

He thought. "I think he was with a nurse, but I'm not sure."

"Where is she?"

An officer in a crisp uniform swept in and faced Gunter. His narrow eyes took in Gunter's rumpled linen suit. "Who are you?"

Gunter flashed his RSD badge. "Gunter Hoffman, Reichssicherheitsdienst. You are . . . ?"

"Kriegsmarine Captain Hinzer, at your service." Hinzer gave a slight bow of his head, clicked his heels. "How may I assist you?"

Good, the type who knew which side to butter. A naval officer a world away from the intrigues at the Kommandantur.

"For reasons of security, I need Antoine Doisneau and a nurse who was accompanying him located. Now." Gunter figured Hinzer would assume this involved Göring's security and treat the search as a priority.

"I saw them not ten minutes ago."

"Good. Gather a team."

MONDAY, JUNE 24, 1940

Place de la Concorde, Paris | 11:25 A.M.

Kate scanned the sidewalk and the people on the stairs of the Métro entrance at Place de la Concorde. No one paid her any attention. Standing sideways so her body shielded her hand, she rooted behind her in the flower box—the dead drop for Philippe's message. Where was it? Panic struck her at the thought Philippe hadn't come through as he'd said he would.

Or maybe he'd been caught.

Then she felt something metal, rectangular, entwined in the plant.

Once the thing was in her palm, she hurried past the Métro entrance and up the pitted stone steps into the Jeu de Paume leading to the Tuileries Gardens. She collapsed on the nearest bench. Leaves rustled in the plane trees overhead; she could hear children laughing.

The tin of Flavigny anise-flavored sweets she'd dug out of the flower box contained a cigarette paper with a message:

Papers cleared. La Felicité *moored at Île de Puteaux leaves at noon. Acknowledge and destroy this.*

So Philippe had fixed her false papers and passage on the barge.

He'd come through, hadn't he?

She smudged the penciled writing and tore off a bit of the

cigarette paper, then shredded the rest into tiny pieces. Dumped them in the nearby bin. That done she sat back down and with the pencil stub left inside the tin she wrote carefully so as not to tear the plain remaining thin bit she'd saved of the cigarette paper.

See you there.

She took a deep breath. Another.

She'd do one thing right. She'd escape with the film roll of Directive 17 Nigel gave his life for. In a small way avenge Dafydd and her little Lisbeth.

Then she'd confront Stepney.

This would happen. She'd find her way to Île de Puteaux.

She had to hurry.

Monday, June 24, 1940

The Kriegsmarine, Place de la Concorde, Paris | 11:25 A.M.

Kriegsmarine captain Hinzer was nothing if not efficient. Within fifteen minutes Gunter studied the building plan Hinzer provided as he listened to a cleaning woman, who was twisting a rag in her fingers.

"If you can believe it," she said, "here's me doing all the mopping and she's got no water in her bucket."

Gunter nodded. "Point out where you were."

"There. But then she's in line to get a new rag."

Gunter traced the route with his finger; the office, the map room, the courtyard.

"And then?"

"Poof, gone."

Antoine Doisneau had disappeared, too.

He re-questioned the young sentry.

"Yes, sir, a cleaning woman showed me her pass at the gate."

"Did she look like this?" He showed both of them the drawing.

"Not exactly. Older. But same eyes."

"You're positive?"

The guard and cleaning woman nodded. "Sir, Captain Hinzer was standing there by the roses . . . I thought you saw her, sir."

Hinzer's mouth pursed. "I saw you pinch a woman's rear end." He shook his head. "I should have followed up but Luftwaffe field marshal Göring needed my unit . . ." He clicked his heels. "My fault. I take full responsibility, sir."

"Not your fault, Hinzer."

Privately, Gunter found the lax security untenable. A saboteur had been allowed to penetrate Naval HQ.

She must have left via the garden service gate. Gone, evaporating in the crowds on rue de Rivoli.

Gunter looked around the room, noting the strategic map of the coast, the diagrams and routes. This room had certainly been her target.

"Is anything missing?"

Before Hinzer could answer, Niels and the adjutant rushed in, breathless. "We found this in a WC on this floor."

A torn nurse's uniform. A small compass. An empty first aid kit.

Gunter turned to Hinzer. "Tell me again what Doisneau told you."

"He was checking on École Polytechnique documents, checking that they'd arrived. But he's been moving documents all week."

"And the nurse?"

Hinzer's cheeks reddened. "To account for some missing first aid supplies."

The adjutant puffed on his cigarette. "That's right, supplies from École Polytechnique got mixed up. It's happened before so nothing seemed unusual."

Gunter hid his shock at this laissez-faire attitude. He checked the open log on the table again. "Show me the documents Doisneau checked."

"It's maps, sir. Charts. Here in this cabinet."

Once the map—showing the coast of England and France with colored lines crisscrossing the Channel—had been unrolled over the diagram on the table, he understood it at once.

The invasion routes.

"Everything here is highly classified, Hinzer. Don't civilians such as Doisneau require security clearance?"

"Of course, sir, Doisneau's part of the project department. He's cleared."

"What do you mean by project?"

"Directive 17, sir. That's all I'm allowed to say."

Of course, and he almost smacked his head. Why hadn't he realized this earlier? Her mission hadn't been to assassinate the Führer; it had been to sabotage the sea invasion of Britain. First, she had killed Admiral Lindau, then she'd tried to steal the invasion plans.

"What's the significance of this?" Gunter pointed to oblong shapes on the diagram covering the table. "These ones marked *B*."

"It refers to Doisneau's project B; that's all I know. But nothing's missing, sir, we've checked," said Hinzer. "All the maps are logged here and accounted for."

Of course not, a professional wouldn't let them suspect.

No doubt she or Doisneau had had a camera to photograph the plans.

He picked up the compass case found near the first aid kit. Thumbed a lever open and found a tiny Minox camera inside. Absent a roll of film.

Gunter had been looking at this all wrong.

He walked to the window and looked out at Place de la Concorde, the obelisk's gold point shimmering in the sun. What better place for her to disappear than in this giant roundabout—she might have gone by *vélo-taxi,* Métro or bus lines.

His gaze was drawn to the Métro entrance directly across the street. To a figure near a flower box.

Monday, June 24, 1940

Place de la Concorde, Paris | 11:45 A.M.

Kate saw a *vélo-taxi* parked along the rue de Rivoli arcade. She approached the lanky cyclist whose short trousers revealed strong calf muscles. He looked capable of pedaling to Île de Puteaux.

"I'm off duty, mademoiselle," he said before she could speak. He took a drink from a thermos.

"Pity," she said. "Would fifty francs up front change your mind?"

"Where to?"

"Île de Puteaux."

"You mean across from Bois de Boulogne?" He wiped the perspiration from his brow. Thought. "Seventy francs."

Not unreasonable.

"Eighty if we leave right now."

"In a hurry, eh?"

She smiled. "You could say that, but I think you'll keep this to yourself, *non*?"

"*D'accord.*" He slipped his thermos in the basket, adjusted his left handlebar. "We're only allowed to pick up passengers on that side." He pointed to where other *vélo-taxis* waited by the Métro. "Meet me over there."

As his *vélo-taxi* joined traffic to loop around the obelisk, Kate crossed back over rue de Rivoli. She lingered by the Métro steps, envisioning the barge up the Seine, crossing the Channel. London.

A curious feeling came over her. Like a dark shadow crossing the sun. Cold, foreboding. She didn't know why. She couldn't say how she knew, but she was being watched.

Her gut screamed at her to move. Leave right now. She looked around quickly, trying to decide which way to go.

There on the opposite side of rue de Rivoli, under the arcade, were several men in uniforms. One wore a rumpled linen suit.

It was the man with gray eyes.

The one who had almost shot her.

And here she had the film roll with the German invasion plans stuck in her bra.

Kate backed up, moving toward the Métro stairs. Her only option was to run and keep on running. But how far could she run? Her legs were shaking; she was lightheaded from the heat and weak with hunger. There was danger at every corner—she felt paralyzed by the fear of being caught, interrogated and tortured. Of what would happen to her if the film was discovered.

She had to get on that barge.

But what if she was caught?

She had to get this film to London.

The *vélo-taxi* driver was motioning to her, but Gray Eyes was crossing the street. What if he'd seen her? She quickly ran down the Métro stairs, took off the lab coat and stuck it in the nearest trash bin. With shaking fingers, she took the risk of removing the film from her bra, pulled a scarf over her head, counted to five, then tagged behind a couple and walked back up the stairs head down.

Now clutching the film roll in her palm, she stayed close behind the couple. Made herself breathe, keeping behind them as she reached into the flower box. She put the film and her return message inside the tin for Philippe, then stuck the box back in the dirt.

Monday, June 24, 1940

Île de Puteaux, Paris | 11:45 A.M.

The Dutch barge captain, moored on Île de Puteaux, read his radio operator's latest deciphered Morse code.

Has package arrived? Acknowledge receipt.

He knew the waiting fishing trawler was at the mercy of the tides on the Normandy coast.

He couldn't moor here for much longer, anyway. A German patrol skiff made hourly passes. But he'd given his word to wait until noon. So he would, and then come hell or high water, he'd pull up anchor.

"An answer, Captain?"

He calculated. If he answered that no package had arrived London would order him out of the area. His package would be stranded. Too cold blooded for him. He had an idea. He'd give the poor bastard or bastards a chance. "Radio back 'Receipt acknowledged ETA 1:45.'"

MONDAY, JUNE 24, 1940

The War Rooms under King Charles Street, London
11:45 A.M. Paris Time

"Professor Fuchs's train has been delayed," said Stepney. "So I've sent a car for him. Meanwhile you have before you a brief recap."

Cathcart, Teague and assorted military sat at the round table.

"Gentleman, do note the study mentioned in the recap. Note that among the names of the authors listed on this University of Birmingham paper are those of then graduate students Nigel Swanson and Antoine Doisneau."

Stepney nodded to Cathcart. Damn fool had only now enlightened him on the stakes of Swanson's mission.

"I'll let Cathcart proceed from here."

"The Jerries got hold of their rather ingenious cavity magnetron design," said Cathcart. "It's able to emit long-range radio waves." Cathcart flipped some pages. "We know Doisneau returned to France in 1935 and carried on research for the French government. The Germans discovered his research at the École Polytechnique. Swanson alerted us when Doisneau contacted him a few days ago."

"Get to the point, Cathcart," said Admiral Wilesdon. "I've got a meeting with the PM."

Stepney loathed the pompous man with his bulbous red-veined nose of a drinker.

"Let me finish, please," said Cathcart. "Doisneau agreed to

exchange the information about the Germans' technical adaptions to the cavity magnetron. Devices we believe contain an adaptation of this technology have washed up on our shores."

Wilesdon leaned forward. "I see the implications of espionage devices washing up on our shores, Cathcart. What have you done about it?"

"Due to the situation in Paris, we didn't have much time. We parachuted Swanson into France to obtain the invasion plans highlighting the deployment of the devices."

"Parachute an engineer into an occupied country?" Wilesdon shook his head. "I can't believe this was sanctioned."

"Doisineau was skittish," said Cathcart. "Through connections at the Portuguese embassy he relayed the information to Swanson via diplomatic pouch. Of course, we saw it first. He was clear he would only deal with Swanson. Insisted we fund his underground connections so he could send his pregnant Jewish wife out of France."

"That's blackmail, sir," said the SIS assistant.

Stepney agreed.

Cathcart tsked. "If we'd known about his role and information, we'd have offered him an incentive before," he said. "He's risking his life, remember. However, Swanson succumbed to wounds sustained in an ambush. Now, according to an Alpha network operative, it's all in place. Stepney's Yank is meeting Doisneau."

"And how's she getting Doisneau's wife out?"

"She furnishes the diamonds to pay their way, the rest is up to him. We sent Swanson in with diamonds, one-carat stones embroidered on a scarf. According to the contact who buried Swanson, it didn't get buried with his corpse so we're assuming she's got it."

"I fail to see how this prevents the invasion."

"We believe these buoy signal devices are part of an all-forces attack."

Wilesdon stood. "Why not disable the damn things?"

"It's not that simple," said Stepney, cutting in. "We need

Professor Fuchs's advice for how to stop this. So far intelligence report buoys have been discovered in Ramsgate, Dover, Bexhill, Brighton, Portsmouth, Ventnor and Lyme Regis."

After Wilesdon left, Cathcart cleared his throat, rustled papers together. "A word, Stepney."

On his aching legs he followed Cathcart outside to the hallway. Cathcart handed him a file.

"Tough news, I'm afraid. Bletchley decoded this during the past hour."

The four snipers' dog tag numbers showed up on the saboteur list transmitted to Berlin. Dead. Men he'd trained, on the mission that could have changed the course of the war.

"They didn't talk, Stepney. Bit the pill. They went out honorably."

Tell that to their widows.

MONDAY, JUNE 24, 1940

Place de la Concorde, Paris | 11:50 A.M.

Kate trembled, eyeing the crowd in the late morning light that haloed the statues of Place de la Concorde. Summer-suited men with dogs on leashes, women in light frocks, children clutching a grandmother's hand.

No gray-eyed man.

Had she imagined seeing him? Reacted in panic? This awful lightheadedness made her prone to mistakes.

Big ones.

As she got in the *vélo-taxi*, she kept watching the faces. Humidity blanketed the air—not even a breath of wind.

Just then she recognized Philippe, wearing a blue cloth cap, standing by the flower box. Hurry, she had to hurry and catch him. She'd recover the film, stick to her first plan.

"Stop!" she shouted at the driver. "Let me out."

"Aren't you in a hurry?" said the *vélo-taxi* driver, braking hard.

"Wait for me." By the time she jumped out of the uncomfortable pod-like box, she had lost sight of Philippe. Heat simmered off the colonnaded facade of the Kriegsmarine and arcaded rue de Rivoli.

Then a firm hand gripped her shoulder. Before she could turn, metal clinked as heavy handcuffs encircled her wrists. Her knees trembled; her thoughts went wobbly. In this heat, all she could register was a weary accented voice in almost pleasant-sounding English. "So we finally meet, mademoiselle."

The man with the gray eyes turned her around to study her.

She stumbled. Strong arms caught her.

"Put her in the car, Niels . . ." was the last thing she heard.

Kate wasn't in a cell. Wasn't handcuffed. Whispers reached her ears but made no sense. She lay bathed in streaming sunlight and reeking of antiseptic. Delicious cool air from an open window ruffled her hair and Gilberte's floral dress, the thin silk slip.

Her arm stung when she tried to sit up. There was a needle in her vein hooked to an intravenous solution. Light danced and prismed through the glass bottles of medicine at her bedside.

Where was she?

"Feeling better?" That same accented English.

Kate registered the man leaning into her view. His gray eyes were red-rimmed and bloodshot, his dark blond hair parted messily on the side. His rumpled brown linen suit looked mismatched with the starched dress shirt he wore underneath.

"Who are you?"

He showed her his badge. "Gunter Hoffman, RSD. And you?"

Fear clamped her heart. Next was a firing squad. But she wouldn't show fear.

Never.

She'd go down fighting.

"I'm an American citizen and demand you notify the embassy. Right now."

He rubbed his neck. "Excuse my bad English, but you're a British national."

"Do I sound English?"

He cocked his head. Grinned. "More like what I've heard in the movies. In cowboy Westerns."

A friendly Nazi? A technique to trick her into lowering her guard? She wouldn't let him see how she quaked inside.

"No doubt. I'm a ranch woman from Oregon. Can't get more Western than that, Mr. Gunter."

"Excuse me, please." He took a handkerchief from his pocket to wipe his runny nose. Sounded like he had a cold. Good.

"Fascinating," he said. "Like a cowboy ranch, roping cattle, shooting Indians? A real Annie Oakley, eh?"

Sly. He wasn't stupid. But he seemed genuinely interested, like she was a specimen he wanted to figure out.

"Cookin' chow for ranch hands and cowboys more like it."

Could she charm him with country-isms while she figured out what he knew?

Face it. She was caught and soon to be quartered no matter what.

A doctor was listening to her chest with his stethoscope.

"Stable," he said in French-accented English. "You're lucky."

He called this luck?

With a deft movement the doctor removed the needle, applied pressure and taped on a bandage. Then he went to the window to stab out his cigarette in the ashtray.

So she was in a French hospital. Everything felt very wrong.

"Now, Doctor, please roll up her right sleeve exposing her shoulder."

Warm fingers probed her upper arm.

"Please note the bruise here." Gunter picked up the Lee-Enfield, which had been reassembled—where had he gotten that? "If I measure the buttstock, like this."

The cold metal brushed her bruise.

"*Ach ja*, the measurements match. Telltale marking of this rifle recoil. A unique piece with a modified telescopic sight." His warm fingers probed her armpit. Kate realized another man was in the room. A youngish soldier, dark haired, with a clipboard and camera slung from his uniformed shoulder. "Niels, photograph this."

A flashbulb went off, blinding her. She had to admire him. The German was damn good. He'd recovered the Lee-Enfield and tracked her down. Disheartened, she realized Philippe must have betrayed her.

"Please swab her hands for gunshot residue in case any remains. Then, Niels, take a full set of fingerprints to match those we've analyzed from the rifle."

What kind of charade was this? How did her fingerprints even matter? The next stop would be the firing squad.

Her anger burned. She had nothing to lose now. Would bang her head against the hospital bed rails before she let him see her scared.

"The methodical type, eh? A German Sherlock Holmes. Only Sherlock Holmes never tortured people."

The man's mouth tightened. "I was a homicide detective in Munich. No case goes to trial without solid evidence; it's the rule of investigation that I was trained on."

Right.

"You call a bruise evidence?"

Gunter consulted a worn brown leather notebook. Thumbed a few pages. "We have two witnesses who saw a woman similar to you in appearance at Sacré-Cœur, where a naval officer was murdered. A building concierge and a melon seller recognized you from this drawing."

The drunken concierge, the terrified melon seller? But she blinked seeing the skillful drawing of her in a blue sweater, her hair clipped by a tortoiseshell comb. Her neck tingled.

Deny. The first rule for a prisoner. Deny everything.

"Under coercion, no doubt," she said.

"The final corroborating factors, miss, are the bullets. You see the lab compared the bullet taken from the victim's brain and the bullet lodged in the pillar of Sacré-Cœur. All consistent with the remaining bullets in the magazine of this Lee-Enfield. Now, with your fingerprints, my work is done."

"Just like that?"

"Instead of the thirty-six hours I was originally given to apprehend you, it's taken me . . ." He consulted his watch. "It's now six o'clock, so it's been thirty-three hours."

"Nice and neat, eh? Expecting a pat on the back from the Gestapo?"

"Depends on the Führer's mood."

Her blood went cold.

"I'll be accompanying you to Germany for the trial."

A crisscross of sunlight played over her dirty toes.

"A trial in Nazi Germany?" she said, trying to sound sure and careless. "I'm an American citizen. We have diplomatic relations. That would be against the Geneva Convention."

"Have a passport to prove it?"

"The embassy will furnish papers. Clear this up."

"You've been talking in your sleep, miss."

"What?" The word caught in her throat.

"How do you say? Talking funny, what's the word?"

"Delirious," said the French doctor.

What had she said?

"*Ja*, the doctor insisted if you were given mild sedation and hydration, you'd be in condition for transport."

The doctor nodded. "You were suffering severe dehydration, erratic heartbeat, extremely low blood pressure. But we treated you in time."

In time to be shot. Her mouth went dry.

Failed again. The boat had sailed, Philippe had betrayed her and the film was lost to German hands.

Trust no one, Stepney had said, time and time again.

Idiot.

She'd accomplished nothing, saved no one and put others in harm's way.

"Your false French papers are enough to imprison you," Gunter Hoffman told her. "But tell me why an American would be an assassin for the British."

Smart again. How had he figured that out?

"Tell me and I can circumvent unpleasant things for you."

Like she believed that.

"You kept calling out for Dafydd. Who's that?"

She swallowed with effort. Said nothing.

"I'm personally escorting you on the plane to Berlin." Gunter wrote something in his notebook. "Then tonight I'll be home with my wife to belatedly celebrate my daughter's second birthday, which you made me miss."

A little teddy bear sat on an attaché case by her hospital bed.

Kate's thoughts went to Lisbeth's rosy cheeks, her sweet breath, her warm baby smell, the last time Kate had held her in her arms. "You're lucky to have your daughter to go home to."

Knocking came from the door. The doctor looked at Gunter, who put his finger to his lips. Then Gunter motioned his aide, Niels. Together they rolled her hospital bed through a door into another room, then through that into yet another. Closed the door.

He'd clasped her hand in his. Those red-rimmed gray eyes probed hers.

"Keep still and cooperate. It's for your safety so I can escort you to the plane."

"Safety?"

"I finish my case. Serve justice."

"By delivering me to your Nazi land of butchers?"

His lips pursed. "I hate loose ends. Why didn't you have a cyanide pill?"

Speechless, she shook her head.

"Why wasn't it in your back molar like the other four snipers?"

"I don't understand."

In this small examining room, Gunter took the contents of her pocket from a paper bag and set them on the aluminum tray. "Nothing makes sense unless . . ." He rooted through the contents. Stared at the small dirty bit of scarf she'd smudged with charcoal and diamonds she'd caked with mascara. Before handing off the scarf to Antoine, she'd kept two for a bribe if she needed it to escape.

Deflect him. Her heart in her mouth, she said, "So, Mr. Gunter, what doesn't make sense to you?"

He looked up. "I got you wrong from the beginning. I underestimated you. My mistake. After you murdered Admiral Lindau, you photographed Directive 17 plans with this . . ." He pulled the Minox out. "To sabotage the invasion."

Terror stricken, she wanted to die right now. She couldn't face prison and torture.

"I always believed the Führer was your target. So did he. But all along you were the distraction for the real assassination, the snipers who were parachuted in to target the High Command arriving at le Bourget. You did your job admirably. We almost missed them *and* lost you."

So it was true. Damn Stepney had used her.

And she had to hear the truth from a Nazi.

"We knew where to find you at the Café Littéraire because the radio operator you arrived with gave you up under torture." He caught her eye. "Not by me. But did you know you were sent here to be captured and interrogated? You were meant to talk."

That matched what Max had said.

"Look, if you're saying all this because you think I'll confess to something, you're wrong. I'm an American citizen."

She heard voices in the adjoining room.

"But you were never caught, as your handlers thought you would be. You've always been a step ahead. When I cornered you, I saw how you killed Max Verdou, who betrayed you. Your training is superb."

Kate met his gaze. "If you expect a compliment in return, forget it."

Gunter watched her, reading her expression with a burning intensity.

Like hell she'd give in to him and confess. Now she felt so full of anger she had no room for fear. "I'm an American citizen. I demand to go to the embassy."

"You're what we call tough as day old bread," he said. "But you know old bread cracks."

Niels motioned to him. "The ambulance arrived. So has Roschmann."

An ambulance? What did that mean? Whatever it was, it didn't sound good.

Visibly annoyed, Gunter slipped the bear inside his case. Took out his pistol, a Luger, and covered the door. Niels lifted her into a stretcher, wheeled her through another door, out of the hospital and into a waiting ambulance.

"We're getting you on the plane. Now." Gunter secured the wheelchair. "You'll get a fair trial. But I want to know why you did what you did."

"Taking me to Germany makes no sense."

"I'm on the Führer's orders. No one will sabotage this."

"So you'll bring your 'spoils of war' home to a pat on the back from the Führer?"

His gray eyes looked faraway. Tired, he sat down on the ambulance bench. His shoulders sagged, but the alertness never left him. And when he spoke, his words came out low. "That's not why. I'm a cop. I do my job to the end. My wife calls me a Rottweiler because I never give up. I can't."

He'd opened a window into himself.

"Just a guy doing his job?"

She wiggled her toes, flexed her calves. Everything seemed to work. Physically she felt better than she had in days after the rest and hydration. She doubted she'd live to enjoy it.

"We're on opposite sides. Still, I admire an opponent like you. I feel sorry for you that you have gotten yourself into this."

"I don't need your pity," she said. "You're to blame, all of you."

"And you're a killer," said Gunter, his voice thin. "Like all killers, you have a reason. Justification, *ja*?"

Why wouldn't she want revenge?

Gunter rapped on the ambulance's door. "Let's go, Niels."

"Looking for the right key, sir," Niels called from the front of the ambulance. "One moment."

She was going to die. What did it matter now if she told him why?

"Then write this down in your little notebook, Mr. Gunter," she said. "Dot the i's, cross the t's and get what I say right."

She hated reliving it yet again. But she made herself.

"My daughter, Lisbeth, was eighteen months old. Almost your daughter's age. We lived on an island and one of your submarines bombed a ship in the harbor. In the chaos my husband and child were in an accident. It shouldn't have happened. Never. In a few minutes my baby and husband were gone. Burnt alive."

Gunter looked away.

"No, you look at me and *you* listen," she said, grabbing his arm. "I couldn't save them. After that, everywhere I looked, everything I smelled and touched reminded me of them. Dafydd's big warm arms, his laugh. He was such a talented artist. My little Lisbeth's sweet smell, her first words, the way she giggled when I blew on her toes. That's why I failed. I hesitated."

"What do you mean?"

"At Sacré-Cœur. It was the little girl with the yellow dress. Her blonde curls—she looked so like my Lisbeth. If I had shot your Führer the bullet would have gone through her cheek. Killed her. She'd be dead and another mother would suffer a hole in her life."

She was nothing—she had failed every attempt to avenge her family.

Telling the story to the enemy would be the only payback she'd ever get. Pathetic.

"I wanted to get back at you Germans."

A sob stuck in the back of her throat.

The siren wailed as the ambulance pulled away into the parking lot. Gunter leaned close to her ear. "I'm sorry you lost the family you loved."

She hated the thoughts coming in her head—that she wanted to trust him. That something told her he was straight up. A family man, albeit a Nazi. A cop who, despite his allegiance, followed the code of the law.

"I trusted someone who betrayed me."

"Who?" Gunter strained to hear.

Suddenly, Kate heard the screech of skidding brakes. Felt a sickening jolt as something crashed into the ambulance. Gunter's arms shot out, shielding her from crunching metal and splintering glass. Time slowed, suspended in heat and glass shards as the crash's force crumpled the back door. She saw Gunter thrown against the window. Kate felt wetness on her hand. Blood.

The stretcher strap ripped loose; then she was smacked against the window, too. Outside she saw a Mercedes had crashed into the ambulance. Then she was falling on the floor. Gunter scrambled toward the driver. Blood dripped from his brow. "We have to get out of here, Niels. Go."

He turned to her. "Stay down."

As she crouched, she saw Gunter's pistol in his pocket. Could she use this accident to escape? The ambulance engine sputtered. Kate scrabbled in the evidence bag, only had time enough to stuff the scarf down her front before she heard shouts in German.

The ambulance door scraped open, and the rest happened in a blur. It happened so quick they hadn't even gotten out of the the parking lot to the street.

A sack was pulled over her head, her wrists tied. She was herded stumbling down a chill passageway back into the hospital from what she could figure out. A church bell pealed and she counted: one, two, three, four, five, six . . . silence.

She doubted she'd hear it peal seven.

KATE SHIVERED, BAREFOOT, ON A bench behind bars in a tall cage-like cell. Cracked plaster veined the scuffed green wall under a sign that read JURIDICTION DE POLICE DE PARIS.

So she was in a police cell for criminals in the hospital facilities. From somewhere came the dull clanging of a boiler.

Dabbing blood off his forehead with a handkerchief, Gunter spoke to a man in a stiff, angry voice. He faced this man, standing legs apart, as if for battle. The man was a black-uniformed SS with meaty paws, thick neck, wide-set dark eyes and thick lips. A thin arched scar replaced half his left eyebrow, giving him a permanent quizzical look.

The SS man set down a fat file on the gouged desk. Smiled. When he spoke it came out in a calm voice.

Was she some pawn in a Nazi power play?

"I'm transporting you to Berlin," Gunter said in English, addressing her. He had picked up the receiver on the black melamine phone and spoke into it, his voice low. Was he requesting backup, an escort to le Bourget?

The SS man turned to her. A smile still on his face. "This is my investigation now, miss," he said in almost unaccented English. "My file already contains a list of evidence, preliminary autopsy, statements, forensic tests and ballistics. The only thing I'm missing is your confession."

He untied a gray felt pouch, unrolling it to reveal a set of surgical scalpels neatly tied in place like a set of carving knives. Fear tingled up her spine. He walked to the cell. Surveyed her with those dark, wide-set eyes like she was an animal in the zoo.

Sweat dripped down her back. She willed her panic down. She'd learned never to show fear in the face of a wild animal.

"You caused such a lot of trouble, miss," A shake of his close-cropped blond head. His words were soft, like a teacher issuing a gentle reprimand. "Now, you know this won't do. I'll need your confession."

Kate stared him down. Kept her mouth shut.

"*Ach,* let's not start out on the wrong foot," he said, wagging a finger.

Don't show fear. That was what his type enjoyed. He thumbed through the file.

"My report won't be complete without your confession. Let's start with a few questions."

"Stand down, Roschmann." Gunter slipped his notebook in his case and nodded to Niels, who waited at the cage door. Niels opened the cell, motioning Kate forward. Her bare feet stuck on the cold tiles. "The escorts will arrive any minute. Everything's been arranged."

"So soon? That of course changes things." The man rolled up his felt pouch, pocketed it and drew a pistol. Kate struggled to hide her fear. The boiler's metallic clanging raked her skin like needles.

"It will go in my report that she was shot while escaping," he said. "You can have the honor, Gunter."

All this was in English. He wanted her to understand. To terrorize her before she died.

He handed Gunter his Luger, an automatic 9mm Parabellum. "You wanted to finish the case. Finish it."

Controlling her terror, she locked eyes with Gunter. He was so close she could smell the coffee on his breath. She couldn't read his gray eyes. Would he actually shoot her after his talk about evidence and justice?

She heard the cock of a trigger. Tore her gaze away to see the SS man holding a second Luger to Gunter's head.

"You'll fire, Gunter, or I shoot you, too, for getting in the way of the Führer's direct orders."

Cold chills traveled from the soles of her feet up her legs.

"Nice try," said Gunter, his voice even. "The Führer gave me thirty-six hours and they aren't up yet."

What deadly game was the SS man playing?

"You think that matters? No one cares."

"I care. I'm a policeman and act according to the law. I know you have no orders to shoot her or me. You won't set me up to murder a prisoner."

Kate marveled at the authority in his voice.

"Niels, open the door," said Gunter.

The SS man turned and fired twice at Niels. Gunter whipped around and slammed the pistol butt against the man's outstretched arm. He yelped in pain. His pistol clattered across the floor, rolling under the desk.

Gunter, Luger in one hand, pulled out his handcuffs, but the next moment both men were on the floor, punching each other. Everything happened so fast—Kate saw the man reaching for the pistol under the desk.

A shot. Then another. She was stuck standing hemmed against the cell bars. A bitterness of burnt powder in the back of her throat.

In horror, she heard Gunter's gurgling breath. Saw the blood dripping from the shot to his neck.

Gasping, she bent down. She saw the helpless look in his eyes, felt the gun in his trembling hand. He was trying to give it to her.

She put her hand over his. Gunter's gray eyes fluttered, then closed.

The man was heaving himself to his feet. He brushed off his black uniform and smiled. "It seems he chose to spare your life, so we have a bit more time together. Shall we hear your confession?"

"Don't count on it."

She fired, hitting him between the eyes, the second shot to his heart. As any ranch girl knew, you shoot twice to make sure. Surprise arched his brow. He was a big man, collapsing over the desk, sending his report cascading onto Gunter's blood-spattered body on the floor at her feet.

Kate checked the magazine. Four bullets left in the Luger. Enough to do some damage. She took Gunter's attaché case and wiped her bloody feet on Roschmann's black jacket.

She gathered the papers, took a last look at the carnage and opened the door, her heart thumping. She expected a volley of bullets, charging troops, but all that met her was the boiler's dull clanging and the whine of an ambulance pulling into the adjoining emergency bay.

She found the nurse's locker room and stared at the blood smudged on her face, her feet. Her hands shook. Her face had gone numb with shock.

Focus.

She splashed water on her face and forced herself to clean up.

In a nurse's locker, she found a pair of worn espadrilles and a sun hat. She put them on. From a surgery supply cabinet she took a needle, catgut thread and a scalpel.

With the scalpel she picked off the teddy bear's eyes and replaced them with the painted diamonds in short tight stitches. She thought of the little girl who wouldn't see her father again and this birthday present he'd tried so hard to bring her.

At the hospital incinerator, when no one was looking, she dumped the papers from Gunter's case, the drawing of her and everything else except his loose change and her French identification papers.

His notebook had fallen to the floor. She picked it up and inside saw his name and address in Munich. She tossed the notebook into the flames. By the time the escort for le Bourget arrived, Kate was gone.

Monday, June 24, 1940

Near Porte de Clichy, Paris | 7:30 P.M.

Near the Porte de Clichy, the linden trees blossomed, perfuming the air like the last time she'd been in Paris. That Paris was gone. Like Dafydd.

Adrenalin coursed through her. She wanted to live. Escape.

In the nearby café, she bought a token and used the telephone downstairs.

"Any radio contact?"

The voice of the sewer worker said, "Meet the fishing trawler anchored in the third cove north of Saint-Malo. It waits until midnight. Avoid the train stations."

"Any suggestions how I get there?"

"Hop a freight car north in the switching yards beyond the Périphérique."

Click.

Troop trucks rumbled on the boulevard outside the café, stopping every so often to let out soldiers who pasted posters on walls and kiosks. Her eye caught on the red bordered poster, in French and German, offering a reward of ten thousand Reichsmarks or two hundred thousand francs for information leading to the capture of . . .

Her image stared back at her.

Fear danced up her spine.

She'd be dead if she didn't get out of here. Kate put her head down and adjusted the sun hat low.

She followed le boulevard de Douaumont paralleling the old wall of Paris. If she remembered right, beyond the south cemetery were the railway yards mentioned by the sewer worker.

Several trains filled with passengers passed, hissing steam. No train stopped at the confluence of tracks. If she'd reasoned wrong, how far away were the freight yards? Heat hovered like wet cotton, perspiration stung her eyes, her muscles ached.

Running on fear now, she followed the tracks beyond the rail sheds. A short snaking line of railcars baked in the sun. A locomotive whistled, backing up, its steam billowing and clouding the air.

Two German soldiers patrolled the freight warehouse platform.

Stuck in the heat and no way out. She heard cranking, the shifting of metal as men in blue work coats loaded wooden crates on open cars. The soldiers turned and marched to the other side.

She waited until the loader's attention focused on an arriving shipment. The minute he turned away she climbed aboard the first railcar.

TUESDAY, JUNE 25, 1940

Saint-Malo, French Coast | 1 A.M.

As the farmer's cart mounted the crest, the road led down past the trees toward a dark expanse of water illuminated by the moon. Kate breathed in the salt air. The sea. So close to freedom.

The cart lumbered toward rocky cliffs overlooking the cove, the night chirping of crickets louder than its wheels. Pine scents mingled with the salt.

A light blinked once, twice from the edge of the cove. She made out the faint outlines of a fishing boat hugging the rocky outcrop.

"You've got ten minutes to get down the path and swim out from that point." The farmer gestured. "It's close."

Swim.

She was a terrible swimmer. Could barely dog-paddle. At Beaverton High School, you had to swim across the ugly green swimming pool to graduate. Terrified, she'd wanted to hide. Forget graduating, she had been that scared. But Jed, her middle brother, a champion swimmer, mocked her in front of her friends. "Katie can't do it. Katie's a chicken."

That's right, she'd been chicken. Damned chicken now.

"It's the only way," the farmer said, getting off the cart. "The path's narrow, but it winds to the point. The trawler can't wait any longer."

She handed him the Steiff teddy bear. It wouldn't help her swim.

He shook his head. "*Mais non, merci,* my children are grown."

"A small repayment, monsieur. His eyes are diamonds."

Kate worked her way down the cliff path, hanging on to scrub brush, her breath coming in short spurts. All she could see was the dark gel of roiling water, cloud wisps over the moon and the blinking boat light. It looked close.

Her heart pounded. *Now or never.*

"I'm not chicken," she yelled as she jumped.

Then she was thrashing in freezing water, her mouth full of salty brine. Her legs cramped, her lungs seized up. Such a bad idea to think she could do this. After everything she'd been through she was going to die by drowning.

She dog-paddled, kicking and kicking to stay above water. Her waterlogged clothes and the damn Luger in her bra pulled her down. She was sinking, panicking and thrashing the water. Choking. Her eyes stung from the salt.

"Grab the life preserver," someone was shouting.

She kicked again, then again, sputtering and inhaling water. Her ankles were knotted in seaweed. She was being sucked under.

Then her hand caught something hard. The life preserver. With one last kick she bobbed up enough to hook her arm around it.

WEDNESDAY, JUNE 26, 1940

Before Dawn on the British Coast

The trawler anchored at Portsmouth in a clammy fog. Kate shivered on deck. She noted the telltale shrouded shape of antiaircraft emplacements. Preparations for the imminent invasion.

She felt lucky for the fisherman's slicker and rubber boots as the sky opened. That dense bone-permeating rain. Welcome to England.

Her eye scanned the wet dock. No one but an older man in a khaki uniform, who stood at the end of the ramp. He was holding an umbrella and a gas mask hung from his belt. "This way, Miss Rees."

"It's Mrs. Rees. Where's Stepney? Isn't he meeting me?"

"Don't know nothing about that. Your boat took longer than expected."

The choppy sea and evading German patrol ships had seen to that.

"My orders are to escort you to London."

She followed him in the rain to the station. He proved to be an untalkative home defense warden who furnished her with a gas mask and looked out the window the entire dawn train ride to London.

Only once did she catch him watching her when he thought

she was asleep. His eyes caught on the Luger sticking out of her pocket. It was the only thing she'd gotten out of France.

In drizzling humid London, a taxi ride took them to an anonymous building, where she was let off.

"Second floor, room 238, missus," said the warden. He gave a doff of his cap, the taxi pulled away and she stood alone on the pavement.

On the second floor, her knock brought a rail-thin man in a brown suit to the door. "I'm Wilson." He gestured for her to sit in a chair before a khaki metal desk bearing a sheaf of blank paper and a pen. "Let's get started, shall we?"

"I want to speak with Stepney, my handler."

"First things first. We have a system, Miss—"

"Mrs. Rees," she said.

He nodded. In a raspy voice he reminded her she'd signed the Official Secrets Act and in this debriefing session she was to write a report of her "overseas activities." No more, no less. And to remember time was of the essence.

Wilson furnished a weak milky tea and refused to answer any questions. Not much of a welcoming committee. Kate did her best to duplicate what she'd seen of the wall map, what she remembered of the charts. She wrote down what she remembered about the network and agents, the traitor. It took all morning.

Wilson looked at his watch. "Splendid. You're expected next door."

With that he ushered her to the stairs, pointed to another anonymous building across the courtyard.

Now she could debrief Stepney herself.

Instead, it turned out to be the Women's Royal Naval Service. Kate was fitted with a navy blue wool serge jacket with brass buttons, a white shirt, blue tie and shapeless skirt. Issued a khaki canvas tote containing a freshly issued Wren identification card, ration coupons, a housing voucher. On her assignment card it read: *orders pending.*

"Where's Stepney? Why isn't he here?" Her questions were met with blank stares. "What does 'orders pending' mean?"

"You'll be contacted."

Contacted?

Fuming inside, she trudged down the steps of the rundown liver-yellow building to another anonymous building—her lodging billet, courtesy of the Royal Navy. Her uniform tickled in the wrong places. She missed the silk of Gilberte's slip in this warm London air.

At the military information office, a receptionist smiled and shook her head. Stepney? Never heard of him. At Kate's insistence she took down Kate's name and promised to query her superiors.

Stepney, it seemed, had vanished off the face of the earth.

Depleted, she saw a line queuing at the shop. Tea was what she needed, strong black tea.

A woman running to the approaching bus had stopped in front of her.

"Kate?"

She hardly recognized the woman in a chic dove-gray suit with stylish matching hat over her chestnut hair.

"Margo?"

"Is that really you, Kate? I heard you were . . ."

"Dead, Margo? Don't believe the rumors. I'm very much alive."

Margo was scanning the street. "Bus is here. Must dash."

Margo had hopped on the back of the double-decker.

"Where's Stepney, Margo?"

Margo blinked. "Haven't you heard?" she said from the platform.

"Heard what?" But the bus took off into traffic. Kate broke into a run, nearly catching up before the double-decker got swallowed in the Piccadilly Circus roundabout.

Finally, she gave up on Marlborough Street in front of the sandbagged windows of a department store. Her lungs heaved, her calves ached.

"In a hurry, luv?" asked a newspaper vendor holding the *Daily Mirror.* The headline read 2 OZ TEA RATION AS OF TODAY.

She nodded, catching her breath.

She needed answers. Now.

KATE GOT THE RUNAROUND AT every army office she tried. Finally, she was given an office address and told to leave a "query" there for Stepney. She tried each of the offices in the dingy hallway.

At the third, a middle-aged woman wearing rimless glasses paused at the typewriter.

"Stepney? No clue. I'm just the department typist. Can't help you, miss."

Kate noticed an envelope next to her typewriter in the outgoing tray.

She pointed. "That's for me."

"You, miss?"

"As in Mrs. Kate R-E-E-S that's printed there on the envelope."

KATE SAT ON A BENCH in Regent's Park. Her view took in the boats rowing on the lake, the gliding swans, the haze of insects in the blossoming buddleia branches. Children's voices and laughter drifted from the playground. Apart from the blacked-out windows in the gardener's cottage, the piled sandbags and posters, the war seemed far away.

Stepney sat down, his cane at his side. "Knew you had moxie, Kate, but you've gone above and beyond your duty."

Stepney looked older, as if he'd aged in the past week. She probably did, too. He grinned. "You put everyone to shame. No one thought you could do it."

He hadn't either. He'd set her up to fail.

"I didn't, Stepney." She stared at the ripples on the lake. "I failed my mission. Didn't shoot the Führer. But that wasn't your intention anyway."

An uncomfortable look crossed his face.

"You took out the admiral," said Stepney. "That turned out more effective than you know."

"Not enough. I photographed and lost the invasion plans. Risked the lives of people helping me." Anger simmered inside her. "I shot a traitor, an admiral and a Nazi sociopath, sure. But accomplished nothing."

"Don't be silly, Kate," said Stepney. "An agent delivered the film. Good job."

She sat up. The hard bench bit into her spine. "Wait a long minute. You're saying Philippe got the film through?"

"Philippe? Is that his code name? No matter, that's unimportant. The film's processed. Of course, once the Germans know we've got it, they'll change the plans. But there's only so many ways to invade an island. Churchill wants to keep everyone on high alert. I wanted you to know and to keep this between us." Stepney gripped his cane. "Last night's RAF bombing missions took out coastal German emplacements for the invasion. You won't see that in the papers or hear it on the BBC. Good work."

Sun-dappled shadows mingled on the grass. She tried to digest this. So Philippe hadn't betrayed her? "There's a lot you're not telling me, Stepney."

"My Section D's about to fold. Ruffled too many feathers," he said. His fingers rubbed his bony wrist.

She saw a wistfulness in his eyes.

"You're young. It's your war. Not mine anymore."

How unlike the Stepney she knew to say that. But then she didn't really know him. Or trust him.

"Why didn't you have me carry a cyanide capsule?" she said. "Like the others?"

"What others?"

"The four snipers I was the diversion for, Stepney."

She watched his reaction.

"That's not quite true." He fielded her question, smooth as always.

"You trained me and signed my death warrant."

"Remember when I found you, Kate. Broken. Ready to jump off the munitions factory roof in Orkney," said Stepney. "You had skills. Volunteered for a way to use them. I gave you a mission, something to live for."

"Isn't that what you tell all the agents you send on suicide missions?"

Stepney's jaw hardened. "It's war."

"I accepted that, Stepney," she said. "But not that you set your stock on those snipers. You never thought I could do it." That hurt the most. "You used me for fodder. A distraction. And the snipers and radio operator paid the price."

"Not the optimal outcome, I agree." Stepney clenched the knob on his cane. "You're well informed."

Such stuffy English understatement. "Come on, ask me how I know."

"How?"

"And ruin the surprise?"

For once Stepney looked flustered.

"Max Verdou, the traitor in your cell, suspected. Even the Nazi detective who arrested me wondered. He thought the fact that there was no cyanide pill said it all. That you intended me to get caught and tortured."

"I underestimated you, Kate. That's the beauty of it. You accomplished the mission to assassinate one of the High Command." Stepney slapped his knee. "Why hasn't an old man like me learned never to underestimate a woman?"

"All that to expose a rat. Max Verdou, my old tutor? Pathetic."

Stepney shook his head. "You assassinated Admiral Lindau, shot this traitor, took over another agent's mission and generally bolloxed up Hitler's invasion. Not that Hitler will ever admit it."

A butterfly alighted on the bench. Diaphanous blue-violet wings fluttered before it took off again. Tears brimmed in her eyes.

"I trusted you, Stepney."

He'd been the one person she'd believed in. The one who'd made her feel she could do something worthwhile and fight back.

"That's a handler's job, Kate." He sighed. "The country owes you."

"Well, they've given me an insignificant job in the boonies to keep me quiet."

Stepney clutched his cane and stood.

"That's right, Stepney, keep your head high. All for King and country, right?" She reached for the Luger and pointed it at him. "You asshole."

No fear showed in Stepney's green eyes. "I understand, Kate."

"You're going to erase me, right? So I'll conveniently never reveal what happened." She leveled the Luger.

"No one would believe you. The file's destroyed." Another sigh. "Anyway I'm not worth it. You'd stain the courageous act you've done. Your future."

Could she kill an old man? She wanted to, but he was worn out, deflated. His group had been disbanded, his slimy techniques banned.

She set down the pistol. "You're right. You're not worth it, Stepney."

A weight lifted from her. She felt lighter, released. She'd been determined to prove her worth and avenge her family. Now she thirsted to live. Do more. No one deserved those oppressors.

The only one she had had to prove her worth to had been herself.

He lifted his cane. A signal. Had he played her again, the old man? Would she be shot in the head before she stood up? Her body disposed of and her story buried forever?

"Don't bollocks this up, Kate."

"What does that mean?"

Stepney raised his arm and saluted her. "It's not an old man's war. You can continue to serve in the memory of your daughter and husband."

Then he set a train ticket on her lap. Scotland.

"Didn't you want to be a rifle instructor?"

She nodded. "I'll make a damn good one, Stepney. The best."

"Of course you will."

And then he was walking slowly away, leaning on his cane.

In King's Cross station, Kate mounted the train steps with her one bag. With no regrets she was leaving London, Kate turned back to check the station clock—the train would leave any minute—and her gaze caught on a group of men in Free French uniforms laughing, smoking and speaking French.

She recognized that smile. It was Philippe, clean shaven and smart in a Free French uniform. Her heart jumped.

Philippe joined his group as they boarded the train one car ahead.

Kate found her seat. Never looked back.

Author's Note

Hitler spent only three hours in Paris in June 1940. Fact. Two of the men with him, Albert Speer and Arno Breker, recorded different dates for this visit in postwar accounts and memoirs. Both men attested to contradictory dates for the rest of their lives.

Why?

The historical discrepancy grabbed me, and the *what if* wouldn't let go.

This is a work of fiction, but it is drawn from a range of real-life inspirations.

In World War II, over two thousand Russian women were trained as sharpshooters and deployed in the defense effort against the Nazis. Lyudmila Mikhailovna Pavlichenko was the most successful female sniper in history. When asked how many German men she had killed, her reply was "I killed three hundred nine Fascists." She toured the US in 1942, when she was twenty-six years old, and met Eleanor Roosevelt in the White House.

Section D, the precursor and forerunner of SOE (Special Operations Executive), was formed in 1938. Section D commenced active operation in March 1939 and was absorbed into the SOE in September 1940. Many Section D and SOE records were destroyed in a London fire—an accident, it was reported. The Lee-Enfield No. 4, Mk. I (T) sniper rifle was in development from 1940, when this story takes place, but was first used in the field in 1942. Starting in 1940, the British special services designed and manufactured the S-Phone that went into documented use in 1942.

Operation Sea Lion, the planned German naval invasion of Britain, was real. Documents, maps and plans have survived. But it never happened. Historical theories exist as to why. This book posits one hypothetical scenario.

Acknowledgments

THIS BOOK OWES MORE GRATITUDE than I can express to so many who encouraged me to write this, to keep going, and to not give up. I'll try with huge mercis to: Jude Callister of the Scapa Flow Museum, Lyness, Orkney Scotland; the Churchill War Rooms of the Imperial War Museum, London; Maureen Battistella of Ashland, Oregon; the librarians at the Cecil. H. Green Library, Stanford University; in Paris to Gilles Thomas; the Ministére de la Marine; Jean-Baptiste O.; Naftali Skrobek, Résistant; Musée de la Libération de Paris; Musée du Général Leclerc; and Musée Jean Moulin; Blake Leyers, J.T. Ellison, and Denise Hamilton, who shifted my view in the best way; Tony Broadbent; Mary Volmer, who shared her family story; Jacqueline Winspear, for her generosity; Rhys Bowen always; Desirée McWhorter; Susanna Solomon; J.T. Morrow; Jean Satzer, my alpha and beta; patient Libby Fischer Hellmann; Dr. Terri Haddix, who answers every medical question and then some; plotmeister James N. Frey who wouldn't let me quit; my agent, Katherine Fausset, who is in my corner every time; my editor, Juliet Grames, for her patience, insight and dedication to making this book better, along with the incredible team at Soho Press, who I'm lucky to work with: amazing Bronwen Hruska,

Paul Oliver, Rudy Martinez, Rachel Kowal, Monica White, Amara Hoshijo, Steven Tran, and Janine Agro. To those who lived under the Occupation and shared their experiences; and to the unsung members of the short lived Section D forerunner of the SOE; and to Hannah, my son, Tate, and Jun, always.